Recycled Love

To Gillian

From George Henry

xx

George Henry

Copyright (C) 2017 George Knox
Layout design and Copyright (C) 2018 Creativia
Published 2018 by Creativia
Cover art by Travis Miles, Pro Book Covers
This book is a work of fiction. Names, characters, places, and incidents are the product of the author's imagination or are used fictitiously. Any resemblance to actual events, locales, or persons, living or dead, is purely coincidental.
All rights reserved. No part of this book may be reproduced or transmitted in any form or by any means, electronic or mechanical, including photocopying, recording, or by any information storage and retrieval system, without the author's permission.

DEDICATED TO ELSIE KNOX

My Mother
1907-2004

The remarkable daughter of a coal miner, she lived through two world wars, the Great Depression, the loss of a child, and always put her family first. My brother and I owe everything to her determination to have her boys educated and succeed in life.

Maps

March 22nd, 1996

Mumbai, India

DAN SPUN AROUND at the scraping sound behind him. Outlined against the bright lights from the main road, a gangly figure shuffled oddly toward him, a big gold crucifix glinting as it swayed on a heavy chain against an ankle-length, black cassock. Dan's pulse shot into his temples at the sight of the gun.

I'm getting mugged by a priest!

He fingered the Buddha talisman in his pocket. Self-defense was OK but with only fifteen days to Kathmandu, he wasn't going to risk his life on a filthy side street in Mumbai. That's not how he'd planned to die. He dropped his bag and held his hands out to the sides. The priest stepped awkwardly toward him, dragging a heavy built-up boot. He used it to kick the bag into the gutter.

"You want money?" Dan unclipped his money belt. "Take it," he said, holding it out at the priest.

The priest ignored it and stumbled closer. His hatchet face caught the light: the unblinking, pallid eyes of an executioner.

He intends to kill me!

Dan caught his breath. His heart thumped. He readied the Buddha statue to throw along with the money belt, preparing to rush the gun and hope for the best.

"Drop your gun, asshole!" barked an American voice.

The priest jerked around. The silhouette of a huge man showed starkly black against the white glare of the lights. The priest moved his gun slightly then hesitated.

An abrasive laugh mocked the priest. "Try it and you're dead, buddy!"

The priest dropped his gun and held his hands out from his sides.

"Vamoose," ordered the American with a jerk of his gun.

The priest maybe didn't understand cowboy English but he got the message. He stepped and dragged his way across the street, giving Dan a definite evil eye. The American kept his gun pointing at the priest until he turned the next corner.

Dan squinted into the light at his imposing savior: wider than Dan and taller even if he took off his boots, a baseball cap pulled down over the lined face of a bearded man in his fifties, this Goliath had to be the heavyweight champion of somewhere. "How can I—?"

"No need, bud. See that cross?" He snorted derisively, sliding his gun under his arm. "He's lucky I'm a better Christian than he is or I'd have shot him to cull the asshole crop." He shook his lantern-jawed head at Dan. "Trying to get killed, you dummy?"

Dummy? Dan let it slide. After all, he'd been one. "Let's get back to the road before he thinks of coming back," he suggested and didn't wait for an answer. He picked up his bag from the gutter and shook the wet dirt off it.

The American picked up the priest's gun and thrust it at Dan butt first. "Here, looks a dope like you'll need it. A souvenir Glock of when I saved your sorry ass in Mumbai, buddy."

Dummy? Dope? Sorry ass?

Dan's taut nerves triggered a sharp response this time. "No thanks. Don't like them. Stick it with the grenades and AK-47 in your toy collection, *buddy.*"

"Frightened of nasty guns?" the American asked mocking him.

"Frightened of nasty India?" Dan snapped back.

The American glowered at him. "Sure you won't need it if you're stupid enough to go down a dark backstreet again?"

Stupid enough? Dan bit his tongue as they walked back toward the main road. The jerk had saved his life after all. He found a couple of pills in his pocket and forced them down his dry throat. He introduced himself to break the silence.

The American said he was William J. Loskota. "Call me Bill," he ordered brusquely.

"How come you were down there?"

"Saw you turn thataway. Reckoned you were a total *tourist ass*. Thought I'd make sure you got to where you were going—other than heaven. Where are you going?"

Dan stopped abruptly. "This *dummy* is heading his *stupid tourist ass* to the Consort Inn," Dan said fixing a wry smile to take the edge off. It fell on Bill's stony ground.

"I hope the *rube* gets there," Bill growled.

"Want to come for a drink as thanks?" Dan offered tonelessly.

"Another time."

Without Dan asking, Bill directed him to the hotel, only about a quarter of a mile away. He ordered him not to stray off the main road until he reached the big church on the right because he had other things to do besides saving Dan's ass again. Dan thought of asking Bill for the Glock since he wanted to shoot him. Instead, he watched Gulliver stride off through the Lilliputians along the sidewalk.

Dan walked slowly toward the church allowing his body and mind to quieten—and the Percodan to dull his throbbing headache. It had been a narrow escape—someone wanted him dead and he could think of only one person. But how had he been traced to Mumbai after a year hiding in Africa? He'd just got off the plane from Cairo and the gunman had been waiting for him? Followed him from the airport and into the side street? Was it the UK passport he'd stolen from a colleague and had doctored for a bargain thousand bucks? No information was safe in India—every kid was a computer hacker or money bought any so-called secure data the criminals wanted. He toyed with the idea of not going to the hotel but he couldn't go back to the airport and fly somewhere else, not if it was the passport. And it was the last thing he wanted to do. Here he was, at the start of a journey across India, a lifetime dream. Mumbai. Jodhpur. Jaipur. Jaisalmer. Agra. Varanasi. Lumbini. Kathmandu. The names had conjured up the exotic in his child's mind: the fortresses of Kipling's Northwest Frontier, maharajas in howdahs atop trumpeting elephants, ferocious tigers, chests of jewels, gold and silver, and vindaloo curries ready to burn a hole in white men's heads. He couldn't see any way Vijay Gill would know he was joining a trip to Kathmandu.

* * *

Kapoor had seen too many bodies floating in the harbor. They'd come in all shapes and sizes: male and female, the young and the old, the skinny and the obese, black, brown and white, stabbed and shot, strangled and drowned, burned and mutilated. One thing they shared in common was their bloated, stinking masses. Only the smell of his aftershave kept him from vomiting at the sight of them. He wished he'd put on more this time but at ten in the evening he'd had to hurry from his tenth-story apartment on the western side of the peninsula and only a quick shave and comb of his crinkly hair had been possible. Still, he'd taken time to select his best uniform from the three clean ones he kept neatly together with his expensive suits: a light khaki shirt with his three golden stars on the epaulettes; khaki trousers creased to perfection by a jeweler with a razor-sharp steam iron; polished brown shoes that could be used as dinner plates.

"Be careful, my sweet," mumbled a voice from the bedroom as it had hundreds of times.

"I will, beloved," he replied just as often.

One last look in the mirror: name badge above his right breast pocket; a rainbow of medal ribbons above the left; his black cap with its red band and silver-grey insignia; its black peak at a rakish angle. His light brown eyes matched the shirt nicely. He didn't forget to strap on the leather holster containing his nine-millimeter Browning.

Nasma sprawled on her back taking up most of the queen-sized bed, a single sheet covering her mound. God, he thought, if she gets any bigger, I'll have to squeeze in a king-sized one. In the *puja*, a small office area they'd put aside for prayer to symbols of their favorite mythical gods, Nasma's goddess Parvati and her son, Kapoor's Ganesha, the scent of the previous evenings incense lingered as Kapoor lit one of the many assorted candles, knelt facing east, head bowed with his hands held together and thumbs to his forehead. The outsized, brass statue of his god on a throne looked down on him from the altar as he repeated a chant eleven times for Lord Ganesha to remove any obstacles for his day and grant him success. Ritual completed patiently, he was soon weaving his way south, blue and white lights flashing, siren clearing a way through the packs of vehicles traveling in the most unexpected directions along the brightly lit, multi-lane Dattaram Lad Path and into the darker streets of downtown Mumbai and to Chowpatty Beach.

A young policeman resting against the white police car he'd stationed halfway across the road leading down to the water jerked to attention and saluted Kapoor before waving him by his own blue and white flashing lights. Kapoor parked behind the old Volkswagen of his assistant superintendent, located a pair of rubber gloves and stepped out onto the pavement being careful to avoid any cow shit. His shoes sank into the soft sand of Chowpatty Beach as he walked toward a group of dark figures with flashlights milling at the water's edge.

Another policeman saluted him and lifted the yellow tape strung on wooden stakes to cordon off a section of the beach. Someone turned on a bright portable light to illuminate two bodies sprawled on the sand. The group of figures dispersed leaving only a short man with a glowing red cigarette sticking out of his face.

Kapoor smiled to himself. *That's right. Look busy when the boss appears.*

With the tide out, the beach was a mess of garbage. Added to it was the pasty white-bluish body of a naked and headless, muscular white man on his back. One wrist was handcuffed to another wrist, one of another headless corpse: a woman with athletic legs, slim hips, no pubic hair, a black knotted mane and pendulous breasts.

"Evening, sah," said Hosseini through drifting gray smoke.

"Good evening, Hosseini." He shook the detective's rubber glove with one of his own and lowered himself to his haunches to examine the bodies.

"White male, about thirty-five, six-feet tall, about two hundred pounds," said Hosseini. "Tortured. Missing several fingers and toes. Heavy abdominal bruising. No rings or jewelry but an interesting tattoo." He shuffled around to the woman's body. "White female, about thirty, five feet six, one hundred and ten pounds. Also tortured. Cigarette burns on her body. No particular distinguishing marks, unfortunately. No heads so no teeth to check. They've both had their fingertips cut off so we can guess criminal records. With the lack of swelling and decomposition in this warm water and little physical damage, I'd say two or three days in the harbor, no longer. Probably dumped from a boat off the point a couple of nights ago." Hosseini jerked his head toward the Raj Bhavan, the state governor's residence at the harbor entrance to the south. "They got it wrong. The current swept the bodies into the bay not out to sea or we'd never have found them in a million years."

Kapoor and Hosseini stood up together. This was why he liked working with Hosseini—he didn't waste time. To the point with all he needed to know. Having worked the murder beat for over thirty years, Hosseini knew more than all the pathologists and medical examiners put together. Also, he knew the currents and tides that moved bodies around the vast harbor. Kapoor had made him his right-hand man despite Chief Dewan's allergy to Muslims.

"We'll check the CCTV cameras out near the point," Hosseini said. He paused then glanced at Kapoor. "Should I talk to Commander Chopra about the traffic in that area?"

Chopra? The boss of the harbor police? That glory sniffer? Kapoor wasn't losing another case to that bastard. "Leave Chopra out of this for now," he ordered.

"The NCB would be interested in killings like this," said Hosseini with a wry smile.

Kapoor showed a jaded eye at the mention of the much hated and totally corrupt Narcotics Control Bureau. Drugs ran in and out of Mumbai faster than a Hindu in Pakistan. The NCB bosses lived particularly well for some reason.

Hosseini nodded knowingly. "Captain Sujat would be better?"

Kapoor nodded at the mention of his "cousin" in the harbor police.

Hosseini crouched down on the wet sand again. The tattoo of a swastika on the man's shoulder was interesting in that it wasn't a good luck Indian Aryan symbol but definitely Nazi Aryan in origin. Hosseini didn't have to tell Kapoor he was a White Supremacist. The tattoo on the forearm was a crude jailhouse design of a skull, a heart with a Christian Cross wrapped in barb wire, and several numbers and letters.

"That's American," said Hosseini fingering the wrinkled skin. "Saw one like that back in ninety-one."

And he'll know the prison I bet, thought Kapoor.

"Walla Walla in Washington State," Hosseini added from his encyclopedic brain.

Kapoor patted Hosseini on the shoulder. There was a superintendent position coming up in Ahmedabad, the nearest big city to the north. Kapoor would make sure Hosseini stayed in Mumbai: promotion and a pay raise would be arranged with Chief Dewan, a man who knew that departmental success trumped his own religious bigotry every time.

March 23rd

CHARLIE SHOOK, UNABLE to stand still in front of the bathroom mirror. Plenty of gel and voila! Fantastic! More makeup to get it just right! A voice told her she was wickedly hot! Better than that fucking Shira and her fucking big tits and fucking huge ass! This'll piss her off! And that fucking bitch Auntie! She's always on my ass and I'm sick of it. She pulled her red tube-top tighter to stick out her nipples. No tits but my legs are fucking awesome! Shira's flexed her cleavage and stolen men who've shown an interest in me. Now it's payback, bitch! Now, I'll steal any man who wants a grab of your tits! She jerked up her black microskirt and giggled at the reflection of her newly dyed and contoured patch. She turned to see how much of her ass was showing and barked a throaty laugh. Fucking, fucking awesome! Showtime!

* * *

Dan woke early to shower, meditate and enjoy the first of his four daily cigarettes while watching the colorful streams of Indians on the sidewalks below from his balcony. He snatched a breakfast of fried eggs and white toast, swallowed his morning pills and took the last of his coffee to the group's meeting scheduled for nine. He arrived early but the small room at the rear of the hotel was already packed with about a dozen tourist-types chatting noisily together at small tables. Two tables next to one another had spare seats: at one sat a broad-shouldered man with a long gray-streaked ponytail while at the other a pale-skinned hawk of an overweight, older woman sat rigidly, her small, cunning eyes scanning the others like a hawk on a fence post looking for its next meal. Brushed-back black hair with a platinum blonde forelock topping a harsh face with a sharp beak of a nose, she fleetingly reminded him of someone. Dan gave her table a pass and sat down next to the stocky man who was flipping through a magazine while chewing on a Twix candy bar between sips of beer.

"We meet again," said Dan.

He'd shared a ride in a taxi with the man who'd maintained a wary silence while checking the taxi's mirrors and a nervous older English woman visiting India for the first time who'd bitten her nails all the way from the airport to the Chhatrapati Shivaji Terminus. Dan got out with the woman at the train station to ensure she wasn't ripped off on her ticket price and caught the right train south to Goa. She thanked him profusely which made it all worthwhile. Afterward, on an almost fatal whim, he decided to stretch his legs with a walk to the hotel instead of hailing another taxi.

The man turned a friendly smile at Dan. "So we do. Ah'm Steve," drawled a hard voice with a twang from south of the Mason-Dixon line. He was a much more relaxed version of his previous self.

"Dan."

"Murican. You?"

"Canadian."

Steve nodded a firm chin. "Canucks are good with me, man." He held out a rock of a fist.

Dan bumped a pound of bone and gristle and thought Steve the kind of guy you didn't want to be not good with. A close look at his sinewed forearms and calloused knuckles and Dan realized he was sitting next to a lethal weapon. The healed wound on his neck interested Dan too. "Americans are good with me" seemed the right reply.

"You guys saved mah life in Afghanistan. Somethin' ah don't forget. Canadians are *real* good with me, *eh?*"

Dan thought that was real good too. Afghanistan. The bullet wound on his neck. The ponytail and silver earrings indicated Steve didn't miss the military that much. Steve was someone with an interesting story to tell and perhaps lubricated enough even at that time of the morning to tell it. "I didn't know the Americans were in Afghanistan."

Steve smiled slyly. "We're not."

Dan wondered if he'd been in US Special Forces. He was built to jump out of planes without a parachute.

"Where were you *not* based?" Dan asked.

Steve chuckled. "We *didn't* fly supplies in Galaxies into Kabul. Fuck, nobody should bother with that shit hole," he said, his voice rising. "The Brits and Russians tried it and copped out. Now it's our turn to fuck up. What a waste of my buddies for—" He cut short his rant and swigged some beer. "Ever been in the military, Dan?"

Dan hated the military more than Steve could ever imagine. But it wasn't the time to rant about his clashes with his ungrieved, alcoholic Navy father who'd had a stroke far too late for the health of his family as well as his sailors.

"No. But I've my grandfather's World War Two Webley," Dan said with an air of amusement. "Does that count?" It weighed more than two pounds and strained Dan's wrist just picking it up.

"A Canuck with a gun? It's lahk meetin' a Yank without one." Steve babbled on, animated as he came back from his virtual tour of duty. "Ah've eight pistols and revolvers: Colts, Smith and Wessons, Rugers, all from the good old US of A." His smugly murderous grin said, "Wanna make mah day?"

"A regular Harry Callahan?" Dan asked without trying to sound too flippant.

"That was a real fine movie, wasn't—?" Steve's train of thought crashed into the buffers when a tall woman with copper-red hair thrown back over her shoulders sashayed the tightest of black yoga pants on a wide rear slowly by their table and slid onto the chair next to the overweight Hawk. The noisy chatter quietened as all the men and even the women glanced her way.

"Jeez," Steve muttered and elbowed Dan. "See that ass?"

Dan couldn't miss it but he had other things in mind: Big Red was stunning, with the type of Hollywood face found on flashing billboards in Times Square and could sell sunlamps in Saudi Arabia. Her heavy breasts amply filling a red tank top advertising NYU easily compensated for her dull eyes and a blank expression. His immediate thought was: fake or a miracle of evolution?

The Hawk smirked at the sound of the door opening behind Dan. He turned to see an even taller redhead, the fringe of her long crimson hair streaked with shocking pink gelled into short spikes that radiated like the Statue of Liberty's crown, bounce by in a butt cheek-revealing, hooker skirt to sit at the Hawk's table and directly in front of him.

"Fuck me. What's that?" said Steve under his breath.

Except for Big Red's rounder head and plumper lips, they were facially similar but not the rest of them. Spikey's small bust and narrow hips packed nowhere near the sexual heat radiating from Big Red.

"You get the punk with no ass," muttered Steve.

Eyes bathed in pools of red and black with clumsy dabs of cheek rouge and wayward scarlet lipstick, Spikey tapped her stilettos, playing with her eyebrow piercings, her hair and constantly fidgeting, eyes dancing around the room. Bored, rebellious punk or high on something? Dan couldn't tell but the circus had come to town with Big Red the major attraction in the Big Top and he had a ringside seat. He ignored Spikey intensely studying him, his eyes drawn back to Big Red like a moth to a flame and he knew the fate of a too-curious moth. He'd worked with the poor and treated the sick, avoided lying as much as possible, didn't steal, swore less and given up drinking—not smoking—but Big Red was the primordial egg-timer archetype that had men getting out their clubs. Raw, primitive instincts flared. Four years in prison and a year in the isolation of the hinterland of Africa hadn't prepared him for such a disturbing physical specimen.

He glanced back at Spikey to find her big black pupils disconcertingly staring through him. She smiled that big slash of lipstick as she slowly and deliberately uncrossed her legs to give him an eyeful of shocking pink.

My God! What a slut!

He looked away quickly and took a deep, cleansing breath that didn't fully cleanse his thoughts about Spikey—that would take a lot more breaths.

A high-pitched "Ladies and gentlemen! Good morning!" interrupted thoughts Dan shouldn't be having. A slight, light-skinned Indian guide spoke on a raised platform from the front of the conference room.

"My name is Loki and I welcome you to Mumbai and the start of our trip across India to Nepal," he told them, his singsong voice rising and falling excitedly. "First of all, I'd like everyone to introduce themselves, please." He looked down to his immediate right at an older man with skin the color of strong tea that blended into an old khaki army shirt with its medals and badges removed. "I am so glad that Major and Missus Drury have been able to join us at the last moment," Loki said, respectfully waving a hand. "Please, sah?"

The major stood quickly to attention. "Major Mark Drury and my wife, Gilly, from Stirling, bonnie Scotland," he bellowed as though on a parade ground. "We retired and it's wonderful to be back visiting the old Raj where we spent so many happy years. I trust we'll all have a jolly good time together."

Dan had to smile. He was pure theater. The wristwatch facing the inside of his wrist indicated a military affectation as did the bushy Victorian mustache extravagance. He sounded English, not Scottish. His silver-haired wife waved a knitting needle and smiled amiably. Dan thought he'd like them.

"Thank you, sah," said Loki. "Missus Jacobs?"

Dan wasn't surprised she didn't attempt to raise her bulk.

"Elaine Jacobs and it's so wunnerful to be with you on this trip," she said in a harsh New York accent. "I'm sure we'll have a real good time together." She encompassed Big Red and Spikey with a wave. "We're from the States. This is my daughter, Shira. Say hi," she ordered with a prod of her shoulder.

"Hi." Shira forced a smile.

"And my niece, Charlene O'Neill."

Spikey sprang to her feet. "Hi!" she exclaimed, bouncing on her toes. "Let's make this trip the greatest ever! I can't wait to get going!" She paused to stare those big pupils at Dan and said, "Let's have fun together!" Her aunt's eyes darted along Spikey's line of sight and narrowed at him.

"Charlene," Missus Jacobs said calmly. "Please sit down, dear. That's enough."

"For fuck's sake, stop telling me what to do!" Spikey shouted down at her aunt.

"Please sit down," repeated Missus Jacobs.

Spikey angrily stamped a foot. "No! I ... will ... not! You fucking bitch!"

A wide-eyed Loki looked like a tiger had entered the room.

"Fuck! Fuck! Fuck!" Spikey dashed out of the room.

"Jesus Christ," said Steve. "I *really* don't like yours."

Punk *and* coke head? thought Dan.

Missus Jacobs' voice boomed over the murmur: "I'm so sorry everyone," she said, waving open palms of resignation. "Charlene's a tad temperamental. Please forgive the disruption, Loki."

Everyone turned to a startled Loki, whose light skin had paled even more. His mouth flapped noiselessly back at them.

Dan threw the poor guy a life jacket. He got to his feet. "Dan Palmer from Canada. Really looking forward to this trip. It's been a dream since I was a kid and I look forward to all you can tell me about your wonderful country, Loki." Missus Jacobs elbowed her daughter and muttered something that had Big Red catch Dan's eye and give him a big smile.

He sat down to a murmur of approval.

"Hear, hear," called out the major.

"Absolutely," said Gilly.

He avoided looking back at Big Red. *What the hell was that?*

"Oh, thank you, thank you, sah," gushed Loki, his color returning.

"Bob Stewart," called out a very short, tanned, grinning bear of an Australian with a bald, bowling ball of a head. No more than five foot four, Bob's shirt strained over a hairy chest above a belly that hadn't missed many desserts. He introduced himself and his glum-faced Indian wife, Rani, without moving his heavy jaw. Apparently a businessman from "Peerth," his broad accent was going to have to get used to but Dan liked Aussies: funny, irreverent, great travel companions and Bob looked like another.

But he had to look at Big Red again. She still eyed him and broadened her perfect smile. An uncomfortable heat flushed his cheeks as his dispassionate theory on the rejection of lust met the reality of an extremely desirable woman coming on to him. Only a few weeks to go and five years of abstinence were under severe pressure. Surely he could dismiss the pleasures of the flesh at this late stage. Or was he whistling past the graveyard?

Steve stood and smiled at Big Red. "Steve Schoenhoff from the US," he said, speaking directly to her. "Great to see some fellow Americans are on the trip—and beautiful ones too ah may say, ladies."

Big Red frowned and glanced at her mother, who regarded him as something she'd scrape off her shoe.

Squeezed into leopard skin Spandex pants and a bulging top, a chubby blonde with Big Hair stood and cocked a hip. Her wide shoulders and thick arms indicated she could easily bench-press Dan. Steve's eyes read her plump rear like an eye chart. "Nice to meet you all. Karen Hunt from Auckland, New Zealand," she said with a broad smile on a world-weary face. "I own a pub back home and I like to party. I hope some of you whackers can keep up with me." Dan instantly liked her.

There was laughter from the men who could see an extrovert woman to have fun with but subdued muttering from the women who could see she was trouble.

"Count me in!" called out Bob. Rani elbowed him but she needn't have bothered—Karen ignored him and sat down.

A young lad, wearing a claret and blue soccer shirt and sporting as much stubble on his head as his sharp chin, got to his feet. "I's Dazza Stevenson," he said in a cockney voice as thin as he was. He had an interesting case of pink eye and a wide smile to match.

"An' this is me china, *Arthur* Penney," he said nodding at a scowling bulldog with a shaved head. Or as we calls 'im ... *Arfa*," he told them with a chuckle at the play on words. "We're from Lunnon, England like."

Arfa blinked bulging eyes that may have had something to do with the open can of Red Bull clenched in his tattooed fingers. Dan wondered if they'd missed their cheap Ryanair flight and flown to India by mistake. Getting pissed with their mates on Ibiza seemed a far more likely destination than this trip to Kathmandu.

Loki checked off the final names on his clipboard. "Jeffrey and Sylvia Thompson?" he called. "More friends from America?" No response. Loki put crosses next to their names. "Duncan?" He looked around the room again. "Duncan Gorkoff?"

The room's doors flew open and a tall, young man with cropped black hair thrust himself into the room. "Sorry I'm late," he told them breathlessly, "the cow broke down." He dropped his bulging backpack with a resounding clatter and took a seat.

The room buzzed again, this time in amusement at the sudden appearance of this handsome lad, all broad shoulders and strong jaw. Dan noticed Duncan got Shira's attention in a hurry.

"What accent is that?" asked someone.

"Canadian," Dan whispered.

"Mister Schoenhoff? Mister Palmer?" Loki called in his high voice. "As single men, you'll be sharing a room on this trip."

Steve turned to Dan and smiled. "No problem."

Loki got their attention again with a wave of his hands. "Ladies and gentlemen! Today, the rest of the day is free so have a look around this wonderful city. I recommend a boat trip to Elephanta Island's magnificent caves. Have a very good day, ladies and—"

Steve coughed like a surfacing whale. His chair crashed back as he jumped to his feet. Red-faced, clutching his throat, he knocked over the table. Dan leaped up, wrapped his arms around Steve's waist and jerked him off the floor as he put all his strength into a powerful thrust under Steve's diaphragm—an inch of a Twix exploded out of his mouth. Steve sank to his knees, whooping air in big gasps. He turned wide eyes up at Dan.

"Fuck!" he rasped.

* * *

The tallest building in the area stuck out on the corner of the street: dark brown and cream bricks with a quadrant of spires of a Gothic-style church. Dan entered through the massive wooden doors into the cool interior and wandered up and down the nave and side aisles taking occasional photos. A purple-robed, wooden statue of Jesus, his head covered by a long, black wig, gave him a jaded look. It was far from the wooden mask of the wild, angry Kali goddess sticking her long, red tongue out at him as Hindus pushed and shoved to see her in the madhouse of her Kolkata temple.

Dan sat down on a well-worn bench blackened by a century of use and relaxed while listening to the distant honking of taxis and buses and the murmur of voices. Something red moved in the corner of his eye—Spikey without the spikes. Her streaked hair was no longer stuck out like Lady Liberty but pulled back in a conservative ponytail. No garish red and black eyeshadow and changed into a white blouse buttoned to her throat and a knee-length black skirt, she looked a freshly scrubbed Catholic schoolgirl. A rosary dangled from one hand while a slim paperback was clutched in the other. Chin down, she walked slowly up to the altar, genuflected and crossed herself with her book. She ambled around the periphery of the church showing no sign of her earlier agitation, stopping at every saint in its own alcove to mumble and play with her beads. Maybe she wasn't a coke head but simply a young woman in emotional turmoil, thought Dan. A wildly rebellious punk one moment and a child needing God's protection the next. His own daughter had gone through a similar stage of revolution, defying him at every turn before pulling back from the edge of a dark, drug-fueled future. He'd been a lousy role model. Spikey had his empathy: the transition from child to adult was a difficult but necessary stage in everyone's development, one that never ended.

Dan closed his eyes and let his mind drift to his children. He was in India not only for his dream journey but to see them for perhaps the last time. His son was close to being a lost cause—he hadn't given up on a reconciliation—but Kathleen had just married an Indian man in Vancouver and held a celebration with his family in Kolkata. Dan had been unable to attend either event for fear of Gill and the police but had hoped to see her and her new husband—who, to Dan's chagrin and Kathleen's amusement, was a year older than he was—when their trips crossed somewhere in northern India. Unfortunately, they'd miss one another by a day in Agra. He wasn't surprised she'd found an older man: Safeer was a mature figure, not some kid trying to find a direction. She'd told Dan she'd found the kind of bond she'd formed with him during the crisis of her mid-teens and his years of incarceration: they knew almost everything about each other and her support had been a major reason he'd survived prison. He took it as a hell of a compliment and hoped Safeer was a far better husband than he had been.

A sweet aroma of roses. He opened his eyes to find a pink-streaked, red ponytail dangling almost directly in front of him. Two gold chain necklaces, one thick, the other thin, encircled a smooth neck tattooed with a small Chinese character. Diamond ear studs. He noticed the title of her book: *The Quiet American*. Graham Greene, one of his favorite authors. She was reading that?

She sighed deeply as she slipped down onto the knee rest and pressed her head on the fingers interlocked around her rosary beads. Her lips mumbled something over and over. She prayed for a few minutes then slid back on the bench before slowly scanning the church until she saw Dan.

"Oh!" She flushed and turned away quickly.

Her embarrassment disarmed Dan. "Hi, I'm Dan," he said softly. "Didn't I see you in the hotel with your aunt and your cousin?"

She turned pink cheeks back to him. "Um … I'm … Charlie. Yes … at the hotel," she stuttered. "I'm so sorry—"

Dan plowed on as though nothing had happened. "We're going on the trip to Kathmandu together, aren't we? Looks to be a good mix in the group. I think we'll have fun."

"I … hope so," she said smiling ruefully.

Dan almost got up to go but instead watched her thoughtfully fingering her beads. Had she deliberately sat in front of him to apologize? It was a big church after all. The change in her was remarkable: aggressive, slutty punk to humble supplicant. Was it sincere or another performance? She intrigued him.

She turned back to him. "Um … are you Catholic too?"

"No."

"Do you believe in God?"

"No. I assume you do."

She sighed deeply. "I try to. I'm not sure."

"Is anyone sure of anything?" He thought of the beliefs he'd adopted to change his life. "Sometimes faith is required, isn't it?"

She nodded. "What do you believe in?"

"I believe in being kind to one another."

"Like you are to me?" Her gold-flecked brown eyes warmed his.

He smiled at them. He was still wary but taken aback by this version of Charlie: a sweet, thoughtful woman under her camouflage of youthful rebellion.

She checked an expensive wristwatch. "I have to get back to Cruella," she told him with a resigned grimace.

"Cruella?"

"Haven't you seen *101 Dalmatians*? Cruella de Vil?"

That's who she was. The black hair and white forelock. "That *fucking bitch*?" he whispered with a grin. She spluttered laughter, flushing again. Heads swiveled and shushed them. They left the church quickly.

Outside the church, a tidal wave of noise rolled over them. There was a sudden silence when the vehicles stopped at the red lights and turned off their motors to save gas and waited for the lights to change. At the green light, engines roared back to life, horns blared and the cacophony started all over again.

She surprised him by taking his arm. "Will you walk me back to the hotel?"

"Let's go."

Dan pushed through the people along the sidewalk, past the stalls piled with fruit, runners, shirts, pants, sheaves of paper, paperback books of all kinds, socks and other clothing.

"Aren't Indians crazy?" he asked.

"Yeah, wonderfully crazy!"

"You like this?" He realized she was almost as tall as him even though she was wearing sandals.

"I've dreamed of being in India since I was a child. I love the exotic mystery of the whole place. The mayhem!"

That's my dream. "And the smell?

"Pity the National Geographics weren't scratch and sniff!" She laughed delightfully girlish. "Have you been to India before?"

"I've just spent a week in Kolkata before coming here. The old Calcutta?"

"Like Mumbai used to be Bombay."

"Wow. An American who knows some geography?"

She chuckled. "Didn't God create war so Americans would learn geography?"

She can quote Mark Twain?

"I have to confess I googled Mumbai before I left home," she told him. "I had no idea where it was. But I did memorize *namaste*."

"That's more Hindi than the entire US knows. *Mera nam* Dan *hai. Apka nam kya hai?*"

"Whoa, you speak Hindi?" She held up an arresting palm. "Let me guess." She frowned and tapped her long fingers on her bright red lips encouraging Dan's attention.

"Charlie. And you're Dan?"

"Easy, isn't it?" Dan pulled a folded sheet of paper out of his pocket. "Especially when I googled a tourist vocabulary." He gave it to her. "Keep it. I have a spare."

"Oh, thanks a lot."

"You like Graham Greene?" he asked.

"Ah, this?" She waved her paperback. "I saw the film and decided to read the book."

"What did you think?"

"Great film and great book so far." A thoughtful look formed as she twisted her mouth. "Helps me understand the foundations of the disastrous Vietnam War."

Dan could see the attraction of Graham Greene with his Catholic perspective on the world's moral and political issues to a young Catholic woman struggling to find her way. Serious stuff when her contemporaries were playing with their phones in the malls to discover the latest pop star's planned wardrobe malfunction.

"And what people will do for love?" he asked.

She held up a cautionary finger. "Don't tell me what happens to Fowler, Pyle and Phuong!"

"OK. Have you read his *Our Man in Havana*?" he asked.

"Uh-huh. It's one of his entertainments, right? But it taught me a bit about Cuba pre-missile crisis. My father talked to me about what happened in 1962. He wasn't surprised in the slightest when the people turned to Castro and booted out that thug Batista we had backed."

"You remind me of Milly."

"Wormold's sixteen-year-old, devoutly Catholic daughter?" She laughed and elbowed him playfully. "I hope I'm not that tight-assed!"

"Just a little," he teased. Her eyes flashed amusement.

In the crowded hotel lobby, Charlie smiled at him. "Thanks so much," she said earnestly. "It was so good talking to you. Please, let's do it again."

"I'd like that," he told her and really meant it. She was surprisingly interesting. "One last thing. I'd leave your necklaces, rings and your watch in the hotel safe or you won't come back with them."

"Oh. OK."

"What have you two been doing?" snapped a harsh voice from across the lobby. Cruella waddled her bulk toward them.

Charlie rolled her eyes. "Oh my God, what's your problem now?"

"Don't talk to me like that!" barked Cruella. "Get to your room!"

"Get to my room?" Charlie flared. "What am I? Fucking ten?"

"Your room, young lady! Now!"

Dan reached out and held Charlie's arm. "I'm so sorry it upset you, Missus Jacobs," he said calmly. "We met while praying in the church at the end of the street. I escorted her back to the hotel to make sure she was safe." Charlie and Cruella blinked at his quiet politeness.

Cruella grabbed Charlie's other arm and pulled her away from him. "Let's go!"

Dan didn't miss Charlie's furtive smile.

* * *

In the air-conditioned sports bar, Dan ordered a ginger ale and parked an elbow on the counter. Inevitably, a cricket game was showing on the big TV above him. Patrons' *oohs* and *aahs* interspersed swearing at umpires' decisions on *lbw*s and *not out*s and *howzat*s.

Steve climbed onto the seat next to Dan and slapped him on the back. "Mah hero! Lahk a beer?"

Dan waved his ginger ale. "I don't drink."

"For real?" Steve shrugged and snapped his fingers for a drink. "Ah sure do owe ya, buddy. Ah almost met mah maker, didn't ah?"

"Sure. For a moment you were *Twix* heaven and hell."

Steve barked like a sea lion. "A Canuck saves me again."

"What did the first one do? Play goalie for your hockey team?"

Steve paused for a moment and smiled, savoring the story. "We were unloading aviation fuel in Kandahar when a raghead wearing an explosive vest drove his motorbike straight toward our Galaxy. If he'd succeeded, parts of me would have been in China."

"What happened?"

"Sergeant John McLean sent parts of *him* to China and forever earned my gratitude."

"Canada has troops there?"

"You don't."

His beer arrived and he drained half of it. "Man that Big Red is really somethin', isn't she?"

Dan had to agree. *Too much something.*

"A woman like that could kill me."

You're not the only one, thought Dan.

"But, man, what a way to go, huh?"

That had occurred to Dan too. About four inches taller than Steve and twice as wide at the hip, Shira killing Steve was a good possibility. "She is a very big girl," he said carefully.

Steve barked another laugh. "Ah get ya but we're all the same height lying down, man!"

Dan had to agree with his physics and admire his ambition.

"Listen up, ah'm a bit of a nighthawk. Old military habit. And if ah'm there in the mornin', ah do at least a half hour of exercises. Ya'll get used to it." Steve finished off his beer. "See ya later."

Dan liked Steve but was sharing with him going to be an excruciating couple of weeks talking about the latest guns and drooling at big girls' asses all the way to Kathmandu? On the positive side, Steve owed him his life. That could come in handy since someone was trying to kill him.

A crushed six over the boundary enlivened the next few overs of rather dull cricket before the major bellied up to the bar and ordered a Glenlivet Scotch and water on the side.

"Cheers," Dan offered.

Major Drury smiled politely and nodded. "Oh, my fellow traveler. Cheers." They clinked glasses. "I think this will be a bloody good trip. Looks like a top bunch of chaps to me."

"The women aren't bad either."

"Ha! Indeed. Those redheads? My God, if only I were younger. But don't tell the wife!" He raised an eyebrow at Dan. "On your own?"

"Yes, just me. Dan Palmer." He offered a hand. "And you're Mark, right? From Scotland. Interesting accent for a Scot."

"Ha! By way of London. As far from those bastard wallies in the fucking—excuse my French—government as I can reasonably get. And you're one of our two Canucks. Is it OK to say Canuck these days? Not offensive or anything in these ghastly PC days?" He wiped some Scotch off his mustache from waxed point to waxed point with a gnarled index finger.

"Not at all."

"It's not like calling you a cunt or—"

Karen Hunt, the lumpy blonde, appeared at their side, beer glass in hand. "Did I hear my name called?" she purred coolly. No hint of a blush, only of a grin. Dan wasn't surprised. She didn't seem to be a shrinking violet.

Mark cleared his throat, his tanned cheeks darkening further. "Um... er..." His eyes mooned Dan. It was like a naked woman had been allowed into his Officers' Mess—without the right tie.

"Nice to meet you. I'm Dan." He held out his hand and received a firm grip in return as she hitched her well-padded bottom up on a barstool. "Care for a drink?" He waved to the bartender. "A frostie?"

"Too right. I'm Karen." She held out her strong hand to Mark. "No worries. I've been called worse. And called people worse. Much worse."

Mark exhaled. "Jolly good. I'm Mark. I've called people a lot worse, too."

A large hand gripped Dan's shoulder. "Howdy, *rube*. Buy me that drink for saving your life?"

Dan looked into William J. Loskota's fierce grin. *Not him again.* Bill took off his New York Yankees ball cap and sunglasses to reveal longish, blond hair and startlingly blue eyes that fired out of a leathery face, slightly rearranged by physical combat. When he shook everyone's hands with a meaty fist, he batted those eyes and held onto Karen's hand a bit longer than Dan thought necessary. *Another Yank who likes big women?* Dan twitched annoyance but he had to show his gratitude, no matter how forced. "What'll you have?" he asked.

"Bourbon. Double on the rocks."

"A bottle of Jack Daniels, please," Dan told the bartender. "And three glasses with ice."

Bill leaned his enormous frame against the bar next to Dan and more than smiled at Karen. "Right on. Who's not drinking?"

Dan lifted his ginger ale to him. "I'm on medications."

"It's not that syphilis again?" asked Mark.

Karen giggled. "Surely not chlamydia?"

"A lovely girl, chlamydia," said Mark.

Bill laughed. "I love those Greek chicks."

Dan opened his palms. "No, I have to confess it's just the clap."

"Oh, boring," said Bill.

Karen chuckled. "Have you lot finished?" She turned to Bill. "What's a rube anyway?"

"A hick from the sticks." He thumped Dan on the back. "A shmuck."

Dan let it go. Saving his life cut Bill a lot of slack and it wasn't the time or place to be bothered by him.

"What was that about saving Dan's life?" Karen asked.

"He was wandering around in darkest Mumbai last night looking to get robbed and I saved his sorry ass."

"Ah, a real dipstick," said Karen.

"A right wally," chimed in Mark.

"I think I'll find another trip," Dan said maintaining his good humor.

The bartender reappeared and poured out the American whiskey. Karen clinked glasses with all of them. "Here's to you cunts then."

Bill choked on his drink. This time, Mark laughed out loud. Dan's turn—he thumped Bill hard on the back as he dribbled down his shirt. *Take that, asshole! Karma!*

Oh, I like Karen. She's going to be a lot of fun if Steve doesn't get in the way.

Half an hour later, they said goodbye to Bill. Dan was thoroughly tired of the loquacious bastard who'd dominated the conversation, particularly with Karen. They'd learned Bill was from Dallas, loved baseball and country and western music, told jokes—some funny—and—in Dan's mind—was an all-around pain in the ass. Dan gladly waved him off in a tuk-tuk and took his giggling companions to the lobby for a lubricated trip to Elephanta Island.

* * *

Wearing a broad-brimmed sun hat and an expectant smile, Charlie found Dan and a few others assembling for the excursion to Elephanta Island. She hesitated, dreading what these people must think of her. Not everyone would be as forgiving as Dan. What a surprise he'd been: understanding, humorous, calm and selfassured—the mature kind of man she gravitated to. He could have embarrassed her big time for flashing him but instead, he'd been so sweet.

She studied him: tall with strong arms ending in large hands; the firm chin of a boxer below a bent nose and crooked eyebrow that may have indicated he had been one. He ran one of those hands back over his slicked black hair that was graying at the temples as he listened attentively to the major, just like he'd listened to her. The thin scar that ran from below his ear across his throat combined with his pugilistic features added to his sexual attraction—why else had she changed into a short sundress to show off her legs?—but she wasn't fifteen anymore, thank God, with fire in her loins and peanut butter for brains. She wanted sex with a man but only as part of a real friendship. A man who'd get her pulse going but who valued her for who she was not what was between her legs. Could it be with Dan after that horror show? They shared an interest in books and she looked forward to more talk about that. He seemed so at peace with his life and it had rubbed off on her within minutes—he was a man to share her thoughts and not patronize or judge. She'd felt herself relaxing with Dan and despite his hard exterior she detected a softer interior that many men would never reveal, especially to a woman. But what if he thought her a nutcase? What did he really think of her childish rant in the hotel? Had he just been nice and would shun her for the rest of the trip? She fingered the cross on her necklace and took a deep breath before putting on a smile.

"Hi," she said, to everyone but sidled up to Dan. All of them except Dan looked a bit tipsy. "Loki told me about your trip to the island. Can I join you?"

"What's your fucking aunt think of this?"

She giggled with relief. *How I like him!* "Fuck my fucking aunt."

Dan popped on his straw hat and smiled. "Let's go then."

The young driver, apparently freshly minted from the rural backwaters, didn't know how to get to the Gateway to India, the most famous landmark in Mumbai, so they had to show him on the hotel's tourist map. In the backseat of the taxi, Charlie squeezed up against Dan, casually hitching up her sundress far enough to reveal more of her thighs. The way to a man's heart wasn't necessarily through his brain. Dan turned more toward her, twitching his nose.

"That's a lovely perfume," he remarked.

"Isn't it?" she replied. "American Beauty."

"Suits you."

She tingled. This was going well. With his arm behind her on the seat, she rested against him and let him fill his nostrils as far as the harbor. Their driver took a side journey to a shop in a backstreet in case they wanted to buy a carpet or anything at all before eventually finding the Gateway to India, a smaller version of the Arc de Triomphe, at the harbor. Fending off ticket touts who hassled them to take tours on "this special religious ceremony day" that didn't exist and persistent ferry-ticket vendors with special ferry deals, they went down the gangplank onto the boat for Elephanta Island. Bob and Rani joined them, falling clumsily out of a taxi and scrambling onto the open-decked ferry just before it embarked.

The ferry cruised through anchored freighters and tankers across the glistening waters of the enormous harbor. Charlie followed Dan and sat in the bow of the boat, with the wind blowing through her light dress and the bright sunshine turning her skin to gold. Dan sat holding an ankle over one knee while reading a thick book in his lap. She took out *The Quiet American* from her bag.

"Back to see what Fowler's up to," she said to invite conversation.

Dan looked up. "Well, he—"

"Don't you dare!" She waved an admonishing finger. "Not far to go. It's making me tense."

"Let's talk about the ending when you finish."

"I'd like to. What's your book?"

"Top Ten Sights in Mumbai by Graham Greene. One of his entertainments."

Without missing a beat she said, "The dissolute, tortured priest did it."

"Damn! Now you've spoiled it!" He snapped the book closed. "For that, I'll tell you Fowler—"

Charlie covered her ears and made gobbledygook noises before giggling. Dan laughed at her. *Oh, this is fun!* He made her feel good. She gave him her biggest smile.

After the ferry docked, they avoided a few stray cows before entering a gauntlet of the ubiquitous stalls selling shirts, jewelry, guidebooks and other tourist bric-a-brac that lined several flights of stone stairs. They emerged out of breath at the entrance to the Elephanta Caves with their famous fifth-century Hindu rock carvings.

"This is great!" said Charlie sticking close to Dan as they wandered into the cool interior of the biggest hand-carved cave, one that could have been used as a ballroom. She looked up at a group of twenty-foot-tall carvings. "What's this? It's amazing."

"They're the three big gods of Hinduism: Shiva, Brahma and Vishnu," he told her.

"Wow. How many gods do they have?"

"Hundreds, possibly three hundred and thirty million—or more."

"You're kidding? No wonder monotheism caught on."

"I once caught monotheism. I felt godawful for weeks."

Karen groaned but Charlie laughed, delighted with him. This was a guy she could have fun with.

"Hinduism is actually monotheistic," Dan said. "All the gods are mythological, many ways of devotional practice to one universal reality, Brahman."

"Just like Christians, Muslims and Jews then?" said Charlie to keep her conversation with Dan going. She was interested anyway. Since her return to Catholicism, she wanted to know more about all religions.

Dan waggled his head a little. "Close enough."

"You know a lot about religions, don't you?" she asked. Nothing like a bit of flattery to loosen men up, she thought.

"Some."

He sounded modest about it. She liked that too.

Dan smiled at her. "You're interested in this stuff?"

"Absolutely. Maybe we can get together and talk about it later?"

Their eyes lingered for just enough time for Charlie to sense he was becoming more interested in her.

"Who's the busty sheila over there?" asked Karen, pointing at another large stone carving.

Dan checked the photos in his book. "Parvati. Shiva's lady. Otherwise known as Kali, Nadiapurna, Annapurna, Durga and other names depending on her day of the month." Charlie giggled. "Kali is the real bitch apparently," he added.

"So we know when that was," said Karen. "Great boobs though! Being a goddess has its advantages."

"You can't be jealous, can you?"

Karen laughed. "Thank you, sweetie."

Was Dan flirting with her? Surely not! Overweight, overloud and over fifty? Was it the boobs? Christ, thought Charlie, how she wished she'd got those implants. Maybe now she would when she got back home. Big ones. Bigger than Shira's damn it! She looked up at the voluptuous goddess. "Nice change from all the male gods, Dan," she said. "Glad to see women get in on it."

"Hindus were very affirmative action in the fifth century."

"You are a dipstick," said Karen with a shake of her head.

"A funny dipstick," said Charlie, catching Dan's eye with a smile. She pointed at a stubby column of gray stone, about three feet high and a couple of feet across. She walked over and rubbed her hand on it. "What's this thing?" she asked and watched a big grin form on Dan's face.

"Be careful," he warned, seriously. "It's Shiva's lingam."

"Lingam?"

Karen barked a laugh. "Quite the stubby!"

"Oh." Charlie felt a surge of warmth in her cheeks but laughed along with them. "Wow. How big was his wife?"

"Big enough apparently. They had a kid. He's over there." Dan pointed at the carving of a human body with an elephant's head. "He's Ganesha, the happy god. You'll see him on houses, cribs and cars, and anywhere you fancy a bit of luck."

"How'd he get the head?" asked Charlie.

"Dad got annoyed when he thought the wife was cheating on him. Thought the kid was her lover so ripped his head off and eventually replaced it with an elephant's."

"I once had a bit of a blue with my ankle-biter and wanted to do that to him too but he called Child Services," said Karen. "Little brown-eyed mullet."

Dan and Charlie looked at each other.

"What?" said Karen.

"Do you actually know any English?" Dan asked.

"I know *bugger off, you whackers!*" Karen punched him not so lightly on the shoulder but laughed herself. "Now let's get a few photos of you with these god things."

Dan put his arm around Charlie's waist and pulled her close. She did the same to him and felt that tingle run through her again. She had no problem smiling into Karen's camera.

* * *

Recycled Love

Six in the evening, the ferry tied up back at the Gateway to India after sailing into a tangerine sun dropping into liquid gold. Low tide and the waters were quiet: leviathans of oil tankers and container-stacked carriers rested at anchor; yachts and powerboats docked for the evening; the white lights of downtown Mumbai lined the bay.

Dan sat with Mark and Gilly avoiding choosing between Charlie and Karen. He felt flattered that Charlie was hitting on him and he liked her too but not now. Karen was a different kettle of fish—or was it sharks: older than him and an experienced woman of the world and probably the underworld. She was easy to like with her bold, devil-may-care attitude about what she said and did and how she looked.

Charlie told Dan she'd better get back to the hotel. Her aunt would be wondering where she'd got to and she could be a mean cow about it. She couldn't defy her aunt too much or who knows what the old bitch would do. She could cancel the whole trip and take them back to the US whenever she felt like it. She was lucky to have even got this trip out of her. It had been a surprising change of what heart she had.

"Thanks for a wonderful day," Charlie told him with a hug and a kiss on the cheek. "This is going to be a great trip!" She joined Mark, Gilly, Bob and Rani for the ride back to the hotel and waved goodbye through the window.

"I think she likes you," said Karen. "Pity she's a child, isn't it?"

"I prefer old women like you anyway."

Karen laughed. "Bastard. So take the old girl to dinner then."

"OK. I'll take you to Chowpatty Beach."

"*Cow patty?*"

* * *

The tide was out and the beach was a mess of plastic bottles and bags, and other garbage, so they curtailed their walk and crossed the road to a restaurant with a view of the lights of the silhouetted buildings and trees on the point. They shared cashew and vegetable plates with spicy naan bread. Karen toasted him with a lime-soda concoction.

"Here's to a great trip even if everyone else turns out to be boring. You're a bit of laugh, mate."

"Thanks, you're not so bad yourself." He clinked his glass with hers. "Always travel on your own?"

"I'm a writer. It's a great way to meet new people and do new things. Learn about new cultures and then write about it."

"Novels?"

"Anything to make money. Short articles, long ones, travel columns, novels, you name it."

"Any book I might have heard of?"

"*Prison Bitches* has sold well. Lots of violence and lesbian sex."

"Lesbian sex?"

"Write what you know. Got something against lickerty splits?"

The weightlifter physique? She's a lesbian? He couldn't have found a more perfect woman: a lot of fun and no complications. "Not at all. I like women too."

She chuckled. "I'm writing a travel blog for this trip to keep my fans engaged. Helps spread my name and sell, sell, sell. You'll be in it. So watch out. What are you doing on the trip?"

"It's been a dream to visit the splendors of India. Thought I'd try a small group for a change."

"Small groups can be bloody awful. I know. I blogged about a trip I had to Bali and pissed off my group when they read it. They were all dickheads anyway."

"What about this lot?"

"Well, you're all right. And Mark and Gilly look fun. The Brit boys probably have a good sense of humor. That Steve guy looks an arsehole. Shira? I think her tits are in *The Guinness Book of Records*. Her mother? Crikey. A fucking medusa. No wonder Charlie skedaddled back to the hotel."

"Why do you think rich Americans like them are on a trip like this?"

"Tired of the suave and sophisticated down at the tennis club? Trolling for a bit of rough?"

"You're not that bad."

Karen poked a fork at him. "Ha ha. Arsehole. I meant you." She eyed his left hand. "No wife or just hiding the ring?"

"Or significant bother. You?"

"Me neither." She clinked glasses with him. "Bonzer! Let's have fun on this bloody trip."

"Absolutely. But may I ask you a favor?"

"Sure, what?"

"Do you think I could sleep with you tonight?"

March 24th

RED-FACED BOB WRESTLED a fridge of a suitcase onto the overhead rack as the group members sorted out their seating in the carriage.

"*Jeesus,* what a shabby troin," he grunted.

Dan knew Bob was only punning—the early morning Shabadhi Express out of Mumbai north to Ahmedabad was comfortable with its cushioned bench seats, clean windows and decent toilets. Coffee and tea were immediately available from an attendant pushing a cart along the middle aisle and a light breakfast was promised.

With much shuddering, the train engine hauled its string of carriages with gathering speed out of the Victorian red-brick crenellations of the Chhatrapati Shivaji Terminus and through the shambles of the almost endless Mumbai slums with weak daylight beginning to show.

Most of the group members immediately tried to catch up on their lost sleep but Dan stayed awake to watch the countryside change as morning came to the great expanse of rural India, the train swaying its way north through misty, green fields of corn, millet and rice and wandering herds of cows and water buffalo.

Dan glanced across at the sleeping Steve Schoenhoff. Thank God Karen had paid the expensive single supplement and got a room of her own. She'd refused his offer of payment but recommended beer to Nepal to keep her from kicking him out. He just wanted to relax but Charlie worried him. She'd scarcely moved a muscle since boarding the train. Trapped against the window by her aunt, it was difficult for her to move anything but it was the way she ignored the book open on her lap and stared sightlessly out at the passing countryside.

George Henry

The bubbly young woman on Elephanta Island had gone into hibernation. At least she wasn't the slut.

* * *

The seat sagged under the heavy pressure of Cruella squeezing her mass onto the seat as far as she could. He recognized her perfume—sweet bourbon that showed in her demi-glace eyes. Ever since Dan had stopped drinking his heightened sense of smell could pick out booze at fifty paces.

"Good morning, young man," she said. "How are you today?"

"Fine thanks. And you?"

With one hand she held her stick vertically between her knees and got quickly to business. "My niece tells me she went to Elephanta Island with you yesterday."

"Yes, we—"

"Don't do that again without my permission," she interjected harshly.

"We weren't alone if that's what worries you. Mark, Gilly, Karen, Bob and Rani were chaperoning us. Nothing untoward happened to your niece's honor, you can be assured," he said quietly, an apologetic English duke on Masterpiece Theater.

"She only mentioned *you*," she said pointedly before softening her tone. "I'm responsible for her on this silly trip. I need to know where she is ... *at all times*,"

"I'll let you know if she's with me again. OK?"

She tilted her head toward him and lowered her voice. "I'd prefer she wasn't with you again. She can be moody ... *unpredictable*. Haven't you noticed how *depressed* she is this morning? Yesterday, she was bouncing off the walls at breakfast," she reminded him. "And there's also a *protection* issue."

He waited her out.

"She's such a problem to herself. And it would be a problem for you if you get too close to her. *Understand?*"

He nodded. He was being warned to keep away from Charlie but it was too late: the bad-good girl had hooked his interest and his Rescue Ranger had saddled up way back on Elephanta Island. She did remind him of his daughter, Kathleen, so maybe that was part of it. He'd been through the madness of her teenage mood swings and risky behavior and she'd become a wonderful young woman. Maybe he could do it again with Charlie: help her deal with growing up and dealing with her anger—and maybe drugs. She just had to learn to love herself first. If he was going to help her, he had to know more about the dynamics of this odd family group.

"You know I'm Dan. You're Elaine, aren't you? Why don't we all have a drink together before dinner to get to know each other?"

She blinked slowly, considering the offer. "That would be agreeable," she decided with an emphatic dip of her beak.

* * *

Dan rubbed his eyes, the back of his neck, exhaled deeply and lay back by the window across the carriage from where Karen had teamed up with Gilly and Mark. Bob and Rani, the woman the humor god had bypassed sat in front of them. Even sleeping, Rani looked miserable, unlike Bob, who joked with the Brit boys in complete contrast to his dour, dead weight of a wife. When the boys moved off to sit with Duncan, Dan moved over.

"You live in Perth you said, Bob?" he asked.

"Been there?"

"No."

"Thought so. No one goes to Perth unless they're lost."

Tucked away on the west coast of Australia separated from the east coast by thousands of miles of desert, to the west from Africa by more thousands of miles of seawater and with Antarctica to the south, Dan could see why. Nice place to hide out from humanity though. He could see a certain attraction.

"Did Rani get lost?" He glanced at Rani but she stayed mummified.

"Nah. Met Rani when I first visited Mumbai back in the mid-eighties." Dan thought it might have been at a garage sale and he'd got done. He should have gone for the bedside lamp.

Bob elbowed her. "Been together now about six years, haven't we, love?"

Rani emitted a low "Mmm" to show she was still alive. Dan couldn't quite see the attraction of a vacuous lump like Rani for a garrulous Aussie like Bob.

"You've traveled a lot?" Dan asked breezily to keep the unnecessary conversation going until he'd been polite long enough to withdraw.

"All over, mate. Wherever there's work to be done."

"You're an engineer, something like that?"

Bob attempted an enigmatic smile that came off creepy. "Business. Import-Export." A sly wink. "That kind of thing."

Dan knew the kind of thing. It's called "One Step ahead of the Law" and having friends in the warehouses and checking the containers out on the docks.

"You and James Bond?" he quipped.

"Yeah, that's us. What do you do?"

He got up to go. "I work for Customs and Excise."

"You bloody what?"

Dan was sure he heard Bob's buttocks squeak.

* * *

"I'm Shira," she said languidly in an unexpectedly childish voice, holding out a hand as she slid a big hip into him along the blue plastic recently warmed by her mother.

Dan shook her long fingers with red nails like Charlie's. "I'm Dan."

She was dressed in a white silk blouse and a pair of matching slacks, each a few sizes too small for their contents, so he kept his eyes up. She smelled faintly of roses like Charlie. No bourbon.

"Mother wants us to be friends. She must like you," she said.

"She does?"

"Wouldn't you like to be?" she asked coyly chewing on a nail.

"Why not?" He could think of a list beginning with what he was not looking at. "Did you see much of Mumbai?" he asked to change the subject and his thoughts.

She turned her mouth upside down. "We stayed with Mother together at the hotel. We didn't go anywhere. We wish we could have gone to that island with you. Take us next time you do something like that? Please?"

We? She's British Royal Family?

"Your mother won't mind?"

"I'm not the one she worries about."

"OK then."

"Oh goody!" She clapped her hands together with delight. "I'm so glad you're on this trip. We think we can have some fun, don't you?"

He tensed like he'd touched an electric fence at the sudden press of a warm, heavy breast on his upper arm as she unexpectedly reached over to hold his left hand. And if that wasn't enough to get his attention, she toyed with his fingers.

"You're not married, right?" she asked.

"Right."

"What's this one?" she asked waggling his index finger playfully.

The carriage began to feel a little warm. "A Greek puzzle ring. A trip to Greece with my first big love when I was twenty-one. Ended in misery like all first loves."

"And these?" Two gold rings were interlocked on the same finger.

"My grandfather and great uncle's twenty-first birthday rings. They're twenty-one karat and almost a hundred years old."

"You've said twenty-one three times!" she cried excitedly as though it meant something. "Twenty-one's my favorite number! It must be yours too!"

"It is now," he said to keep her as happy as his arm and fingers.

"Goody!" She ran a fingernail flirtatiously along his pinky. "Now, how about this one?" She turned the outer ring on the inner one.

"Most likely twenty-one karat tin. It's a Buddhist ring."

He took it off and gave it to her for a closer look.

"What's the inscription say?" she asked.

"It's a mantra. *Om Mani Padme Hum.* The six syllables cover the search for perfection in generosity, ethics, tolerance and patience, perseverance, concentration, and the practice of wisdom," he explained but he could tell by the way she played coquettishly with a long strand of hair and flapped her eyelashes at him she wasn't listening.

She was more beautiful than Charlie: crimson lips plumped and shaped by Cupid himself; a flawless skin with not a wrinkle to be seen around her large eyes and wide mouth; Charlie's thin nose and high cheekbones but more perfectly balanced; plucked eyebrows that arced symmetrically across her smooth forehead above brown eyes speckled with gold. Charlie's eyes.

She caught him staring and smiled. "You think Shira's beautiful, don't you?"

"You and Charlie are two beaut—"

"Charlie!" She snorted her annoyance. "Charlie copies almost everything I do and I'm sick of it," she hissed. "You'll see. She's obsessed with me. Never got the boys like I did." She tilted her head up at him, running her fingers from her smooth neck to her open blouse. "I like you, Dan. Do you like me?"

"I think we'll have a good trip together."

She beamed. "Would you like to meet with me later?" she asked fingering the gold Star of David resting in her cleavage.

"I've already got a date with your mother," he said, "but I'd love you to join us."

She kissed him quickly on the cheek and breathed, "Later then."

On her way back up the carriage, Dan noticed Cruella lifted her eyes from her book to nod at her daughter. He also noticed Shira had kept his Buddhist ring. And Charlie had surfaced with the eyes of a blast furnace: her look at Shira was meant to kill. Her look at him wasn't much different.

Ahmedabad

Charlie burst through the door wearing a cool, cream wrap dress and a hard frown. She threw herself on the end of the bed and stared angrily at the carpet. Cruella having chosen an imperial purple kaftan and looking as coldly indifferent to Charlie as a polar bear to a snowstorm was suitably given a stuffed leather throne all to herself. A smug Shira sank her rear on the sofa next to Karen and smiled at Dan. Dressed for a night at the casino with James Bond, she glittered in a garishly maroon, sequined top that was open for business and a slitted, black skirt she hitched above her knee.

"Charlene she can only have fruit juice," declared Cruella.

Charlie cut the air with a razor sharp "Must you treat me like a child? I'm almost twenty-one!"

Dan winced. *She's only twenty? She's younger than Kathleen! Charlie's underage drinking? That's what it's all about? She can own a semi-automatic assault rifle but can't drink?*

Shira rolled her eyes at Dan.

"Almost," Cruella snapped back. "You're still a minor, young lady."

Charlie's face flared. "Oh, fuck it!" She jumped up and propelled herself from the room, slamming the door behind her.

Cruella sighed and held her palms up to the others. "She's a handful that silly—"

Dan didn't wait for the rest. He paused at the hotel entrance and looked quickly both ways. Down the crowded street, a red head bobbed above the mass of black hair, taqiya caps and hijabs. Pushing bodies brusquely aside, he caught up with her in a nearby square where she'd stopped, gasping with her head in her hands.

"Charlie!" He grabbed her and pulled her out of the crowd.

"I'm sorry," she blurted. "They humiliate me!"

He reached for a large tissue in his pocket. She took it, dabbed her face and blew her nose.

"Let's stroll to calm down. OK?" Dan took her arm and led her by stalls piled with clothes and general junk for sale. He pointed to a stack of cricket bats on the ground. "Next time, take one of these. You might need one to hit your aunt for six."

"Hit for six?"

"It's a cricket term. Something like a home run."

"You bet! I'd like to hit both of them out of the park!"

He held both her arms and looked straight into her reddened eyes. "Take it easy. I see your aunt's point—she's responsible for you and you're not drinking age in her eyes."

"What? You're on her side?"

"You kidding? Have a drink with me later. How's that?"

"That'd be great!" Her broad smile slipped into anger again. "Did you see that fucking Shira smirking at me? Ugh, she's such a bitch! Any man I—" She stopped abruptly and looked away.

A bony cow forced its head between them. Charlie cooled as she patted the cow's head and stroked its back. Dan rubbed the animal's head between its big black eyes.

"Do you like her?" Charlie asked without looking at Dan.

"The cow?"

"You idiot!" She slapped his arm playfully. "The other fucking cow! Shira!"

He pulled her into the flow of bodies back toward the hotel. "Charlie, forget about her and just be. Enjoy the mayhem of India, Toto. Isn't that what you came for? I've a feeling we're not in Kansas anymore."

"Woof!" She giggled and slipped her arm around his. "It is amazing, isn't it?"

Sweating women used long wooden ladles to stir pans of heated milk while others stirred bubbling cauldrons of soups. A man slept on a pile of bolts of silk and cotton, surrounded by shelves of skeins of yarn while his tea water boiled itself to dryness in a copper pot on a gas ring. Charlie woke him up and pointed to the pot—he immediately offered them tea and tried to sell them something.

Charlie gasped. "Wow! Look at those!"

She stopped at a women's underwear stall where a throng of well-covered women was sifting through piles of bras and panties. The only server was a long-bearded man who enthusiastically waved the underwear in both hands at his customers.

"That's my kind of job," he told her.

"Wow. How about those?" Sexy, colored bras and panties fluttered from hangers alongside sequin-covered robes above the stall.

Dan grinned. "All is not what it appears, huh?"

Charlie giggled. "Ooh! Behind closed beaded curtains? I like the red bra."

The owner followed their eyes and was over in a flash waving the bra, babbling something incomprehensible except for "beautiful one" and "lovely *memsahib*".

She took the bra and held it over her small breasts. "What d'you think?" she asked, pink rising in her face. The owner knew his sizes.

"Mmm. Far too big."

"Bastard!" She waved an open palm at him but only tapped him lightly on the cheek.

He hesitated but the Devil made him do it. "How about I buy it for you. Think of it as a souvenir."

The owner became frenetic over a possible sale. He peppered his Hindi with "lovely lady" and "most gorgeous" as he waved matching panties and a negligible thong.

"Might as well take the panties too," Dan suggested.

When she took the panties from the owner and held them against her hips, the owner's voice jumped an octave. "OK. They'll do," she said, her cheeks now glowing.

"They certainly will," said Dan, his imagination off the leash. He took out a bunch of notes, haggled halfheartedly and had the almost epileptically happy owner throw in the minuscule thong as part of the deal. He handed the plastic bag with all the lingerie to a beaming Charlie. "Feeling better?" he asked. He was certainly feeling better.

"Yes, thanks so much. You're so sweet." She kissed him on the cheek and excitedly swung her bag. "And to think we're not even dating yet," she said in a tone that promised something Dan hadn't expected.

Dan had definitely flirted too much. "Let's go back," he suggested to cool things down. "Don't let your aunt and cousin control your happiness. They can't make you suffer, only you can."

"Yeah, screw 'em!" She laughed and took his arm again, continuing to happily swing her gifts.

* * *

The buffet was in a full noisy swing. In the high-ceilinged restaurant, its walls decorated with framed sepia photographs of portly maharajahs and British chaps in howdahs atop elephants, and dead tigers slung under poles, air-conditioning units blew cool air over white tablecloths and red napkins. In a room big enough for up to a hundred guests, about half that number were either seated or lined up at the silver warming trays and open cold plates. If it tasted as good as the food smelled, Dan knew they were in for a treat. He turned when he heard the click of metal on wood. Cruella tapped her ebony walking stick toward them across the parquet with Shira in tow. She ignored Dan and glowered at Charlie.

"Tantrum over, Charlene?"

Charlie glanced at Dan and bit her lip. "Yes, Auntie. I'm better now. Sorry to everyone."

"We're used to it," said Shira with affected weariness.

Cruella turned a sour expression at Dan "What did you get up to out there?"

"I bought Charlie some nice underwear," he informed her as if he'd bought her a loaf of bread.

"*Underwear?*" Cruella's eyes turned sharply at a smiling Charlie.

Charlie waved her shopping bag. "Really nice, sexy red lingerie," she explained. "A lovely bra and panties and a teensy, tiny thong."

Shira frowned her annoyance.

"I don't think you should have done that," Cruella said coldly to Dan.

"Ha! Let's eat, Dan. I'm hungry after all this excitement." Charlie turned and deliberately slid her arm through his to lead him away.

"Nicely done," he whispered. Charlie giggled.

They piled their plates from the assorted dishes before Dan guided her to where Gilly and Mark had artfully maneuvered themselves to their own table. Several opened bottles of wine stood next to a spray of plastic flowers.

Gilly patted Charlie's hand. "Nice to see you back again, dear. You look so much better."

Charlie nodded with a big smile at Dan. "Thank you, Missus Drury. Dan's been very nice to me."

"Has he now?" said Mark with an innocent smile.

"Call me Gilly, dear. Now, don't worry yourself. We all have our little meltdowns from time to time."

"You should see Gilly when I annoy her too much," commented Mark from the safety of the other side of the table. "Then it's tin hat time in our house!"

"Or in India, Mark." Gilly gave him a theatrical wave of her knife.

Dan could see these two had an easy relationship. Old Brits, divorce not an option, give and take, keep calm and carry on with the marriage. He was envious. A stone-faced Cruella surprised him by sitting down with Shira on the chairs next to them. Was it to keep a close eye on Charlie? And him? It wasn't social—she silently radiated frost, forking languidly at plain rice and a small dollop of bland vegetables while Shira glumly picked at a few pieces of fruit. Better not antagonize the old bat too much, thought Dan. That won't help Charlie. He played nice, attempting to pour a glass of red wine for Cruella. She stopped him with a slash of her hand.

"Where's this wine from?" she asked curtly.

Dan checked the bottle. A good California Zinfandel. "Chateau Delhi. A spicy, little brew from the south slopes of the Ganges," he told her adding "Travels well with notes of cumin and cloves." He heard Mark clearing his throat but avoided looking at him.

Cruella snatched at the bottle and read the label. "Pour, funny man," she said mirthlessly.

He poured before offering the wine to Shira, tipping the bottle to her glass. Cruella's hand moved quickly to cover Shira's glass. "She doesn't drink."

Shira shook her head and said, "I don't drink."

Dan caught Mark rolling his eyes. "I assume you're retired from the Brit Army, Mark?" he asked to lighten the mood around the table.

Mark wiped his mustache with the back of his index finger. "After thirty years, Dan. It was a wonderful career traveling the world until the Empire got a lot smaller. Ended up in bloody awful Sussex instead of knocking back Singapore Slings at the Raffles."

"What made you move to Stirling? The sunshine?"

"Sarky bugger," Mark answered genially. He glanced at Gilly who jumped in.

"My father was born there. I remembered it a little from my childhood, the castle and the Church of the Holy Rood up on the hill. It's where all the kings of Scotland were crowned, you know. Seemed a nice place to retire."

"Saw action here in India?" Dan asked.

"Just old enough to get some with my father's brigade," said Mark proudly.

"Fighting those—" Gilly elbowed him professionally as all good wives do.

Mark cleared his throat. "Our little friends in Burma."

"My grandfather fought in the war," said Dan. "Dieppe."

"We really cocked that one up for you," Mark said with a regretful shake of his head. "Canadians really bought it."

"He was lucky. Spent the next few years learning German in a POW camp just in case we lost." Dan's grin triggered hearty laughs from Gilly and Mark.

Karen appeared with a small bowl of ice cream and a beer that didn't look like her first. She sat down next to Mark and glanced around the table. "Good evening everyone. You should try the ice cream. Not hokey pokey but it's mint."

"I think we will," said Mark. "May I bring some for anyone?"

"Hokey what?" Cruella asked Karen.

"Never heard of New Zealand's favorite ice cream?"

"Of course not. And I don't like mint."

Karen, Dan and Mark laughed. An irritated Cruella looked around at them. "And what's so funny?" she demanded.

"She means it's awesome," Mark told her. "Kiwi slang, don't you know?"

Cruella stared down her nose at Karen. "We're going to need a translator for all the Australians and Kiwis, aren't we? You people are real difficult to understand.

"Get used to it," said Karen without looking up from her bowl.

Cruella's face darkened. Charlie broke in quickly. "Where are you from in New Zealand, Karen?"

"Auckland. North Island. Know it?"

"Heard of it. You have family there?"

Dan sensed where this was going. So did Karen by the look in her eyes.

"No." She smiled faintly at Dan.

"Really?" said Cruella not hiding her sarcasm. "Still on the shelf at your age? Pity."

"Not really." She grinned. "I take the ferret for a root whenever I can."

Cruella gasped and waved her open palms. "Good God, I can't understand anything you say! What on earth does a ferret have to do with it?" She turned sharply to Dan when he started laughing. Charlie chuckled. Gilly giggled. Shira chewed a nail.

"Google it," Karen told her dismissively. She pushed the empty bowl away from her with a satisfied sigh.

Cruella sat back and went silently dull-eyed. The quiet when you hold your breath before something big happens, thought Dan. Like watching a fuse burn toward a barrel of gunpowder. Karen had joined him on her hit list.

Silence descended as they picked at their meals. Dan was grateful when Mark returned with a tray loaded with six bowls of ice cream, looked around at their faces and melted the frost.

"My father was a military adviser on India to Churchill during the war," he informed them jauntily. "Met my mother in Poona and the result was me. The old girl was getting on but it's marvelous what that curry can do."

Dan grinned at Mark and toasted him. *What a splendid chap in the crunch.*

"So you're *Indian?*" The word slid off Cruella's tongue like slime off a frog's back. "Oh dear." She'd bided her time waiting to dig her knife into someone.

Mark flushed angrily looking like he was going to tee off on her but was too well mannered to do so. Not so Karen.

"What's wrong with Indians?" she demanded.

"Such dirty people. Of course, not whites like you, Major," she added with a curt nod in Mark's direction.

Karen angrily shoved her face at Cruella. "I thought you Jews would be the last people to be racist!"

"Just selective."

"So am I." Karen slammed her ice cream bowl on the table, scraped her chair back on the parquet and left. Karen just moved up to number one on the hit list, thought Dan.

Cruella sighed. Just another day looking down from her castle turret at the great unwashed. The ice cream must have been warmer than her minuscule heart. "Kiwis," she sniffed. "Such ignorant people. Sensitive, isn't she?"

"*Great* soldiers!" Mark retorted stiffly. "*Wonderful* people. Entered the war in thirty-nine. Not late again, like some," he added pointedly.

Cruella blinked slowly at him. Was Mark now number three?

"What does your father do," Dan asked Charlie to avoid another cold silence developing.

She swallowed hard and cleared her throat. "My father and mother died in a car crash two years ago."

"Oh. How awful, dear," said Gilly.

"I'm so sorry, Charlie," Dan said and reached for her hand under the table.

Charlie turned damp eyes on him, her hand tightening on his. "I'm slowly getting over it."

"So you live with your aunt now?" he asked.

Her voice hardened. "If you call it living."

"Charlene, that's really uncalled for," Cruella chided. "I take—"

"Isn't it true?" Charlie scowled. "You keep me locked up in your prison?"

"What do you expect when no respectable school will have you?"

Charlie wiped her fingers across her cheeks. "But next year, when I'm twenty-one, I'll be off. You won't be able to stop me."

"Is that so?" Cruella said, so sardonic it piqued Dan's interest. The smug glances she exchanged with Shira told him Charlie wasn't going anywhere.

Gilly jumped in to lighten the mood. "My father and mother met at boarding school in England. There was a bit of an age difference but it worked out quite well. They had four children. I was the first."

"A mixed boarding school?" Dan asked. Out the corner of his eye, he noticed Mark smiling in anticipation—he'd been set up.

"No, my father was a teacher there. My mother was his eighteen-year-old pupil. Ah, such sixth-form love."

Mark laughed on cue. Cruella joined far too heartily. Shira smirked behind her fingers. Charlie flushed crimson, her hand still holding his tightly.

What's this all about?

"Charlie tells me you work at NYU," he quickly asked Cruella to change the conversation away from Charlie's obvious embarrassment.

"A professor of history at the prestigious NYU," she corrected haughtily.

"Any future in history?" asked Mark.

"Future in history?" Cruella frowned her confusion. "What's that mean?"

"It's a joke, Elaine," explained Dan. "History is the past so it can't—"

Cruella glared at Mark and spoke slowly through tight lips. "The Jewish story isn't funny, Major."

"Oh, I wouldn't say that. Comedians like Groucho? Milton Berle? Bob Newhart?" Mark looked innocently at Dan. "Funny as hell, Dan?"

"He's right," said Dan.

"Don't be stupid, you two," Cruella snapped when she saw everyone was laughing at her. "I study twenty thousand years of Jewish ancestry all the way back to Abraham. Two thousand of them with Christians trying to kill us!"

Dan groaned. She really knew how to kill a party. Mark and Dan avoided each other's eyes. Charlie fidgeted uncomfortably. Shira was hypnotized by her finger nails.

"Good for you, Elaine," chipped in Gilly. "Must be lots of work to do in the future if you're not wiped out by those blighters." She motioned to Mark. "Please pass the wine, Mark. I think I need it."

Cruella stared at Gilly for a moment before turning her inquisitor's eyes to Dan. "You're not married, Shira tells me," she said brusquely. She cast a critical eye over him. "Not *gay* are you?" she asked rudely. "You look like one."

"Thanks. I take that as a compliment. You're not married, Shira tells me. Are you a lesbian?" he replied with equanimity. "You look like a one."

In the hushed silence that fell as sharp as an executioner's guillotine, Cruella held Dan in the coldest of stares before snorting away her annoyance. He'd moved above Karen, Mark and Gilly on her hit list. "Tell me what *you* do for a living," she demanded.

"I'm an old-fashioned doctor. Coughs and sneezes. That sort of thing."

"Really?" Charlie gaped at him. "A medical doctor?"

"Is it that hard to believe? You were thinking astronaut or lion tamer?"

"Well, I was hoping." She smiled and squeezed the hand she hadn't let go. He liked it and squeezed back.

"Not smart enough to be a professor?" Cruella sneered. "M.D.'s admission test scores are way below Ph.D.'s like mine."

Her put-down rankled but he shrugged. "I think you might be right."

"I am, of course."

"OK then. Let's make a deal. I'll call you if I have an emergency question about the Jews at Masada and you call me if you have a heart attack or a stroke. Sounds fair?"

Cruella's expression turned glacial. Mark smiled. Gilly grinned. Shira's eyes showed a lot of white. Charlie stifled a nervous giggle. Dan just stared at Cruella until she blinked and heaved herself to her feet. He was definitely number one again—with a bullet. Hopefully metaphorical.

"Time for bed, girls!" she ordered with a sharp crack of her stick.

Charlie mumbled, "Soon."

Another crack. "*Now*, young lady!"

There was a few seconds silence while everyone glanced from Cruella to Charlie.

"Go to hell!" Charlie cried, leaped to her feet and ran across the floor between the tables and out of the door.

Cruella sighed. "Oh dear. Here we go again. Now you see what I have to put up with?" She snapped her fingers at Shira. "Come on, you." Shira quickly stood up.

Cruella shook her head sadly. "Don't be too harsh on Charlene. I've been taking care of her ever since her parents died and it hasn't been easy."

Mumbai

Kapoor fixed himself a fist of single malt Bowmore with a dash of water and lay in only his *chuddies* on a wicker lounger on his balcony overlooking the enormous sweep of the Indian Ocean. The sun had finally sunk its red rim and a purple curtain descended on another blisteringly hot day. He drank a hefty slug of the fiery Scotch, closed his stinging eyes and looked forward to a relaxing few hours without Nasma and any of her chatty girlfriends to disturb him. Appropriately, the soaring violins, violas and cellos of Mozart's *Eine Kleine Nachtmusik* swept in vibrant waves through the screen on the sliding door behind him. Beethoven's *Moonlight Sonata* would soon follow and he'd drift off until Nasma returned and helped him to bed. He doubted he'd make it to Debussy. Life was good but something had been missing for far too long—someone to love and be loved in return. His eyes began to tear up at old memories but he caught himself. He was getting bloody maudlin. Turning fifty was proving quite a transition. Time was passing him by.

Nasma. In order to have the right social image and avoid suspicion, Kapoor had married well, financially anyway. Nasma wasn't the most attractive woman he could have chosen but she was rich, of the right clan and caste and, most importantly, only interested in sex for procreative reasons. He could rest easy now he'd pleased his father and hers by completing the three functions of marriage: *prajaa* for the perpetuation of one's family, *dharma* for the fulfillment of responsibilities and *rati* for companionship as friends and mutual pleasure as lovers. The last one was a stretch but having closed his eyes and done his duty early in their marriage, he now had a wife happily menopausal, occupied with her tea-swilling friends and laudable charities, and two teenage boys sent off to boarding school for most of the year. Sex between them had never reared its ugly head again. Both of them were content with that.

He was drinking too much again but what the hell. The last strains of Mozart faded as he stood up unsteadily and went inside to pour another fistful and find the bottle was now a lot closer to the bottom than the top. He wandered briefly around his living room, its walls decorated with fine Modern Art paintings and sculptures of nudes: plenty of nude females for male guests to appreciate but enough males to interest him. On a whim, he picked up the red-tagged, beige file he'd dropped on a side table with no intention of reading it. It was the file folder with the latest material on the Harbor Murders, as the media had dubbed the bodies found at Chowpatty Beach. Hosseini had delivered it into his reluctant hand as he left the office. He had files on four new murders in his attache case never mind more on those two. He lay down again and casually flipped through the typed pages to review them for anything he might have missed and before he drank so much he'd fall asleep on the balcony again.

The case appeared to be literally a dead end at this point: it had taken only two days for the bodies found in the harbor to be identified as Dwayne and Tracey Koepke, violent American criminals who'd traveled on false passports from Washington DC in the United States only the day before their murders, but nothing new since then. India's frontiers were built of Swiss cheese. Kapoor shook his head again at the continuing incompetence of Border Security. India had a border of Swiss cheese.

Hosseini's poorly typed report was easy to spot—Kapoor gritted his teeth through his assistant's general illiteracy. The Koepkes had been scheduled to join a group trip across India out of Mumbai? His detective's antennae twitched—had the Koepkes been hired to kill someone on that trip? Was it as simple as someone had killed them first? Kapoor checked the tour's itinerary. It had left for Ahmedabad that morning, heading north toward Rajasthan. Too late. A pursuit of the group might be a wild goose chase and his boss would not appreciate anything like that draining the department's budget, especially with the new murders.

Twelve pages were stapled together: the group's itinerary, the tourists and the leader. Passport details, addresses, sketchy biographies, photos—Kapoor jerked bolt upright, spilling his Scotch into the crotch of his *chuddies*. He stared at the image of the brown-green eyed Dan Palmer, his pulse jumping in an uncontainable rush of emotion. *My God!* He was Monty Clive Miles! Surely, Monty's twin soul—what he'd prayed for from Lord Ganesha! Memories flooded back of secret fondles at bedtime and getting wonderfully drunk together before making truly mad teenage love.

Despite all his forensic science, Kapoor the Hindu believed in the divine powers of thousands of gods, more than one for any occasion. Had the happy god eventually brought him success in his quest for his childhood lover?

Ahmedabad

"I hate that bitch!" seethed Charlie, interrupting the clicking cicadas, chirping birds and the humming air-conditioners on their window perches. "Next year, I'm off for sure!"

In the dark beside the pool house, she and Dan sat together on a low brick wall across the swimming pool reflecting the lights from the hotel's blue, pink, yellow and green stained-glass windows. She couldn't stop the valve in her head from letting it all out. At least it wasn't what she'd done after the nadir of her life: drink her face off; find a guy, any guy to fuck her brains out; take uppers, downers, and mind-blowers that floated her off to see the Yellow Submarine. Her life had become meaningless and emotionally dead until wandering alone one evening by a church and hearing familiar singing escaping from within, she took the Eucharist and drank the wine at her first evening mass in several years. She'd taken confession and choked on her litany of sins, expecting to shock the priest out of the box. It hadn't, of course. She'd come back from the brink, back to God and was wearing out her novenas. And now she'd found Dan. God was looking out for her—unless Dan was gay. He hadn't answered her aunt's question and he was so unusually clean cut, well dressed and gentle for a man. He even smelled good. He was so easy to talk with and—she put it out of her mind when she felt his touch.

"Take it easy." Dan rested his hand on her arm. The gesture, small as it was, sent an exciting ripple through her. "Let it go," he whispered. "It's hurting you more than her."

"That's easy to say," she hissed. "They've made my life hell these last few years!"

"I know it's hard to let it go. But they win when you're angry and unhappy." He stroked her arm lightly. "Why let them win?"

Dan sounded like her priest back home but Father Fenton's wrinkled hand hadn't generated electricity inside her. It was sexually intimate, more than her father's soothing touch that calmed the sea raging inside her when she'd returned home in pieces. Someone she'd rested her head on with his arm around her shoulders and made her feel secure. The shared cigarettes and beer on the sun deck when her mother wasn't around. How she missed him and their easy relationship. Dan's soft words and gentle touch drained her anger in the same way but it also triggered a deeper need, one she'd been unable to satisfy for far too long.

She sipped from her beer bottle. "Don't you drink?" she asked.

He drank Coke? With a bent nose and scars, surely he had to drink like Hemingway or her image of a tough, worldly guy would be shattered. He removed his hand and held his together, resting on his knees. She missed it already. She knew he wouldn't come on to her like men who'd have their tongues down her throat and their hands on her boobs within minutes of meeting. But he was going to need the Chinese water torture. Drip ... drip ... drip.

"I can't mix it with my medicines."

Medicines? "I hope you're OK." A woman's way of asking what's wrong with him.

"Just a bug I picked up in Africa. I'll be OK."

Africa? Hemingway couldn't have said it better. "Wow. Africa? You were traveling?"

"I worked at a refugee camp in northern Nigeria."

Helping refugees? Who was this? Saint Dan?

"I've always wanted to tour Africa. What was it like?"

He paused for a moment before looking at her with eyes she thought must have seen far too much. "Don't go there. It's a terrible place. Dangerous as hell for men. Worse for women. Fatal for white women like you." He shook his head despairingly. "If there is a benevolent God, he's not in Africa."

"And yet you went to help save lives." She brushed the light brown hairs on his forearm and it just came out of nowhere: "That makes you a special person to me."

His eyes met hers and there was a moment when she thought he might kiss her. He didn't but she'd seen the spark and knew it was only a matter of time. Their intimacy was growing. She wanted to know all about him. What made Dan tick? Why did he go to Africa? "People often do things like that as a form of penance, don't they?" she asked boldly hoping he'd open up.

Dan eyed her thoughtfully. "You're very perceptive. It was of a sort. Something I needed to do for my bad behavior."

"It's something I understand. Sure you're not a Cathoholic drunk on guilt like me?"

Dan laughed. "A Cathoholic? Never heard that one." He took a red and gold packet out of the breast pocket of his shirt. "Mind if I smoke?" he asked,

"Only if I do."

"It'll stunt your growth."

"Ha! Funny man. I should have started at twelve." She raised her eyebrows. "A doctor who smokes?"

"You'd be surprised by how many do. It's the stress." He shrugged. "I'm working on perfect."

"Tell me about it," she murmured. If only he knew. She looked at the box. "Gold Flake? Never heard of them."

He gave her one and lit it. "They're not Kools, believe me."

She inhaled lightly and grimaced at the harsh smoke. "Oh, they're strong. Funny taste."

Dan inhaled deeply then blew out a long gray-blue stream into the night air. "A certain *je ne sais quoi*. Probably cow shit."

She coughed and giggled. "You idiot." She smacked him on the shoulder, hoping he took it as an intimate gesture.

"Enjoy, young lady. It's the biggest selling brand in the world. Another adventure into the unknown." They clinked bottles again. "A billion Indians can't be wrong. Just wait 'til you try beedies."

"Beedies? What are they?"

"Ah! Patience grasshopper," he said mimicking an Oriental voice. "Another adventure awaits you."

Charlie inhaled more and they enjoyed their cigarettes and sipped the drinks. They chatted about this and that, Charlie probing him for similarities and differences, not steering clear of the potentially divisive subject of politics. Besides books, they shared a love of old black and white movies: flamboyant dance musicals with Fred and Ginger; Bogart and Bacall seducing one another over smoldering cigarettes in smoky bars; Jimmy Cagney going yellow to the electric chair; romances with Cary Grant and Katherine Hepburn. She'd enjoyed them with her father in their personal movie theatre at their mansion on Long Island. Kids' Disney movies had never been for her.

She was relieved he shared her lefty politics too and the same somewhat depressing global viewpoint: humans were so selfish they'd wipe themselves out rather than work with each other to maintain the planet—greed would end human civilization. They agreed they needed not to just complain about it but to do something. She was more than impressed he'd put his life where his mouth was: he'd gone to Africa to make a difference, save lives in a hellish place. She wondered what bad behavior had instigated the penance. It must have been something big. She'd work on him.

She noticed him occasionally studying her and smiled to help his thinking. She wondered how to phrase what had been gnawing at her all day. A smirking Shira had passed on the information over breakfast on the train that morning: there was a rumor Dan had slept last night with chubby Karen. Shira and Cruella had reveled in her anger when she'd already descended in one of those black moods that sucked all the life out of her and left her in lead boots. When Shira had cozied up to him and laid—literally—her usual boob trick on him on the train and returned sneering at her, she'd had to grit her teeth—and vow revenge on that bitch. How could he have chosen Karen? That lump of lard over her? Damn! Was it boobs again? Another big ass?

"Karen seems to like you," she said, mentally crossing her fingers.

Dan cast amused eyes at her. "It's OK. We just sleep together," he said carelessly.

Charlie caught her breath as though she'd been punched in the stomach. "Really?" She'd been beaten to him by an old bag more than twice her age! It just had to be the tits!

Dan laughed. "We just share a room. Separate beds. I couldn't stand being with that Steve guy. Karen's a writer and a lot more fun and more interesting to be with." He smiled wryly. "She's a lesbian, you know."

"A lesbian?" Charlie couldn't believe her ears. She took a deep breath and held back a whoop of delight. Now to get rid of that bitch Shira! She leaned back into him and breathed warmly on his ear like a concubine's flapping veil. "You know why I like you?" she asked.

"Why?"

"You treat me like a woman, not a girl," she whispered, her hand feeling for his again. Drip ... drip ... drip. "How come you haven't told me to take out the piercings? Asked what that stupid tattoo's for?"

"What's that stupid tattoo for?" he asked.

She giggled. He made her feel good. "You really want to know?"

He grinned. "Not really."

"You are a jerk, aren't you?" she said, with a gentle rub of his shoulder that moved to his neck. Drip ... drip ... drip. "It actually says 'Kiss My Ass.'"

"Wordsworth, right?"

"Oscar Wilde."

Dan laughed so hard he spilled his Coke. She joined in with him.

He finds me funny!

Unexpectedly, his arm went around her shoulders and shook her. "You are probably one of the few Americans who don't think Oscar Wilde makes sausages!"

Charlie's heart jumped. Was he just being friendly or was there more to it? "I'm so glad you're on this trip. I can't stand being with Auntie and Shira all the time. We can have fun, can't we?" Dan's arm abruptly withdrew as though jolted by a cattle prod.

Oh damn. Have I blown it?

"You know, go on side excursions, things like that?" she went on quickly. "Shira's a huge pain in my ass and no fun at all. We can have a smoke together. Talk about books, politics, movies. What do you think?"

Dan crackled his cigarette with an extra deep intake and exhaled the smoke slowly. "Even though I'm twice your age?"

She laughed. "You *are* too old for me but I've got to know you and we get on well, don't we?"

Dan nodded thoughtfully. Charlie tensed. Which way would he go?

"It's a pity that Duncan is the only young guy on the trip, isn't it?" he asked.

"Yeah, it is." *He's trying to palm me off?*

"He did tell me he liked the look of you—a lot."

Charlie caught her breath. "He did? You talked about me?"

"We Canucks stick together." Dan grinned. "You're worth talking about."

Heat rose in her cheeks but she steadied her voice. Duncan's interest was flattering but Dan was *her* interest. "Would you feel better if I had fun with both you and Duncan?" She smiled broadly and held out her hand. "It would reduce your average age to about thirty."

Dan laughed at that. "OK, fun as friends," he said taking her hand.

"Charlene?" Cruella's harsh voice called from an invisible window. "Are you out there? Damn it, where are you?"

"Better go before the old bat flies out of her cave," Charlie whispered. "Thanks again for the lingerie. That was very sweet of you. It made me feel so much better."

"You're very welcome."

"Smoke tomorrow night after dinner?"

"OK."

She kissed him on the cheek, lingering a little, and left him blinking his bemusement. She giggled all the way up to her room. *Yes!* He was on the ropes with plenty of rounds left for the KO.

March 25th

Mumbai

UNLIKE THE OTHERS in the modern wing recently added to the Gothic, red and white-bricked Maharashtra Police Headquarters, Kapoor kept the air-conditioning low and the window open enough to capture the smell of vegetables rotting and meats warming in the heat of the busy nearby Crawford Market. It was the India he loved! It was quieter now in the early afternoon as the swarms of *dabbawallas* on their bicycles bringing containers of hot lunches to thousands of Mumbai offices had come and gone for another day. The air had helped his hangover recede to a low drumming as well as remind him of his childhood in a much poorer part of Mumbai.

In a dog-eat-dog world, he'd been born Dipak Dhilan, a scrawny pi dog, learned how to be a ferocious Bully Kutta in a private school and fought his way to the heights of the sixth floor of the Maharashtra. Not bad for fourth-class *Shudra* rubbish they'd sneer at if they knew his maternal origin. How lucky he was to have been the bastard child of his servant mother's married and wealthy *Kshatriya* second-class master, a bluff Army general of otherwise outstanding rectitude. The death of the General Kapoor's childless wife changed Dipak's life: the aging general finally did the right thing—maybe to improve his karma—by adopting him and implanting his morals into the uneducated five-year-old.

The general soon dispatched him to a boys' school to become another of the military and ruling elite. But more than ten years in the Lord of the Flies environment of his private school molded the young Kapoor into something more suitable for battling liars, bullies, thieves and perverts. Disappointed but supportive, the general used his influence to have him jump the queue into the National Police Academy at Hyderabad where he excelled. Kapoor had escaped the passive, exploited underclass—the "Rooster Coop" of India as that author had put it—and he hated what he'd found in their masters: amoral, extreme greed overcoming the basic decency of Hinduism. However, being one of the foxes guarding the "Rooster Coop" certainly helped in that regard. There was something he could do about it.

The open window's pungent draft was a perfect antidote to the sterility of his glass-topped, chromed-steel desk, white-walled office and bland associates who had nothing to do except discuss cricket: test, one-day, twenty-twenty, forty-overs, the league. God, how it bored him! Did any of the Philistine men care about culture beyond bowling a ball down twenty-two yards of baked dirt to knock down wooden sticks? He heard a low-pitched growl over the excited voice of a babbling television commentator—apparently not. It was coming from Chief Dewan's office down the wide hallway, his sloth-like boss enjoying a break between his lunch and another strenuous committee meeting. A sleepy-eyed boss but as ruthless as a manager of a car lot who fired the employee at the bottom of the sales numbers at the end of each month to encourage the others. All he wanted was quick arrests and got rid of any underling who didn't fulfill that function. The innocence or guilt of those arrested was of no consequence. The only two good things about Dewan were that he never asked about operational details and was a closet homo. Kapoor had sensed Dewan undressing him with his eyes. His clumsy passes had not gone unnoticed and certainly not unrecorded, stored away with all the other sexual predilections and peccadilloes of Kapoor's associates for future reference.

Nasma had helped him to bed but unable to sleep, not because of the Scotch but because of Dan Palmer, he'd left for work even earlier than usual to miss the morning traffic warfare. On his arrival, Hara, his secretary the size of two normal Indian women, had maternally eyed him and quickly prepared a cup of Marsala chai just the way he wanted with plenty of whole milk, ginger root and a touch of cinnamon, and with a typical patronizing snort pressed aspirins into his hand.

Unwanted by others who preferred pliable, beddable, incompetent, eye-candy females, Hara was more than a mother hen to Kapoor, she was a mother whale whose loyalty knew no bounds and he rewarded her every way possible, such as ignoring her tardiness, leaving-earliness, smoking in the smoke-free building, occasional hangovers and generally ignoring every rule of being a secretary. They trusted one another in this rat's nest of backstabbing, duplicitous arseholes and she passed on all the important gossip that flowed through the secretarial grapevine from one floor to the next, that clandestine network that rivaled the CIA—and was probably more reliable. In fact, she'd spent so long with Kapoor she fancied herself an unofficial detective, casting her critical eye over the reams of documentation she sent Kapoor's way.

A second cup quickly followed the first. He re-opened the beige folder containing the group members' personal data from the travel company. They were from the US, UK, Australia, New Zealand, India and Canada. He called in Hara and gave her formal requests to those countries and international agencies for all they had on the group's members. She paused and looked back from the doorway.

"It was the brother in the honor killing," she told Kapoor over her half-rim glasses. "You heard it here, boss." She turned and left.

He watched her big arse waddle off while he nibbled on a shortbread biscuit, sipped his chai and rehearsed his story for the chief.

* * *

Kapoor found the corpulent chief in his plush leather throne, shoes off, feet up, in front of a blaring flat-screen TV in an office smelling of socks, cigars and spicy wafts from the remains of the hot lunch brought by the *dabbawalla*. It was the office of a man with no taste except in what cricket offered to Indian culture. Framed and autographed photos of a grinning Dewan with leading players both old and new; a cricket bat laid horizontally on a window sill like the mace of Parliament; several battered cricket balls on individual plinths as though they were Roman emperors' busts.

"How's the test cricket going, sah?" Kapoor asked, standing to attention on the other side of the boss's desk. "Whipping those Aussie arses?"

"Excellently!" cried the florid chief, beaming at the flat-screen as he dabbed his mouth with a tablecloth of a handkerchief. He didn't bother to turn to Kapoor. "Hitting the buggers for six!"

"First class, sah!" enthused Kapoor.

"Anything on the Harbor—?" A sharp crack of a hard ball on a willow bat. Dewan abruptly shook a fist at the TV. "*Madachord!* Motherfucker!" he shouted at the Aussie who'd just hit a boundary. Despite the cool of the office, Dewan wiped beads of perspiration from his forehead with the sauce-stained hankie before he continued: "The Harbor Murders? The goat-fucking media's all over my arse!" He shoveled another spoon of rice into his maw.

Kapoor had the sense not to tell him that meant he was a goat. "I've cracked the case!" he declared instead.

Dewan's head snapped around on its thick neck as quickly as his chair. "*What?* You have?" he spluttered, firing bits of rice at Kapoor.

"I need to catch up with a travel group the murdered Koepkes were going to join and arrest my man for you," Kapoor continued in a rush to maintain his momentum.

A heavy Dewan fist pounded the desktop. "Wonderful!" he exclaimed. "Where is he now?"

"On the way to Udaipur today," Kapoor said. "It'll only take a couple of days for me to arrest him and bring him back."

Dewan examined Kapoor as he paused to thoughtfully lick his fingers with his thick lips. Kapoor could sense the manipulative cogs whirring—his boss was a shrewd apparatchik who got what he wanted by leverage and Kapoor had been careful never given him any.

Dewan blinked his heavy lids slowly. "Solving a high-profile case like this will be good for your career, won't it?"

"And *your* department, sah."

"Contact the police there." Dewan turned back to the TV but glanced at Kapoor.

"Wouldn't it be better for your department to do the arrest, sah? You really want Chief Prekash in Ahmedabad to get all the glory?"

Dewan's face darkened. "That fuck?"

"I can have him back by Wednesday," Kapoor said, "and you'll have him to parade before those goatfuckers."

He remained patient while Dewan stalled, tapping his fingers on the desktop while his flickering eyes indicated his personal cost-benefit analysis was ongoing.

The chief's cunning eyes narrowed at Kapoor. "Don't I need you here solving the latest murders?"

"They've all been solved, sah," Kapoor lied.

They were the kind of murders he'd have Hosseini wrap up inside twenty-four hours: a family honor killing of a bride suspected of not being a virgin, a sister disfigured because of something her brother did, a wife was found with a cleaver in her head, and a gang-raped woman had died in hospital. Women didn't have it easy in India.

Thank Ganesha, I'm a man. Don't reincarnate me as a woman in India!

Dewan continued to tap his fat fingers while Kapoor waited for him to hint at what he needed in exchange for releasing him.

"And I'm sure Assistant Superintendent Hosseini can deal with anything while I'm away," he said. Hara had already solved one.

Dewan's big head swayed from side to side. "But I could always send Hosseini to represent the department," he mused tilting his head. "We've never had that drink, have we?"

"Should we discuss it at your place tonight, sah?"

Dewan's piggy eyes sparkled like fireworks at Diwali.

"And I'll bring a friend."

Perhaps I am a woman in India.

Ahmedabad

Charlie, Shira and Cruella sat in silence finishing their breakfasts across the patio from where Karen and Dan had found some shade under the dry, yellowing fronds of a maltreated palm. Shira was partially covered by a strained halter top and Bermuda shorts while Charlie was disconcertingly gorgeous in another short sundress that showed off her slim, tanned body. She caught his eye and smiled before looking away. Cruella looked straight through Dan as they all got up to leave. Shira paraded languidly across his line of sight. When Charlie caught him following Shira's rear closely, she chilled him with a harsh glare that recoiled him back to his hot breakfast of tea, eggs on toast, yogurt and honey.

The tall Duncan appeared and glanced at Karen and Dan sitting under the palm. He hesitated before striding across the flagstones to their table where he snatched at a plastic chair and sat down.

"This is Duncan," Dan told a surprised Karen.

"Oh, I remember. Morning, Duncan." She extended her hand but he ignored her, fixing his eyes on Dan. She frowned at Dan out the side of her head.

Duncan poured some coffee into a spare cup. He grimaced and pushed it to one side. "God, Nescafé shit."

"Duncan runs a coffee business in Vancouver," Dan told Karen.

"Oh, that's interesting. How'd you get into that?" Karen asked, keeping her cool.

Duncan waved a hand carelessly. "I escaped my crappy family when I was sixteen. Worked on tankers, saved my money and quit after a few years. Bought a coffee roaster and started a café." He glanced sourly at Dan. "Nobody helped me. Did it all myself."

"Good for you. My family was shit too. My dad booted me out the door." Karen blew out annoyance between her tight lips. "Told me I was sitting on a gold mine. Can you believe that? What a bastard."

Duncan glanced a goading sneer at Dan. "Perhaps you are."

"I'm *what*?" Karen dropped her fork. She cast a fierce look at Dan, ready to deck Duncan. He wanted to tell her to go right ahead.

"What do you think, *Dad*? Is she?"

Karen's head spun. "This shit's your son?"

Duncan could no longer pull Dan's chain about anything but he was smart enough to know embarrassing Karen in front of him was an effective substitute.

"Find another table for your crap manners," Dan said evenly, not letting Duncan needle him.

"A shit? Son like father?" Duncan smirked still trying to piss Dan off.

"Leave," Dan told him.

"Or what? Gonna punch me?"

"No, but she will."

"And I bloody well will!" growled Karen.

Duncan jumped to his feet, jerking a thumb at Karen. "Is this the latest woman you're fucking, *Dad*? You don't waste much time getting laid, do you?" He turned on his heel and stomped off.

Karen pushed her chair back to get to her feet. Dan beat her to it.

"Allow me," he said. His metal chair clattered back over the flagstones as Buddhism took a back seat to shaking some sense into Duncan. He stood up quickly and staggered as he tried to take a step. The world swirled. His vision narrowed. He leaned on the table to stay vertical.

"Dan!" Karen grabbed his arm.

He shook her off. "I'm..." He took another step. The table turned sideways. His legs gave way. *Clunk.* On his hands and knees on the stones. Breathing hard, head swimming.

"Are you OK?" Karen kneeled beside him, arm over his shoulders.

"Give ... me ... a moment." He took a few deep breaths to help clear his head before Karen helped him slowly back onto his chair.

Karen handed Dan a wet paper napkin to clean his hands. "Does this happen often?"

"Wanting to kill my son?"

"That too."

"It's the medicine for a parasite I contracted in Africa. Lousy side effects. I've OD'd on it."

"Take it easy then. You don't want to do this kind of thing on the edge of a cliff, do you?"

"It would ruin my trip, wouldn't it?"

"And mine. Who'd I have to sleep with?"

He rubbed the dust off his pants. "Sorry about that little bastard."

"Not so little." Karen rubbed the back of his neck. "No worries, Dan. I'll kick his arse later."

Dan half-smiled at her and sank back into the chair. Let it go. Didn't he tell Charlie that? It had harmed him more than Duncan.

Karen lowered her voice. "Duncan's your son?"

"We don't get along."

"I can see that. What's he doing on this trip?"

Dan rubbed his temples, wooziness receding. "I paid for him. Bad idea by the look of things."

Karen shrugged. "It's one of those bonding trips?"

"I hoped it might help melt some of the ice."

"Looks like a lot of ice to melt. Don't give up yet. We've barely got going. You never know what can happen by Kathmandu. You might become the best of buddies."

"More likely kill each other."

Karen looked across at a miserable Duncan, sitting at a table on his own. "He doesn't look that much like you."

"You mean he's ruggedly handsome?"

"Yes."

Dan glanced at Duncan's somewhat Asian face with its almond-shaped, blue-green eyes and wavy hair that were more Nadia. The stubbled chin was his. Did Duncan remember any good times or had they been flushed even before Dan had gone to jail? The good times when they'd had fun on vacations to cabins by lakes and beaches? Getting drenched at Niagara Falls on the *Maid of the Mist*? Did he recall the year they'd spent on Saint Lucia in the West Indies when Dan had worked at the hospital in Castries for a change of pace and he'd taught Duncan how to swim so he could snorkel and scuba dive in the coral reefs? When he'd been Duncan's soccer coach every weekend until the usual battles with kids in their early teens began and Duncan had drifted away to experiment with drink and drugs with a group of no-hopers and discover girls. No communication so he'd thrown boxes of condoms in Duncan's room and hoped for the best. One thing they'd shared was an explosive temperament.

Karen patted his hand. "Just wait 'til I tell the little bastard how you're bonking my arse off."

Dan chuckled and clinked cups with her. The next two weeks with Karen were going to be a lot of fun. A large shadow passed over them and he looked up into a familiar face.

"Well, if it isn't the rube," it said.

"Bill!" said Karen, delighted.

"What are you doing here?" asked Dan, not as delighted.

"You were such a great group of guys—and gal." Bill winked at Karen and took her outstretched hand. "I decided to join the wagon train." He took a seat next to a very smiley Karen and waved for some coffee.

"Lovely! Just lovely!" Karen squeezed his arm. Dan didn't want her to do that.

"I saw Loki," said Bill. "He arranged it all. I caught a later train and only got in around midnight." After the waiter poured his coffee, Bill raised the cup. "Here's to you cunts," he said, keeping his voice low.

Karen laughed if Dan didn't.

* * *

"Ladies and gentlemen! Get ready for the ride to Rajasthan!" called Loki.

The dusty red Parshwanath public bus trailing acrid, diesel fumes arrived in the small square in front of the white-painted facade of their three-story, brick hotel that leaned toward Pakistan and began to disgorge passengers and their luggage. Honking and shouting began when traffic was forced to a halt as tuk-tuks and taxis parked anywhere, their drivers competing to grab cardboard boxes, battered suitcases, treasure chests and bags of all shapes to help customers' decision-making. New passengers were milling around trying to get on before everyone had got off. No one formed orderly lines in India—unless you wanted to be left behind.

The crimson, plastic Ganesha statue glued to the driver's console amused Dan. On Indian roads, you needed all the luck you could get. A window sticker of a purple Shiva with his trident was going to help too. Nice to have Ganesha's dad along. The swastika painted on the windshield was a little disconcerting to anyone who didn't know the ancient Hindu symbol means "All is Well" and confers good luck.

Dessicated gray and brown rubble and low rocky hills whipped by. Hardy trees and succulents formed fences, dividing up the barren land for people in the stone farmhouses who had to be tougher than the rubble. Occasionally, a few fields appeared that grew more than rocks but the area hadn't seen much rainfall since Ashoka the Great had ruled his mogul empire more than two thousand years ago.

Charlie still wouldn't hold his eye after their breakfast contretemps. Watching a woman's plump rear sway across your field of vision and not pay attention? He wasn't dead. He turned his attention to Duncan staring morosely out the window. His height was Dan's but he looked far more like his mother, the raven-haired beauty with the sloe eyes who had been the belle of the ball or at least of the religious Doukhobor community in the Slocan Valley in British Columbia. The competition hadn't been fierce since most of the women were from Russian plow-pulling stock but Nadia had been a slim corker and with her uninhibited acceptance of the group's professed sex egalitarianism had been pursued by more than Dan—and boys as tall as Dan. Much as Dan wanted to throw Duncan off the bus after making him apologize to Karen, he moved over next to him.

"Is this going to be like in Kolkata when you wouldn't talk to me?" he asked.

Duncan continued to look out of the window like Dan was invisible and talking at the frequency of bats. Nadia had done a good job of turning him against Dan although she'd had plenty of ammunition to work with. Kathleen had passed on Dan's secret invitation of a free trip for Duncan across India at the wedding celebration in Kolkata and it had unexpectedly been taken up. Was it a tiny crack in his wall?

"It's a good group of people, isn't it?" Dan asked but Duncan's interest remained with piles of cow patties the size of houses and women walking by the side of the road with piles of firewood on their heads.

Dan tried again. "You didn't mind coming with me?"

"Couldn't turn down a free trip," Duncan replied sulkily still looking away. "What do you want? A bit of father-son bonding after five years of nothing?"

Dan smiled inwardly at the breakthrough, bitter as it was. "I wrote to you many times, didn't I?" he said evenly. "I hoped you'd write back,"

No reply except a twist of the mouth.

"What do you think of Charlie?" Dan asked the dead air.

Duncan turned and looked over the seat at her but wouldn't look at Dan. "You seem very friendly with her," he muttered and returned to the scenery going by.

"I am. She's a nice kid."

Now he eyed Dan and snorted. "Can't stop yourself, can you?" He looked away again but he'd actually spoken directly to Dan.

"By the way, don't tell her I told you but Charlie wants you to ask her out," Dan said casually. Duncan turned sharply. Bull's eye!

Dan moved back to his seat having planted his time bomb. Duncan looked at Charlie again, longer this time. Tick tock. Dan rested back as the bus continued to speed along the uneven blacktop through the bone-dry mountainous wasteland of rocks and past the occasional herd of skinny goats.

Halfway to Udaipur, Charlie moved over to talk to Duncan. They were soon deep in animated conversation, both of them smiling and gesticulating with their hands. Charlie's occasional glance at him and her giggle interspersing Duncan's deeper laughs made Dan wince. He was trying to get that little bastard laid with Charlie? What a dad!

Udaipur: City of Lakes

The bus arrived in Udaipur just as the city began to sparkle a spider's web of white and yellow lights. After a stop at the hotel for a refreshingly cool swim, an hour's rest with air-conditioners on turbo and changes of clothes, they were loaded into tuk-tuks decorated in anything silver and gold that rattled and shimmered. They flowed into the turbulent river of vehicles cascading to the market where the tuk-tuks disgorged them outside a massive red-stone arch. The market was a riot of lights, smells and colors: strings of bare light bulbs and glowing oil lamps flickering within the stall covers; the aromas of cooking oils and barrels of spices; browns, yellows and reds, in particular, of the cloth stalls; and the illuminated clock tower that ran its lights through the spectrum above it all.

Bob stopped at a stall that sold only turbans. He picked out a big, blood-orange one, more suitable for warning low-flying aircraft.

"Whad'ya think," he asked while looking in the mirror the obsequious shop-keeper held up for him. Dan gave Bob the thumbs up. He looked like a beach ball with an orange stuck on the top.

"He looks a right knob," whispered Mark in Dan's ear.

"Bonzer, mate," called Karen suppressing a giggle.

Why Bob was wearing a lightweight jacket on such a warm evening became apparent when he reached into his breast pocket for his wallet: a gun under his armpit. Bob bought the turban, kept it on and grinned his way through the crowd. He'd never get separated from the rest of them.

Charlie brushed up against him. "What a fabulous market. I've never seen anything like it." She'd dyed her hair a darker red to remove the pink streaks and it hung back over her bare shoulders like Shira's. Removing her eyebrow piercings had removed her last vestiges of a punk. This Charlie was getting better.

"Fabulous," he said and he wasn't looking at the market.

"Sorry about this morning," she whispered. "I saw the way you were looking at Shira's jiggles and swishes and it pissed me off."

"Haven't you noticed me following every jiggle and swish of yours?" he said before he caught himself.

Charlie held his arm to pull him closer. "Now that I like."

"Let it go, Charlie. OK? Don't be so competitive with Shira. There's no need for you to get envious."

She beamed a lock-picking smile as she ran her hand gently down his bare forearm. "Let's keep it that way," she told him with an edge he didn't miss.

He moved away to examine something—anything—on a nearby stall. A copper pot looked interesting. *God, she's so much trouble.* Dan was so distracted by Charlie he almost fell over a woman squatting with her three children on a carpet amid barrels of cereals and spices. Embroidered headscarves hung from a rail above them. Her husband snored, rattling his cot at the rear of the stall. Dan noticed Duncan hovering morbidly in the distance drawing occasionally on a shared joint with Dazza and Arfa.

The Indian woman stood and placed a red scarf over Charlie's head and wrapped it around her shoulders. "Most pretty," she told her.

"What do you think?" Charlie asked Dan.

Far more than pretty. Red hair, red scarf, golden eyes and peach skin. Little Red Riding Hood with a hell of a lot of sex appeal. "I like it."

"I'll get it then." Charlie grinned provocatively. "It'll match my lingerie, won't it?"

Did she have to say that? Dan doused the thought of Charlie wearing only the headscarf, bra and panties that set fire to his imagination—he recalled what happened to the wolf. "Would you like to bargain for it? Do you have your sheet of phrases?"

"I'm sorry. I lost it."

"No problem, I'll get you another."

He bargained the woman down from six hundred rupees to four hundred and gave her five hundred. The woman gave him a quizzical frown until she saw his expectant smile. She immediately offered them a fragrant tea in small clay pots that they gratefully sipped to complete the deal.

Charlie gave him a kiss. "Thank you, *sweetie*." She laughed loudly before whispering, "I have to go. I have a date with Duncan. See you."

Dan sighed slowly as Charlie skipped over to a glassy-eyed Duncan and felt a pang of regret when she giggled at something he said and took him by the arm.

"I see Charlie's into you," said Bob, bumping into him. "What a babe, eh?"

"You think so?"

"Very attractive sheila, that one. Those legs and a tight arse like that? Chroist."

"Bit tall for you? You dirty old man. Rani will have your nuts."

"Ha! That'll be the day, mate."

After browsing a few stalls together, Bob bumped him again, this time toward a narrow alley that led to another street. "The restaurant's this way," he said.

Dan had no reason not to follow him but a sixth sense he'd developed in prison caused him to get ready for trouble. Bob was a jolly kind of guy, ready with a quick quip, but Dan was wary of him. The way he rolled as he walked with his hands dangling far out to the sides of his body indicated inside the tubby clown was a much harder man. He'd go with his attribute: strength. He'd come at anyone with brute force swinging his heavy paws, throwing his bulk to overpower his victims. Dan hung back far enough to stay out of arm's length although he wondered about the gun having a range of more than three feet. The dark alley was wet and strewn with garbage. A radio blared from an open window. Singing and dance music echoed from an unseen party in a backyard. Bob paused halfway to the next street and turned. His face was half lit and it looked like he'd stepped in something nasty.

"Shira's into you too," he said.

"Some guys have all the luck."

"Are you *into* her?" Bob leered. "If so, you really are a lucky man."

"You think so?" Dan edged back as Bob moved closer.

"Go for the tits. They're dangerous mothers but much safer for you, believe me."

Bob's right fist clenched. No gun. He must reckon he can easily take me in a fist fight, thought Dan. Cause no injury or harm but Dan had the right to defend himself if attacked. He moved back farther to get away from any sudden moves to his head or groin. His pulse quickened, his skin tingling as the adrenaline flowed.

"I'm a fatherly figure, Bob. What's this all about?"

Dan had learned how to fight—and fight dirty—after being on the receiving end of a few beatings that had left their marks. No Marquess of Queensberry rules where he'd been and needed to survive. The Marquess would have been dead in no time. He turned a little sideways, widening his stance and lining up what would look like a right hook. Bob shuffled closer, sneering the smile of the schoolyard bully.

"Keep away from Charlie," ordered Bob, viciously jabbing a fat finger.

"What business is that of yours?" Dan asked calmly, eyes focused on Bob's chin. Bob would throw a right and he'd counter with a left hook.

Bob's growl deepened. "It is my business. Stay away from the Yanks. Go fuck that fat Kiwi."

Dan waited to deflect Bob's punch, knowing the one who didn't get in the first blow might never get another chance. His pulse thudded in his ears. His body wound itself tighter.

"What's up, Bob? Prurient interest? Do you whack off to them when Rani's asleep in her cave?" Dan goaded, his left fist tight on a bunch of hard rupee coins.

"Fucker!" Bob barged at Dan, head down throwing a roundhouse right that narrowly missed as Dan switched feet and swayed away.

Dan's thudding punch missed Bob's chin. It pounded the side of his throat as he lurched by. Bob collapsed like a Wall Street sure-thing pyramid scheme, his momentum carrying him onto the ground. Round Two was not needed unless Jesus was in Bob's corner.

"*Ooooh!*" Bob growled and gurgled. He clutched his throat, coughing and gasping for breath. His turban rolled away in the filth.

Had he killed him? Dan dropped to his knees and rolled him over.

Bob rasped, "I'll ... kill ... you!" out of a raspberry face.

Dan took in a huge breath of relief and sat Bob up. He'd missed crushing Bob's Adam's apple—death a certainty. He'd be OK if talking like a frog for a while. Dan's heart thumped, thumped, thumped, a pounding headache on the way. He felt sick and suppressed an urge to vomit but wasn't distracted enough to miss Bob edging a hand inside his jacket. Dan beat him to his gun.

"Twat!" growled Bob, grabbing for the Walther before it disappeared into Dan's pocket.

Dan ran up the street to stop a tuk-tuk. Down the lane, the driver helped him pile a struggling Bob in the back.

"Hospital!" he told the driver, shoving a wad of rupees in his hand. Better to be on the safe side.

* * *

Dan washed down a few pills for his nausea and walked off the evening's madness through streets still a hive of activity—shops would not close until the last person with a rupee had gone to bed. He avoided collisions with the bulls and cows, monkeys swinging from awnings, and being electrocuted by wires strung in dangling loops from pole to pole along the street.

After a few flash photos and some video of street scenes, the unobtrusive beer outlet between a big clothing shop and a stall piled with fruits and vegetables swung into his viewfinder. Dazza, Arfa and Duncan and—impossible to miss—Charlie were backed off into a shadowy area, the glow of what had to be a joint moving from head to head. Boys will be boys but cops would see a nice earner in fining them whatever they had in their wallets. Dazza exchanged gesticulations with an Indian with a face that had run into a propeller. He had more scar tissue than a pack mule's ass. Dazza shook the man's hand and exchanged a package for a bulky backpack he threw over his shoulder.

Oh, Jesus! An icy finger of fear stroked Dan's spine. Charlie and Duncan are at a dope deal? Please God, let it be hash, not opium, he thought, although he knew a quick death might be preferable to a longer one with a life sentence in an Indian prison.

Deal done, the boys and Charlie walked back toward the hotel. Dan followed hoping like hell the cops didn't appear. He watched the boys' backs and saw no—*Christ!* A man wearing a hooded robe trailed them by ten yards, keeping his distance in the stream of bodies. It did Dan's headache no good at all as his body surged with adrenalinee again. He darted through the weaving tuk-tuks and honking cars to cross the street and closed up within five yards of the man. Like a jittery lioness guarding her cubs, he steeled himself to jump him if he tried to collar Charlie and the boys. In the illumination of the hotel's portico, the small man paused and turned away as the boys and Charlie entered the lobby. The light caught his face—Steve.

March 26th

Somewhere over Rajasthan

THE STREAMING WISPS of clouds covering the dark-blue expanse of the Indian Ocean disappeared behind the two-engined Fokker as it buzzed north with its half-empty load of twenty passengers into buffeting headwinds descending from the ragged colossus of Kashmir. Below, the land buckled in jagged ridges, becoming more and more desolate, the greens of river valleys gradually replaced by the browns and grays of desiccated, rocky land and the endless sandy reach of the Thar Desert toward the shimmering haze of Pakistan.

Unable to sleep, Kapoor had caught the 0600 plane out of Mumbai for the hour and a quarter flight and sat at the rear of the plane, intensely contemplative as for once in his carefully controlled life he had no plan. He had taken a big leap into the dark with no idea as to where he was going to land but he couldn't stop himself. Dan Palmer had reset his brain circuits into operating on pure emotion, the greatest enemy of the logical thinking that had served him well for over two decades as a detective. Dewan had given him only three days to return with the Harbor Killer to Mumbai. He had no idea who the killer was but if Dan were gay or bisexual, he was sure he could seduce him in no time at all. That was all that mattered.

Udaipur

Kapoor's camera clicked epileptically. Just one jaw-dropping sight of Dan Palmer and he cast aside his concerns about his rash decision. Dan Palmer was beyond his expectations: tall and athletic, wearing a tropical shirt loose on his broad shoulders and khaki cargo pants on a tight arse. Dan Palmer's glossy, black hair was much neater than the tousled mass in the passport photo: cut shorter and combed back like Freddie Mercury. He looked so damn *jhakaas!* Perfect!

Kapoor thanked the gods he'd dressed even better than usual for the special occasion in his best light brown suit with a white shirt and a cream silk tie. The suit's lapels and creases were sharpened with a file and pressed to perfection. He took a Panama-style hat off his beautifully oiled and parted hair as he unfolded his unusually tall Indian frame out of the taxi and loped flamingo steps toward Dan.

"Mis'r... Palmer?" stuck in Kapoor's throat. Dan stopped and turned toward him in the hotel's portico. "Good morning, I'm Superintendent Kapoor. May I talk with you for a moment, sah?" he asked with his most disarming smile and an outstretched hand Dan shook firmly.

Dan noticeably tensed. Perhaps it was the typical reaction to being stopped out of the blue by a policeman, Kapoor thought. Everyone had something to hide—sometimes something as insignificant as parking tickets and sometimes something far more serious.

"About what?" Dan asked and glanced at his watch. "I have to join my group."

"Murder, sah," Kapoor intoned in a low voice for dramatic effect.

Dan missed a beat before throwing open his palms. "Superintendent, if it's about that pestering monkey on Elephanta Island, I plead guilty."

Kapoor smiled at Dan's quick sense of humor. "Nossah, nossah," he assured him. "I deal with homicides ... not pesticides."

Dan laughed. Somewhat nervously, thought Kapoor. "How can I help you, Superintendent?"

"Shall we go and find somewhere cooler? It won't take too long, sah."

Dan ordered them both cold fruit juices in the hotel's air-conditioned bar since Kapoor told him he didn't drink on duty. He waited for Dan to speak first. It was an old habit of his to leave his subjects waiting, give them time to think, get nervous—and observe them.

"Mind if I smoke?" Dan asked.

"Only if I do," replied Kapoor affably, appreciating his manners. Another box checked.

Kapoor had experienced many a guilty suspect hiding behind the smokescreen of a cigarette: it gave their mouth and hands something to do besides fidget. Kapoor took a proffered cigarette and reached out unnecessarily to hold Dan's hand while he lit it for him. He noticed it was nicely manicured, just like his. And he detected a pleasant musk cologne on Dan's manly stubble. Dan was his kind of clean man. He began to feel as nervous as Dan appeared to be.

"You're investigating a murder?" Dan asked.

Kapoor nodded but his mind was elsewhere, scanning Dan from head to toe for clues. Was he a homo? He tried a simple ploy, leaning closer to finger the collar on Dan's shirt. "May I say that's a very nice shirt? Silk?"

Dan blinked surprise. "Yes, it is."

"Cool in this climate. And it matches your lovely brown-green eyes."

Dan reached to feel the hem of Kapoor's jacket. "Thanks, you're looking very dapper yourself, Superintendent. I love linen suits too. Lovely color and it matches your tie perfectly. You have great taste." He sat back smiling. "We make quite a pair, don't we?"

Quite a pair? Heat prickled Kapoor's cheeks. Everything about Dan told him he was a homo! The manly type he liked. It was his turn to draw heavily on his cigarette to calm his frayed nerves while he kept his eyes down on his notebook. When he looked up into Dan's brown-green eyes, his mouth stalled, the heat rising. He was in lust again.

Kapoor cleared his throat as he adjusted his tie and took a deep breath. "There were ... two murders in Mumbai. Two Americans ... due to join your group were ... were found dead in the harbor."

Oh god, I must sound such an idiot!

Dan had burned through one cigarette like a vacuum cleaner. He lit another and sat back with one ankle crossed over the other leg's knee, abruptly far more relaxed. Kapoor held his breath. It was the English way. Monty's way. Was he Monty's twin soul? Had Ganesha blessed him?

"Loki mentioned the Thompsons," said Dan.

"The Americans were traveling on false passports," Kapoor said stringing his words together better. "They were actually the Koepkes. Both had been horribly tortured. He had a record in America as long as one's arm, mostly for violence. She wasn't much better. No crimes in the last five years or so. They'd either gone straight or were smarter about what they did."

Kapoor sipped the last of his juice and needed something stronger to relax him. He never drank alcohol on the job but this was an exception—and a reason to celebrate. He ordered a peaty Lagavulin Scotch, no water.

Dan stuck with juice and asked, "So why are you talking to me?"

"You've read about the Harbor Murders?"

"I caught a bit of it on TV."

"I believe the Harbor Murderers are in this group."

"*Jesus*," Dan replied. "How many are we talking here?"

"Four."

"*Four?*"

"Just joking, sah. Only two. Maybe just one."

"Oh, only one? Great."

"See how much better one sounds now?" Kapoor said playfully.

"Hilariously witty," Dan replied with a wry shake of his head. "I should have you arrested for that!"

"I'll arrest myself after I've finished this great Scotch, sah."

Dan laughed genuinely for the first time, Kapoor thought. And when he did, there was a glint of his unforgettable Monty.

"Why are you asking me to help you?" asked Dan. "Hell, how do you know I didn't do it?"

"When did you arrive in Mumbai?"

"Um ... Monday."

For Kapoor, there was too much hesitation. It made him curious. "You flew in?"

"From Cairo. Fantastic city. Ever been there?"

Is he attempting to digress?

"Before Cairo?"

"Nigeria."

"Vacation?"

"Work."

Kapoor waved his palms. "There you go. The bodies were found in the harbor the night you arrived from Kolkata so you couldn't have done it. They'd been dead at least twenty-four hours."

"OK, I confess it wasn't me."

Kapoor chuckled. "Hilariously witty, sah."

Dan clinked his glass on Kapoor's. "*Touché, mon ami.* A lot of people have lost their sense of humor these days—or aren't allowed to have one. You remind me of an old friend I loved."

"Really?... Oh... *Touché,*" stuttered Kapoor. *An old friend he loved?* Tingling with a rush of blood, he hid for a moment behind gulping his drink. "And you remind me of one of my friends, an English boy with whom I attended a boarding school for many years. He was a handsome rogue, too. Got along with everyone—male and female." He smiled at Dan, sensing the possibility he was as bisexual as his promiscuous, teenage lover, the beautiful white boy who had teased him beyond endurance. "You'd be a perfect fit."

"Fit for what?"

"I have suspects traveling in this group and I need an informant inside it."

"You mean me? Working for the police?"

"Be my inside source, sah. Just like those English public schoolboys in the John le Carré novels I love so much. Together we can solve the Harbor Murders."

"Sure," Dan said sarcastically. "I noticed a few ended up betrayed and dead in the books I read."

"Betrayed by falling in love. That most powerful and dangerous of human emotions," remarked Kapoor guiding the conversation. "Humans will do anything for love. Believe me, I've seen it all from murdered wives, girlfriends, boyfriends, husbands to disfigured women and even the occasional man who's woken up without his penis. Don't you agree?"

"You're right, it is the most dangerous of emotions. Also the most wonderful, isn't it? It's what makes us human. But it makes fools of us all. We do irrational things when love rears its beautiful head and seduces us into foolishness."

Kapoor's stomach fluttered at Dan's eloquence. How his thoughts matched his own. "Well put. I assume you must have experienced the highs and lows of love."

"Ha! Certainly the lows."

"Never a high? It's never too late, is it? To love other women—and men too of course."

Dan smiled faintly, his eyes drifting to the ceiling.

Is he thinking about women and men? Lost loves?

Kapoor caught himself staring at Dan's enigmatic expression until Dan gave him a quizzical look.

"You seem quite the romantic, Superintendent," said Dan.

"I am a romantic, indeed, but a realistic one. As John Lennon sang: love is all you need."

"Although Buddha had a hit with it 2500 years ago?"

"And Parvati, our goddess of love and devotion recorded it long before that, of course. The Kama Sutra wasn't written by a Canadian, was it?"

"Explains over a billion of you."

"We Indians like our sex, sah." Kapoor smiled suggestively. "Any way we can get it too. Did you know in the ancient scripts of Hinduism we view hetero and homosexuality as just part of love making?"

Dan raised his drink to Kapoor. "I didn't but it's something we can agree on. It's all loving one another."

It's all loving one another? Excitement fizzed through Kapoor.

Dan smoked more then slowly shook his head. "I'm sorry but I've become a Buddhist pacifist, Superintendent. This sounds like I might tangle with someone who isn't and end up a dead one."

Buddhists were OK as far as Kapoor was concerned. Hindus and Buddhists believed in reincarnation and karma. "Hindus and Buddhists shun violence but they are allowed to defend themselves. Correct?" Kapoor asked. Dan nodded. "The murders were particularly vicious and any help to bring this disgusting monster to justice would improve your karma, your future happiness, your next life?"

"Correct."

"Perhaps I can explain more," Kapoor said lightly. "Just talk normally to your fellow travelers. Listen in on their conversations. Report anything of interest. Don't play Sherlock Holmes. Leave that to me." He patted Dan's knee. "No one will hurt you as long as I'm around."

"I'd really like to help but ..." Dan trailed off with a shrug.

Kapoor felt a surge of anxiety. He was losing him. "Would it help if I told you my suspects?" He plowed on without waiting for an answer. "First of all, Mis'r and Missus Stewart—"

"Bob Stewart's a suspect?" Dan interjected.

"This trip is not where I'd expect to find such a character," Kapoor continued quickly now he had hooked Dan's interest. "He arrived in Mumbai two years ago with enough money to set himself up in a small security business. He's garnered an ugly reputation for violence. Not bad advertising in that field, of course. He's been smart enough to avoid getting into trouble with the law. Implicated in a few murders but never charged."

"Bob is a nasty piece of work. He's the American women's bodyguard and he's bloody serious about it."

"Why do you think he's their bodyguard?"

"We had a disagreement over the young American women last night."

"Disagreement?" Kapoor's fingers formed a steeple against his smoothly shaved chin.

"He warned me off them and physically attacked me."

"What happened?"

"I defended myself."

Kapoor smiled broadly unable to stop himself patting Dan several times on the knee. "Well done, sah," he gushed before taking a drink of his fiery Scotch to gather himself together. Damn, he was an excited teenager next to the prettiest girl—or boy—in the class. Dan knew how to fight if he could do ward off a thug like Stewart. Impressive. Dan ticked another Monty box.

Kapoor thought while scribbling in his notebook as a cover before asking, "May I ask why he felt it necessary to warn you off the American ladies?"

"He thought I was too friendly with them."

"Ladies can be dangerous, can they not?" Kapoor asked with a wink and a conspiratorial chuckle. "Perhaps you should keep your distance from the ladies and avoid trouble. Bob Stewart is a hard case and will want his revenge no doubt. A lot of things can happen between here and Kathmandu."

"He's threatened to kill me. He's a bad loser."

"Kill you?" Kapoor stiffened down to his Gucci shoes. Bob Stewart grew a bull's eye the size of the Taj Mahal on his head.

"He has a Walther with him. I'm afraid he'll use it sooner rather than later."

"How do you know?"

"He threatened me with it at our fight."

Kapoor didn't bother to consult his notes. "He has a three-year license for a registered Walther. His wife has a permit for a Beretta Nano."

"Rani Stewart?" Dan laughed. "Obviously not rape prevention."

"Indeed not, sah," Kapoor agreed with a laugh of his own but raised an eyebrow at Dan's ignorance—some Indian men would rape anything with a *yoni*. He thought every Indian woman should carry a small Nano regardless of physical attractiveness. It slipped nicely into the purse amongst the female knickknacks but could remove a testicle at forty paces. He'd wangled one for Nasma, his wife, and taught her how to use it.

Dan leaned close enough for Kapoor to feel a disturbance in his magnetic field. "Don't you think it's him? A professional thug with a Walther?"

"There are other suspects. Do you recall who joined the group at the last minute and after the murders?"

"The major and his wife?"

"Drury has a permit for a Browning and his wife carries a Nano."

"Gilly, that little old lady, is packing heat too? We have enough guns to invade Tibet," Dan joked then got serious. "How come tourists like the Drurys have permits for guns?"

"Tourists? They've been residents of Delhi for the last twenty years."

"The last twenty years?" A deflated Dan blew out between tight lips. "They don't live in bonnie Scotland?"

"Not any longer. Mis'r Drury was born here in India but joined the British Army after his family moved to Stirling in 1964."

"Wasn't his father an officer in the British Army in the big war?"

"Sorry to disappoint you but his father was a cook based at a divisional HQ on the Burma Front."

"Never a brigadier?"

"Only a sergeant. Drury was kicked out for violent insubordination. Punched a captain who'd overstepped it with his wife. And that kind of thing has dogged him ever since."

"What's he done?"

"Let's say he put his violent tendencies to work for him. Delhi's the nation's capital and there are lots of people there who need intelligent protection or underhand operations discreetly performed. Not just muscle like Mis'r Stewart."

"And Gilly? Don't tell me she was a shoplifter."

"Securities fraud when they lived briefly in London. After Mis'r Drury was cashiered and his wife had served a few months at Her Majesty's pleasure, they moved to Delhi. Missus Drury has lived on the dodgy edge of the financial laws ever since."

"So they're on the trip for violent and/or financial reasons?"

"It's quite possible they are the murderers."

Dan crushed the stub of his cigarette and lit a third. "You think they may have got rid of the Koepkes to replace them?"

Kapoor shrugged. "I want you to find out. But you'll need to be careful. There are at least four guns in this group and only the gods know how many others you'll have to watch out for."

"You should have mentioned that earlier in the brochure, Superintendent."

Kapoor chuckled. "We'll need a code name for you. How about Monty?"

"Monty the Mole. Sounds right out of a kid's storybook." Dan stood up. "When will we talk again?"

Kapoor stood up too and held Dan's hand as long as possible. "I'll contact you tomorrow, sah."

He slipped his camera from his pocket and clicked several photos as Dan walked away. Mmm. A very nice tight arse, too. It was time for another offering at the temple. The god deserved a weighty bunch of fresh marigolds and a cornucopia of fruit. He'd rub some coconut oil on Shiva's lingam too—and then on his own.

* * *

The group spent the late morning touring the City Palace, a blindingly white, fortified mansion on a crag, with its towers high above the almost black waters of Lake Pichola. Rani and Bob were absent when they jumped off the bus and followed Loki to the wedding-cake palace's courtyard, overshadowed on three sides by four or five layers of balconies and windows beneath curving, pagoda-style roofs.

Udaipur was losing its cool. Only a few hundred miles from the Thar desert to the northwest, Udaipur simmered under the rising sun in a light blue sky that hadn't seen a wisp of cloud for months. Dan looked down at the white palaces on the islands in the long lake that bordered the city and moderated its rising temperature. Families gathered by the lake on the ghats, the stone steps below the overhanging royal palace, to wash and play in its warm water.

"Did you hear about Bob?" Mark asked Dan.

"What about him?"

"He was attacked near the market last night."

"Must have been the turban."

"Ha! Bloody awful wasn't it? Anyway, the poor chap spent the night in hospital."

"Is he going to be OK?"

"He's going to be fine. We'll pick him up at the hospital. Apparently, he fought off a gang of louts, " said Mark. "You have to be careful in this bloody country. Indians are a rough bunch."

Dan had not slept well. He'd taken a risk on Bob not reporting him to the police and have them arrive in the middle of the night to use their sticks to beat him—and find out more about him. It would have been a quick way for Bob to get him out of the way of Charlie and Shira but whining to the cops wouldn't be his style. Revenge would be. And Bob wouldn't want a boxing match the next time.

The group followed Loki by the parking lot of bollards and mounds in the yard where elephants took a load off to the terrace overlooking the lake. Near the main entrance, Loki patted the curled trunk of one of the many carved elephants that supported the palace for good luck then clapped his hands several times.

"Ladies and gentlemen!" he exclaimed. "This is our Venice of India. Or perhaps Venice is the Udaipur of Europe! It is our most romantic spot, I tell you. People come from all over India to have their romance here. Is it not most wonderful?"

Dan leaned over the scalloped Islamic parapet and looked down almost five hundred feet at the ghats and the shimmering water. Far above, black kites soared and circled on the updraft over the pagoda towers with their decorated window arches.

A languid voice said, "Have their romance?"

He turned to find Shira dressed in a cool, white dress with a neckline that plunged to a waistband. It looked like the dress Marilyn Monroe had worn in that iconic photo when the draft from the subway grate sent her skirt flying to immortality. Shira filled it better.

"It is a lovely place for that, isn't it?" she said, twirling a long hank of hair in her fingers.

"It is," he replied, taking in her familiarly glazed morning eyes.

She tilted her head, fingering a thin shoulder strap. "Would you like to take me to dinner tonight?" she asked, raising her big eyes, inviting him to take the plunge.

"Hasn't Loki arranged dinner for us?"

"Really? Well, we can sit next to one another, can't we?"

He could think of a lot of reasons pro and con to be next to her. He was sure he could resist the cons and admire her scenery. "Why not?"

"Later tonight then," she breathed with a lazy smile and departed by running her hand down his forearm. Whether it was an invitation to check out her bed springs or assemble a doll's house out of Lego blocks, Dan found it hard to tell. He wondered what Charlie could come up with to rival that piece of theater.

"That shirt's a bit gay, bud."

Dressed in a blue and white batik shirt with white jeans and sandals, Bill would not have been out of place on a sundeck in Hawaii. His aviator sunglasses reflected back Dan's pink-flowered, beige Indian shirt.

"Where's your parrot?" Dan asked without interest.

Bill rested back against the parapet. "Whaddya think of the women in the group?"

"Why would a gay guy like me care?"

"Sensitive type, aren't you?" said Bill carelessly. He nodded toward Shira idling at her mother's side. "I'm going to take a run at the big girl."

"No, you won't. We have a date for later." Dan planted his flag in Shira.

Bill barked a gloating laugh. "I don't give a shit about her, rube! It's your bunk muffin I'm after!"

Bastard, thought Dan. "Not too fat and loud for you?"

"Maybe for you. Not for me. I like them funny ... and pneumatic for a soft landing."

Dan smiled smugly. "Pity she's a lesbian then."

Bill's face sagged his disappointment. "Aw, no. You're kidding?"

"Try anything and you'll find your balls in Pakistan."

Ranakpur

It was fewer than two hours to Ranakpur from Udaipur. The twelve of them lounged in an air-conditioned bus designed for about forty so there was plenty of room for everyone to spread out and relax and watch the countryside get drier and higher. White and gray stone houses clustered occasionally into small villages. Slanted, gnarled telephone poles with their sagging wires lined the road looking more alive than the leafless trees.

Cameras starting clicking when the gray stone Adinath Jain temple rose like a fantasy Oz out of the flat, sparsely treed land. With so many curved roofs, it resembled an upside-down egg box and was surrounded by spires displaying red banners with swastikas. White monkeys greeted them, swinging through the leafy branches and fiery red flowers of the flame trees, looking for a camera to pinch.

The monks served lunch on long, wooden tables in a spartan, low-level building next to the great temple itself. Seconds of the vegetable stew was offered but Loki warned them not to accept more and then leave it—unless anyone wanted to come back as untouchable, fourth-class human refuse. Bad karma. No one did.

The group assembled at the bottom of a broad flight of stone steps that rose into an elaborately carved portico. Charlie and Shira drank from their water bottles while a pink-faced Cruella stood guard with a spiked parasol at the ready. Loki led them up into the cavernous structure supported by a myriad of carved, stone columns that hadn't been rushed jobs.

The stunning beauty of the elaborate interior of the temple was disrupted by a constant, loud hammering that drove its visitors to distraction: rattling, banging and shouting echoed throughout the more than fourteen hundred individually unique pillars and the towering, fabulously detailed ceiling of its central dome.

"Ladies and gentlemen, you'll never, ever see anything like this again. The greatest architecture in the world, right here in India," Loki called loudly and proudly in that singsong of his over the background cacophony. "The rich merchant Jains, an offshoot of Hinduism, created the most fabulous temples in India. It's built from the same marble as the Taj Mahal but this makes the Taj look like a Lego set, I tell you!"

Dan wandered on his own, snapping close-ups of the carvings, some interestingly erotic. He heard a stick rapping the stones. It was Cruella with Shira following like a mindless gosling among the pillars in the persistently annoying racket of the workmen. When Cruella noticed him, he expected sour indifference after the previous evening's jousting but she tapped toward him. He got ready for combat.

"Have you seen our Charlene?" she asked unexpectedly and remarkably solicitous of her problem child. "She looked real agitated after lunch."

"Not lately. She seems really good today."

She pressed a palm against a cheek to emphasize her anxiety. "We never know what she'll be like. Up one day, down the next. She can be such a bitch. As you well know, of course."

Dan glanced at Shira.

"She's a bitch," Shira murmured with little lip movement.

"Is this her unpredictability?" he asked Cruella.

She paused to release a deep sigh. "I don't know how much to tell you." She lowered her voice. "She had a serious breakdown after her mother and father died. She'll deny it but she went …" She twirled a finger around on the side of her head. "The drugs? And her promiscuity? Don't get me started. Keep that to yourself but better you stay away from her for your own safety. She's a dangerous girl … for older men in particular."

"How old?"

She stared coldly at him. "Whatever age you are." She turned and walked away.

He went in search of Charlie, passing hushed tour groups and a few loitering red and yellow-robed monks mumbling with their wide-eyed acolytes. He saw her disappear behind a group of pillars.

* * *

Charlie's head exploded with excitement. She sweated, her heart pounded, breath rasped. She could see the pounding noise—everything vibrated to a xylophone of ringing hammers—colours flashed. An electric shock touched her arm as she aimed her camera at the elaborate ceiling.

"Hi. How are you?" asked a voice.

A pair of concerned brown-green eyes drilled into hers.

"I … I … I feel great! Aren't these … amazing … remarkable?" she babbled, bouncing on her spring-loaded toes like a Jack-in-the-Box. "They're so … detailed and look at this one … the people in this, and the elephants … and that one … Isn't it wonderful, and this one." She paused briefly to take a deep breath between her gasps. "How long ago was this? A long time? How many centuries?"

"Slow down a bit." Dan held onto her trembling arm. "My ears don't work that fast."

She ran her hands quickly over the stones, feeling at the carvings of the voluptuous women in particular. "Look how sexy these women are! I wish I had boobs like them! Those butts! Wow!"

Dan tried to hold her steady but she pulled away.

"What's this all for?" she asked.

"The temples are sites of education," he told her soothingly, putting an arm around her quivering shoulders. "The rows tell people how to lead their lives. Look at the bottom, we have—"

"Like how to fuck their brains out?" she blurted. "Look at that! You don't see this in America ... not New York anyway ... and what about this one!" A carving of another voluptuous woman with a well-endowed man and a horse. "Wow. They do anything, don't they?"

When he said, "I guess they love their pets" she barked a laugh that echoed louder than the hammering.

"*Shhh* for Christ's sake!" Dan slapped his hand across her mouth and pulled her into him.

She enjoyed his arms around her but she pushed him away. Moving from one column to another, she ran her trembling hands over the reliefs of the sexual menagerie. "Gotta get shots of all of these. Look at them. Those boobs! Butts!" She grinned at him. "Those enormous cocks!"

She remembered in elementary school seeing illustrations from the *Kama Sutra*—it had frightened the hell out of her. She'd lain in bed and prayed it wasn't true. What a dope!

"Do you think I should have my boobs done like Shira?" she asked. "She had boobs worse than me."

"Shira's are fake?"

She brayed a laugh. "You think they're human?" She let go of him and jiggled her small breasts. "Mine are so ... nothing. You like breasts, don't you? You're a man you must! I'll have them done for you if you want. You'd like that?"

"Charlie, Charlie!" Dan held her trembling shoulders to get her full attention. "Don't ever do that. This is the genuine you."

"So you like them? Really?"

"Yes, yes, yes! Look, there's nothing fake about you. I like you just this way. Don't fall for that cosmetic crap—or I'll dump you!"

She smiled so much her face hurt. *How I want this guy!* "OK! Yes! OK!"

"Never ask that again. Let's take a rest outside."

"OK! Great!"

Dan grabbed her hand and led her down the long entry staircase toward a bench seat under one of the flame trees with those long red blossoms and the odd monkey to keep an eye on. A woman rocked her baby in a hammock contraption in the shade while her husband ground knives using a foot treadle. He had an array of knives from a big Gurkha kukri that could behead a tiger to a small one for cleaning nails laid out on a blanket.

Charlie paced backward and forward in front of the knives. "That one! That one! I really like that one! *Kitane kah hay?*" How much is this? Charlie handed a few bills to the grinder when he held up some fingers. She picked up a miniature knife in a decorative, metal scabbard with a length of leather for its attachment. It would be a nice souvenir and a bit of jewelry too.

Dan took the knife from her and said: "It's a kirpan Sikhs carry as an article of faith." He ran a thumb along its curved, two-inch blade. "Be careful, it's sharp. Anyone in mind?"

"Several!" She swished the blade in the air before sliding it into its scabbard. After tying the strip behind her neck, she slipped the knife inside her blouse.

"It's for protection or peeling fruit?"

She giggled. "Rapists and dangerous fruit!" She looked down at the knives again. "I'd *really* like the kukri. What I could do with that!"

"And a kukri book?"

Charlie laughed so hard she almost puked. "You're just *sooo* funny!"

She had to kiss him! Catching him unawares, she quickly raised her mouth and pulled his lips to hers. His lips burned, her insides melting in a warm rush until Dan pressed her away. "Wow! Wasn't … wasn't that great?" *Dan looks as though he's been hit by a truck!* She tried to kiss him again but Dan held her shoulders and guided her onto the bench seat.

"Let's have a rest before we get back on the bus," he told her.

"Really? Do we have to? Let's stay here together! There's so—"

Dan's arm tightened around her and she gladly fell into him. "Let's do a bit of meditation to turn our brains off. Get into the eternal now," he said softly.

"Wow! The eternal now. Oh, that rhymes, too! That's amazing! Who said that?"

"Me about five seconds ago."

"Ha! Before you, idiot!" She fidgeted, unable to stop her legs moving.

"It was a book I read in ... a few years ago. About freeing the spirit from the controlling power of sin and the acceptance of the certainty of the eternal. Something like that."

"The eternal now," she repeated. "Wow. Have you sinned?" She expected he had. The scars? How much of a bad boy had he been? And here she was a Catholic girl loaded to the gills with guilty baggage, condemned to hell.

"I don't believe in sin. I believe in just trying to get better. Reduce my karma so I have a good rebirth. How about you?"

"John Lennon sang "Instant Karma," didn't he?" she asked in a moment of calm between her brainstorms. "What is karma? I just remember he said it would knock you on the head."

"It's the enemy of the soul. It's your actions. Good actions lead to happiness while bad actions result in misery and pain."

"Sort of like 'whatever one sows, that will he also reap,'" she quoted from the Bible.

"That's right. Improving your karma leads to a good rebirth until you achieve perfection and are not reborn but have become an enlightened soul. That's the Buddhist brochure in a nutshell."

"Nirvana? Right?"

"Well done. Christians, Muslims and Jews are so boringly linear. Life ends in heaven or hell." He chuckled. "Hindus and Buddhists recycle and have more chances."

"I never thought of that." Her face slipped as she looked up at the heavens. "They spiral to their heaven while we believe if you've led a good life you'll not be reborn but go to heaven and to hell if you haven't."

"How's it going?"

She was sure the answer was written in her damp eyes. "I'm going to hell, for sure."

"You've been a bad girl?"

Was this a way to get Dan's attention? "Bad? Ha! You name it I've done it! Sex, drugs, rock'n roll!"

Those chaotic years—rebellion, pain, suicidal thoughts, blackouts, bad sex even orgies with shitty men, almost every drug she could cram down her throat flashed by. "Yes, yes and yes!" she exclaimed. Would Dan be impressed with that?

"Ever done Ecstasy?"

"Who hasn't? Do you have any with you?"

"I do." He reached into a pocket and opened his palm to show her five blue pills. "Try these."

"Oh wow. Blue ones?" She herded them around his palm with a finger.

"They're Indian. Picked them up in Mumbai."

"Can I have one?"

He put three in her hand. "No more than that." He passed her the water bottle and she flushed them down.

"You having any?" she asked.

"Had a couple in the temple."

"Wow."

"You've used a lot of pills?"

"Well, duh. My last school was a meth lab. Rich kids can get anything. How about you? What's your favorite?"

"Acid. Magic Bus shit."

"Oh yeah."

Pete Townshend's power cords vibrated in what was left of those memories. She'd actually tried it and had bad experiences—too many flashbacks—so she'd stopped before she'd turned into an addled Timothy Leary.

Dan felt for her pulse. "Now, close your eyes," he ordered.

As they sat with their arms around each other, she sensed her breathing slowing and the tremble slackening. Time ceased to matter. When he said she could open her eyes all the fidgeting had ceased.

"Better?" he asked, running his fingers across her forehead.

She licked her dry lips. "Mmm. That's nice." She wanted to stay under his arm forever.

Jodhpur: The Blue City

On the last leg of the long bus trip to Jodhpur, Dan relaxed as Charlie dozed on the seat in front of him where he could keep an eye on her. The tranquilizers he'd given her continued to do their job. It was getting late when the bus descended from the mountains. A black blanket rolled over the flat land and left them sitting in the fluorescent glow of their reading lights.

"Is dear Charlene all right, doctor?" Cruella asked as cloyingly solicitous as at the temple.

"Dan, please, Elaine. What makes you ask?"

"I'm worried sick about her already and we've only started this awful tour." She paused. "I saw you with her outside the temple."

"We were doing a bit of meditation. She's interested in that kind of thing. She's a bright kid."

"Mmm. She wasn't acting strange in any way?"

"Strange?"

"She seemed quite *agitated* in the temple."

"Maybe she was just excited. She seemed very happy to be visiting such a place."

"Oh, good," Cruella said. "I'm just so fearful when she's out of my sight."

"I can see that."

"I'm so glad you understand. I thought she might be having another *manic episode*. She could end up really hurting herself." She threw her hands in the air, despairing. "Get lost. God knows what."

He took the offered bait. "Manic episode?"

"I didn't want to tell you everything but I guess I'd better, you being a doctor an'all. She's been diagnosed as bipolar."

Dan sat up. "How long has she been like this?"

"She's never got over losing her mother and father in that crash. I thought she was recovering but I can see episodes of depression and mania beginning again. If it gets worse we'll have to rush her to the clinic. Perhaps you can help me deal with her."

"Of course. I'll help all I can. What treatment has she received?"

"Therapy, drugs, you name it. I've tried everything but nothing's worked."

"Not even lithium?"

"She's a stubborn girl. She tried it, hated how she felt and now refuses to take it."

"What's going to happen if you have to take her home?"

Cruella sighed deeply. "I'm afraid it'll be into special care now. I've lined up an exclusive center near Jodhpur should she need it while we're over here."

"Jodhpur? That's where we're going."

"It's run by a Doctor Pathan. *Wonderful* credentials. Somewhere she can get twenty-four-hour treatment and she'll have no choice in the matter. She's been so disruptive we can't find a school that will take her until she's under control." She lowered her voice and leaned in close enough for a mist of bourbon to float at Dan. "Nothing appears to work with her. I'm considering Doctor Pathan's recommendation of ECT as a last resort."

"ECT? You can make her do that?"

"She's my ward." She paused as though to let that sink in.

"ECT's getting extreme, isn't it? It'll cause memory and cognitive dysfunction." *Blow her brains out!*

"Well ..." Cruella sounded exasperated and opened her palms. "If it comes to the last resort, that's what we'll do. It's coming back in favor for cases like hers. I hope we don't have to do it but what can we do to protect her from herself, poor child?"

"Whose idea was this trip?" he asked. "She could be somewhere safer right now."

"You mean it doesn't look our type of vacation?"

"Frankly, I'd expect you to be drinking champers in the presidential suite of a cruise ship."

"Ha! If only. Charlene's call. I indulged her since it got her away from her problems at home and she desperately wanted to travel on a simple tour to get immersed in a foreign culture." She twisted her mouth with distaste. "Such as it is."

* * *

Jodhpur greeted them with strings of multi-colored gems tangled around the base of the towering Mehrangarh fortress, its dark orange mass glowing in yellow arc lights.

"We're here." Dan nudged Charlie awake.

Charlie blinked and rubbed her eyes. "Where?"

"Downtown Jodhpur."

"How long have I been asleep?"

"About three hours."

Charlie frowned. "I had one of those moments, didn't I?"

"Don't worry yourself. You were a little excited. No big deal."

"I'm sorry. I can't seem to control them."

"Don't sweat it. You didn't flash me again."

"Oh, you jerk!" she hissed, blushing furiously, subconsciously pulling her thighs together.

He chuckled. "If you feel like that again, I have more Ecstasy for you."

She snorted. "You lying skunk."

"Listen. If I'd given you Ecstasy you'd be somewhere near the top of Mount Everest right now salsa dancing with the Sherpas. How often do you get that way?"

"Since my parents died two years ago. It's been getting worse recently. Let's not talk about it, please."

The last thing he wanted was another nutbar in his life but he couldn't stop his Rescue Ranger from saddling up. ECT? It'd blow her brains out. Not happening.

* * *

The bus squealed to a halt in the dirt-brown gravel outside a low, red-stone building set back behind a lawn with scattered lounge chairs and bordered by bushes. A latticed arch festooned in vines welcomed them down a path to its porch and loggia.

No swimming pool at the small hotel so a quick shower before the warm water was all used up did its job of refreshing Dan. He arrived deliberately late at the restaurant to stay away from Charlie but it was impossible to avoid looking her way. She was in animated conversation with Duncan and the other boys whose eyes danced as they hung on her every word. It was easy to see why: swaths of red hair over her bare shoulders and dressed elegantly in a black choli over her small breasts and baring her belly above folds of a black sari trimmed with sparkling red, she had them hypnotized. With Karen hanging around with Bill, he found a chair with Mark and Gilly at one of the tables. While Cruella drank a cocktail, Shira sat idly sucking a finger tip until Dan caught her eye while admiring how partially dressed she was. She swooped in quickly onto the plastic seat next to him.

"Hi, how's your day been?" she asked in a little voice.

"Great. Would you like a drink?" he asked casting an eye quickly over her glistening hair that flowed over bare shoulders like the cascading Nile in the rainy season. The stressed black choli left a bare belly for disturbing eye candy above a hip-hugging black sari. It all looked remarkably familiar.

"Bottled water, please."

He ordered for the table: an amusing "child" beer for Mark, a G and T for Gilly and bottled water for Shira and himself. He toasted Shira. "You look *osum!*"

He envied the folded sheet of paper she withdrew from her deep cleavage and scanned.

"Awesome? Really?" Her smile widened as she glanced back at the sheet. "*Dhan ... ya ... bad?* Right?"

"Very good." He thought *he* should do all the thanking. "Is that a copy of the sheet I gave Charlie?"

"I borrowed hers."

Dan turned more toward Shira, and found her knees quickly rubbed his like firestarters. "OK. How about *tuma bahuta khubasurata ho?*"

"I'm not sure about the *ho*."

"You'll never know." He smiled slyly. "*Tuma sundara amkhem hai.*"

She held his forearm. "And that too."

"I can say all kinds of naughty things and you'll never know."

She giggled. "How naughty?"

Mark interrupted. "Shira? He just said you are very beautiful and—"

"You have beautiful eyes," completed Gilly.

A rosacea-in-full-bloom Mark raised his beer glass. "And I jolly well agree! You look simply super."

"Lovely, dear," added Gilly.

"Oh ... thank you." She kept her eyes on Dan as she folded the sheet and slid it slowly and deliberately back in her cleavage.

"I forgot about you two buggers." Dan shook his head and a fist at Gilly and Mark.

"That's so sweet, Dan." She clinked her water with his and pecked a kiss on his cheek.

Across the dining area, there was laughter followed by a crashing sound. Charlie was enjoying herself with the boys. Arfa and Dazza were doing a comedy act that involved sticking spoons on their noses and dropping dinner plates onto a stone floor. Duncan glared at him whenever he caught Dan looking his way.

Shira followed his gaze. "It's a *pity* about Charlie," she whispered like a schoolgirl to her friends in the washroom. "So *troubled* even before her parents died. And she'd *run away* for a year before that and ... *well.*" The cadence, the emphasis on key words, and the eye roll were all her mother.

Dan bit his tongue at Shira's churlish behavior. "That's a double whammy in all our lives. What's bigger than losing parents when you're young?"

She snorted. "*I lost my father and didn't go nuts.*"

Dan decided not to argue the point. "She must have been close to them."

"Such a *daddy's girl*," she sneered. "It all went *wrong* at her last boarding school. In and out of trouble. Got *expelled* for a *teacher thing*. The other kids nicknamed her *Lolita*."

Dan looked across the tables at a giggling, troubled and parentless Charlie. *Lolita?* No wonder Charlie had blanched and run for it after Gilly had told her story about her father having an affair with her schoolgirl mother.

"Look how she's dressed! Didn't I tell you she copies me?"

Dan glanced back at Charlie. Was she copying her more beautiful and well-endowed cousin? Was she that competitive?

Shira placed her hand on his arm. "But I look better, don't I?"

Dan gave her a deliberately admiring look that took no effort. "Absolutely no comparison," he told her. "You look more than *osom*."

When she planted a much longer kiss on his cheek, he didn't miss Gilly grinning and Mark winking at him from across the table.

"Would you like to take us for a walk?" Shira asked brightly.

* * *

No sooner had they left the restaurant and entered the main street than Shira became the center of attention from passing men. They stopped abruptly to stare without inhibition at her undulating Parvati-like attributes, their leers revealing the contents of their muttered asides to one another. The fist-pumping needed no translator. If Shira noticed, she didn't show it. She held his arm tighter as they kept out of the way of the honking tuk-tuks and bell-ringing bicycles. Without warning, she pulled him off the main street into the entrance to a dark alley and withdrew a silver thermal flask from her shoulder bag. She unscrewed the cap and drank deeply. The way she rolled her eyes and smacked her lips told him it wasn't Perrier. With Cruella for a mother, who could blame her?

She rattled the ice in the flask at him. "Like some?"

"Not with my medicines."

"Drink with me!" she snapped, thrusting the flask hard into his chest.

All the softness had melted from her and been replaced by lips drawn tightly across bared white teeth and her piercing eyes of black diamonds. The chilling sensation of being in a haunted house and something touching him on the shoulder shot through Dan. He knew very well the changes in personality that could occur in alcoholics—for the good, the bad and, far more likely, the ugly—but this was different: much quicker and frightening. He shuddered at her simmering violence as much as the bite of the small amount of cold vodka.

"Drink for fuck's sake!" she barked.

He took a bigger swallow and was hit by a dangerous friend he'd avoided revisiting for years. It must have shown in his face.

"Ha! That's better!" She grinned and finished the flask. "Gotta ciggie?"

He fumbled a cigarette between her lips and lit it for her. All that vodka in a couple of minutes and she didn't seem to be affected while he, after so long clean and sober, reeled at its impact. His brain went as slack as his neck muscles.

He wasn't dealing with milquetoast Shira. Whoever this was scared the hell out of him. Why hadn't he seen what was going on inside her head earlier? Shira had said "we" and "us." Talked about herself in the third person. Her slips into a different speech pattern and attitude. He steadied himself and remained calm. Other personalities were coping mechanisms to dissociate from experiences too violent, traumatic or painful to assimilate with the conscious self. Shira's other personality might be harmless but what if it wasn't?

She eyed him as she dribbled smoke out of her nostrils. "Let's have some fun," she said, taking his arm and leading him without a wobble in her heels farther into the alley.

He never walked down dark alleys, especially one running with dirty water and particularly in Third World countries, but with an unexploded bomb on his arm, he made an exception. Shira stopped when they were far enough away from the street not to be seen.

"Kiss me and it better good," she said. She threw away her cigarette, wrapped both her arms around his neck and pulled his head toward her.

He hadn't kissed a woman—no matter what her personality—in more than five years. What the hell, she was a woman worth kissing. He threw away his cigarette too. She tilted her head back, opened her plump lips and closed her eyes. The intense rush he felt when he drew her long body to him and kissed her deeply, feeling the erotic crush of her breasts put the vodka in the shade.

The sound of footsteps on stone cobbles. He broke the clinch and looked back up the alley toward the main road. Something moved in shadows. It wasn't only Bob and Rani he needed to watch out for. This was India and they were filthy rich by Indians' standard.

Shira pulled him back again. "Gimme some more," she purred.

Another quick movement. Feet shuffled.

"C'mon, kiss me again before I go off the boil," she demanded, holding her face up but he wasn't paying attention.

Over her shoulder, a figure stumbled out of the dark. It pointed a gun straight at them. Shira caught his wide-eyed stare and twisted quickly in his arms. Dan expected a scream but instead, she startled him with a low growl, tensing in his hands.

The man dragged his foot closer. A hatchet face with dull eyes. A gold crucifix swayed against a black cassock.

"Let her go," Dan said, holding Shira tightly in front of him. Her snarl intensified. "She's got nothing to do with this."

The priest shook his head. Dan got ready to throw Shira to one side. One more clunk of the priest's boot closer and he'd—Shira uncoiled like a striking cobra, ripping up her dress and thrusting her hips at him.

"You wanna fuck with me?" she screamed. "Show me what you've got, cripple!

Dan gasped. The thug froze.

Dan was the first to react—in one quick movement he pulled Bob's Walther out of the back of his pants, thumbed the safety off and aimed it over Shira's shoulder at the priest's chest.

"Drop it!" he shouted.

"Kill him!" Shira grabbed the gun out of Dan's hand. The priest saw his chance. His gun came up quickly.

Bang! BANG! Bang!

A bullet whined off the cobbles at their feet. The priest lurched forward, gun skittering toward them across the cobblestones. The man's body convulsed, his head a mass of blood. Shira swayed and fell to her hands and knees in the pool of filthy water at their feet. Lights went on above them and in the houses across the alley. A window flew open. Voices shouted. Dan picked up the man's gun at his feet and stuffed it in his pocket.

"Let's get out of here!" He pulled Shira to her feet and prised Bob's gun from her clenched hand.

George Henry

The following five minutes was a stomach-churning stumble with Dan's finger twitching on the trigger of Bob's Walther. His surge of adrenaline had his heart thumping and his head pounding as he half-carried a dumbstruck Shira to the hotel only a block away.

The desk clerk arched an eyebrow at him stumbling a barefoot Shira across the lobby to the elevator until Dan forced a grin and shot him a conspiratorial wink. The clerk's return thumbs-up indicated a happy man carrying a drunk woman up to his room was nothing new.

Dan propped her white-faced, blinking sightlessly, on the toilet in her bathroom before vomiting in her washbasin. He washed the bitterness from his mouth, drank from the tap and swallowed his Percodan to attack a splitting headache. The run from the alley had come as close to killing him as the priest. He pulled back the shower curtain and turned the bath taps on full before turning to find Shira blinking confused eyes at him.

"You're safe," he told her reassuringly, kneeling beside her to hold a dirty, trembling hand. "What's the last thing you remember?"

Her eyes looked around searching for something. "We ... were in the restaurant ... we went for a walk." She blinked a few more times. "Then ..." She frowned at her filthy hands and feet and wet dress.

"You fainted. I brought you back here to your hotel. Have a nice long bath and clean yourself up. It'll do you good."

She nodded slowly as he helped her get unsteadily to her feet. He held her shoulders to keep her vertical while her shaking hands fumbled with her dress. He unzipped the back of it, said, "I'll be right outside" and left before the dress hit the tiles.

In the bedroom, he moved a Raggedy Ann doll with long, red woolen hair out of the way and flopped onto her bed. He lay back with his hands behind his painful head while the water began to slosh behind the door. He closed his eyes and his mind went back to the priest and the fear that had shot through him, Shira's banshee screaming, the thug's head pouring blood from a huge head wound, running for their lives. Crazy as it was, Shira had saved them, distracting the priest enough for him to pull out the Walther. And then—*Jesus Christ!*—she'd shot the priest dead! Shira's alternate personality was violently protective of the other one. Who the hell was going to come out of the bathroom?

"D ... Dan?"

He opened his eyes to find Shira standing over him wrapped in a bath towel, chewing a thumb to the bone. Her red hair hung in wet clumps over her trembling shoulders, the shock of the incident still reverberating. She looked harmless.

"Get into bed," he told her.

She dropped the towel and slid under the duvet.

"Have you fainted like this before?" he asked sitting next to her and holding her hand.

"Just now and again. Where's Carla?" she suddenly asked anxiously in her small voice.

"The doll?" Dan passed it to her and she crushed it into her bosom.

He found a zopiclone pill in his wallet medicine cabinet and gave it to her with a glass of water. "Here. It'll help you sleep."

She looked at it as he held it out in his palm. "It's blue like one of those Mother gives me."

Dan closed his palm. "Your mother gives you pills?"

Shira frowned, biting her lip. "We don't talk about them. OK? I shouldn't have said anything. Don't tell Mother. Please?"

"OK." He opened his palm. "It's just a sleeping pill."

Her eyes held his. "Can we trust you? Men haven't been nice to us."

"You can."

She swallowed it with some water. He reached for the bedside light switch.

"Please … leave it on."

He tucked the duvet around her shoulders. It was another warm night but she'd need it. He kissed her on a cheek and started to leave.

She gripped his forearm and raised anxious eyes. "Please stay with us … Please?"

Didn't he have a bag to pack and an escape tunnel to burrow? But wasn't she a damsel in distress? His forte? He slipped off his sandals and lay on the duvet next to her. She turned toward him, chewing a thumb, clutching her doll and curling her legs up beneath her.

"OK. Just until you fall asleep," he told her.

"Oh, goody. We like you, Dan. Please be our friend."

"OK."

"You're so good to us," she mumbled dreamily. "Mother said you can touch our boobies if you want."

George Henry

* * *

Without an air-conditioner and only an overhead fan whirring slowly, Dan lay on his bed in his shorts, sweating, calming his nerves and sipping a cold fruit juice. He ran through his options as he stared up at the red, yellow, green and blue-stained glass of the windows scattering a colorful mosaic across the ceiling. There were three options and one was off the table: report what had happened to the police and claim self-defense. One look at his past and he'd be in an Indian Black Hole of Calcutta dungeon before being shipped back to Canada. And heaven help a voluptuous white woman like Shira caught up in the Indian prison system: the guards would rape her before the inmates—and maybe the judge. The second was to stay and hope no one had seen them in the alley. It had been dark. They'd seen no one but the priest, run off before anyone had appeared to find out what was going on and they'd be gone after only another night. But hope was not a strategy he cared for. He preferred his last option: the certainty of leaving the trip and disappearing into a billion people. Vijay Gill wouldn't immediately know the murder attempt had failed so Dan reckoned he had time to get some sleep. He'd pack and leave after breakfast. Just in case he was wrong about Gill, Bob's Walther lay on the bedside table out of Karen's sight. He heard Karen fidgeting.

"Just get in?" she mumbled, rubbing her eyes.

"Yes, Mom. Didn't mean to wake you."

"I was worried. She could have smothered you."

"They're not that lethal. Just a few chin bruises and ear damage. Next time, I'll take a snorkel."

"I hope you used a frenchie."

A rubber? Dan thought that pretty funny. He rolled toward Karen and caught sight an extensive amount of color-dappled bare flesh. After an evening to forget, Dan paid it little attention.

"D'you mind if I ask you about Duncan?" she asked.

"What would you like to know?"

"He didn't appear happy to see you."

Dan breathed out deeply and gave her the partial truth. "He thinks I was responsible for wrecking the marriage and his home by screwing around."

"Were you?"

"No. Not that I didn't think about it. My daughter understood what was going on and sided with me but Duncan sided with his mother. Pretty typical really."

"Girls are far more perceptive than boys, aren't they? They grow up quicker and get relationship issues quickly. Boys have to be hit on the head to know they have one. Jesus, it's bloody hot." Karen flapped her nightshirt to cool off. "I lost contact with my three kids for a long time after my husband died but we got back together a few years ago. My son and his girlfriend live with me. It's funny to have him worrying about me. Too many different men coming home with his drunk mum from the pub. He lost track of the names." She chuckled. "Started calling them all Dick which was a bit off-putting."

Dan laughed. "Yeah, I can see that. Pity your husband died."

"He thought so too."

Dan laughed louder at her dry wit. *I'm going to really miss her.* "So no new guy?"

"Came close." He saw the light catch her pensive face. "But not yet. As I said, I'm an acquired taste."

"Well, I like you." *Whoa!* He bolted upright. "You're not a lesbian?"

She snorted derisively. "What the hell gave you that idea?"

"The *Prison Bitches* book? Write what you know?"

"Believe me I saw a lot of the carpet munchers in the slammer! Too much! Believe me, I like dick." Karen grated her harshest laugh. "So that's why you asked to sleep in my room? I wouldn't be interested in you? Ha! Ha! You better watch out, sweetie pie!" she barked. "You've got a cute arse."

Not a lesbian? She didn't need to know about Bill. Screw him. Oh shit! He'd forgotten he was meeting Charlie.

Karma points today? Lust minus being a good boy? Minus one. Four cigarettes and no booze? Plus two. Lies? Minus one. What's this? Brigit Jones' karma?

Karen rolled toward him. "One last thing before sleepy time. I think someone searched our room."

"How do you know?"

"Things have been moved. Someone's been in my drawers."

"You would notice that."

"Not my knickers, you whacker!"

"Anything missing? Surely not your bras. None of these Indian women would steal one. What would they do with one? Share it?"

"You're a riot, you bugger. Carry watermelons from the market?" She cackled at her own humor. "Anyway, nothing's missing that I can tell."

A thieving servant or someone else? Did Karen have anything they'd be looking for? Dan let that mystery go but his anxious mind hung tenaciously onto the flashing images of the thug approaching with his gun, Shira's craziness and the thin man's head streaming blood onto the cobbles. Dan put that out of his mind and fell asleep to the warm sensations of Shira's wet lips and soft cushions of breasts, and the bite of the cold vodka.

March 27th

KAREN WENT FOR for breakfast and left Dan behind for a shower and to meditate. Would Shira get into big trouble if the police somehow connected her with the killing? She wouldn't know what she'd done and if he'd gone she'd have no witness to tell the cops what had really happened. Uncomfortable as he felt, it was a risk he'd have to take. How to say goodbye to Charlie without wanting to say goodbye? What would happen to her? His conflicting thoughts about her tumbled around in his mind without resolution as he showered but his meditation calmed him into going through with his decision: he packed his bag and slid it out of the way under the bed.

With the thug's gun in the back of his belt, he sat on a well-pounded sofa watching Shira, Charlie and Cruella having breakfast in the sunlit courtyard. Cruella read a newspaper. Shira looked dopey, her morning usual. A blank Charlie silently drank her coffee. It had been easier to think of abandoning Shira to her fate and leaving Charlie behind when they weren't there. Now that they were real, a depressing paralysis set in about making the wrong decision over them. Why hadn't he just walked out of the hotel and got a taxi to the airport?

He was about to leave and get something to eat at the airport when Shira and Cruella got up from their table and went to get ready for their visit to the fortress. Charlie was left to finish a piece of white toast she'd slathered with a green jam of some kind. She ate it while burying her nose in a thick book. She looked grumpy. He walked over and stood defensively behind an empty chair. He wanted the last time he saw her go well.

"May I join you for a moment?" he asked.

She flapped a palm carelessly at the seat but he saw the suppressed anger in the set of her jaw. She remained engrossed in the book and less fascinated by his presence.

"May I have some of your coffee?"

She still didn't look up. "Knock yourself out."

He followed her eyes but they weren't moving along a line—they were trying to burn a hole through to the back cover. He poured some coffee into a spare cup and drank it black with no sugar. "How are you feeling?"

"How do you think I should be feeling?"

"I'm sorry I forgot about—"

"You disappeared with bitch Shira," she burst out, her voice tightening a garotte around his neck. "What happened? Mistake her for me? Did you see how she copied me to get your attention? The choli and sari. Fuck, how she pisses me off!"

Who was copying whom? Dan shrugged. It wasn't his concern any longer. "While you were busy flirting with the boys?" he asked.

"While I wandered the streets on my own wishing I had my gun!" she snapped, slamming down her book on her thigh.

"You wouldn't have killed her in a million years."

Her fiery eyes found his. "*You*, I'd have killed with my Magnum in a minute!"

"A Magnum? Isn't it a big gun?"

"Too big for a girl?" She snorted. "It would have blown your head off!"

Americans. Guns. Dan tried to change the conversation away from Charlie shooting him. "What were you doing walking the streets on your own late at night? Do you have a rape wish, you idiot?"

She thrust her head at him. "Now I'm a fucking idiot?"

"Yes, you are! Tall, white, beautiful. A gang's wet dream. Rape you every which way then kill you?"

The steam abruptly went out of Charlie. Her reddened cheeks cooled as reality forced itself through a crack in her angry veneer. Deflated, she chewed her lips, silent again.

"What happened to Bob?" he asked.

"Him?" she said in a softer tone. "I took off from the restaurant and left the fat bastard behind."

"The fat bastard who could have saved you from being mugged or raped?"

Charlie ignored him. A few minutes passed while they drank their coffees in silence. He spent it taking in every part of her for later recall: red hair, smooth skin; studded ears; long body, red fingernails. Her brown eyes flecked with gold. And that mouth: wide, thick crimson lips. Charlie was pretending to read her book again. He decided to clear the air and leave no misunderstanding.

"What did Shira tell you?" he asked.

"She didn't have to say anything," she told the book.

Dan wondered why Shira hadn't sunk his boat with the broadside revelation he'd slept—albeit on top of the duvet—with her part of the night. She hadn't remembered that either?

"We had dinner and—"

She cut in sharply. "Tell me you fucked her and I *will* kill you!"

Dan flinched. Was she having some morning mania? He took out a pack of cigarettes to slow down the conversation. "I didn't," he replied calmly and lit a cigarette. "Would you like one?" he asked, offering the pack.

She swatted the pack away. "I don't believe you! I bet you did. They all do. Every man I want has to fight her off—and they don't!"

Want? Dan took his time resting back to cross his legs and take a slow draw on his Gold Flake. He said nothing to let her continue to blow off steam.

"I thought you were *my* friend," she pouted. "Not *hers*. I thought *we* were going to have fun. Damn it, I waited and waited for you."

"I'm very sorry, Charlie. I really am. So now you think I'm not your friend?"

"And don't talk that shrink garbage to me! I've heard too much of it!"

"Sorry."

She threw her head back and growled at the sky. "Stop saying *sorry* for Christ's sake. You Canadians!"

"It's a myth. Some of us are assholes."

"Tell me about it! Are you *my* friend or *hers*? You'd better decide. Right now!" On the verge of a major crying jag, she slapped the table. "Keep away from her or else. It pisses me off!"

She was an emotional teenager berating her two-timing boyfriend—three-timing if she included Karen—and too young for him. He bit his tongue and reached for his coffee cup. "After last night, I might. I didn't know she had such a foul temper. Never seen anything like it."

"Shira? She—?" Charlie blinked as though a memory was replaying in her eyes. She collected herself and mocked him. "What did you do? *Not* grab her boobs?"

"You must have seen her angry before."

Charlie blew out derisively. "Not Shira. Her mother's filleted her into a spineless jellyfish. Play-Doh with boobs. Wouldn't hurt a fly."

Dan sensed she knew Shira was more than a simpleton with dangerous curves—she had a violent side. He checked the cover of the paperback opened across Charlie's thigh. She was partially through *A Passage to India*.

"Finished *The Quiet American*?" he asked.

"What's this? Shrink deflection?"

"Curiosity. Unless you want to talk about Shira again. I'll leave if you want me to," he offered evenly, hoping she didn't end things that way.

She took a deep breath. "I loved it."

"Even though Fowler set up Pyle's death?"

"He did it because of his intense love for Phuong. He didn't want to lose her, did he?"

"Does that justify it?"

She waggled her head from side to side. "I understand it."

Did she? An inexperienced twenty-year-old and she understood what men have done for a woman's love? The potent, sexual power women have over men? How the pursuit of love had changed the world? Just ask Paris starting the Trojan War.

"I might kill for love." She settled her golden eyes on him. "Wouldn't you?"

"No," he lied. How could he tell her he already had?

"Are you sure?" she asked.

Their eyes held each other's in a poignant moment of silence until Dan tapped her book. "How's *A Passage to India* going?"

"It gives me some cultural background for the trip. Have you read it?"

"I've just seen the film. I'll watch anything David Lean ever filmed. His great sweeping ones in particular."

"So will I."

"*Lawrence of Arabia* and *Doctor Zhivago*. *Bridge on the River Kwai*."

She nodded, expression softening.

"Did you like *Ryan's Daughter*?" he asked. "Critics panned it."

"Of course. It was very romantic. You?"

He waved a hand, palm down. "So-so. I'm not a fan of Robert Mitchum."

"Me neither."

"But I fancied Sarah Miles," he added. "She was so cute. The freckles and the reddish hair. Like you."

A snort. "I hate freckles! Are you trying to charm me?"

"Who? Insensitive *moi*?"

"Yes, *vous*."

"Did you know David Lean didn't make another film for fifteen years because of the criticism he received for that movie?"

"Really?"

"Then he made *A Passage to India*. He died before he could make another." He looked at her place in the book. "Have you got to the part about Miss Quested in the Marabar Caves yet?"

"Her sexual awakening? It really came out in the cave, didn't it?"

"Happens to us all but not necessarily so hysterically or in a cave. Mine was up against a wooden fence in a back garden. Not quite so romantic. More rustic. I was seventeen and ... now I'm afraid of fences—and tunnels."

She was unable to suppress a smile. "You're bad."

He wondered if she'd share. "You? Afraid of trains?"

She pursed her lips then glanced at him. "Front seat of a convertible Stingray in a beach parking lot. I was only fifteen and terrified what might be put in *my* tunnel."

Dan laughed to keep the mood light. "A Stingray? Classy. You Yanks had bigger cars to fool around in. I was more of a Hyundai Pony kind of guy. Involved a few yoga positions and avoiding being reamed out by the gear shift."

"Ha! Believe me, a Stingray bucket seat was not a good choice!" She giggled. "My legs were splayed over the top of the front windshield!" She laughed louder at the memory while Dan took a moment to quench the fire of that image. "I should have chosen a guy with a Caddy Eldorado, the back seat of those things could launch a Jumbo jet."

Reluctantly, Dan got his mind out of a car's back seat and said, "The downside is he probably would have been a bank tax accountant named Hymie who lived with his mother."

"At least he might have done my taxes!"

"Sounds like me and Linda Tait against the fence," he admitted wryly. "I felt so used."

"Sure, I bet you did," she said with amused sarcasm. She breathed out a long, dissatisfied sigh. "I wish I'd never got in that car with David Hamlish. I did the cheerleader bit and he was the Senior High School quarterback. I was a big girl at fifteen and had a virgin's bull's eye on my forehead. David took aim and I let him do it. He chased me and I was ready to lose it. He was the handsome prince."

"Even though you're Catholic?"

She threw her head back and laughed. "Ha! Catholic girls? Forbidden fruit? All my cheerleader friends but me had lost it to footballers and bragged about it. Guess who was left as the scared pussy? Who better than the biggest stud on campus? The American *fucking* dream, right?" she punned with a wry smile.

"It didn't end well?"

"That was it. The end. I had to promise not to tell his team he'd lasted less than a quarterback sneak into my end zone. He bragged we'd done it three times and he'd driven me wild. What a bastard."

"What did you tell your girlfriends?"

She twisted a smile. "We'd done it three times and he'd driven me wild."

"We can only hope karma will get him."

"Now I understand karma but I wish him no harm." She shrugged. "We were both young and stupid. He's now the quarterback at Yale and working on a political career just like his dad."

"Is that when you ran away?"

She blinked. "Who told you that?"

"Auntie mentioned you'd run away for a year."

"She did? Bitch. Loves to tell stories about me. I think she lives through my misfortunes."

"Did you enjoy California?" Dan asked, keeping the conversation going in the right direction.

The waiter came by and refilled their cups, giving them time to reload their thoughts.

"Sure I did. All that sun. Those beaches. Fantastic."

"Where did you live?"

"Venice."

"Really? I used to live in Santa Monica, right next door to Venice," he lied but knew the area from visiting friends.

"You did?"

"I loved the beach life. You must have gone to Pacific Ocean Park near the pier? Good place to hang out and get ripped as I recall."

"Yeah."

"Became a total beach bum like me? Drugs, sex, the usual?"

She picked invisible hairs off her light cotton blouse. "It was great. Such freedom. But I was broke, living in a commune of dropouts. Stealing from grocery stores. The guys in the commune wanted me to start hooking to bring in some money." She laughed bitterly. "Bastards. Free love wasn't enough for them. That's when I decided to go home."

He nodded and smoked his cigarette, letting her talk.

"My parents—I should say, my mother—sent me straight to a tough boarding school: Saint Beat Your Ass Raw for the Criminally Insane."

"Where you fitted in."

"You're a real bastard at times," she said with a gentle slap on his forearm.

"Do you often travel with your aunt?" he asked.

She groaned. "You kidding? It's like traveling with the Spanish Inquisition. She wants to know everything I do every minute of the day and doesn't believe anything I tell her." She leaned closer. "And if she's not watching me, she has her personal drone, Loony Shira."

"Loony?"

"Just an expression," she said carelessly. "I guess I'm loony now too."

"You mean your bipolar episodes? When did they start? When you were doing drugs?"

"No." She thought for a moment. "They started after my parents died. Just now and again but Auntie took me for examinations and I ended up in therapy, on antidepressants, tranquilizers and that awful lithium."

"And nothing worked?"

"I felt stoned on all of them."

"Maybe it's the stress of the car accident that's brought this on. Both your parents killed at once? My God, that's a terrible thing to happen to anyone, especially when they're young." Her eyes glistened and they reached his heart.

"My father was a senator in Washington. My mother was his second wife." She gave Dan a wry look. "I think he learned a lot from the first."

"Marriage isn't easy. The death of hope as Woody Allen called it."

Charlie dabbed her eyes while she mulled that over. "The triumph of hope over experience as Samuel Johnston said?" She suddenly smiled at him. "I still want to try it though."

"A nice thought," he agreed.

Anxiety flooded her face and she grabbed his hand. "I'm frightened of never having my special day. Don't let me go mad."

"I won't," he told her not knowing if it were possible. Pacific Ocean Park had been demolished in 1975 after a series of fires. Perhaps she could time travel. He'd stay to protect Shira and Charlie. Perhaps hope would triumph after all.

* * *

It took a few minutes for the groggy Kapoor to realize where his room smelling of warm coconut oil, stale cigarette smoke and booze was. Warm sunlight beamed brightly through the gap in the curtains as he lay flat on his back, naked, hugging an empty half-bottle of Scotch. He sat up too quickly and his head ached its objection. He checked his watch—10.32! He quickly switched on his phone for messages. Hara had texted a typically brief, teasing message between her cigarettes: *News at Police Jodhpur Interested?* He didn't reply. He knew she'd be sitting back waiting to text another enigmatic message.

Kapoor wore one of his better suits and his queasy stomach told him to skip breakfast even though he hadn't eaten since yesterday's lunch at a roadside restaurant on the way from Udaipur. He drove about a mile through late morning traffic to the single-story police headquarters where the local chief turned out to be the antithesis of a Northwest Frontier, cowboy sheriff: a refreshingly amiable, wiry man wearing a crisp uniform and without the usual small-town chip on his shoulder that Kapoor usually had to deal with when his Mumbai City Slicker rode into town. Did the chief have information that would help him solve the Harbor Murders? That damnable Hara must think so. But did the chief know it? He might want to keep it for himself and take all the glory.

The chief blinked at him behind owl spectacles as they shook hands before leading Kapoor into a sunny room with a huge wall map of Rajasthan and windows that faced directly at the colossal fort that dominated the city.

The chief caught Kapoor's gaze. "Can't get away from the bloody thing," he complained. "Please, take a seat, superintendent."

"But good for tourism or you'd still be hoping the Silk Road comes back," suggested Kapoor sitting down across a tidy desk from the chief.

"Quite. Keep those tours coming or we'll return to sand. Tea and a biscuit?"

They exchanged the usual police banter about crime and punishment over excellent Marsala chai, Rich Tea biscuits and American cigarettes before the chief said, "I don't think we've ever had a superintendent visit from Mumbai."

"Just on holiday with my wife. A break from the stresses of the big city. It's a wonderful area you have."

"Indeed."

"I dropped her off at the market. Feeling a bit bored so I thought I'd drop by and touch base with a fellow policeman." The chief nodded thoughtfully at him over his teacup. "Anything happen of interest recently we can chat about before I meet the wife for lunch?"

"We did have a murder last night."

"A murder?" *Whose? If Dan had been ...* Kapoor's pulse jumped but he remained expressionless. "That's interesting."

The chief put down the cup. "Your personal assistant thought so. It's lucky you're in Jodhpur, superintendent, isn't it?"

Personal assistant? That bloody Hara! What was she doing talking to the Chief of Police? He was busted.

"Can you fill me in, sah?" Kapoor asked respectfully. "Share information for our mutual benefit?"

The chief nodded a smile. "I've just received the autopsy report." He reached across his desk to an orderly stack of folders and selected a red one. He held it out to Kapoor. "Would you like to see the file so far?"

Kapoor nodded and held the end of the file. The chief kept hold of the other end.

"Anything in particular I can immediately help you with?" Kapoor asked.

"I have a cousin who's applying to the Maharashtra police force in Mumbai."

"I'd be pleased to recommend him, sah." The chief let go of the file.

"One bullet to the head," said the chief.

Despite the dead man missing part of his skull and looking like an exsanguinated ghoul, Kapoor was electrified—he recognized the long face with sunken eyes so close together they only needed a single, thick eyebrow, and a nose sharp enough to open cans. He was a well-known Mumbai thug—Amir "The Club" Pinto. What was he doing in Jodhpur and getting topped to boot?

"We identified him by his fingerprints through your personal assistant." Kapoor shuddered with annoyance again. "Lovely woman. She picked up right away on the murder being one you'd be interested in. And bingo! Here you are."

"So I am."

"I wish I had someone as efficient as her in Jodhpur," the chief remarked.

"It can be arranged," Kapoor mumbled under his breath.

"Now, how is this useful to Mumbai?"

Kapoor took a moment to make his announcement. "I believe the Harbor Murderers are with a travel group in your city," he intoned with gravitas.

The chief jerked up in his captain's chair, slopping his tea into the saucer, jolted by the gruesome murders that had been splashed across the news media. "That's why you're here?" he exclaimed. Kapoor nodded. "Could the dead man have been the Harbor Murderer?"

"Unfortunately, no," answered Kapoor. "The victims in the murders were mutilated and killed by a knife. Given the chance the Club—as one might expect—preferred to kick his victims to death with his big boot. Some kind of delusional revenge on humanity or his God, I guess." Kapoor stood up and walked across to the window. The impressive fort looked back at him as it had on others for four hundred years. He turned back to the expectant chief and said slowly in a deep voice, "This is confidential, chief. Not even my boss in Mumbai knows this. Will it remain confidential until we release the information together? No leaks?"

"You have my word," said the chief solemnly.

"Thank you, sah. I have four suspects for those murders and I wouldn't be surprised if one of them killed this man too."

"Could he have been sent from Mumbai to kill the murderer?"

"The murderer who could reveal who'd ordered the hit?" mused Kapoor.

"Or a simple case of revenge?"

"Good thinking," Kapoor said ingratiatingly.

The chief beamed like a lighthouse in a pitch-black night. "I'll have everyone in that part of the city interviewed!" he said, picking up his phone.

"Please leave the group at the hotel to me, sah," Kapoor requested with heavy politeness.

Kapoor could see the headline in the chief's eyes: "Harbor Murderer Captured by Jodhpur Police Chief." But "Harbor Murderer Captured by Superintendent Kapoor" would be even better.

Kapoor left the chief in a state of red-faced grace barking orders down the line. He drove straight to the temple to give effusive thanks to Ganesha for his overwhelming blessings with even more marigolds and fresh fruit than usual.

The stall owners called out "You must be having a most lucky day, sah!"

"A very lucky day!" shouted Kapoor bouncing up the steep stone stairs between Shiva's bulls and into the temple's entrance.

* * *

A fortress as big and impressive as the Mehrangarh was hard to imagine. It made Scotland's granite Edinburgh Castle look like a brick outhouse.

"Mister Kipling thought so," Loki told them, beaming with pride. "He called the monster construction the work of *giants!*" he informed them excitedly. "And said the palaces up there must have been designed by Titans. *Titans!* Can you imagine that?"

Dan could. On the rock crag rising four hundred feet above them, the fortress added another one hundred feet of red-gray sandstone to the enormous mass. The maharajas had lived in safety for over three hundred years—no army invading the northwest of India had been able to break in. As he paused outside the first gateway where babbling vendors enticed him to buy a living room-sized carpet, a decorative bedspread or a three-foot-tall, wooden maharaja, Shira ghosted to his side. What had she remembered? What had she told the police?

"You slept with us last night, didn't you?" she asked in an anxious whisper even though her mother was twenty yards away with Charlie, prodding her stick into a hanging carpet. "*Please* don't tell Mother."

It was really the last thing that was bothering him. He looked into the dull eyes of someone who still didn't know she was a killer. "I won't. But 'slept' is the operative word, Shira. Do you remember anything after our dinner?"

"Only going to bed with Carla—and you." She shook her head as if to blow away a fog.

Stay foggy, thought Dan, until at least we get out of Jodhpur. *Never remember* was OK by him.

"Mother will punish us if we did such a thing without her permission," she said. "If you don't tell her, I won't tell Charlie you stayed with me."

So that's why Shira hadn't said anything to Charlie, thought Dan. "Deal. Surely your mother wouldn't punish you."

"Oh, she would. She'd take Carla from me."

"Your doll's that special?"

"My best and longest friend." She chewed a thumb. "We share all our secrets. We trust each other—and we trust you. You were very nice to us last night. You took care of us. Carla knows that and so do I." She scurried off to catch up with her mother.

Loki, Bob and Rani led them through a stone-arched gateway to a second bigger and more formidable gate pock-marked by cannon balls and up the narrow road that rose and wound around a hairpin bend to the fortress walls. They'd separated themselves off from the group and had been chatting together all the way from the minibus. When they saw Dan coming, Loki strode off to head up the rest of the approaching group. Bob's red face sweated profusely into his white neck brace. He shuffled away a stone-faced Rani with his eyes.

Dan opened his backpack and handed Bob a bulky hotel hand-towel. "Merry Christmas," he said. "Be careful, the towel's stolen."

"Funny bastard, aren't you?" Bob croaked mirthlessly as he hefted the gift. "Come to your senses, have you?"

"I prefer fist fights, don't you?"

"Twat," snapped Bob.

"It'll save you searching through my undies again. Although you might have liked fondling Karen's bras and panties."

Bob twisted a smile. "There is that."

"Pity I lost one of the bullets."

"You what?"

"Had a shot at a kite," Dan said pointing a finger and cocked thumb at a squadron of the big birds flying overhead. "Missed the bugger. Never been any good with guns."

Bob eased his collar off his sweating neck and grimaced before prodding a finger at Dan. "Still chasing after pussy even though I told you not to? You've really got a death wish."

"Better get in as much as I can then before Kathmandu," Dan quickly retorted. "Still beating off over Charlie and Shira?"

Bob winced, growling a laugh. "As much as you do, wanker. If I didn't want to kill you, I'd like a cunt like you. You'd make a good Aussie."

"Just because you tried to whack me and I almost killed you doesn't mean we can't be friends."

"Aw, that's nice, mate. Just think every day might be your last." He held up digits on both hands. "Nine days left, mate."

"Still counting on your fingers?"

"Fuck off," snarled Bob, clenching his fingers back into meaty fists.

"I might get you first," he said leaving Bob with something to think about. But the last thing he wanted was a shootout with a career gunman like Bob.

Loki called them together with waves of his hands above his head. "Let us go into these magnificent buildings and see the fabulous architecture, furnishings and wealth these moguls accumulated over the centuries! Be sure to see all the jeweled howdahs for the elephants and the gold and silver palanquins for conveying the maharinas around the city in most seclusion. Not even an ankle of the ladies was to be seen or there was hell to pay!"

Loki led the group to the stairway up to the entrance to the biggest of the palaces in the fort. Its four levels rose high above them, a series of covered balconies baking the biggest, brown wedding cake they'd ever seen. Inside, Charlie, Shira and Cruella stopped for lunch in a small café that was already half full of tourists. Karen was all geared up for the palace tour but Dan persuaded her to have a cup of tea with Mark and Gilly. He wanted to watch out for any craziness from Charlie and Shira.

"You're becoming a mother hen," said Karen. "Stop worrying for Christ's sake. Charlie isn't nuts today."

And Shira hasn't killed anyone, he thought. "It's you I'm worried about. Didn't you just pocket a teaspoon?"

"Bugger! Busted! It's for my travel collection. It'll look good with the one from Buckingham Palace." She chuckled and pulled on his arm. "Come on, Mother Goose. Let's go see any treasures I can steal."

Red cordons and carpets guided them along hallways to the maharaja's stunningly ostentatious personal chamber: it reflected light from every tiny, blue, white, green and golden mosaic tile in patterns and scenes, small rectangular mirrors, and the pieces of precious metals and jewels in its walls. Framed paintings of elephants, horses and dead maharajas littered the high walls.

"Man, did those maharajas live well!" exclaimed Karen. "In the day, shoot some tigers, attend an elephant tug o' war in the courtyard and bet at the horse races."

"And in the evening," Dan added with a grin, "ten wives to choose from and a covered walkway to their individual bedrooms to keep them on their toes. *Whoo hoo!*"

He left Karen taking photos in the elegant Pool Mahal, a spacious, low-ceilinged reception room with plush, red carpets, comfy divans, plump pillows and stained-glass windows that opened onto the Queens' Courtyard and entered the Hall of Mirrors. The Sheesha Mahal reflected well on the wealth of the moguls with its walls and ceiling embedded with hundreds of small mirrors. A hundred Duncans came up behind him in the mirrors. A hundred sour faces he was getting tired of.

Duncan's voice was harsh. "Charlie told me you said I wanted to ask her out but I was *shy?*"

"That's right." Dan concentrated taking a photo of the pair of them in the wall of reflections. "How are you getting along with her?"

"*She* asked *me* out!"

"Saved you time then."

"You pimped for me!"

"No payment necessary."

Duncan pulled on his arm to spin him around. "Stay out of my life!"

Dan suppressed an urge to ask Duncan how his free trip was going and if he didn't like it to shove off. Instead, he said, "OK" and walked toward the exit and the next room of elaborate gold and silver-sheeted howdahs that had sat on the elephants for the maharajas to take a ride to the shops or shoot those pesky tigers. Duncan followed him like a Jack Russell sniffing a rabbit.

He pulled on Dan's arm again. "Why did you do that? I can see she really likes you not me."

Dan stopped the tactical withdrawal and turned on Duncan. "And I really like her too. The only problem is I'm old enough to be her dad. She's younger than Kathleen, for Christ's sake."

"I don't want her to be with me because you won't have her."

"Is that happening?" Dan said losing his patience. "Do you like her?"

"Yes."

"Well, have fun with her. I'm not competing with you. I repeat: I'm too—"

"She says she likes older men."

"What do you want me to do?" Dan waved his arms with exasperation. "Get younger, for fuck's sake?"

Duncan glared. "I hate talking to you. You always turn things around."

"Look, have fun with her but she's a very moody kid. She—"

"What are you doing now? Something wrong with her?"

He *was* a Jack Russell! Dan gritted his teeth. "I was simply—"

"You never simply anything. It's all calculated, cold. Scared she's like *Mom?*"

Dan bristled at the trigger word. "Mom's problems—"

"Throwing her away because you think she's defective. *Just like Mom?*"

Dan stopped himself saying something he'd regret. "That's not—"

"What a bastard you are!" Duncan spun on his heel.

* * *

From the windows, it was easy to see why Jodhpur was called the Blue City: a quilt of houses of various colors, notably blue, the color the highest caste, the scholarly Brahmin.

"How long have you been doing this guiding?" Dan asked Loki as they trailed behind the others.

"About five years."

"So you like it? Doesn't get boring dealing with people like us?"

"Oh no, sah. It's a most enjoyable occupation. I was turned down by the Army due to my lack of family connections so I will do this until I get enough money together."

"To start your own business of some kind?"

"To do that, of course, but I want to get married." He sighed frustration. "And that takes a lot of money for the right lady."

"There must be about a couple of hundred million to choose from."

"Ah, not so. I must marry within my caste and then within my clan of close family members. This becomes very limiting indeed."

"Have you any lady in mind?"

"Oh yes. But her father expects me to be far wealthier than I am. I need a lot of money."

They caught up with Cruella and Shira mingling with fellow tourists in a cavernous room of tile mosaics lit by chandeliers. Cruella's broad-brimmed straw hat cast a shadow over a short man in a smart white linen suit she'd backed up against a wall. He was sweating and dabbing his glistening forehead with a large white hankie.

Loki caught Dan's quizzical gaze. "That's Doctor Pathan. He's one of India's finest psychiatrists. Missus Jacobs has him along as a guest today."

Dan snatched a breath. The clinic in Jodhpur! Where was Charlie? With the palace a maze of rooms and corridors filled with tourists, Dan's chance of finding Charlie before Cruella, Shira, Rani and Bob cornered her was slim to none. He forced his way back against the tide of visitors through the Hall of Mirrors, the courtyard and the Pool Mahal. No Charlie anywhere.

Ten minutes of running up and down stairs and along hallways later, the pain behind his eyes had his stomach roiling. It was bad enough to fell him to his knees out of sight behind a silver howdah and force down a double dose of pills. A clatter of feet.

"God Almighty ... Where is the lass?" Mark, out of breath, sounding more Scottish.

"Go t'other way ... ah'll go this," replied a panting Gilly, sounding like a Yorkshire barmaid.

They dashed off.

He'd wasted valuable time. The thought of Charlie putting her head in a power socket drove him on. Opposite him, a narrow flight of stone steps led up to somewhere he hadn't been. Just what he needed: a steep staircase worn into a series of valleys by millions of feet. It took a monumental effort to climb up to what turned out to be the maharinas' living quarters from where they could look out across the fort ramparts at the city, as isolated as prisoners on Alcatraz looking at the lights of San Francisco across the bay.

Charlie! His thumping heart leaped into his throat. Got her! She paced backward and forward, muttering to herself and running her hands over the stonework, her breath rasping like her insides were on fire. She jumped cat-like at his footsteps and swiveled crazy eyes toward him.

"Isn't this amazing? Fantastic? Wow!" She grabbed at Dan and kissed him repeatedly before bouncing back toward the window. She ran her shaking fingers the stone-laced veil of the windows. "Who ... lived here?" she asked breathlessly. "Was it the king? Was it?"

Dan firmly held her shoulders from behind and spoke calmly, slowly. "The queens were isolated here in purdah. This is where they looked out from the palace into the real world."

"Poor bitches. And I thought New York was bad!"

"How bad?" asked Dan, not loosening his grip.

Her fingers tightened on the stone lace as she banged her head against it. "That bitch aunt never allows me out alone. Always a fucking guard wherever I go. Here it's that fucking Bob."

She jerked herself loose and spun around. Black pupils the size of gambling chips. "When I ran away I should have stayed away forever!"

"Why did you run away? The Hamlish thing?"

"I just fell apart. I needed to get myself back together. Canada was the only place to go."

He held her tightly again. "So then Catholic prison, right?"

"Christ! Those nuns! What miserable bitches!"

"And then the teacher thing?"

She stiffened. "Shira told you about that?"

"You must have been lonely after losing your parents. Having an affair—"

"An *affair*? Jim was a great guy. It was more than a fucking *affair*!" She laughed bitterly. "What I did for that bitch! If only you knew!"

"Knew what?"

"Christ, how I hate her! And now you're letting Big Boobs lead you on? Gonna fuck her are you?"

"Never."

"You'll fuck her all right! Just wait 'til her feet are behind her ears! Stay away from Shira! She's big trouble. I'm warning you!"

"We just went for a walk."

"Liar! Liar!"

"OK, we kissed."

"I knew it!" She grabbed Dan by his shirt and pulled him into her. "Kiss me like you did her!"

He took her face in his hands and kissed her as gently as he could on her lips. She had her tongue in his mouth before he knew it. She pressed herself hard against him until Dan pushed her away.

"Better than that bitch?" Her glare demanded an answer.

"Much better. I don't like kissing New Jersey anyway."

"What?"

"You have real lips," he explained.

"Everything about me's real unlike that—"

The sound of voices and feet. A tapping stick. Cruella and Shira. Bob's croak.

"Where's that crazy kid?" Cruella's shrill voice echoed up the ascending staircase.

"She's given us the slip," Bob rasped.

"Damn it!" Cruella cracked her stick on the stones in her annoyance. "And where's that little worm Pathan? Shira? Come with me. Bob? Go look up there!" Footsteps and heavy breathing as Bob began to heave himself up the stone steps.

Dan grabbed Charlie's hand and forced her toward the exit. "Let's get out of here or you'll be in a padded cell tomorrow."

On the battlements overlooking the broad expanse of Jodhpur's crowded warren of buildings, Dan shoved a wriggling Charlie into the shade under the wooden wheels of a huge cannon pointing its business end at the city. He fed her tranquilizers before they hid in drugged silence for an hour while the legs of chattering tourists ambled by. His pain dulled and his pulse slowed while Charlie ceased fidgeting and went limp under his arm, her head resting on his chest. He smiled through a fading headache—he'd saved Charlie. He kissed her forehead, stroked her cheek and ran his fingers through her hair like she was a child who needed comforting affection, just as he had with Kathleen. The similarity wasn't lost on him. But something wasn't similar: he wanted to kiss her—and not in a fatherly way.

* * *

Dan stood in the hotel pool watching the other hotel guests splash around in the pale blue water. Shira lay on a lounger near an umbrella with a speaker that murmured sitar and tabla muzak. Dan's mind returned to Shira or whoever it was in the alley and the kiss that warmed the ice wall he'd built to protect his emotions. Charlie had melted it even more. By the look of Shira's glistening cappuccino body almost wearing a black bikini, the wall wasn't about to freeze again soon. A beached Moby Dick lay next to her in the shade of the umbrella: Cruella in a voluminous white robe that covered her from her neck to her toes. She wore white gloves up to her elbows. A white sunhat shaded a face wearing big alien-eyed sunglasses and painted white with sunscreen. The way her head moved, she was watching him, expressionless, no sign of anger at having missed out on shipping Charlie off with Pathan.

Karen joined him in the water. She'd slipped into a loose, long-sleeved t-shirt over what looked like a colorful paisley, one-piece swimsuit. "You hurt yourself?" She nodded at the scar on Dan's right side, just below the ribs.

He ran his fingers over the livid scar that stretched around to where there used to be a kidney. "I was rescuing a disabled child from a raging house fire and fell on a knife."

The late Bohan Gill's knife. He'd never forget him. And his brother had never forgotten Dan.

"You should be more careful. They're all over the place, aren't they?" She touched the scar that ran down the side of his neck. Bohan Gill had come that close to lowering his blood pressure to zero in a few seconds. "And what about that one?" she asked. "Another kid in a wheelchair?"

"Saved a blind nun crossing a road."

He didn't want to talk about knives or scars. He still had occasional nightmares to remind me of how close he'd come to being recycled early. When Karen dunked herself and rose out of the water, it was immediately apparent Karen wasn't wearing a swimsuit underneath the wet t-shirt—her upper body was heavily decorated in reds, greens and blues.

"Impressive tattoos," said Dan.

"They *are* really impressive," said a voice from above. They both looked up at Charlie wearing a black bikini. The tranquilizer had done its magic but dark circles around her eyes and her pallor showed her tiredness from the brainstorm at the palace. "Hello, you two," she said with forced breeziness and jumped in the water between Dan and Karen. A faded, pink scar ran from below Charlie's left breast to under her arm. Dan guessed a ruptured spleen had exited through it.

"Ooh. Love that tattoo," said Karen.

Charlie ran her fingers over the head of a fierce red and green snake that twisted over her shoulder, back around her waist and down her belly. "I was a rebellious, little bitch," she told them. "A bit over the top, I know."

"Been there," said Karen.

"Not only over the top." Dan lowered his eyes to where the python entered her bikini bottom.

Some color returned to Charlie's cheeks. "Not my best idea. But I liked the strangeness of it."

"I love it," said Karen. "Where did you get it done?"

She glanced at Dan. "Venice beach. I was a bit stoned."

"Quite the souvenir. Couldn't you have just bought a t-shirt?" Dan asked.

"Not the same is it, dear," said Karen. She took Charlie's arm and pulled her toward the steps out of the pool. "Come with me to the Ladies for a moment and I'll show you *all* of mine."

"Can I have a look too?" Dan asked, grinning solicitously.

"Only if I get pissed," said Karen, wagging a finger at him as she reached for the stairs.

Charlie lowered her voice. "Thank you for taking care of me today. Did I say any horrible things?"

"You called me a bastard again. But I'm getting to like it."

"Idiot." She slapped his chest playfully but her face quickly fell again. "I just couldn't control myself. I am nuts, aren't I?"

Dan looked into a confused face desperately wanting him to say "No."

"No. You're going to be fine," he said confidently.

Yet he wondered if the sanity boat had already sailed and she'd been left waving her little flag on the dock. He knew she'd lied about Venice beach. Was she lying about Canada too? What else had she lied about?

The rest of the group dribbled down to the pool. Mark arrived wearing a pair of Speedos that many older men with potbellies and flaccid buttocks feared. He obviously kept his body up to snuff and it matched his sharp brain: perfect for, as Kapoor had put it, "intelligent protection."

Dan watched Mark dive into the pool and begin stroking lengths as though born to the water. Was he friend or foe? He recalled Mark and Gilly's faces when he and Charlie had reappeared after going AWOL at the fort. They'd had the looks of acrobats who had just finished a walk on a slippery wire across Niagara Falls. What had they been doing at the fort? Were they hired guards who had replaced the murdered Thompsons or had they murdered the Thompsons and had their own nefarious agenda in mind? A third possibility was they had murdered the Thompsons since they had been a threat to Charlie and Shira. Whatever they were up to he knew they were armed and as potentially dangerous as Bob and Rani who appeared chastened in Cruella's icy presence for losing Charlie in the fort. However, after she left to go back to her room—for a swim in Jim Beam, thought Dan—they visibly relaxed as if it had been another day at the office. In fact, they looked strangely pleased with themselves.

Dazza, Arfa and Duncan arrived together, the Brits in their red, white and blue Union Jack Speedos. Dazza was skinny and sunken chested but Arfa was a ripped fire hydrant. Duncan, the tallest of the three, showed off a fine athletic body that rolled Shira's head toward him for a good look. Duncan's scowl at Dan melted into a big smile as he made a beeline for Charlie when she called to him from where she'd stretched out on a lounger. He slid his arm around her shoulders and she pecked him on the cheek to evoke a disturbing sense of envy in Dan but deep inside he knew it was for the best. Good luck to them.

A splash next to him. "Ah haven't seen ya for a while, man," said a surfacing Steve, water streaming down his impressive torso.

"Same here. What've you been up to?"

"This and that." Steve watched Karen walk back with more bottles and spread herself like a Rubens model on the lounge. "Ah know what ya've been up to. Fuckin' the big girl instead of sleepin' with me?" he said with a wry shake of his head. "Ah'm real jealous, man.

Dan winked. "She's great. The best."

"Ya lucky dog. Ah love her big butt."

"I'm getting the distinct feeling fat-bottomed girls make your world go round, Steve."

Steve chuckled as he humped a pair of invisible buttocks. "Ya bet. Any chance of a threesome?"

"Mark and Gilly are up for it."

Steve barked a laugh. "Ya're a real asshole!" He glanced over Dan's shoulder at Shira applying more blocker to her glistening thighs and sighed deeply. "No double date with the redheads, huh?"

"You've got a problem there. And it's not how ugly you are."

"Couldn't be."

"I've been warned off by their bodyguard. Bob."

"Fuck no! That butterball? Ya're kiddin'?"

"Nope. Tried to punch me out."

"He did? What happ—ah! The neck brace?" Steve threw his head back and barked again. He ran a respectful eye over Dan and raised his hand for a fist bump. "Right on, man."

Dan bumped, his chest puffing just a little. "He wants revenge. He's threatened to kill me."

Steve's face hardened with a flick of a switch. He looked at Bob sunning himself by the pool. "The fat fuck did, did he?"

"You could always change his mind about Shira," Dan suggested.

"No doubt, man, but ah don't need the hassle."

Pity, thought Dan.

"Why do they need a bodyguard? They rich or somethin'?" Steve asked.

Dan shrugged. "Yanks scared it isn't Disneyland?"

"Wouldn't surprise me." Steve leaned closer and lowered his voice. "Ah saw y'out walkin' other night. Down in that market below the hotel."

"I saw you too," Dan said, prepared for this possibility. "Watching the Brit boys, Charlie and the Canadian kid at that dope deal. You a cop?"

Steve's wide forehead furrowed for a moment, his mouth wrestling with his next words. "Listen, man, ah work for a nameless agency, OK? Ah'm trackin' those Brits to Kathmandu, findin' their contacts, and when they get there ah'm gonna have the locals arrest 'em. They're relatively small time but a part of an organization shippin' dope to the States out of Nepal and India. Get these guys and we can squeeze 'em on their boss. Just lahk on TV. *Capisce?*"

"OK," said Dan, surprised at how Steve had confided in him.

"Ah know ah can trust ya to keep this to yerself." Steve smiled knowingly. "Ah had HQ check y'out. Ya're cool with me."

Dan stiffened. Steve gripped a strong hand on Dan's shoulder. "Don't freak out, man. Ah lahk to know who ah'm dealin' with." He went Clint Eastwood. "Ya got lucky with me, punk. Ah can keep mah hero's secret ... if ya do somethin' for me in return, o'course."

"What do you want?"

"What do ya know about that Bill? Ah've seen him talkin' with those boys and he disappears a lot when they're not around either. He bothers me and ah don't lahk to be bothered in this business."

Dan's thoughts stuttered. *Bill? Trafficking dope?* "You think he could be working with them?"

"Joined the trip after we left Mumbah? Maybe he's their boss or a link to the boss. Work with me, Dan. Keep an eye on him and let me know if ya see anythin' suspicious. Ah'd real appreciate it. Be careful, the drug business isn't for sissies."

"OK. You just want the Brit lads, don't you? Charlie and that Canadian kid were just hanging with them."

"Keep 'em out of the way or they could get killed. And ya stay clear of any deals too, man. Ya could get killed too."

"OK."

"Mah man," growled Steve with a fist of Dan's shoulder before hauling himself out of the pool and walking away close enough to Karen to check her out again.

Dan shuddered in the warm pool. What had he done by staying? One word from Steve to the wrong people and he'd be shipped back to Canada. Something cold tapping his shoulder jolted him. He turned quickly to find Karen kneeling down on the side of the pool, passing him a water bottle.

"Here you go." She flashed a smile that instantly made him feel better and forget the danger he was in. "That Steve creeps me out," she continued in a low voice. "He's always looking at me like I'm a piece of meat."

"You are. Prime rib."

"Ha! Smooth bugger!" Karen chuckled. She looked up and grinned. "Now here's a great piece of beef."

Although he had developed a bit of a middle-age paunch above his bright yellow Bermuda shorts, Bill was an intimidating specimen with his massive, muscular physique, blond hair, blue eyes and short beard—only a battleax short of leading a Viking raid. Over his shoulder, Dan heard Karen purring as her camera fired a burst of clicks. Bill took some photos of the swimmers in the pool, put his Nikon digital with its big lens down on a lounger and dived in. When his water-plastered, blond head surfaced, Dan noticed his hair was thinning. He liked that.

Karen chirped, "Hello, Bill. Here, have a frostie!"

He took a beer from her and said, "Cheers!" before drinking half the bottle. He gave her a big smile and a wink before turning to Dan. "Lovely woman that Karen," he said under his breath.

Bill was far more trouble than he'd thought. A drug trafficker with a gun? He wanted Karen nowhere near him. He didn't want to be anywhere near him either. Bill had saved his life in Mumbai but had it really been a lucky break? Had he in fact been following Dan? But why would he? He hadn't spoken to Bill since briefly in Udaipur. Bill had made no effort either. He must want something.

Bill leaned closer with a pained expression. "Are you sure she's a lesbian?"

"Hard core. Checked out those muscles and tats? She fancies Shira herself."

Bill glanced back at Karen, sighed and drank more beer. Dan noticed he wasn't wearing a wedding band although that didn't mean anything.

"What if I tell her I'm disgustingly rich?" Bill suggested. "She might change teams for a while?"

"Are you?"

"Rich enough. I run a tour company out of New York. I get to travel the world spying out places for interesting trips. Then I go home and sell the idea to the wealthiest people I can find."

"Not trips like this then?"

"This?" He snorted derisively. "I'm slumming with you lot."

"Glad you could tag along with the peasants," Dan said tonelessly.

"Listen up, I have people who will pay up to one hundred thousand dollars for jet trips around the world staying occasionally at twenty-star hotels but mostly in luxurious apartments on hermetically sealed Boeings. You wouldn't believe it."

Dan believed it would be a great cover for shipping drugs around the world. If he were in the drug trade, he might be disgustingly rich. Dan stopped thinking when Shira got up off her lounger and stood by the pool adjusting her negligible bikini. Shira smiled her afternoon smile down at Dan and waved to him. It was the "Look at me!" of a child wanting to show her parents what she could do.

"You're screwing that?" Bill said out the side of his mouth, keeping his eyes on Shira.

"You bet," Dan lied to stick a knife into Bill's groin.

Shira plunged in after bouncing up and down on her toes enough to come close to diving topless.

"Holy fuck," said Bill.

"You need to get laid," said Dan, enjoying the misplaced envy. Bill grunted. "Dating the palm sisters?" Bill gave him a dirty look. "I'm sure an ugly *rube* like you can buy it somewhere if your hands get tired."

"Fuck you, asshole," Bill snarled and waded off across the pool.

Maybe continuing to make an enemy of a gun-toting dealer wasn't smart but he couldn't help himself needle the bastard. Karen rolled off her lounger and knelt at the edge of the pool.

"Bill looks in great shape," Karen said breathily.

"If you like that kind of hunky, bronzed thing."

"And I do. It looked like you were talking about me. Bill kept glancing my way."

"Why would we be talking about you? You voluptuous, sex siren?"

She frowned theatrically. "Is voluptuous a compliment?"

"You bet it is. Plenty to hold onto. Who wants a coat stand?"

"Thank you, sweetie."

"Pity Bill's just not into you."

"Ah well," she said offhandedly. "Oh-oh. Here comes trouble."

Dan turned to find Shira's sleek red head rising from the water. The rest of her followed as glisteningly smooth as a surfacing mermaid. He found his arms around her waist as she gripped him tightly around the neck. Over her shoulder, Charlie stood by the pool, arms folded tightly, glowering at him.

"Let me take you to dinner to make up for last night," she asked in her innocent voice. "Please?"

He hesitated. Did he have to try and help her? She was a childish alcoholic with a personality disorder and needed anger management. The press of her body triggered a memory and suggested an answer. "What time?"

"Eight in the lobby." She kissed him on the lips and swam away.

Charlie immediately jumped into the water and threw her arms around a surprised Duncan, kissed him hard on the lips and turned a *quid pro quo* glare at Dan.

* * *

Kapoor loved the Turkish-style baths. It was a great place to get the dirt of the day sloughed off, have a relaxing massage of tired muscles and the scenery wasn't bad either. If only the baths had a bar, it'd be nirvana. Drinking? He'd been drinking a lot lately in hotel bars and in lonely rooms since he'd left Mumbai and without any physical release, a volcano was building inside him and about to erupt.

He'd inquired at his hotel about the quietest *hamam* in the city and the recommendation turned out to be just what he wanted: a secluded, single-story, red-brick building. He descended a stone staircase under a rusted archway into a humid half-basement smelling strongly of coffee and harsh cigarettes. A grizzled attendant in a green-striped kaftan and two men in muscle shirts and shorts—one a heavyweight, the other more of a middleweight—were the smokers, all drinking from small cups behind a wooden counter.

The old man smiled semi-toothlessly when Kapoor paid him for the whole menu on offer for both him and his soon-to-arrive guest. The boxers—their fingers and arms thick with muscle and tendons indicating they had to be masseurs—gave him a rough bath towel and a pair of flipflops. Kapoor looked forward to the beating to come. He removed his clothes, stored them neatly in a locker and made his way down a narrow hallway into the *hararet*, the hot room.

A towel around his waist, he sat on the blue and white tiles of the central heating dome, sweating as he waited excitedly for Dan. He'd fallen madly, stupidly, wonderfully in lust with this Monty surrogate. But with only two more days to arrest someone for the Harbor Murders before Dewan would force him back to Mumbai his anxiety was growing. Could he seduce Dan in forty-eight hours?

When Dan shuffled in and sat down next to him wearing only his towel, Kapoor ran his eyes quickly over Dan's bare upper body and long thighs.

"Couldn't you find anywhere hotter?" Dan asked.

Kapoor placed his hand on Dan's shoulder and felt the electricity flow. "You've been in a steam bath surely?"

Dan flicked a hank of sweat off his forehead. "I've only been in a steam bath once. Felt faint through hyperthermia in no time at all and almost fainted. Never been back."

"This is a lot better than a simple steam bath." Kapoor patted his hand on Dan's exposed thigh, a move that excited him even more. "A scrub and massage in this hot room, cool off for a while and then a cold shower. You'll be invigorated in an hour, believe me!" He was invigorated already by a potentially embarrassing surge in his loins at Dan's semi-naked presence. He stood up to cool his face in some cold tap water at a sink and quieten his ardor before turning back to Dan. It was a forlorn hope that Dan had discovered anything in such a short space of time to be of use but he asked anyway. "Discovered anything that points to the Harbor Murderer?"

"Bob confessed."

"Excellent! Anything else?"

"Rani's a man."

"Ha! Now that I believe!"

"Seriously, I'm sorry to say I have nothing to connect anyone with the Harbor Murders. But Bob did threaten to kill me again."

He didn't care one jot about no progress on the Murders. Here he was with a throbbing chubby and a semi-naked Dan with a shower together to come. Excellent progress! Bob Stewart had threatened him again? He'd be neutralized somehow even if he weren't the Harbor Murderer.

Kapoor loosened his towel and paced around the room slowly. "Could it be the Koepkes were murdered by the Stewarts to protect the Americans from them?"

"Or for their own nefarious reasons?"

"And the Drurys replaced the Koepkes to complete their mission?"

"For good or for bad? Maybe they didn't replace them at all."

Kapoor shook his head and sighed from the soles of his warming feet on the slippery tiles. "We'll eliminate some of these possibilities when Hosseini sends me his investigations into the Stewarts' and Drurys' whereabouts and communications around the time of the murders."

The two masseurs appeared and waved them to lie down on the benches at the sides of the room.

"Time for a jolly good wash and massage then!" exclaimed Kapoor delighted with how this was going.

What followed was ten minutes of being scrubbed with a soaped, rough towel mitt that peeled off anything that wasn't nailed down. Dan's masseur looked at his mitt, scowled and mumbled something. Kapoor had a fit of the giggles.

"What did he say?" Dan asked.

"He said ... dirty man!"

Dan laughed between the winces as the masseur scoured him.

"Enjoying yourself?"

"It's great, Dipak! I've never felt so clean ... and brutalized."

"It'll get better. Just wait 'til these guys beat and twist the hell out of you!"

In the next room, they lay face down with their towels wrapped around their waists on padded tables so close together Kapoor felt he and Dan were on the same bed. Uncomfortable as it was, he was glad he was facing down.

"Aaagh!" The boxer had pulled Dan's arm around behind his back. "Fuck that hurt!"

"Wait till he does that to your leg!"

Dan howled and groaned as the masseurs rubbed, beat and stretched every muscle they could find. "Never again, Dipak!" he gasped as the boxer rhythmically thumbed deep into his thighs.

"That's what I said and look at me now." *Big men rubbing their hands all over me? Not to be missed!*

Dan and Kapoor stumbled out of the room as though they'd lost the use of all of their joints. Dan rested up against a corridor wall. "They killed me!"

"It's not over! Time for a cold shower!" *A shower with Dan?* Damn, he was giddy!

Dan stared at him. "You're kidding?"

"Cold first and then hot!" Kapoor giggled as he led Dan into the common shower area where they threw away their towels onto a bench.

Dan flipped his shower to hot. "No chance. Hot first and last!"

When Dan stood in the steaming water next to him, Kapoor quickly dialed up a cold-water blast to quell his rising embarrassment. Hitting him like a shower of hailstones, it was instantly effective. "I have some very good news," he said, teeth chattering. "Listen to this. Remember I told you a man was shot and killed on a street near your hotel in Jaipur?"

A moment's silence before Dan said, "Yes."

Well and truly cooled off, a shivering and shriveled Kapoor turned, kept his eyes up in Dan's and lowered his voice to promote intimacy. "He was a hired assassin from Mumbai. And it ties in with the Harbor Murders. I think he was following your group and was killed by the Harbor Murderers before he was able to get revenge on them."

"Sounds good to me," Dan said as he turned and backed up to the nozzle to wash his hair.

Kapoor eyes couldn't help but follow the bubbles streaming down Dan's toned torso. The cold shower called again. "The Drurys and Missus Stewart left the dinner in the company of Missus Jacobs and had a drink together back at the hotel," he said over his shoulder. "It's impossible either of them was involved. Mis'r Stewart says he followed Miss O'Neill when she went out walking alone. As her presumed bodyguard, this is plausible. But ..." He paused before he said, "But she says she deliberately shook him off."

"So my friend Bob is the only one of your suspects without an alibi? This is getting better!"

Recycled Love

Was Dan going to respond to this obvious ploy of a meeting at the bath? Here they were standing naked in the showers and he hadn't made any kind of move to show an interest in him. A final try. Kapoor made a show of being unable to get his arms around his shoulders. "Would you wash my back, please?" he asked, backing up toward Dan.

"Sure," Dan said with no hesitation.

Kapoor gasped as Dan ran his soapy fingers around his neck and over his shoulders. When Dan slid his hands down to the small of his back and onto his hips, his legs weakened and began to shake. He staggered back into the icy stream, biting his lower lip so hard to avoid moaning his teeth sank into its flesh.

* * *

Kapoor licked his stinging lip, glancing at Michelangelo's naked David toweling himself dry. The thought of never seeing that body again was painful but not as painful as the deep throb in his abdomen that was unlike anything he'd ever experienced, even with Monty. So unexpected and so powerful, the pleasure must have been sent by Brahmin from nirvana. Twenty years had been worth the wait!

Dan confused him: it hadn't been an obvious homo ploy to bring him to the *hamam* and have them strip naked but asking him to soap his back certainly was. It had been a homo's invitation for even greater intimacy but Dan hadn't taken it up or seemed to have noticed the erotic effect on him. He wasn't a homo or bisexual after all? Or Dan wasn't sexually attracted to him despite their growing camaraderie? Kapoor knew now he wasn't going to be able to seduce Dan. But what next? In his mental jumble, he did know one thing very clearly: he had to have Dan in his bed and nothing was going to stop him.

Dan popped a cigarette in his mouth and offered one to Kapoor who gladly accepted to hide his bleeding, swollen lip. Dan lit the cigarettes before reaching for his cargo pants. "That was amazing, Dipak. I feel like I've been beaten up but I'll be back."

Kapoor sat with his towel in his lap, emotionally drained but managed a smile and said, "Told you so."

Reluctantly, he began to get dressed too. In the bath's entrance, they ordered coffees and sat smoking their cigarettes under the watchful eyes of the attendant and the masseurs.

"Did you ever play Clue as a child like I did?" Dan asked, stirring some sugar into the strong coffee.

"I loved it," Kapoor replied, the throb in his belly having faded sufficiently for his mind to string thoughts together. He lowered his voice into a solemn, mystery-movie voiceover: "It was Colonel Mustard with a knife in the library!" he intoned. "I preferred it to cricket. I even made up my own cards and board."

"And probably carved your own dice," Dan said with a shake of his head. "You're something else, Dipak."

Kapoor flushed. "We even play the same games."

"Ha! How about this then? It was Bob the Harbor Murderer with a Walther in the alley!"

Indeed, Bob Stewart was his prime suspect. But why was Dan so over-the-top sure about it? Just the personal animosity? Kapoor voiced his skepticism: "I'd be surprised any intelligent killer would have kept the murder weapon."

"Bob *is* an Aussie," Dan deadpanned.

Kapoor chuckled. "There is that."

"I bet he thinks he's got away with it. Believe it or not, I saw his Walther in his holster today. A silver and blue one with black tape on the handle. He carries it all the time. It's there for the taking. Why not take him in for questioning and check out the gun to see if the ballistics match?"

"Now there's a good idea, Dan," Kapoor said with more humor than sarcasm. "I'll get CSI Jodhpur right on it."

Dan winced theatrically. "Sorry. Seen too many models solving crime between the adverts."

"Quite. I'm still waiting on the ballistics," Kapoor said. He took a slow drag on the cigarette as he recalled the latest report from the chief. "The bullet passed through the side of the assassin's head and they're looking for it. Probably stuck in a wall somewhere. Be patient. I expect the models will send the ballistics results soon. If it's a nine-millimeter from a Walther and he's dumb enough to have kept the weapon, I'll nab him. Let's not alert him to our interest or he could disappear."

Kapoor clinked his coffee cup with Dan's. Would a pro like Bob Stewart keep the murder weapon? That would be far too risky but maybe he was as overconfident as Dan had suggested. He knew what an ambitious bureaucrat Dewan would want him to do in these circumstances: if the bullet didn't match, arrest a thug like Bob Stewart anyway. A suitable bullet could be found. Reports altered for a few favors. Criminals Dewan hadn't been able to nail for some crimes, he had nailed for others. Justice had been served. Stewart off the street for twenty years? Good riddance. Harbor Murders solved. Dewan ecstatic for the department. Kapoor would get the kudos, promoted and become famous for a media cycle. It was the corruption that destroyed citizens' belief in their government. It happened all over the world but India had refined it into an art form: expedient law.

But its practicality and immorality weren't in Kapoor's ethos. He prided himself on something called credible evidence and the rule of law. He wanted Bob Stewart to be the Harbor Killer and to drag him back in chains to Mumbai but not an innocent man at the behest of a corrupt system and its lackeys. Match the bullet to the gun in his possession and Bob was toast. Bob had no alibi for the Jaipur murder and he had the motive, means and opportunity. But another thought crossed his mind: Bob Stewart had threatened to kill Dan—twice. Would he break his own moral code to protect Dan? He looked over his coffee at him, now relaxed, smiling thoughtfully at the ash growing on his cigarette. He was in love, not just the lust he'd had for him in the shower. Shakespeare came to mind: "Love is blind, and lovers cannot see, the pretty follies that themselves commit." What "pretty follies" would he commit for Dan's love? Dan caught him staring.

"Earth to Dipak," said Dan. "Penny for your thoughts."

Kapoor blinked. "Ah, yes." He held back on the answer.

Dan raised his cup to Kapoor. "Here's to you arresting Bob Stewart, carting the bastard back to Mumbai and getting your promotion and maybe a few medals thrown in." He grinned from ear to ear. "You've got your man!"

Kapoor ran his eyes over Dan. *My man? Not yet.*

* * *

The restaurant was what he'd expected Shira to choose: five-stars, perched on an open rooftop with a panoramic view of the city dominated by the fortress glowing in the floodlights and where the meals cost a year's wages for an average Indian. At the sight of Shira on his arm, the place came alive. It was as if the Elizabeth Taylor at her most seductively beautiful had walked in with Richard Burton in their heyday as *the* couple. The portly headwaiter in a white dinner jacket and black satin trousers appeared quickly to show them to what had to be the best table, by itself under an arbor of sweet-smelling, flowering creepers. The headwaiter developed a sheen of perspiration on his bald head as he took over control of the table, snapping out orders to his underlings in their neck-throttling, white shirts and shiny black suits, although ogling Shira's five-star cleavage seemed to be more his main interest.

The restaurant oozed opulence that made Dan uncomfortable but not so much as Shira when she eyed him like a hungry tiger stalking a tethered goat and rubbed her foot on his ankles. She'd dressed to kill and it was killing Dan in the best way: a gold, ankle-length dress with sparkling silver trim hugged her waist and accentuated her broad hips. It was off-the-shoulder, with a v-neck exploiting her large bosom coming perilously close to a major spillage. Had he really been naive enough to imagine he was going to have a pleasant dinner with her and the alcoholic, sexually aggressive killer wouldn't be back for another piece of him? Maybe all of him? Or had that piece of him wanted her back? Another rub of her foot on his ankle and he knew the answer: part of him was asking for it.

Shira glugged her double vodka on the rocks and licked her lips appreciatively. She'd been drinking when he'd met her in the lobby and showed no sign of putting on the brakes. Although drinking hadn't worked for him and he'd ended up in a jail cell instead of a palace, the road of excess to wisdom was hers to tread. He was sure it wasn't a new journey for her. He put away his nerves and looked on the bright side: inebriated, she might cough up a lot more about herself and her whacky family—if she didn't kill anyone before dessert, of course.

"Glad to see you drinking with me," Shira said and drank from her glass.

Proud of himself for having resisted an urge to drink after the vodka with Shira in the alley, he'd ordered a single vodka with lots of ice. He could handle that. "You load up whenever Elaine's not around?" he asked.

"You bet." She rattled her ice cubes. "I could do with 'nother too."

The headwaiter appeared like magic to take her order and Dan amused himself watching him try to hide his glance at Shira's assets.

"I'll be carrying you home at this rate," he told her. There was no stopping her on the road of excess and at this rate she'd do a Thelma and Louise at the end of it. He was in two minds about that.

She rubbed her bare foot higher up his leg, sharpening an eyebrow. "Maybe I'll let you take me to bed," she breathed.

He let that hang in the air for a moment like a nuclear bomb. "Booze makes you naughty, doesn't it?"

"I like drinking—and being *very* naughty." She looked at him over the rim of her glass. "I like you. You haven't pawed Shira. You don't need Charlie. I'm much more fun."

"Shira doesn't know about you, does she? She can't recall anything you do."

She shook her head. "But she talks to me a lot. I know *all* her secrets."

"I bet they're interesting."

"Wouldn't you like to know?" she asked slyly. "Be nice to me and maybe I'll let you in on some."

"Do you have a name?"

She tilted her head coyly. "Can't you guess? You slept with us."

Dan rubbed his chin for a moment watching her grin. "Ah. Good evening, Carla."

"I knew you were a clever boy."

"You get all her pillow talk?"

"She's told me all about you." Penetrating eyes held Dan's. "Why didn't you fondle her boobs? She would have liked it and I like her to be happy. Do it next time or I'll get angry."

He thought he could manage that. "You protect her? Like last night?"

"You bet. Anyone who hurts her in any way better watch out—including you." She paused to run an eye over him. "But I don't think you will, will you? You didn't take advantage of her. I respect you for that."

It was a good time for the headwaiter to arrive with her drink.

"Nice place you brought me," he told her.

"A fitting reward for my hero."

"It took two of us remember? Without your crazy flamenco, we mightn't be here at all."

She laughed, waving her glass. "I guess we make a good team. My pussy power and your gun."

Sure, they were a regular Nick and Nora Charles—all they needed was a cute dog—but this time she'd killed the thin man. "Pussy power" wasn't in Nora's lexicon but she had a point.

"I was surprised you had a gun," she said.

"What gun?"

"The one I used to kill that thug."

"What thug?"

Nora Charles chuckled at Nick.

"Have you shot a man before?" he asked, hoping the priest had been a one-off.

She snorted. "Only those bastards who've deserved it."

Good God, she has. How many? Was he drinking with a serial killer? "I'll be on my best behavior," he told her.

"Do that and I *will* shoot you! I want to have some fun!" She chuckled. "Maybe we can find a dark alley and do it properly. Got that gun with you?"

The Walther was uncomfortable in the back of his belt but that was OK after last night. "Isn't that what Bob's for?" he asked.

She scowled. "That fat bastard? He's easier to lose than a blind man. He doesn't follow *me* around." She dismissed Bob with a wave of her hand. "Let's talk about you. I love men with scars—they excite me." She reached over to stroke the back of her fingers erotically along the keloid ridge across his neck "How did you get it?" she asked with a sensuous edge.

"A sharp can of beans." His sharpened glass against Gill's shiv made from a tin can. He'd got lucky.

She frowned. "Whatever that means." She rattled her empty glass. "Know what that means?"

You're on a record pace to oblivion, thought Dan. A new drink was delivered immediately by the hovering headwaiter, who had professionally spotted a lush.

All the menu was missing was a stuffed tiger's head. He whistled softly. "I hope to hell you didn't forget your purse or we could be working in the kitchen for a month."

She eyed him over her drink and said, "I have other plans for us" in a tone that suggested something more interesting than washing dishes.

Dan didn't feel that hungry considering what he knew was on offer and neither was Carla apparently so they decided to share a *thali*: a big silver platter of bowls and cups of yogurt, spicy dips, eggplant, rice, dal, chutney and pickles with *puri* bread. The hot and spicy aromas of the foods perked up his appetite but Carla only picked at the selection between sips of her vodka.

"Tell me about a bit about your life and I'll tell you a bit about mine," Dan said after they'd decided to share a *jalebi* dessert.

"OK but only if you don't nurse that drink all night," Shira said with a sharp edge. "It's like I'm drinking alone here."

The first one had relaxed him and he felt less anxious about Carla. He ordered another from the headwaiter but just a single with lots of ice again. "I'll start. I'm thirty-nine," he told her.

"Twenty-five."

"I've been married once with two children."

"Shira's been married twice," she said, toying with the yard of hair hanging over a shoulder. "At eighteen and at twenty-two. Now, she lives with Charlie in Elaine's mansion in the Hamptons in the summer and in a barb-wired Jewish concentration camp in Palm Beach in the winter."

"I was married for almost twenty years."

"About two years each time."

"I found my wife in bed with someone else—God. He made me feel quite inadequate."

"I bet he did! My husbands *died* in bed." She sniggered. "They were both real old. The last one was eighty-four." She gurgled a harsh chuckle. "Both natural causes!"

She screwed them and naturally they died? He just had to ask. "Killed them with kindness?"

"Blew their minds and their stents!" She laughed liquidly, far happier drinking despite double widowhood. "Elaine did OK out of both of them."

Her mother was pimping her out to old rich guys on their deathbeds?

"She chose well?" he asked.

She laughed. "*Unwell* more like it. Both Jewish, pacemakers, emphysema, and impotent. Life expectancy zero. Her kind of long-term commitments."

"No children?"

"You kidding? Neither of them couldn't get it up the flagpole even with a truckload of Viagra and an oil derrick!" She washed back more vodka.

"Had fun with *goys* like me?"

She grinned sloppily, swaying her head from side to side. "Sure when Elaine wasn't looking. Jewish boys are incredibly boring believe me."

"You prefer them *dead* boring?"

"Ha! The deader the better." She giggled. "I like you. Pity you're not Jewish. Elaine would dislike you less."

"*Oy vey*, I'm glad I'm not Jewish. Too much pressure to marry within the clan."

"You can say that again. Poor Shira. At least the next one Elaine's picked is going to be a whole lot better."

The next one? thought Dan. Shira had been lined up for another payday?

The jalebi spirals of deep-fried flour covered in sugar syrup arrived and invited their immediate attention. When she quickly polished off her share, he realized it was the first time he'd seen Shira really eat.

"Have 'nother drink with me," she slurred. "And then ... I want my romance." Her hand went under the table. Dan flinched. She giggled and unsteadily got to her feet to wobble off to the washroom leaving Dan to cool from the hand she'd rubbed along his thigh. How would she react if he didn't give her some *romance*? Was she armed? Another woman with a Nano in her purse? His Glock might come in handy.

The soothing vodka helped him justify loosening his Buddhism a notch: Carla had to be appeased, hadn't she? And it would be his absolutely last kick at the biggest cans he'd ever get to kick. But if she wanted sex, he was in big trouble. Dan poured water into the remains of his ice cubes but ordered a triple vodka for Carla and hoped she'd crash and burn before she raped him. The headwaiter's eyebrows lifted at the order and gave Dan a conspiratorial grin. Dan smiled back at the envy. It made him feel like Richard Burton about to bed Elizabeth Taylor. Awesome. Carla reappeared with a roughly touched-up face, her lipstick having gone off track.

"D'you see ... those lights?" She waved a hand at a white building, lower down to the right of the orange-glowing Mehrangarh. "I want to go ... go there ... for you."

"Are you going to finish your drink?"

She downed it in one and grabbed his hand.

* * *

The tuk-tuk, a virtual Hindu temple on wheels, jangled to a halt at the white marble memorial to a long-dead maharaja. Instead of returning to pick them up in an hour, the driver parked, put his feet up and started chewing some paan.

Carla stumbled alongside Dan as he guided her with an arm around her waist along a narrow bridge over a small lake with the bright moon reflecting off the exquisitely carved gazebos and pointed dome. A flock of white pigeons heard them coming and soared in a fluttering swarm around the memorial and darted off toward the fortress.

When Carla stopped Dan and pressed her breasts into him as she pulled his face down to hers to give him another of her sloppy kisses and he felt her hand on his thigh again, it was the erotic straw that broke the reticent camel's back.

"Why don't you search me … ," she burped unromantically, "… for your … ring?"

He didn't have to be asked twice. He caught his breath as he cushioned her heavy breasts in his palms and thumbed her prominent nipples. One of them felt odd.

"Like … them?" she mumbled, swaying into him.

Woolf!

Carla vomited yellowish jalebi onto his shirt and down onto his shoes.

"Oh!" She sagged her dead weight against him.

A wave of the bitter stink of booze and stomach acid made his guts churn. He turned her quickly and she sagged over the balustrade, heaved again onto the bushes below and moaned. Dan took out a pack of travel tissues and wiped himself down while she had a final retch. He dabbed the drool from her chin.

"Let's get you home," he told her and threw one of her arms over his shoulder.

They staggered back along the walkway to the tuk-tuk. When he folded her over a low wall to return to pick up both the stilettos she'd stumbled out of, he heard footsteps. About twenty yards away, two black figures, one tall and one short, moved toward them. Guns dangled by their sides. A shock wave of adrenaline blasted his heart out of his chest and his pulse shot into his head. A third attempt to kill him? Someone kidnapping Shira?

His shaking hand quickly pulled out his gun. No Carla to save them this time—not unless she puked on them. He reckoned they were almost invisible up against the dark of the trees. They stood a chance. Moving slowly farther into the dark, he knelt down by Shira groaning over the wall and loaded the chamber with a click.

At the sound, the figures stopped abruptly. Dan got ready to shoot first and ask questions of the dead later. The figures said something indistinct to one another before sliding their guns out of sight.

"Need some help, old boy?"

The Drurys? "Mark! You scared me!" Dan kept his gun pointed at them.

"Don't shoot us for interrupting your canoodling," said Mark, glancing at the gun then at Shira. "She's had enough anyway for one night, you dog."

"I think she's in a spot of bother, poor girl," said Gilly.

"My medical opinion is she's pissed," Dan informed her.

"I thought she didn't drink."

"Teaching her evil ways?" asked Mark putting an arm around Shira to help Dan hoist her to her feet. "Or is the poor girl just exhausted by your attentions?"

"Ha, ha. What are you doing up here?" Dan kept his gun hand free and his eyes on Mark and Gilly as they staggered Shira back toward the tuk-tuk.

"Lovely spot," said Gilly. "Thought we'd come up here for a romantic snog. We're not that old you know."

"Could have fooled me," Dan said and dodged an elbow.

The driver finished relieving himself against a wall, smiled red teeth, squirted a stream of spit onto the road and started up his motor. Mark and Gilly followed them in their own tuk-tuk. Carla groaned against Dan all the way back to the hotel where Mark helped carry her up to her room.

"I'm surprised to see you've brought a gun along," Mark said eyeing the Glock Dan still held in his hand.

"Like you said, it's a dangerous place, isn't it?"

Splayed out on the bed like a doll with broken limbs, Carla mumbled occasionally, her head flopping from side to side. Dan couldn't leave her lying there with vomit down her front but he felt a bit creepy removing her wet dress. Her bra and matching panties shocked him—and not because of their contents. They were red lace like Charlie's. Charlie had chosen the red lingerie to copy her more beautiful, better-endowed cousin? Not only did she dress outwardly like her, she had to compete even with her underwear? He could see how a pathological level of envy had developed: the older more desirable Shira had got all the male attention from when they'd been children at school and Charlie had been left to take her scraps. Dan cleaned Shira up with a face cloth before drying her off with a bath towel and rolling her into the recovery position—no one choked to death on a date with him. After placing a metal waste bin next to the bed in case she needed to throw up again, he set a glass of water on the nightstand and when she was breathing steadily and it was safe to leave her he kissed her cheek goodnight.

* * *

Dan lay on his bed propped up against a pillow, writing in his journal and drinking from a bottle of ginger ale while Karen lay resting on an elbow on her bed, looking at him with a sloppy grin. Empties were lined up on her bedside table, along with an open bottle of Scotch.

"Don't you have something better to do?" he asked.

"Nope."

Dan finished the bottle, placed it on the side table and gave her exposed tattoos his full attention.

"How did your evening go with ... bobbling Barbie?" she slurred.

"Are we going to have a girlie conversation about our nights out?"

"Why not? I'll tell you about mine."

"Ken slid into second base."

"Well done, Ken. Your mother's proud of you."

"What did you get up to?"

"Just stayed in ... played with my toy."

Dan didn't ask for details. A surge of guilt hit him below the belt. He'd been kissing and fondling Shira when Karen could have been getting laid by Bill instead of being on her own in the hotel room. What right had he to lie about her to Bill? What did he feel for Karen? More than protecting her? What was it about him that he always wanted to help others whether they asked for it or not?

Karen swung her legs off the bed and sort of sat up as she drank from what was left in her beer bottle. "Tell me about your ex," she said.

"I don't talk about her."

"Oh, come on, Dan. Isn't talking ... good? Clears the brain? Brings it out into the open?"

"So those shrinks say."

"I tell you what ... why don't we swap details?"

She tried to pass him the bottle of Scotch but he reluctantly held up a palm and took a lemonade instead. She downed a hefty swig from the bottle. She leaned unsteadily forward showing him more of the technicolor tattoos that emblazoned her upper reaches: dragons, skulls, blood, barb wire, daggers and a prominent "LARRY" in Gothic script over her heart.

"I married at twenty-four when I got pregnant. Larry turn'out to be ... not great ... but he treated me OK. Had a couple of kids. I screwed around during the marriage since I was bored. Larry died about a dozen years ago. My kids aren't in prison so I'm happy with that." She waved her bottle at him. " I do own that pub by the way and I'm the busty barmaid with a broad shoulder for drunks to cry on before they go home to their crappy families. I get hit on by loads of blokes so no shortage of rooting there. You?"

Dan stood up and walked across to the window to gaze out at the reflections dancing in the pool. Nadia. She'd seduced him so easily with her black eyes and a personality as dark as her long black hair.

"Nadia was wickedly exotic," he said to the night recalling the thrill of those early days when she'd taken his virginity and made him a very tired but happy man. "Unlike any woman I've ever known before or since. She was born into the Sons of Freedom, radical Russian Doukhobors, Christians who rebelled against secular government, protested in the nude against the conventional Canadian lifestyle and experimented with open marriage and sex long before the hippies." He turned back to Karen. "Nadia was born into it and grabbed it with open legs."

Karen barked a laugh. "Fuck it, Dan! You could be talking about me! I met Larry when I woke up in bed with him and another guy! He looked better." She swigged more Scotch. "How'd you meet this ... you know ... Morgan le Fay witch?"

The enchantress from the Knights of the Roundtable? She wasn't far wrong: sexually aggressive with many lovers but rigidly Christian she'd consumed him in his naivety. Dan's mind drifted off to the first time he'd seen Nadia, stark naked, waving a poster at the front of a group of naked men and women of all shapes, sizes and ages that was marching to city hall to rail against something or other: flowing black hair, small breasts, slim hips, a thick bush and no shame. How she'd seen him ogling her as she'd passed by and her sloe-eyed smile that had been only for him. He'd been thunderstruck when she'd sat beside him in the campus cafe a few days later after her release on bail for public nudity and had struck up a conversation that had led to him missing a microbiology laboratory with three hours of something much better. After a priapismic month of Nadia's sexual ministrations, she'd surprised him: she was pregnant. He didn't mind. He'd won the lottery.

"We met at a protest rally and had two kids," he told her. "We lasted eighteen years. People get less for murder,"

"Don't I know it? And ... you couldn't ... leave because of the kids ... Sir Dan?"

"Uh-huh. In the end, we came close to killing each other."

Karen threw her head back and laughed so hard her nightshirt slipped completely off her shoulders revealing her upper body that was an amazing work of art. "Ha! I ... can beat that! *I did kill Larry!*" She slid off the bed onto the floor with a thump and passed out.

Dan heaved her back onto the bed. What had she said? He could only see her tattoos if she was pissed? A labyrinth of colorful tattoos circled her torso like an erotic Bayeux tapestry. What a gal! Something caught his eye: the tattoos on her arms hid networks of scars where her veins had been punctured far too many times. Her toes weren't much better. He rolled her onto her side and covered her with a sheet.

A search of Karen's bags revealed nothing of interest until he peeled up a false bottom hiding a thin, brown-leather case containing a small plastic bag of a whitish powder—he suspected heroin—a syringe and other drug paraphernalia.

March 28th

THE BRICK PATIO at the rear of the hotel stayed cool in the shade of overhanging trees, leafy palms and a three-story apartment block from which curious children stared down at the rich foreigners having their breakfasts. Dan avoided Charlie and Duncan immersed in an animated conversation over their coffees. Close enough to listen in, Cruella sat head angled pretending to read an article in a magazine while her ears flapped. Shira slouched lifeless at her side, eyes obscured by large wrap-around sunglasses. He collared a waiter, ordered buttered toast and black coffee, and pulled out a chair next to Shira.

"Mind if I join you, ladies?" Dan asked without waiting for a reply.

Cruella scowled her irritation at having her snooping interrupted.

"How are you today?" he asked Shira. "Last night was a lot of fun."

Shira nodded slowly just in case her head fell off.

"You should have eaten somewhere better," Cruella scolded. "Her tummy's been real upset this morning, poor child."

"Next time we'll find a McDonald's. They have a great Maharaja veggie burger."

Cruella's narrowed eyes checked him for sarcasm and couldn't find any. "Shira told me all about it. She tells me everything she does with men," she said pointedly. "I'm glad you both had a good time." Cruella stroked Shira's hand like she would a pet cat. "Shira wants to go out with you again, doesn't she?"

Shira nodded, her eyes flickering at him behind her shades. He wondered what she'd made up for her mother to fill in the blank after she'd left the hotel. Obviously enough to keep her happy.

"You two are going to have a real good time together on this trip," Cruella stated as a matter of fact. "Right, Shira?"

Shira nodded again.

"I look forward to more of the same," he said just to catch her frown.

Dan chased away a bird pecking at the sugar in the bowl and savored the caffeine jolt of his sweetened coffee and quickly poured a second cup. When Karen wearing her own big sunglasses walked shakily across the patio, Dan waved her over. She hesitated at the sight of Cruella but put aside their mutual distaste and headed over to his table.

He didn't think she'd been shooting up before breakfast. He'd seen plenty of the needle and the damage done and Karen was hungover, not blotto on heroin. He'd never detected her in post-injection bliss and it fitted with her scar tissue looking old, mostly faded into almost nothing. Why did she have the dope with her? For an emergency hit if she relapsed?

Cruella lowered her cup and muttered unpleasantly, "Does she have to?"

"Good morning," said a barely audible Karen without looking at Cruella. Dan pulled out a plastic chair for her to collapse onto with a low groan. "Coffee, please," she mumbled at Dan. "Lots of sugar."

Dan poured her a cup and added several spoonfuls of sugar and she drank it like her mouth had struck gold.

"Oh ... bugger me ... fuckin' grouse," sighed Karen, lolling back in her chair as if she *had* received a hit of her heroin.

Cruella rolled her eyes out of her head. She knew better than to ask what it meant.

Dan topped up Karen's coffee and offered some toast. She stared at the plate practicing swallowing before pulling a small bottle of Vegemite out of her shoulder bag to spread some of the dark brown paste on a slice. Cruella looked so disgusted, Dan thought she might pull out a gun.

"It's good to see Charlene having fun," said Cruella, matter-of-factly, looking across at Charlie and Duncan noisily chatting at their table. She couldn't resist eyeing Dan over her cup. "She seems quite happy with boys *her own age*."

"Duncan seems a great kid. Do I hear wedding bells?"

"Ha!" Cruella released a Brahma bull snort. "Not on my watch! Do you know how many gold diggers have chased Charlie and got the worst of it?"

"He's not that kind."

"How would you know?" Cruella flapped a palm at him and clinked down her coffee cup. "Children! They all need to be spanked from time to time to smarten them up." She swiveled ice-cold gray eyes at Shira. "Why haven't you eaten any breakfast?" Shira flinched, her eyes darting around behind her fishbowl shades. "For God's sake, eat that toast! Stop picking at it! You drive me crazy, you stupid girl."

Karen's chair grated as her hand gripped Dan's arm. Shira snatched at the burned offering and nibbled on its crust.

Cruella threw her head back in despair. "Oh, help me, God. Why do I have an idiot daughter like you?" She snatched the sunglasses off Shira's face. "And take those damn things off. I can't see you!"

Shira squinted, cowering in the seat. Dan resisted an urge to intervene. Not so Karen. She scraped her chair back, her face boiling.

"You fucking cunt of a mother!" she roared. She furiously threw her napkin on the table, turned on her heel and marched away across the patio. Dan reckoned Cruella wouldn't have to google any of that. If Cruella had a shit list, Karen had made Number One with a bullet. He'd slipped to second place.

Charlie and Duncan looked at Karen in surprise when she dumped herself on a chair next to them and didn't hold back when she let rip again at Cruella from a distance.

Cruella coolly regarded her with a dismissive wave of her hand. "Good riddance to that one."

"What?" Charlie barked angrily, jumped to her feet and came at Dan with her arms windmilling. "You bastard! Duncan's your son?"

The slap across his face stung his ear as she stomped off. His other ear heard Cruella's mocking laugh.

* * *

Kapoor phoned Dewan.

"Got him?" Dewan growled impatiently.

"Yes, sah. I'll have him back on Tuesday."

"Excellent! Who is he?"

"Robert John Stewart, a fifty-year-old Australian."

"Robert Stewart? Mmm. Where have I heard that name?"

"Stewart Security in Mumbai. Suspected of two murders in Mumbai but never charged. Hosseini has his details for you."

"Damn good work, Kapoor! I'll line up the media! Keep in touch!"

Jaisalmer: The Golden City

The two-hundred-mile drive west toward Jaisalmer and the Thar desert flew by. The desolate, flat scenery got worse as they headed farther into drier land with fewer trees and more sage-type bushes. The ground turned into crushed, gray rock and dirty beige sand. A sparse forest of slowly turning wind turbines contrasted with the litter of decaying runners and sandals by the side of the road.

"Left by pilgrims to a nearby Hindu temple who walk the last ten miles on bare feet to show their devotion!" Loki explained enthusiastically.

It reminded Dan of the pilgrims who walked—or insanely knelt—up and down the almost four thousand steps of the Stairs of Repentance on Mount Sinai. The sight of such religious obsession had reinforced his rejection of sin as a worthwhile concept. Self-punishment achieved nothing positive. Much better to simply try harder to improve oneself by helping others.

He spent most of the time reading in the cool of the air-conditioning. Philip Kerr's Bernie Gunther thrillers usually kept his attention but not today. Bernie solving crimes while dodging Nazis didn't keep his mind away from thinking about Charlie. She sat grimly reading her book, studiously avoiding any visual contact with him and Duncan. He caught sight of the book's title. It could have been a lighter read: *Sophie's Choice*. Nothing like a Holocaust story to while away the hours on the bus, was there? She just wasn't a *Horse Whisperer* kind of gal.

"I'm sorry," said Karen. "It just came out when I lost it over that fucking bitch."

"Just a matter of time. No worries." He felt a relief of sorts at Charlie having solved his dilemma but it didn't make him feel better. Duncan didn't look so thrilled.

* * *

Dan walked around the new hotel pool to where Shira lay in her black bikini. She opened tired eyes when he sat down on the lounger next to her.

"Feeling OK now?" he asked.

She nodded slowly, squinting under her palm into the setting sun. "I woke up feeling terrible," she said in her little voice. "I'd been drinking, hadn't I?"

He laughed. "You drank all the vodka in the city."

She ran her fingers across her forehead. "My head feels like it did. I remember meeting you at the hotel and ... that's all until I woke up feeling like death. I told mother the food had made me unwell." She frowned. "You took my dress off?"

"You threw up on it."

She made a face as she shook her head. "Ugh. How embarrassing. What must you think of me?"

"Only good things. You're so interesting after you've relaxed with a drink," he charmed. "I cleaned you and put you to bed. I am a doctor you know. I was very professional."

She played with her hair, tilting her head coyly. "It's the second time you've put me to bed, isn't it?"

"I don't mind. Nice underwear by the way. Where did you get it?"

"Well, sad Charlie may get it off a stall in India but I shop in New York," she sneered dismissively. She leaned her loaded bikini top toward him. "I need to have it custom-made, you understand."

Dan didn't need another look to understand that very well. Perhaps after his success with Jane Russell, Howard Hughes was still alive and well, designing bras in New York.

"Did you feel my boobies?" she asked abruptly with the wide-eyed, naïve curiosity of an innocent five-year-old girl that surprised him, heat rushing into his face, sticking his mouth in neutral. Feeling Carla's breasts was one thing but feeling Shira's made him feel as dirty as an old guy in a raincoat taking advantage of a child on her way to school.

She laughed behind a hand. "I never imagined I'd see you blush! That's so cute!" She reached out and held his forearm. "It's OK. Mother said you could." She cocked her head. "So you did."

He cleared his throat. "They're great," he confessed, sort of, and felt dirtier still.

"Goody, Mother will be pleased!" She clapped her hands together before kissing him on the cheek. "Better than Charlie's, aren't they?"

"Far better. They're the best," he told her wishing he had somewhere to hide until his face cooled and he'd showered.

She smiled proudly and stroked his forearm. "Mother will be pleased."

"Did you know tomorrow is *Holi*?" Dan asked to change the subject to safer ground.

"Holy what?"

"*Holi* is the Festival of Colors. There'll be fires and people throw colored powder at each other." He left out "maybe kill each other."

"What's it for?"

"It celebrates an old Hindu myth but most people don't care. It's just fun. Want to go with us?"

"We'll have to ask Mother, won't we?" She stood up, covered her eyes with a pair of sunglasses and wrapped herself in a robe. "We didn't have sex, did we?"

He shook his head. "I would have remembered."

"Goody," she said, brightening. "Mother said we can't do that yet."

Dan blinked. "When will she?" It was useful information.

She shrugged. "Oh, when she thinks the time is right."

* * *

Kapoor slurped more Scotch before he got into the shower. His mind was a blur of indecision. Sleepless nights of erotic thoughts about Dan had worn him down. He'd hardly eaten and drank far too much since their last meeting but the images and the sensations wouldn't leave him in peace. The bath memories wouldn't die. He was a love alcoholic who couldn't stop at his first drink of Dan and he intended to get totally drunk on him.

It was now or never. Dewan wanted him back in Mumbai with Bob Stewart the next day. He was in love, just like the gods Krishna and Radha whose romantic adventures were celebrated in Indian dance, theater, music and poetry. He wanted *shringara*, rapturous love not physical lust. He thought he'd understood crimes of passion but it had been only in the abstract, dispassionately judging from the outside the violence of others. All those (almost all men) he'd arrested for attacking and often killing unfaithful spouses and lovers, spouses' lovers and the honor killings of family members (almost all women) came into sharp focus. He now understood the loss of control, the primeval madness that overwhelmed otherwise rational humans.

Several sharp knocks on the door. "It's Dan."

Kapoor took a deep breath and shouted, "Come in."

While drying off, Kapoor watched through a crack in the bathroom door as Dan walked into the room. His heart pounded in anticipation. He finished off the large Scotch he'd poured to take the edge off his anxiety before slipping on a silk robe with fiery, red dragons and slithering, emerald serpents that matched his mood.

"Pour yourself a drink," Kapoor called out in a thick voice. "And a neat whiskey for me, please. No ice. Make it a double." A touch of lipgloss, a final comb of his hair and he smiled at his reflection.

On one of the two single beds, Kapoor had laid a tan suit's jacket and trousers, a sandy silk shirt with a fawn tie. Contrastingly colorful underwear and socks were ready for a final inspection should they be needed. On the other bed lay an empty leather suitcase with his Browning in a shoulder holster next to it. In the open closet, tidily grouped choices of other attire were organized according to color from grayish yellow to pale sandy. Kapoor liked beige. Lena Horne oozed cool, sultry lyrics from his Walkman. The room smelled like a flower shop without a flower in sight.

Dan opened the small fridge and took out a can of Schweppes tonic water and a tray of ice cubes. He poured his own drink before fixing Kapoor a few fingers of Scotch from a bottle of Glenlivet.

"Any news on the ballistics?" Dan asked. Kapoor detected a hint of anxiety. Not surprising. Getting rid of Bob Stewart who'd threatened to kill him would be a relief—for both of them.

"I'm expecting a call any moment." Kapoor left his robe hanging open. "I was just about to get dressed."

Dan turned from the window, two glasses in his hands. His eyes slid down Kapoor's buff body and back up into Kapoor's sloppy grin. "I think I've seen this movie," he said.

Kapoor giggled. "Didn't you like it?"

"The Turkish bath? I have to admit I did." He averted his eyes into his swirling drink.

"You bet! I wish we had time to do it again." Kapoor's giggle became a lusty laugh. He took his glass, clinked it with Dan's, sipped it and smacked his lips. "Would you like a cigarette?" Kapoor took a couple from his silver case by the Scotch bottle, placed one between Dan's lips and another into his own glossy ones. He held Dan's hands as he flicked the lighter, inhaling a tropical island of tangy lime and coconut cologne.

Dan turned away, wandered over to the window and exhaled smoke at the glass. "You're not a typical Indian, are you?" he asked the pedestrian crowds and vehicles streaming along the road below.

"Handsome and brilliantly witty?" Kapoor followed him.

"There is that," said Dan, turning back. "I find you have a different sensibility to so many I've met. You're well educated, extremely well mannered, dress beautifully, humorous, a fun conversationalist. You're a..." He sought for the word. "A *polished* man."

"Oh, you're making me blush," said Kapoor, feeling heat in his cheeks. He placed his hand on Dan's shoulder and looked up in his eyes. "I'm certainly not a typical Indian in so many ways." He attempted an air of sultry mystery. "I like art, music and fine wine. The company of educated men. You like that kind of thing, don't you?"

"I do." Dan took a deep drag on his cigarette. "But I'm not gay, Dipak."

"Is that so?" asked Kapoor. "You think I am?"

"As gay as The Village People singing "YMCA" on a float in a Gay Pride parade in San Francisco."

Kapoor laughed and finished off his Scotch. "It's a pity I have to return to Mumbai with Bob Stewart tomorrow as soon as the ballistics confirm it's a Walther."

"I'll miss you, Dipak. You're my kind of guy."

"You're my kind of man, too." He tilted his head again. "Not even a teensy bit bisexual?" he asked hopefully, grasping at a final straw before he took the plunge in a dark place he didn't want to go. He raised his glass to his lips but found it empty.

"Aren't we all?"

Kapoor's heart flubbed a beat. What did that mean? "Ah, now you're teasing me. You're wasted on those young American fish."

"Missus Jacobs thinks it's the other way around."

Kapoor took Dan's empty glass from him and went to refill it with tonic. He needed even more Scotch to settle his increasing nervousness. "Do you have any problem with my being a homo?" he asked over his shoulder while pouring the drinks.

"Not at all. I once had a good homo friend."

Kapoor turned quickly. "Really? I'm pleased you feel that way. Some men get very uncomfortable around us." He came close to Dan again. "You don't seem that way at all."

Dan toasted him. "You're no better or worse than the rest of us."

Kapoor sat down on the end of the bed, picked up the Browning and placed it on his thigh, pointing at Dan. Kapoor's hand began to tremble slightly, the tension in his mind and body coming to a climax. He swallowed, his lips sticking to his cigarette. His pulse thudded. Sweat dribbled down his forehead.

"Are you OK?" asked Dan.

It had come to this? A knock at the door broke Kapoor's trance. He cursed under his breath. "Who the fuck is it?" he shouted.

"An important message for you, sah."

"It'll be the report from the chief in Jodhpur!" Kapoor laid the gun down quickly and jumped to his feet. "Now, we'll get somewhere." He felt a great relief at delaying what he had to do.

"Great," said Dan. "Let's nail that Bob bastard."

Kapoor stood reading to the end of the report on the ballistics and witness interviews with gathering confusion before looking anew at Dan who was chewing his lips between burns of his cigarette.

"It was a Walther, right?" asked Dan.

Something had niggled at Kapoor since the Turkish baths but he'd disregarded it. "It was Bob the Harbor Murderer with a Walther in the alley!" Dan had chortled. Why not a park, a road, a house, anywhere but an alley? Had his love for Dan made a fool of him? Making him careless, stupidly disregarding it as a wild guess from a man who obsessed him. It hadn't been a wild guess after all—he'd been there! Worst of all, had he killed the priest and blamed it on Bob Stewart? After a heavy drag on his cigarette, he examined its dying red cone as if it were the cooling lust within him before crushing the butt to death in the glass ashtray on the bed. And no more booze. He had thinking to do.

"I've been wondering about that murder in Jodhpur," he said.

Dan missed a breath. "In what way?"

Kapoor scratched his head in apparent frustration. "I never asked … what you were doing that night?"

"Me?"

"The shooting was at ten-thirty. Where were you at that time?"

"I was out for a walk after dinner with Shira about then. I don't know what time we got back to the hotel."

"Ten-thirty-five. The desk clerk remembers you staggering in with a worse-for-wear Miss Jacobs. She's a memorable lady as you know."

Dan nodded blankly.

Kapoor got up, lit a new cigarette out of his case and offered one to Dan that he accepted. "She can remember very little about your walk." He lit the cigarette in Dan's tense face.

"She was very drunk."

"The police interviewed the nearby street vendors and to a man and boy all had noticed a man and woman, both tall and white, enter the alley just before the shooting."

Dan nodded and continued smoking. "Tall and white? Narrows it down to a few thousand couples I guess."

"According to the police chief, one of the vendors actually said the tall woman had—I quote—*enormous booblays*."

He'd also used hand gestures and the expression of a man having seen the buxom goddess Parvati descending from the heavens to fulfill his erotic wishes. Kapoor had just never seen the attraction of breasts—on a woman anyway. As the twelfth and final child, he'd rarely got to the head of the queue for one of his exhausted mother's nipples. Maybe that was it. Give him broad shoulders and firm buttocks any day. He snatched a glance at Dan's exposed strong neck and hairless, muscular chest in his open-necked shirt. He forced his mind back to the killing.

He didn't expect Dan to turn white with fear of arrest or slash his wrists or run for the door either but he certainly never expected Dan to simply smile ruefully and say, "Good sleuthing, Dipak" and continue to smoke his cigarette at ease.

That was impressively cool, thought Kapoor. "Not really great detective work," he confessed. "Walking around with a woman with the biggest tits in Asia has its disadvantages, doesn't it? No Indian man misses them. We build temples to *booblays* like them."

Dan nodded, smiling wryly.

"Tell me about it," Kapoor said, tying his robe tightly around his waist.

* * *

Kapoor drank several glasses of water while Dan related his story about taking the Walther from Bob Stewart in Udaipur, using it to kill the thug when they'd been attacked then giving it back to Bob to incriminate him. It all made perfect sense except for one important fact he decided not to share.

"You can put the gun away," said Dan. "You won't need it to arrest me."

Kapoor slid the gun back in the holster. "I couldn't shoot you no matter what."

"I was hoping you'd say that. You had me worried for a moment."

Kapoor stood up. Pacing helped his thinking. "So you killed a murderous thug while defending yourself and that fish. Tried to pin it on Mis'r Stewart for me to get rid of him." He tapped his nose. "Cunning."

"Pity it didn't work."

"Why didn't you go to the police? It was self-defense."

"You're kidding? In India? The snail-like grind of your so-called justice system? I'd be dead—and broke—before I got to trial!"

Kapoor sighed his agreement. "Yes, the statistics show we *are* the number one corrupt country in *The Guinness Book*. It accounts for an amazing fifty percent of our GDP. Although the data are probably cooked!"

Kapoor refilled his water glass. His mind cleared, thoughts coming faster. "What was this thug up to? Why you?"

Dan shrugged as he opened another can of tonic water. "Shira must have been the target. Kidnap her for ransom money? American so she must be worth a few dollars. Her mother doesn't wear Walmart. Or maybe he was a rapist."

"The Club wasn't a kidnapper or a papist rapist. More of a Trappist." Kapoor chuckled at his own humor. "A deranged Catholic who came to Mumbai from Goa, got into petty crime then discovered his passion: killing people he thought deserved it to make money to spread the Word. Became a paid assassin and a damn good one. Thought to have had at least fifty to his credit over five years before you ended his career and hopefully sent him to his Christian hell. Pity he wasn't Hindu—returning as a filthy pig would have been much better," he added bitterly. "He was a killer. I don't think he wanted to kill Miss Jacobs. He wanted to kill you."

"Me?" Dan threw out his hands. "If he did, it must be a case of mistaken identity. I've never been to India before so who could possibly want to kill me?"

It was a good point but I'll find out, thought Kapoor. What was Dan hiding? Where are all those bloody reports on the group members from Hara? "The chief in Jodhpur has already put the hotel and street evidence together and wants you arrested," he lied.

Dan slowly blew out a lungful of smoke. "Time to make a run for Tibet?"

"Bhutan is much nicer. Happiest place on Earth they say."

"Sounds better."

"I've told the chief to hold off since you're probably one of the Harbor Killers."

"You *what?*"

"Don't worry, Dan. I want the Harbor Murderer and I'm not going to lose Monty the mole to anyone!" He stepped in to hug Dan and plant a big kiss on his cheek.

"So you're not going to arrest me for killing that thug?"

"You'll never go to jail or be killed by anyone as long as I'm around to protect you."

* * *

The shower hissed. Karen sang some unintelligible antipodean sea chanty that echoed from the bathroom. Not a bad soprano voice. She must be happy about something. Dan settled down on his bed with a ginger ale and turned on the small, black and white television. After ten minutes of the old *Forsyte Saga*, he wondered how many countries didn't have it on loop. Bored, he changed the channels on the remote bypassing mindless game shows and talent contests until he found the inevitable cricket match.

Barely had he settled into the calm rhythm of the overs when Karen breezed out of the bathroom looking like the easy winner of one of those talent contests: a short, strapless black dress that hugged and supported in the right places, showing enough cleavage and thigh to get his vote even if she couldn't hold a tune. He'd never seen her in stilettos and they did a good job of thrusting her broad hips forward and lengthening her thick calves. She gave him a sultry look out of a face she'd spent a long time decorating with thin black eyebrows, dark eyeshadow and scarlet cushions of lips. Her hair was different, blonder in a tight chignon. She stuck a cigarette in her lips and lit it with a sharp snap of a thumb on her lighter.

"Well?" she breathed, smoke drifting from her red mouth like sultry Lauren Bacall on fire in *To Have and Have Not*. He knew now why Bogey had folded.

"You look fantastic! For me? You shouldn't have."

"Ha! I didn't. I'm going out to get laid." She sashayed to the end of the bed, placed a hand on a hip to show off her rear and looked back at him over her bare shoulder. "It's been a long time since any roo's drunk at my waterhole."

The imagery that triggered had Dan moving on quickly. "Anyone I should call an ambulance for?"

She strolled back like a runway model. "I've reserved a table at a swanky restaurant and asked Bill out to dinner. If he doesn't make a move on me, I'll make one on him. Don't wait up, darling." She headed for the door, swinging her black-sequinned, evening handbag.

He knew he was going to crush her. "Do you think you should do that?" he asked sounding more like a priest than he intended.

Karen paused with her hand on the doorknob and looked quizzically back at him.

"I'm worried Bill might be part of a drug gang," he explained.

Her face and her handbag dropped simultaneously. She released the doorknob, kicked her stilettos across the room knocking over things no one cared about and plonked down on the bed next to him. She held her head in her hands and scowled her disappointment. "There is no fucking God. Shit, I really like this guy!"

It was enough to weaken Dan just at his moment of success. He put his arm around her shoulders. "I said *might*. I'm not absolutely sure."

She turned damp eyes to him and sniffled. "Really?"

Dan told her everything about Bill but left out everything about Steve.

Karen listened, gradually brightening. "So he may be OK?"

"I'm just worried about you."

"I have an idea. Go have dinner and find out what he's into. OK?"

She chuckled with relief, drying her eyes on with the back of her fingers. "I'll keep my eyes open as well as my legs, eh?"

Dan laughed along with her. She could be coarse, funny and vulnerable all at the same time. "Now go and tidy up the lovely face, close your eyes and think of New Zealand."

* * *

A knock on the room door.

"Who is it?"

"A message, sah."

Dan put down his book and unlocked it. Bill took one step toward Dan and punched him in the belly with enough force to fold him in the middle like a newspaper. Dan fell to his knees taking great whoops of air. Why the hell hadn't he minded his own business?

March 29th

Pushkar

THREE IN THE morning, a time for owls to be chasing rats and snakes across the desert not for shagged-out tourists to be forced out of bed into a bus and bumped along a pothole-strewn track but there they were, bleary-eyed and snoozing between bone-jarring crash landings after attempts at temporary flight.

Karen and Bill sat together ahead of Dan. Getting laid hadn't done anything for Bill's demeanor: his hard stare at Dan promised more of the same—or worse—if he got in his way again. On the other hand, a very smiley Karen winked at him before making a show of snuggling up under Bill's arm and sleeping across his chest. Across the aisle, Charlie had gone out of her way to stick the revenge knife into Dan. She'd cuddled up to a surprised Duncan, laughing excessively and pawing him to shove in the sharp knife of sweet revenge. Duncan flashed a gloating glance at Dan while sliding his arm around her shoulders to twist the knife. How long to Kathmandu? Nine days? Sooner the better, thought Dan.

"Ladies and gentlemen," called Loki. "I am so sorry we've had to leave so early and travel on some of the back roads. It has to be done to avoid gangs of reveling brigands who will stop us and demand tolls."

A general mumble of discontent indicated Loki's attempts to mollify his grumpy band fell on stony ground.

"Surely a toll wouldn't be a problem," someone complained.

"For a bus of tourists like us. Maybe fifty dollars each."

"Drive on, Loki."

Loki warned them: "This day can be most outrageous, I tell you. The untoward displays of fun can get out of hand and people can get ... hurt."

They went back to sleep as best they could when the road leveled out and ran more smoothly to the sleeping city of Pushkar. Dan gazed at the black skeletons of trees passing by with another reason to be unable to sleep: Kapoor and that gun in his bedroom. Had the drunk, excited Kapoor been on the verge of arresting him? Keeping Kapoor happy would keep him safe and let him escape to Nepal.

* * *

Drugs gave Dan four hours of a deep sleep in the cool room at the new hotel. He awoke to find the ibuprofen and Percodan flowing in his bloodstream and a bag of ice on his sore belly had reduced the pain in a red-brown bruise the shape of Antarctica to a dull burn. Showered, shaved and dressed in fresh clothes, he picked his way slowly up the stairs to the canvas-covered, roof restaurant that overlooked the large swimming pool. He ordered fried eggs, juice and toast, before gulping several cups of harsh black coffee laced with plenty of sugar to give himself a welcome jolt into the new day: hot with a fantastically clear, blue sky. The weather report was no rain for another twenty-five years but Dan had unpacked his rain cape anyway. The eggs arrived but he lost his appetite when his abs started throbbing again. After a bite of the toast, he pushed the plate to one side and ordered another carafe of coffee.

When Karen arrived, he could instantly see how happy she was. Rosy cheeks. The bounce in her step. Frustration lifted. Desire quenched for a while. Waking up to an empty bed across the room had been a downer. No funny Karen to banter with. How much she cheered him up at times he got too pensive. She readily laughed at his jokes, no matter how bad. She was great to be around. She saw him, smiled broadly and came over to pull out a chair at his table.

"That looks good," she said. "I could eat a horse."

Dan suppressed a ribald thought. He poured her some coffee and slid his breakfast toward her. "You can have mine. My stomach's just not right today."

"Really? Thanks, sweetie." A pot of Vegemite appeared in her fingers like a magician's dove. She spread the brown paste thickly on the toast and took a bite, closed her eyes and said, "Mmm."

He envied her surface contentment: the mind-clearing afterglow of satisfaction, her tongue licking the salty Vegemite, the bite of strong coffee, the stimulating hit from a cigarette. But not what was bubbling inside her: a dark mate with a syringe and heroin.

He couldn't resist commenting on her mood: "I see your evening went well."

She grinned over the lip of her cup. "Do I look less grumpy?"

"Is Bill still alive?"

"Am I dumb enough to be a female Praying Mantis?" She snorted then giggled. "He's still got his head! Never kill the golden goose who lays you!"

Dan would have preferred her to be a Praying Mantis. "Did you find out anything of interest?"

She laughed lasciviously. "You bet I did. Bill's a bloody stallion."

"Besides his equine qualities?" he asked testily.

"His what?"

"Oh for Christ's sake, what did you find out? No heroin free samples in the lining of his jacket? Go through his wallet like a good wife?"

Karen's expression suddenly darkened.

Dan connected the dots in a few seconds. Wife ... wallet. "Find pics of his family?"

She sighed with a shake of her head. "Another married guy. Just my luck, huh?"

"You'll dump him, right?"

"You kidding? The sex is the best ever."

* * *

Kapoor texted Dewan this time: Not returning today. Need another week to nail the Harbor Murderer.

Dewan: The media have been arranged! I order you back with Stewart. Now!

Kapoor: Sure? Would you like to see a photo of you and my friend?

Dewan: Goat fucker! Sister fucker! Sweat of a lizard's cunt!

Kapoor clicked off his phone. Why didn't Dewan like a photo of him playing leapfrog with a handsome boy?

He texted Hara: Reports on the group members?

Hara: Soon. I told you it was the brother.

Kapoor gritted his teeth.

* * *

"I hope you're wearing your worst clothes!" Loki told them. "They will get ruined!"

Dan didn't have any to spare but he was wearing his least favored and knew he could get cheap replacements from any Indian street stall. He wore his plastic rain cape over a t-shirt and shorts since he knew what was going to happen. He left the gun in the hotel safe. There was no way he'd take it into the mayhem ahead of them. He joined the other oddly dressed group members as they assembled with a host of other hotel occupants near a leafless tree decorated with brown doughnuts on its dried branches. Loki told them it was a tree that would be burned in the celebrations.

"What are the doughnuts?" someone asked.

"They're made of cow dung," Loki informed them without cracking a smile, Hindu to his core.

"And what do they symbolize, Loki?" Mark asked drily with a wink at Dan who had a thought of his own that wasn't for mixed company.

"Um ... well ... nothing really. They just burn so jolly damn well."

"So it's a *Holi* shit tree?" Mark deadpanned. Everyone groaned and laughed in that order.

Charlie rushed up in a skimpy crop top and a pair of shorts that had run out of material. Her long legs alone would create more of a stir under the men's sherwanis than the entire festival. Dan was shocked at her naivety: she had no idea the danger she might get into among crowds of men whose idea of pornography was a bare ankle never mind three feet of naked legs and a bare belly. He thought of intercepting her and advising more appropriate clothes but she cast him a dirty look that told him he'd better not and headed straight for Duncan. Ostentatious kisses on both Duncan's cheeks and a big hug completed the bravura performance. "Sophie" had made her choice. Good for Duncan but he did recall the fate of both Sophie's children—and Sophie. Over her shoulder, Duncan shot Dan dead with his eyes as he slid his hands to squeeze her butt. He was proving to be a royal pain in the ass but thankfully he wasn't hanging around with the Brit lads all the time. He was finding girls were a lot more fun—until they weren't. Dan winked and jerked him a thumbs-up. Duncan's face flashed confusion. Excellent.

Loki waved his hands again. "Ladies—"

"And gentlemen!" the group cried out in ritualized amusement.

Loki laughed and kept his hands waving. "Please take care! The town will be so very much crazy today—most rambunctious, I tell you. Now, go have fun!" Loki flashed a concerned glance with Bob and Rani who hadn't dressed for the onslaught to come. Dan thought they should know better too. No Arfa and Dazza so no surprise Steve and Bill weren't there either. Shira wore a silver Versace blouse and black Vera Wang super-stretchy denim jeans. She didn't look ready for *Holi.*

"You're not coming with us?" he asked.

She pouted, arms folded tightly under her bosom. "Mother doesn't want me to come. She says it's dangerous for women."

Dan knew Cruella was right but didn't Shira need to get away from her mother and test the world for herself? He'd be with her all the way.

"Don't you want to have fun with me?" he asked.

"Are you sure it's safe for me? Mother will be angry if—"

"You'll be fine if you stay close to me."

"I'm not dressed for it."

It was too late for her to change out of her designer outfit.

"Here's my cape." He peeled it off over his head, slipped it over her shoulders and covered her head with the hood. "There you go. That'll keep most of you protected from the colored powder and water. OK?" He held out his arm with an inviting smile.

Her face brightened into that of a teenage daughter given her father's credit card and let loose in Barney's in New York. Dan assumed it had probably happened to her. "OK!" she beamed and held on to him firmly. "Let's have fun!"

"See you later, children," called Gilly, patting Dan on the back and pointing at Mark. "Take care. Don't get into any trouble like the last time!" she added with a warning frown and a final wave—of her fist.

Mark winked. "Righty-ho, dear! See you for tiffin." He wore an old-style military shirt and trousers and had put on a pair of sturdy army boots. Stick handy and prepared to kick arse, he was ready for an assault on the Khyber Pass. Dan would stay close.

"Let's load up on powder!" Mark shouted like Captain Morgan attacking Havana after a skinful of rum.

They stopped at several wagon stalls on the way into the city and bought plastic bags of powders of all the colors available. Loki informed them they were all toxic.

Fearing for Charlie's safety—gang-rape was unlikely but not out of the question since she was the only woman he could see ahead of him—Dan followed closely behind her and Duncan as the crowd flowed into the city center. Men's hands were already tugging at what clothes she had and she was swatting them away. Duncan occasionally turned to smack at someone. Dan knew it was only a taste of what was to come.

Horns blared. Symbols crashed. Drums rhythmically thudded.

A surging mass of chanting men poured out of a side street and sucked them into a bigger street where even more crazed and powdered men were waving their hands in the air, spraying water and throwing powder in rainbow clouds.

Charlie turned a scared face back at Dan.

"Get behind me!" He pulled her behind him before she had a chance to resist.

Duncan viciously grabbed his arm. "What the fuck are—?"

"Shut up and help the women!"

Charlie stuck close behind him. Duncan held onto to Shira and Karen. Mark at the rear.

"Hold on tight to each other!" Dan shouted above the increasingly louder din.

"The buggers are feeling me up!" Karen shouted as a hand tore her shirt open. She flattened the man's nose with her elbow. He staggered with the bleeding nose and was finished off by a whack from Mark's stick. Dan had no need to worry about Karen.

The surging mass turned a corner and into full-blown mayhem. It was total madness: the crazed crowd swirled, a whirlpool of wet, multi-colored bodies. Clothes were torn off and thrown in the air, water and powders showered from the overlooking buildings. Half-naked men danced in a space in the middle of the human pool. Steam rose from the teeming bodies. If ever they needed fat Bob around for a bit of muscle—or even scary Rani—it was now. Where were they?

"Bastards!" Dan heard behind him and twisted around to find a yellow-faced Charlie had lost her crop top. With one arm covering her purple-green breasts, she batted away groping hands. At least she still had her shorts—for now.

Dan expected to find Shira cowering under Duncan's arm but instead she was grinning ferociously. Carla. Her plastic cape protected her and Duncan thrashed away with his fists at the men who wanted any part of her as a souvenir.

The current carried them toward another street opening. Dan pushed that way so they had a chance of getting out of the square before the women were stripped naked.

A blast of wet powder hit Dan in the face and he let go of Charlie to wipe his face of the muck. A loud scream. Charlie. By the time, he'd clawed the slime from his eyes she was gone.

"Where's Charlie?" Dan screamed at Duncan.

"There! Toward that street!"

One thought leaped into Dan's mind: *rape*. He'd never be able to forgive himself for not warning her about the way she was so provocatively dressed. He threw bodies out the way as he hurtled like a runaway train. If these bastards were crazy, he could be crazier. Being bigger helped as he crashed headlong into the bodies and toward the side street off the square.

Dan couldn't see Charlie until he blasted out of the swirling mass. She was a glistening sheen of paint—still in her shorts—and fighting furiously with two men who were dragging her toward a pickup truck idling on the sidewalk. The men were having a hell of a time with the bigger Charlie kicking at them and scratching at their faces until one of them slugged her and she collapsed like a marionette with its strings cut. They grabbed her arms and legs, swung her onto the flatbed and jumped in after her.

Dan gasped, muscles of rubber, pulse thudding, headache growing, but there was a renewed adrenaline rush at seeing Charlie. He threw himself onto the back of the pickup just in time to receive a kick to the head that sent him sprawling back onto the stones. Scrambling to his feet, he dodged around the side of the truck as it began to move. Jumping on the running board, he punched the startled driver as hard as he could. His right-hand knuckles cracked painfully on the side of the man's forehead. The stunned driver let go of the steering wheel and fell to the side over the gearshift. The truck swerved slowly to the side of the street, scattering paint-soaked revelers, and crashed into a stall, sending the produce scattering over the sidewalk and the stall's old owner flying.

The bigger thug jumped out the back of the truck and came at Dan swinging a tire iron. The blow deflected off his raised forearm and narrowly missed braining him. Dan staggered back against a wall, hitting out with his left fist at the thug's heavy jaw to no effect except hurting his hand. The tire iron hovered in the air again.

Clang! A metal pan glanced across the thug's head as the old stall owner vented his fury.

The thug staggered but struck out sending the old guy sprawling. He twisted back to Dan ready to crush his skull. A fat, white guy waving a big revolver burst through the crowd.

"*Bob!*" Dan screamed.

The thug froze and darted a look at Bob, who pointed his gun at them for a second. Mark crashed out of the crowd of shocked onlookers thrashing his stick at anyone in his way. Bob saw him, turned quickly and fired once into the chest of the thug on the pickup.

Bang!

The big thug gasped as his accomplice tumbled off the flatbed onto the road. He turned sharply back to Bob, eyes blazing. He screamed a string of what had to be obscenities as he threw the tire iron. Bob ducked the spinning weapon.

Bang!

Bob blew the big thug backward with a shot to the chest. He swiveled to the driver who was staring, dazed, through the truck's open window.

Bang!

The man's punctured head flew back into the cab. The stall owner and his maddened friends ran to the crashed truck, opened the door and dragged the dead driver out onto the road. Shouting with delight, they began beating the corpse to death even more.

Dan ran over to where Mark had already helped a dazed but furious Charlie off the truck.

"I'll ... kill those ... bastards!" she snarled, holding the back of her head.

"Too bloody late," said Mark bitterly. He left her with Dan and strode over toward Bob, scattering bystanders like skittles. "What the hell, Bob?" he bellowed, beating the men away from the dead driver's bloody body. His cheeks were almost violet under the sheen of colors. "You had to kill all of them?"

"Yeah." A stone-faced Bob holstered his gun. "Fucking rapists got what they deserved."

"They didn't have guns, damn it!"

"What if they had?"

Panting and swearing, Karen, Shira and Duncan burst out of the crowd and stared at the scene in amazement. Police sirens ripped the air, getting closer. Dan took off his sodden shirt and wrapped it around a shaking Charlie. He'd told her not to wear the crop top. Some Hindu had already framed it and hung it next to Ganesha. She was lucky to still have the shorts.

* * *

In the morning, the hotel pool had been full of clear, blue water but in the evening, after the hours they'd spent getting grilled by livid policemen who'd expected only a few broken bones and far more drunks, the group relaxed in a purple-reddish soup. They drank Coke, beer, and G and T's, revisiting the unholy mess they'd got themselves into. Loki sat by the pool looking unhappy with the day's events. Didn't reflect well on him, Dan supposed.

In the shallow end of the pool, Dan sipped from a Coke he held unsteadily in his bandaged hands, the knuckles on both sore and swollen from separately punching a stone head and a cast-iron jaw. More painkillers and anti-inflammatories were soothing the pain—and his brain—to help him smile after being a second away from discovering if reincarnation did exist. Below the waterline, his sore belly had turned more yellowy brown but he couldn't feel it anymore.

Charlie's face lit up like a New Year's Eve fireworks display when she saw him. She swam over from where she'd been standing in the shallow end, smoking dope, drinking and joking with the Brits and Duncan, and threw her arms around his neck.

"My hero!" she said breathlessly, bloodshot eyes, as stoned as the Wailing Wall, giving him a tight hug. Over her shoulder, he caught a bleary-eyed Duncan grimly watching them.

Instead of telling her to go away and play with her new boyfriend, he found his hands on her hips and said, "So I'm forgiven over Duncan?"

"I'm thinking about it, you jerk. I like him but you're a bastard for fixing me up with your son to get rid of me." She flashed a mile-wide stoner's grin. "It's not that easy, Dan." She planted a big kiss on his lips to emphasize the point.

"How are you?" he asked, pressing her away, amazed she wasn't in a fetal position sucking her thumb in bed. She was made of far stronger stuff than he'd imagined. "You need to put some ice on that jaw," he told her, running his fingers lightly over the swelling.

"I'm really great!" She reciprocated by touching the graze on his forehead. *Mm. That's nice.*

"Is that sore?" she asked.

Not now.

She was young enough to feel invincible. Dan knew the post-traumatic stress would set in later when the horrific violence surged back with a vengeance and she realized how she might have been gang-raped and possibly murdered. It had been a close call. Being stoned and drunk now was just what the doctor ordered.

She slowly ran a velvet-gloved finger down the scar on his neck.

That's very nice.

"What happened here?" she asked.

"I was in a fight." He didn't mention it had almost been a pyrrhic victory. He'd barely survived the slash that came within an inch of exsanguinating him in the prison laundry. Resisting touching her, he pointed one of his workable fingers at the scar beneath her ribs. "And you?"

She fingered the scar that ran backward under her arm. "Ugly, isn't it? Someone didn't like my father's politics. Tried to kill him and got me instead. I was lucky, the bullet just passed through my spleen," she said matter-of-factly.

"Who needs a spleen anyway?"

Charlie guffawed. "Or a neck." She held one of his damaged hands and smiled slyly. "I hope these get back into working order soon."

"They'll have to amputate but besides that, they should be fine." He fell into her sparkling eyes. "The things I do for you" escaped from his lips.

Damn. Flirting again.

"And I like them."

She moved to kiss him again but he quickly put his lips to the bottle of Coke instead of on hers. It was a poor substitute but much safer.

"Duncan's a good guy, Charlie. Don't blame him for what I did. He really likes you."

She slid her hands around his waist to pull him close. "I know what you were trying to do but we made a deal to Kathmandu, didn't we?"

"Uh-huh."

"Stick to it," she said with steel in her voice despite her smile and waded back to where the boys were still whooping it up.

Dan heard her loud giggle as she threw her head back and slid an arm around Duncan's neck to gave him a big kiss too. If Charlie wanted to play with his vulnerable emotions to make him envious and more receptive to her advances, she was doing a great job.

He leaned back against the side of the pool and with the sun warming his face, closed his eyes and to think of anything else but Charlie. Thoughts of her were vaporized by a re-run of the fight with the thugs and Bob killing all three of them. Dan shook slightly as the terror of it all seeped back. Charlie and he were both lucky Bob had saved their lives.

* * *

Bob had lodged his sweating bulk in a lounger, a paperback resting on his oily curls of black chest hair and a bottle of beer for his reading breaks. He'd removed the collar and a dark brown pattern decorated the side of his unshaven throat. Folds of white, hairy blubber undulated down to a pair of almost invisible Speedos, contrasting starkly with his glistening red dome. Dan decided not to give advice about a hat. Next to Bob, a dozing Rani—Dan wasn't sure which way she was facing—was catching up on her beauty sleep and would be out a long, long time.

Bob was like many of the men Dan had met in prison—knew what he was doing was wrong but didn't care. He was entertaining for a sociopath but he had to remember he was a funny, homicidal thug who planned on killing him as a souvenir of the trip. Bob was a man of few words so Dan didn't waste any.

"Thanks." He extended his left hand, the one that hurt less.

Bob lowered his book and looked over his sunglasses. "It isn't the one you wipe your arse with, is it?"

"And pick my nose."

He shook Dan's hand with his very strong right hand and chuckled. "I use my right."

"Missus Jacobs must be very pleased with you. Give you a gold star and a pat on the head?"

Bob laughed. "It's what I live for!" he exclaimed with a toast of his glass. "No gang rapes Charlie on my watch!"

"Another three dead men to tell the grandkids down at the billabong?"

"There is that!" He sloshed back more beer.

"Why didn't you kill me?" Dan asked equably. "You could have got away with it. Stray bullet and all that."

Bob looked up at Dan with a smile that didn't reach his eyes. "Plenty of time to Kathmandu," he said.

"Yes, there is. And you'd better be careful. You mightn't make it."

Bob snorted smugly. "That'll be the day, mate."

"How's the neck?" Just a reminder he'd have to work for his money.

Bob's smile vaporized. "Go write your fucking will, mate."

Dan lowered his voice: "Ever thought we might be more useful to one another alive?"

"I doubt it," Bob said carelessly but Dan could tell he was interested when his beady eyes met his.

"I can help you with your Import-Export."

Bob folded his open book over his sweaty belly. "Since you're in Customs and Excise?"

"Crossborder shopping really."

Bob eyed him up and down, blinking slowly as he chewed his teeth. He patted the lounger next to him. "Take a pew."

Dan sat and lit up a Classic.

"Only cigars," Bob said wrinkling his snout, waving away the offer of a cigarette like a fat, Hollywood mogul rejecting another crap script.

"I have contacts who want to run a product to Oz from Jakarta. Interested in getting a cut?" Dan asked, baiting the hook.

"Who in Jakarta?"

Dan ignored the question. "Starting a route into Oz would be useful for my friends."

"Where do your mates want to use?"

"Where would you suggest?"

"I've always thought somewhere north like Darwin would be a good spot," Bob mused, watching for a response. "Only saltwater crocs give a shit about Darwin."

"That's a smart idea," Dan said to be ingratiating. "Easy access from Indonesia."

"I *am* smart," said Bob smugly.

"Think we can work something out if we don't try to kill each other?"

"Only if we make one by Kathmandu or I'll do more than try."

"Deal?" Dan held out his hand again.

Bob reached out and shook hands but didn't let go. His grip tightened as he pulled Dan closer. His voice cooled, losing its previous jollity. "Ever been inside, kid?" Dan nodded. "What for?"

"Something violent."

Bob grunted again. "I'll have you checked out."

"Like my contacts did you?"

"There's nothin' on me, mate."

"That's what impressed them."

Bob smiled again. "Told you I was smart. Never been inside and never will," he bragged, his ego stroked. "If you're shittin' me on the deal," he warned, cocking a thumb on a pointed finger.

"What? You'll kill me twice?"

Bob deliberately twisted Dan's bandaged hand, grinning when Dan winced in pain. "You've got seven days. Get to work if you want to live," he warned and went back to his book and beer.

Dan rubbed his sore knuckles and smiled to himself. Hooked the bastard. He was safe from Bob for a week. A lot could happen between now and then. Not necessarily to the good, of course.

* * *

Dan knocked lightly on Cruella's door. If Shira was asleep, he didn't want to disturb her.

"Who is it?" A harsh squawk meant Cruella didn't care about waking up Shira.

"The man who helped save—"

The door swung open sharply. A rose-cheeked Cruella, her platinum quiff dangling askew, filled the doorway. "If it isn't Superman," she said sourly.

"You wanted to see me?" He didn't normally do house calls but this seemed an interesting invitation into the dragon's den—unless he came out toast.

She jerked a finger at him to follow her waddle to the balcony where a plastic table and chairs, a pair of binoculars, a camera, a white paper-wrapped package the size of a house brick and a half-empty bottle of Jack Daniels with a partially filled glass waited for them. She dumped her bulk onto a complaining chair and glowered at Dan across from her.

"What do you mean by taking Shira to that riot without my permission?" she demanded, slurring slightly to show where the bourbon had gone. "My daughter could have been raped out there, you son of a bitch!"

"How is Charlie?" Dan asked, staying cool.

"Charlie?" She frowned dumbly. "You've just been—"

Dan picked up the binoculars and theatrically scanned the pool below. "Nice view," he said and turned back to her. "Your niece. Remember her?"

"Sarcasm." She sneered sloppily. "Last bastion of the witless."

"Why aren't you thanking me for helping save Charlie? Or does it matter that she was almost abducted by a gang of thugs?"

"Of course—"

"And all you think about is poor Shira? Got your priorities straight?"

She eased her bulk back, the seat creaking its disapproval. "You're an insolent bastard, aren't you?"

"You want my opinion or is that rhetorical?" Before she could say anything he moved on sarcastically. "Aren't you going to thank me for helping save Charlie?"

"You're a snarky bastard too. Didn't Bob save the men from getting away with her?"

"You mean after I stopped Charlie being driven off and got the shit beaten out of me?" Dan laughed, holding up his wrapped hands. "You're lucky he saved the day then, aren't you? There was more kryptonite than I could handle out there. Are you going to give Bob the bodyguard a pay raise?"

"Very observant."

"Not really. Not many men have such a big left breast, follow Charlie and Shira around and threaten me if I get too close to them. You shouldn't have sent him to beat me up in Udaipur."

She sipped her drink, smacked her lips and put down the glass. "You think I need to beat you up to get what I want?"

"He tried."

"Idiot. What happened? You seem still in one piece."

"Seen his neck brace?"

"That was you? He said—"

Dan smiled smugly. "I was a gang of one."

Surprisingly, she toasted him. "Perhaps I should have hired *you*. You're proving quite a handful—as well as a pain in my ass."

Dan restrained his observation that her ass was big enough to take it. He stood up, rested back against the rail and took out a Gold Flake.

"Don't smoke around me," she ordered. "Disgusting habit."

He put the cigarette back in the pack. "Booze is a better habit?"

"Much better." She raised her glass to him again, drank and pursed her thick lips in thought. "Charlene was all over you in the pool. After that bust-up over that Duncan kid being your son, I thought she'd never speak to you again. Then you go playing the fucking hero."

"I thought so."

She wiped a dribble of bourbon off her lip. "Didn't Shira tell you Charlene had an affair a teacher—an *older* man—two years ago? It didn't end well. Think you're the first father substitute?" She toasted him. "Congratulations. *You* are the current *older man*."

She must have seen something in Dan's face.

"Don't look so bad," she continued mockingly. "Besides that, she suffers from sporadic, uncontrollable manic-depression and she won't take her lithium. She's a basket case who needs careful handling and a doctor can surely see that." She shook her head. "She's not even twenty-one. Don't you think that besides being too young, she's mentally unstable too?"

Cruella had pressed a reality button Dan felt cut through his indecision about Charlie. She was right on both counts. Cruella didn't know Charlie only had a week's shelf life so she had nothing to fear from him—whatever that was. Medical treatment? He'd saved her from ECT for now but what Cruella would do with her after Kathmandu was out of his hands.

"She needs treatment not more emotional upset," Cruella insisted, her eyes and voice softening. "Unless you distance yourself from her when the trip ends she'll be off home with a broken heart to add to her troubles. I'll have to deal with the wreckage you've left behind. Is that what you want? I didn't think so." She topped up her glass. "Now Shira is another matter."

Dan rested back on the rail and waited her out. What was the devious hag up to?

She smiled conspiratorially. "I can see Shira likes you a lot. She told me so. Did you know that?"

"I like her."

"I have an offer that could be very rewarding ... in so many ways. I can be very grateful where my daughter's concerned." She raised her glass and slurped from it never taking her amused eyes off him. "You've been out with her twice and she can't remember you squeezing her boobs even once."

"What boobs?"

She smiled thinly. "My daughter tells me everything she does. You've been remarkably gentlemanly with her and I'm impressed you didn't just grab for the motherlode."

"Never crossed my mind," Dan said evenly, wondering where this was going.

"You're the kind of man I've never encountered—one who can resist Shira's boobs." She arched a doubting eyebrow. "Sure you're not gay?" she asked but didn't wait for a reply. "*That* would save me a lot of bother." She shoved the package into the middle of the table. "Here's my carrot. Interested in twenty thousand in expenses to guard Shira and entertain her to Kathmandu as a consolation for letting Charlene down gently?"

"Guard?"

"As I said, I should have hired you instead of Bob. She's giving Bob and Rani the slip and I don't like their incompetence one little bit. She doesn't run away from you, does she?"

"Entertain?"

"You have my permission to have sex with her. She told you she couldn't unless I allowed it." She waved a dismissive Marie Antoinette hand. "Now you can. She's on the pill by the way."

Dan blinked under Cruella's amused gaze. He couldn't believe he was having this conversation with a woman's mother—or was she her madam? "You've been renting her out to alter kockers for their cash, haven't you?"

"I've made a bit," she admitted, apparently unhappy with her return on investment.

"But not enough?"

"Oh, do I detect disapproval for what I do with my own daughter when you've a son who hates you while my daughter loves me?" she asked in a sweet tone and saw the knife strike home as Dan winced.

"Touché," he said to hide a surge of regret.

"You'd be surprised how much I've made out of deals clinched by ... a date with Shira. It's your turn now. That's if you want it."

Her patronizing sneer was galling; her casual psychopathy toward Shira chilling.

"Twenty thousand what? Not rupees, surely," he asked.

"Dollars, of course."

He turned his back on her to look down across the pool. Its underwater lights glowed a soft yellow. He was being offered a main course of Shira with a side dish of green bills. He just had to dump Charlie. The last thing he wanted was to give Cruella what she wanted but he could see an upside if he played it right. He turned back into her supercilious grin.

"It's a deal," he said.

Cruella threw her head back and barked her victory. "Of course! Men will do anything for tits and ass!" She reached for the bottle again. "And don't welch on the deal," she advised. "A bird in the hand as they say."

"Is better than being found floating in the Ganges?"

She pooh-poohed the idea with a disdainful sniff. "Violence shows a lack of intelligence, don't you think? But things could get difficult for you ... *and your son.*"

Dan's voice sliced the air between them: "Don't drag Duncan into this."

"Too bad. It's called *leverage*. You lose. I win. It's how I play the game," she declared. "And win."

Dan stood up. "I'll see Shira before I go."

She smirked and waved her hand dismissively. "Go see your new lover."

He slowly pushed at the open bedroom door and found Shira awake, partially under a sheet. She wore pink-flowered pajamas and stared out of the window.

"Hi, beautiful."

She turned slowly as he disturbed her reverie and smiled lazily.

"Are you OK?" She nodded as he sat down on her bed. "I won't stay. I just wanted to check on you."

"Oh, your poor hands!" she said in a small voice taking his bandaged hands in hers.

"Nothing broken. They'll be fine after the pills do their job and I've iced them some more." He gently squeezed her hands in return. "That's something for you to remember, isn't it?"

"That was amazing!"

He recalled her furious grin as she struck out at men harassing her. That wasn't the old Shira who would have collapsed like a house of cards in a gentle breeze.

"You can strike it off your bucket list then. When you're a hundred you'll have a good laugh about it with the Glicksteins down at the home in Florida. They'll show their slides of Saint Thomas and you can tell them about getting attacked and painted by a thousand crazy Indians in Udaipur. No contest."

She giggled. "Mother thinks I'm shocked but I'm not." She shook her head in her disbelief. "I was *so* excited. I don't know what came over me."

Dan did and it unnerved him. In the stress of the chaos, Carla had shown herself briefly to protect Shira and Shira remembered what she'd been doing. Her personalities were shifting—potentially dangerously if she became as violent as Carla.

Her eyelids fluttered. "Duncan came to see me."

"He did a good job protecting you. I told you he liked you."

"He actually talks to me about all kinds of things. Like you do. Instead of just ... you know." She giggled and chewed on her thumb thoughtfully. Her cheeks colored. "He kissed me. Do you mind?"

"Not since it's within the family."

She giggled again. "Will you kiss me too?" She faked a disappointed pout. "Pretty please?"

He kissed her raised lips and let her rest against his shoulder.

"Charlie was so disappointed she didn't get to go to Egypt," she murmured. "But I'm glad we came here otherwise I'd never have met you and Duncan."

"Charlie didn't want to come to India?"

"Mother insisted on Mumbai if we were going to go anywhere."

Dan gave her an extra kiss for the information. "See you later. Get your rest."

She pulled the sheets up to her neck and smiled beatifically.

Cruella hovered outside the bedroom door. "I see you cheered her up," she said. "Take her to dinner. Do what you want with her. Here." She pressed the package of bills in his hand, enough to buy dinner for everyone in Udaipur. Maybe he should have held out for the Ferrari.

"Mind if I use the bathroom?" he asked.

"Better than peeing on my floor."

The sink cabinet contained the usual feminine hygiene stuff, a plunger, spare toilet rolls, bars of soap and shower gels. What was Cruella giving Shira every day for her blackouts? He rifled through one of the two big toiletry bags: makeup stuff, pads, plastic containers of pills of all kinds from laxatives—on this trip?—to antacids to sleeping pills and boxes of birth control pills. The other bag he assumed was post-menopausal Cruella's. He unzipped it and tubes of pills rolled out. A Pandora's pharmacy box: a small bottle of migraine pills and seven large plastic canisters.

Two of the tubes were labeled Stelazine and Risperidone—enough major tranquilizers to calm Hurricane Psycho blowing through the population of Miami. Another was an antiepileptic drug. An unlabeled one he recognized as containing red 100 mg capsules of Seconal barbiturates that would take out the rest of Florida. A full one of lithium pills Charlie needed to get down her neck. Three types of pill he couldn't identify: one unmarked orange while the others were marked with odd symbols. He didn't recall the symbols as being from Big Pharma.

Dan was staggered. Cruella was zapping Shira with a smorgasbord of drugs—she thought she was both a schizophrenic and an epileptic? And God knows what else? Hence the dopey child with porridge for brains as the pills kicked in. Add vodka and stir well? Anything could happen when you threw Carla into the volatile mix. He shuddered at the thought of the mental knife-edge she was teetering on. He suppressed an urge to leave the bathroom, choke Cruella with her own little pharmacy and throw her off the balcony. *Oooom.* That would have to wait. He took one of each of the unknown pills and flushed.

On the way out Cruella stopped him at the door. "Be sure to use a condom," she told him snootily. "I don't know where you've been."

* * *

The air-conditioned club could have been transplanted from Mumbai's upscale financial district. It had the wealthy look Kapoor liked: lots of shiny chrome and polished, tinted glass, arty tables and chairs designed by arty people who didn't understand how non-arty people actually sat. Cool young men smoking cool American cigarettes—no beedies here—whispered cool things in each other's ears while the cool jazzy blues of Billie Holiday singing "Easy Living" chilled the air even more. Despite flashing his credentials and adopting a hard detective persona, he doubted the hotel clerk had believed his story of having tracked a gay murderer to Jaipur but money always trumped morality. The smirking clerk hadn't seen him wrong with his directions to the most popular "male only" club in the city.

Kapoor wasn't in a hurry to get down to business until he'd fully assimilated Dan's exciting biographical information. Hara's reports on each member of the group had finally arrived after Hara had been officially designated the Superintendent's Associate with the same job description and same salary and no doubt she couldn't wait to laud it over her colleagues—and he couldn't wait to share the information with Dan. He sipped his Scotch and re-read Hara's emailed reports while surreptitiously absorbing Dan in his black, cashmere sweater under a cream, linen jacket, the carefully groomed hair, the whiff of manly cologne, and his trimmed and clean fingernails. Hara's reports had been typically thorough—he *had* to be Monty's twin spirit. He looked with concern at Dan's bandaged hands. What a man! How brave he'd been to tackle those thugs by himself. "Foolhardy" was maybe a better word. He was lucky to be alive. It was terrible to think he'd almost lost Dan just when he'd found him. He had to make the most of the time they had together.

"We have quite a lot in common, don't we?" Kapoor suggested.

"Both tall and handsome?"

"Of course. At least you are."

"Coming from Mister Bollywood that's quite a compliment, Dipak." Dan's brown-green eyes crinkled. "You're by far the best-dressed man I've seen in India."

"Oh, thank you." Kapoor suppressed a blush and moved on quickly. "I see we both went to boarding school for most of our childhood. I in Darjeeling and you near Ottawa." Dan winced. "Not happy times? Too many bullies and not enough chums?"

"That's about it."

"I had a crush on a boy a few years younger named Monty."

"Monty? I suspected as much," said Dan, amusingly wagging a reproachful finger. "But I'm honored all the same."

"I'm pleased you feel that way. Montague Miles Barrett was his full name," Kapoor recalled wistfully. "I protected him from bullies and canings. He loved me for that."

"And it became more than a teenage experiment?"

"Far beyond that. We remained lovers long after we left school." He regarded Dan closely. "Did you have a *special* friend like my Monty?" Kapoor crossed his fingers.

"Not at boarding school. I hated every minute of it." Dan went back to his cold juice with a colder expression.

Not at boarding school? Somewhere else?

"To business then," Kapoor said. "First of all, I must congratulate you on your bravery in saving the young woman from those brigands in the festival."

"You didn't come to give me a medal, did you?"

"Or the freedom of the city although you deserve it, I may say."

"Don't forget Bob Stewart's intervention. He saved Charlie and the bastard even saved me!"

"Lucky for you I didn't rush to arrest him when you wanted me to," Kapoor commented wryly.

"We were lucky but I've been thinking about what happened. Those thugs weren't trying to rape Charlie. It was an attempted kidnapping."

"Oh? What makes you think that?"

"It was a prepared abduction with the getaway truck parked ready to whisk her away to a dungeon with a bag over her head. No spur-of-the-moment 'let's rape the white woman we happened to have noticed in the huge crowd' by a group of horny bastards. *They* would have had her in a back alley pronto. Not that a farewell rape after getting a nice ransom wouldn't have been tempting. It was a kidnapping for a very nice payday. Missus Jacobs' family doesn't look like it lives on food stamps."

"My thoughts exactly!" Kapoor said, smiling broadly. "We think alike too. You would have made a good detective, Dan."

"But it lets Bob out of being a kidnapper, unfortunately."

"No matter. I'll be quite happy to get him for murder." He paused to sip his drink. "The police here tell me a local gang has been robbing tourists for the last few years and getting bolder in their actions. They prey on tourist groups including your travel company, Trans-India Adventure Tours. And with one guide in particular."

"Don't tell me he's Loki."

"Pity Mis'r Stewart killed the thugs," Kapoor said with a heavy sigh. "They were small-time, no history of rape, not gang leaders, replaceable but we could have squeezed something out of them about how involved Loki Malik was. We've searched Mis'r Malik's room and luggage here at the hotel and his house in Mumbai but found nothing incriminating."

"Loki needs money," Dan told him. "He said as much so maybe he found out how rich the Americans are and arranged the kidnapping for a big haul with his friends."

"How do *you* know Missus Jacobs is a wealthy woman?"

"With all that jewelry, she looked rich and she mentioned keeping gold diggers away from Charlie."

Kapoor raised an eyebrow. "Missus Jacobs no doubt wants to warn off amorous suitors for her niece who have dubious intentions."

A quick grin from Dan before he snarled, "Those bastards!"

Kapoor chuckled. It was Monty's wry humor.

"Anything more on Bob to connect him with the Harbor Murders?" asked Dan.

"My deputy has checked their phone records for their locations and contacts around the time of the murders. The phones were silent at the time of the murders and haven't been used since. It isn't illegal to not use your own phone but suspicious, don't you think?"

"Sounds like it to me. They must be using other phones."

"Something else showed up. Phone calls between Missus Jacobs and the Stewarts before they arrived in Mumbai. The Stewarts had worked in Washington and New York so they probably knew her from there."

"It would explain why Missus Jacobs brought the girls to Mumbai instead of Egypt where Charlie wanted to go."

"Guards she could trust?" mused Kapoor.

"What were the Stewarts doing in the US?" Dan asked.

"They worked for various companies but spent most of their time working for a Presidential Election Committee."

"As in doing what?"

"Mis'r Stewart was listed as security and his wife support staff."

"Which probably means he was strong-arming and she was embezzling donations. Who for?"

"One of those puffed-up American billionaires who fancies a crack at being the most powerful man in the world," Kapoor said with sneering deprecation.

Dan examined his burning ash while rolling the cigarette in his fingers. "But the murderers could still be the Drurys, couldn't they?" he asked gloomily.

Kapoor tapped his finger on one of Hara's reports. "The Drurys cannot be the Harbor Murderers. They arrived in Mumbai after the murders had taken place. Hosseini found all their cell phones operating as usual in Delhi until they reused them in Mumbai after flying in shortly after the murders. He found them on airport CCTV too."

Dan blew a smoke cloud of relief. "That's great! I've got to like them. But it begs the question: who hired the Drurys and why?"

"The Drurys' phone records show they had calls to and from an untraceable number in Washington DC shortly *after* the Harbor Murders. Nothing before. And quite a few since. All aboveboard. No one's trying to hide their communications like the Stewarts."

"Washington," mused Dan, toying thoughtfully with his cigarette. "How about this: the Koepkes were to protect the Americans and the Drurys are their last-minute replacements."

"All because someone doesn't trust the Stewarts to guard the women."

"Or do them harm?" Dan leaned forward. "Which gives us Bob Stewart's motivation for killing the Koepkes. He's up to something and doesn't want anyone around who'll get in his way."

Kapoor nodded his agreement. It was coming together slowly. The circumstantial noose was tightening around Bob Stewart but he would no doubt have some cast-iron alibi for the time of the Harbor Murders. He had nothing to directly connect Bob Stewart to the scene. No fingerprints, no witnesses. But he would plow on regardless. He would get Bob Stewart in the end. It was his fate.

While they sipped their drinks, Kapoor noticed Dan thoughtfully running his cool brown-green eyes over him.

"I like you very much, Dipak," Dan said quietly. "You remind me of a special friend. One I loved very much."

Hairs prickled down the back of Kapoor's neck into his shoulders. His mouth opened to blurt, "Oh?"

"His name was Paul."

"Your ... cell mate?"

"Yes," Dan said wistfully. He drew on his cigarette, eyes softening as they searched the past. "You'll know why I was in prison, of course. I'm not proud of that."

"Why you became Buddhist?"

"You're a perceptive man. Paul taught me Buddhism to keep my sanity and get off booze to create a new life. Without him, I would have died in there."

Observing Dan's pensive mood, Kapoor took a deep breath and cleared his throat. This was the part of Dan's record that had kept him awake the previous night. "He was a homo convicted of assaulting his lover in a jealous rage. He was your 'good homo friend,' wasn't he?"

Dan barely nodded.

"Paul was murdered the day after you were released. Drowned in a toilet bowl with a prodigious length of hose up his arse. They never identified the killer. Correct?"

Dan's face became a wall as he blinked slowly.

"The man who's thought to have murdered him was a Bholan Singh Gill, a member of a powerful Sikh gang in Vancouver with whom you had a number of altercations in prison—and almost killed each other apparently." Kapoor's eyes wandered to Dan's face and neck. "The scars?"

Dan's eyes held Kapoor's as he nodded again.

"He'd attacked your cell mate several times because he was a homo and you'd defended him when others wouldn't."

Dan's mouth tightened.

"You were very close to your cell mate?"

"Saved my life so I saved his," Dan said with firm conviction. He asked Kapoor's unsaid question almost casually but Kapoor heard the anguish in his voice. "You want to know if we were lovers?" He didn't wait for an answer. "He had HIV."

HIV? The three letters spelled "hell." Kapoor had done everything to avoid that nightmare. He shuddered at the memories of friends who'd wasted away into emaciated, cancer-stricken, horribly blemished skeletons.

"Gill was murdered when he was released a few months after you," Kapoor continued. "Drowned in a toilet bowl of a Vancouver nightclub with a copper pipe up his arse."

"The circle of life," said Dan grimly. "What goes around comes up behind you. Gill was Sikh. He should have expected it. He'd vowed to kill me when he got out. He cornered me. I had no choice. I got him first."

Kapoor nodded his approval. "So the Gill family sent the Club to kill you when he found out you were in Jaipur."

"I have no idea how Vijay Gill found out where I was. He tried to kill me in Mumbai the night I arrived."

"In Mumbai?" Kapoor frowned his displeasure. "It would have been useful information to rule the Club out of being involved with the Harbor Murders."

"Sorry about that but I didn't want to tell a cop I was on the run from Canada, did I? I didn't think he'd know I was on this trip and took a chance I could outrun him. I'm waiting for another attempt. Gill will find out I'm not dead and try again."

Kapoor stared at him, incredulous at Dan's nonchalance. "Waiting for another attempt? Why haven't you made yourself scarce?"

"It's complicated, Dipak," Dan said. "There are people I cannot leave behind. I'm sticking it out to Kathmandu."

"To protect the American women. Chivalry is not dead, is it?"

"No, but it's a little bit sick these days."

Kapoor laughed. "You disappeared before the Canadian police had a chance to interview you."

Dan aimed a finger and a cocked thumb at his own head. "The Gills put a hit out on me—and many others by the way in a shotgun approach to avenging the murder. It got like the end of *The Godfather*, killings from Vancouver to Montreal. I thought a vacation anywhere but Canada was a good idea."

"Dan Palmer has an international warrant out for his return to Canada as a significant person of interest in that murder."

"So back to watching *Hockey Night in Canada* on TV in my cell? I prefer that to a return trip to the delights of a Jodhpur cell with inmates hanging off the walls." Dan exhaled deeply and held out his wrists. "Well, Louie. Is this the end of a beautiful friendship?"

Kapoor ignored the wrists. "Not so quick, Rick," he replied with a flash of his own wit then surprised himself at his rage over what had happened to Paul resurfaced in his voice. That kind of physical abuse was constantly meted out on homos throughout India and he'd seen the disgusting results far too many times—death must have come gratefully. "I'd have killed the daughter fucker for what he did," he said in an angry rush.

"You'd have liked Paul," Dan told him. "He was your kind of homo. Smart as a whip, educated, worldly and compassionate." He gave Kapoor an admiring look that hypnotized him into silence. "Someone like you, in fact. My kind of man. Someone I can look up to, learn from. Even though you think Jackson Pollock had no more than one dead-end painting in him. Pigeon shit in a frame. Isn't that what you called it?"

Their gazes remained locked for so long, Kapoor blushed under the blessing of those brown-green eyes. "Ha! Now *you* don't know *me*," he commented quickly to cover his embarrassment.

"Bullshit," said Dan succinctly. "I see so much of Paul in you. Perhaps that's why I like you."

Kapoor blinked in astonishment at Dan finding Paul in him and his finding so much Monty in Dan. Lord Ganesha was working overtime!

"Where were you hiding the last year?" Kapoor asked. "Your passport trail ended in Singapore before Riley showed up in Mumbai."

"I caught a Korean rust bucket as its doctor to Mombasa. No questions asked. In Africa, I showed them my old medical credentials. They didn't care anyway. They needed help with the AIDS epidemic infecting and killing millions. They didn't care if I was a vet."

"May I ask what it was like in Africa?"

Dan's eyes lost their glint. They faded into darkness before he closed them for a moment. "Worse than you can imagine. Much, much worse."

"Wasn't it dangerous ... you know ... exposure for you?"

"We took precautions," Dan said seriously before adding: "I always wore a condom while operating."

Kapoor spurted a laugh. "Thank the gods for that!"

Dan's quick smile slipped. "But there were body fluids everywhere. Some weren't lucky. I helped bury them," he said, his voice as cold as the corpses.

"You're a special person, indeed."

"Never think that," chided Dan amiably. "I was just being human. Think of the other doctors, nurses and volunteers who weren't lucky."

"Humanity is becoming a rare commodity, isn't it? You were there." Kapoor wanted to tell Dan how much it made him love him even more.

"You shouldn't say that. You don't know me. I was hiding out."

Kapoor laughed. "You didn't you choose a beach resort in Thailand to cater to your every whim, did you?"

"It was a close-run thing."

Kapoor scanned every inch of Dan's scarred neck and tanned face, the soft eyes and the kind mouth. He'd worked around evil all his career and sensed none in Dan. Maybe it was the alcohol swirling in his tormented brain or maybe just falling in love and wanting honesty between them but Kapoor wet his dry lips and held onto Dan's forearm to steady himself.

"There's ... something come up neither of us expected," Kapoor said hoarsely before taking a big enough gulp of his drink to make his eyes water. "The ballistics report from Jodhpur. I'm ashamed to say I didn't tell you everything. The bullet came from a forty-four Magnum, not a Walther."

Dan's jaw fell. "That's ... not possible! A ... Magnum?" He looked at Kapoor as though he'd been shot himself, right in the middle of his forehead. "I saw him killed!"

"You haven't killed anyone." Kapoor gripped his hand. "I'm so sorry. Forgive me for being ... so cruel." He couldn't believe the emotional surge that brought tears to his eyes and tightened his throat.

Dan stared his green-brown eyes hard into Kapoor's. "So why didn't you tell me?" He crackled his cigarette with a deep drag. His face lit up with a sudden revelation. "You bugger! You were going to force me into bed, weren't you? That was what the gun was for!"

Kapoor opened his mouth to protest but couldn't lie. The blood gushed into his face. "I'm ... ashamed ... I—"

"Well, that's a fucking relief, you bastard!" Dan put his arm around Kapoor's shoulders and held him tightly. "So who killed the Club?"

Ganesha! I love this man! He forgives me in a second!

Kapoor swallowed his emotions and a big gulp of Scotch. His heart still pumped furiously. "Who ... had a motive to save you ... and Miss Jacobs?" he stuttered. *Whom do I have to thank?*

"Beats the hell out of me," said Dan, leaning back flabbergasted to take another deep drag on his cigarette.

Kapoor took yet another drink even though his head was beginning to swim. "Excuse me for asking. Have you and Miss O'Neill become lovers? It's not prurient interest," he added quickly.

"Your rival? No."

"That's perhaps wise since she has a history of mental instability and gun violence, I'm afraid," Kapoor said with the utmost sincerity yet not too unhappy to share that bit of news about Miss O'Neill.

"Gun violence?"

Kapoor noticed he didn't ask about her mental instability. "Sad to say," he intoned, "Miss O'Neill shot her school teacher to death in strange circumstances almost two years ago. Claimed he'd abducted her from her private school and shot him with his own gun." Kapoor saw the pain in Dan's face. "In fact, Miss Jacobs is just as violent."

"Shira?"

"She killed a man who was sexually assaulting her several years before that."

"My God. She killed a man too?"

Kapoor waited a moment before his *coup de grace*. "You'll realize now Miss O'Neill doesn't have an alibi for that evening in Jodhpur."

Dan's eyes blinked he hadn't.

"Do you think she might have followed you and Miss Jacobs into that alley?" Kapoor asked, aware of turning the knife.

"And shot the thug to save us?" Dan ran his hands back through his hair, exhaling deeply as he did so. "That would be unbelievable."

"But perhaps she shot him by mistake."

"What do you mean?"

"From the angle she had behind the thug, she could have been shooting at her cousin—or even you. Those big guns are hard to aim."

Dan hit the heels of his palms on his forehead. "This is too much."

"Perhaps you should be very careful around these women," Kapoor advised. "These ladies may be sharper than a serpent's tooth and not make the best of friends. I will not be a happy man if one of them kills you now, will I?"

Dan went quiet, smoking and blowing thoughtful plumes of smoke as he took in Kapoor's information. Couples performed sexy, slow dances on the small dance floor in a dark corner. Oh to be there with Dan's long body up against his, thought Kapoor. A glitter ball began flashing over the dance floor when Donna Summer belted out "Hot Stuff"—men swaying together to the music, some kissing, some more entwined, everyone enjoying it.

Dan removed his jacket and broke his silence. "Would you like to dance?" he asked.

Kapoor almost swallowed his cigarette. Ten minutes dancing with Dan blew Kapoor's mind—holding each other close enough to feel one another's bodies. How could he have ever have thought of raping this lovely man? He pressed into Dan on the slow "Last Dance." He was sweating, excited, in love! He recalled putting records on the hi-fi to dance with Monty in their secret place, a dusty room in an unused wing of the school. They'd danced and kissed and eventually made love listening to Eric Clapton's soaring guitar on "Layla" and watching the crystal stars emerge from the velvet black Himalayan night through the dormer window. He swallowed hard as he held back tears. He'd thought life couldn't get any better than that. And now it was. Monty. It was happening again. They sat down, breathing hard after their gyrations.

"I danced with Paul in our cell," Dan said gazing into space. "He had two left feet and I had two right. We worked it out by dancing in circles."

Kapoor had a thousand thoughts but only one of reached his lips. "You must have at least kissed Paul," he said, quietly, using Paul's name reverentially. It was how he felt about Monty. Someone to be placed on an altar, unforgettable, treasured.

"Occasionally."

"Other men?"

"No, only Paul. Never anyone else."

Kapoor collected himself as best he could. Without the air-conditioning, he would have become a puddle of nervous sweat. "No one kills my ... friends," Kapoor said determinedly. He lightly placed his hand on Dan's shoulder. "I'll contact the RCMP in Vancouver and they can tell me what this Vijay character is up to. I've had previous business with members of the large Sikh community there. Two can play at this game. I'll protect you. Just like you did Paul."

After Dan left, Kapoor ordered another double Scotch to drown out the circus of his mind. Kapoor had spent many hours in deliberately spartan, intimidating interview rooms learning to ask the right questions and listen closely to the answers of the interrogated, watching out for the nuances of the verbal responses and body languages of the innocent and the guilty, the subconscious physical movements and speech tones and patterns that revealed inner emotional thoughts the logical brain failed to mask. The revealing slips of the tongue. He'd found no obfuscation and deceit in Dan but "I saw him killed?" Why had Dan chosen those words? I shot him. I killed him. But not "I saw him killed." It was revealing: he'd been covering up for Shira Jacobs, a woman who'd already killed. Chivalry indeed. What else was he lying about?

March 30th

Jaipur: The Pink City

ACROSS THE LOBBY, a thin woman whose long, black sari hung loosely on her like a Paris model on a catwalk smirked at him. Dan's blood drained out a hole in his feet and into the Ganges.

Christ, Nadia! Deep breaths. He gripped his talisman and called on his years of emotional control.

He was as shocked at seeing her after five years as he much as he was by her aged appearance: short, cropped, steel-gray hair had replaced her luxurious black tresses and exposed a sour face with a lopsided jaw and the heavily tanned and prematurely wrinkled skin of a face too long in the tropical sun. She'd always followed Doukhobor vegetarianism but the Christian ashram Kathleen had told him Nadia had attended in India before her wedding must have had a lousy smorgasbord. Next to her stood an athletic Indian woman with the scary head of a jack o'lantern and the same harsh haircut. Cruella's moon face flickered excitement under a floppy hat, her eyes darting from one to the other as she listened intently.

How the hell did she know where he was? Not Kathleen. It had to be Duncan's big mouth. His acceptance of Dan's offer of a free trip must have enraged Nadia as much as it had surprised Dan. Had she pursued him across India just to poison any chance of his reconciliation with Duncan or was it something far more rewarding? It wasn't to shop him to the cops—she could have told them already where he was. So what did she have planned? The ostentatiously large crucifix she hung around her neck like a declaration of war showed how far she'd strayed from the pacifist Doukhobors and their rejection of religious symbols—it matched the one around the scowling tall woman's thick neck. In their matching black saris, they could easily have been mistaken for a pair of nuns.

At least six inches taller than Dan, the heavyweight Indian woman interrupted crouching over to fix Dan with a glare so hateful it only lacked a death ray—Nadia wasn't sharing stories about her good times with him. Cruella, dressed as a pink-laced muffin top, followed the Indian woman's glare—her eyes danced on seeing him. She lumbered across the lobby and bore down on him with undisguised glee.

"You're *married*? That woman's your *wife*? Ha!" she barked with delight.

Before Dan could say anything, Charlie bounced down the stairs, saw him and skipped across the lobby. Dan steeled himself.

Charlie caught her aunt's gloating grin. "What's going on?"

"You can't marry him, Charlene."

Dan shot a startled glance at Charlie. "Marry me?"

"She says she's in love, the silly girl. Pity you're already married, isn't it?" Cruella chortled as she pointed her stick. "His wife's over there!"

Charlie paled, glancing across the lobby at the sneering Nadia then back, eyes welling with a painful devastation that filled Dan with lead. "You lied to me like all the other bastards, didn't you?" she said bitterly in such an accusing manner he felt execution should be his punishment.

Dan's guilt choked him up, unable to say anything meaningful. He readied himself for a slap, a punch, something hysterical as she released her anger. Instead, she turned on her heel and ran back up the stairs. He'd have preferred the slap or the punch.

"Oh dear. I guess it's bye, bye then," Cruella scoffed to rub it in.

Dan turned to her, crushing the Buddha in his fist, struggling to contain his anger at her malevolence. "You paid me to stay away from her," he said, gritting his teeth. "You didn't have to do that."

Cruella sneered at him. "No, but I enjoyed it. Insurance in case you thought of reneging on the deal. She hates you now." She flapped a dismissive hand. "You can keep the money but stay away from Shira or I'll have your balls. That's if your wife doesn't have them first." Cruella cackled away from him across the lobby toward a sniggering Nadia.

* * *

Outside the hotel, Dan roughly pushed people out of the way to lose himself in the swirling crowd. He loosened fists he'd subconsciously clenched and burned through a beedie in a couple of minutes as he aimlessly wandered. The Rule of Four was not going to last the day. Why the hell had Charlie been stupid enough to tell her aunt she loved him and was going to marry him? Had she blurted it in another manic moment? When she'd been miserably depressed? He cursed himself for getting so involved with such a young woman. But he did allow himself a brief self-congratulation: the sociopathic control freak was nervous. It explained Cruella's bribe to stay away from Charlie and switch to Shira. He doubted it was simply her motherly concern for Charlie's mental health. There was some other agenda in play but it was too late now to care. Charlie would despise him so Cruella had won—she had nothing to worry about.

He ran his hands roughly back and forth through his hair in angry frustration. Was it time to get out of Dodge? He'd only stayed for Charlie and Shira. He saw an empty tuk-tuk with its radio blaring chugging by and jumped in.

"Where to, sah?" asked a young driver in sunglasses.

"Doesn't matter. I'll tell you when to stop."

"Biki give tour of city! All day for one thousand rupees, sah!"

Dan bargained him down to five hundred after threatening to get out. "The grand tour, Biki, and shut off that fucking noise."

The driver laughed, honked and swerved off into the traffic-choked grid of broad streets of the Old City. No matter how wide the roads though, India had enough vehicles and animals of all kinds that would fill them like nature abhorring a vacuum. The pink-painted buildings that gave the city its nickname since the Prince of Wales dropped by to check out the Raj a long, long time ago zipped by. Flocks of birds lined up on telephone lines and buildings; monkeys ran along power lines in families that would swoop down to steal whatever they could with those opposable thumbs.

Biki soon stopped outside a narrow entrance between racks of shoes and sandals and a shop selling every type of t-shirt possible.

"I don't want a fucking carpet!"

"It's my cousin's bar, sah. Best in Jaipur!"

Why not? He'd drunk vodka with Shira and not fallen off the wagon.

Biki visited all the major monuments and palaces and waited patiently while Dan wandered around the sites or dropped in for a cold Kingfisher at another of Biki's bars. The beer made him feel so much better: his stresses vaporized and the more he drank the less Nadia, Charlie and the rest of them mattered. Biki drove him out to the sprawling Amer Fort with its impressive Ganesh Pol, the multi-colored, mosaic-covered gate, and see the famous cannon.

"It is the biggest cannon in the world. It's in *The Guinness Book*!" Biki told him. Dan thought he'd sat under it in Jodhpur but no matter.

He sat underneath the cannon drinking and smoking, wishing he could have climbed into its long, ornate barrel and like a circus performer been fired far, far away from the Big Top of what was happening in Jodhpur. The journey had turned into a nightmare of a carnival: he was the clown surrounded by characters throwing more than custard pies. Bob wanted to kill him; Steve was blackmailing him into spying on Bill's drug trafficking and that could get him killed; Kapoor knew his past too and could hand him over to the Candian cops and a long stay at Her Majesty's pleasure. Each was a good reason to get the hell out of the trip and save himself.

The tuk-tuk stopped outside the Hawa Mahal, the pink and white Breeze Palace where royal ladies looked out through fenestrated-stone windows at the world they weren't allowed. A snake charmer charmed Dan until he wanted money for just looking at his cobra from twenty feet away. At the enormous, decorated cake of the City Palace, a sign proclaimed that a huge silver pot, as tall as Dan, had been used to carry holy water from the Mother Ganges to London on the behalf of a long-dead maharaja.

"He most probably died in London from drinking water from the Mother Ganges!" Biki joked. "And it's the biggest pot in the world! It's in *The Guinness Book*!"

Dan laughed: if you want to know the history of India, it's all in *The Guinness Book*.

Biki took Dan to a cousin's "restaurant" in the business district: a tiny part of a wall where two young men fried up everything in big steel pans for anyone at any time all day and night. He sat at a plastic table at the side of the busy street and ate the spicy fried rice and vegetables and avoided the lassi, the yogurt drink that could give your guts a real run for their money. More beer.

The booze brought on a pessimistic character he'd avoided for years. His thoughts grew darker the more he consumed. Shira didn't need him. She was a psychiatric basket case and her mother was incompetently drugging her but she'd be back in the States in a week so what did it matter if he didn't stick around? His relationship with Duncan was irredeemable. He hated Dan now more than ever so to hell with him. Charlie? In love with him and wanted to get married? My God, that friendship had got too out of hand. She had no chance of a future with him and vice versa. Wasn't she too young and crazy anyway? Christ, she'd killed someone and maybe another! Now she was angry with him it was a good time to leave.

Biki offered him some paan from the pushcart nearby. Dan had noticed Biki was an addict: his red lips, red teeth and red tongue were a giveaway. He'd been chewing it all day and leaving streams of red spit on walls and the road for three hours. The paan maker sat in his traditional cross-legged position under the cover, wrapping his slices of areca nut and tobacco in betel-leaved triangles on the stall. Absolutely. Bring it on. The buzz of the powerful paan jerked him out of slipping into being so maudlin and into making a decision. One of his passports would work. The hotel could have his bag and dirty clothes.

"The airport, Biki."

Within a couple of hours, he'd be in Kathmandu and near his final destination. Wasn't that what he'd planned before all these people had got in the way? When Biki rattled the tuk-tuk to a halt outside Departures, Dan handed him a thousand rupees and accepted an abundance of thanks that ensured him and his descendants eternal happiness and financial success.

But Dan couldn't move as a deep sense of cowardice froze him to the bench seat. How had he ended up running away again? Hadn't he learned to stay, dig his heels in and fight for what he wanted? Vijay Gill had learned that. And Bob. Fucking, fucking Nadia. She'd triggered emotional circuits he thought he'd re-wired with his Buddhist tool kit. Was he that mentally weak she just had to show up to tip the scales and shock him into drinking heavily again after five years of hard-earned sobriety? But it was Charlie who despite all his misgivings was the conundrum: he couldn't leave her with Cruella but she couldn't come with him either. It was an impossible situation: his "Sophie's Choice." Her devastating hurt still reverberated but it was his devastation that hurt even more.

"Are you OK, sah?" Biki asked.

* * *

At the hotel's entrance, Biki readily accepted another hundred rupees, handed over a bent card and waved his BlackBerry, insisting he be called day or night or any other time and he would be there "in a jiffy, sah."

A taxi screeched to a halt next to them. Charlie jumped out.

"Dan!" she shouted, her face stained with tears, and leaped to hug him in a death grip.

Over her shoulder, Biki grinned his palisade of pearly whites. "Oh, happy days, sah!" he sang with a clap of his hands.

"Find us ... somewhere quiet ... my friend," said Dan and tightened his arms around Charlie.

"Anything for you, sah. Biki find anything!" Biki gunned the motor and laid rubber as he accelerated into the traffic with his horn blaring.

* * *

Biki parked the tuk-tuk just off the busy Amer Road and pointed them down a stone-paved path toward the black expanse of the Man Sagar lake. Dan felt Charlie shiver under his arm even though it was another balmy evening with a light breeze shuffling dry leaves.

"It frightened me to think I'd never see you again," she said, her voice rough, her eyes red with crying.

"Did you have to tell Cruella you were in love and wanted to marry me? A red rag to a bull?"

"She was *ragging* on me and I let her have it."

"Charlie—"

"Listen to me," she interrupted, her voice strong and determined. She stopped their unsteady wandering and held him close. "As I searched all over the city for you, I realized how much I love you. I know what love is," she told him eyes now glistening, "and I've seen what it isn't." She tightened her grip on him and it all spilled out in a rush. "I'm ashamed to say I looked for happiness through sex and drugs and they only led me to misery. I think you guessed that already, don't you?"

He nodded. "Been there," he said.

"You're not like other men. You listen to me. You try to understand me. Talk to me as an equal. You're my friend, a real man I can look up to not just a boy who wants to screw me and move on. I've never met a man who cares for me like you do, wants to protect me, keep me safe. I trust you. I know you love me even if you don't."

Her emotional intensity took Dan's breath away. No woman had ever said those things to him—all those things he'd want a woman who loved him to feel—and it unnerved him. She had a far wiser and experienced head on her shoulders than any normal twenty-year-old. He dreaded the moment of having to say goodbye. It took several deep breaths to shove his emotions back in their box. He firmed his voice.

"I can't love you."

"I can wait," she said matter-of-factly.

"Ever."

"That's a long time and I have a lot of patience."

She reached up to kiss him gently and began walking again with her arm looped in his. Across the black lake, the yellow-pink cupolas and walls of the Jal Mahal palace floated magically in the glow of the setting tangerine sun. Dan glanced at Charlie's determined face catching the sunset, amazed by her poise, the maturity of a forty-year-old in a young woman but her emotional volatility bothered him more than a little. Although she may not have killed the priest in the alley, there was no doubt she'd shot and killed her lover in the Las Vegas motel when that affair had gone wrong. The hell of a woman scorned had been written into human history and it didn't make for good reading for men. He had to let her down lightly.

A bit of magic crystallized in Dan's thoughts. He thought it brilliant considering his condition. "Here's the plan until Kathmandu. Auntie thinks you hate me. Let her believe it. We'll keep away from each other in public but still meet occasionally to have a cigarette and a drink. OK?"

"I'd love that," she breathed now in much better spirits.

Charlie led him to a wooden bench seat where she flared a lighter and ignited two cigarettes. Dan inhaled the nicotine like a camel drinking its fill at an oasis.

Charlie regarded him with concern. "When we were looking for you, Duncan told me you and his mother had split up a long time ago. He blamed your drug taking and fucking around, as he put it. We have a lot in common besides Graham Greene, don't we?"

"Made for each other, huh?" he murmured as a jolt of nicotine sparked him into life.

She laughed for the first time. "Glad you think so."

Dan smiled at her. How could he not? "I bet he was happy to run me down."

She shook her head. "He wasn't. I could see through all the bravado it made him very sad."

"Ah well," he answered, sighing a deep breath of smoke that lingered in the cooling air like old memories best forgotten. "I've screwed up a lot of things with Duncan. I think we may be done."

"Don't give up hope." She gently held a bandaged hand as though she were his mother. "Kids need their parents no matter what they say and do. I wish I had a couple. I told him that. He'll come around. I know it."

"You know a lot of things, don't you?"

"I know you should have told me you were still married."

"Well, I didn't think I'd have to, did I?"

"Now you don't. But someone will have to get rid of that bitch," she added pointedly with a slap on his thigh.

Someone will have to get rid of that bitch? He imagined her gripping a Magnum and blowing Nadia's head off. "Planning ahead are we?"

"Don't let the grass grow under those feet."

"*Carpe diem?*"

"Exactly! Seize the day!" she cried with a ferocity matched by her fierce hold on his hand. "Let's live for today. In the Eternal Now. Didn't you tell me that? And that's right now!"

Nadia, Bob and Rani better keep out of her way or they might be joining that teacher. Bill and Bob were beginning to be the least of his problems.

He fumbled the half-smoked Classic in his fingers. "It's five years since Nadia and I lived together—by that I mean swore and threw things at each other. She hadn't mattered for a long time before that."

"You've thought of getting a divorce?"

A woman's way of asking, "Why haven't you?" Dan thought. He said, "Tried it and she attempted suicide."

"Pity she failed," Charlie said darkly. "Was the bitch serious or was it just a ploy?"

Dan shrugged. "Who knows? But she almost died so I called it off. If she'd been successful, it would have hurt the kids far too much. And I'd have felt a murderer." The irony wasn't lost on him.

"But doesn't she hate you? Why does she cling onto you?"

Dan blew out a stream of smoke that mimicked exhaling all his frustrations of too long with Nadia's madness. "Marriage vows to God. She's always been religious but now she's become a religious nutcase."

"She'll have to be dealt with, won't she?"

"I'll take care of her," he told her. "Leave it to me. I feel guilty over what we went through. We were both to blame."

"Guilt?" She looked wistfully up into the heavens. "You've got nothing on Catholics like me." A dark shadow crossed her face as she exhaled smoke. She suddenly brightened and turned to him. "That's why I want to *carpe diem*. I don't want to dwell on the past."

They slipped into several minutes of quiet stargazing. Sobriety began to surface in his storm-tossed sea of thoughts. He took a half bottle of whiskey from his jacket pocket and made it go away. Charlie took a slug too.

"So now you know more of my secrets. Feel better?" he asked.

Her arm tightened on his. "I want to know all your important secrets. That's true intimacy, isn't it?"

He said nothing. She was entering dangerous territory.

"Little ones don't matter to me." Her jaw stiffened as her eyes wandered off into the past. "I'd been lied to by so many men who've just used me I'd lost my ability to trust them. In my worst time, I was beaten up and abused and I'll never let that happen again. Look at me, Dan," she ordered. She held his eyes in hers, now diamond hard, peering into his soul for who he truly was. "Now I'm trusting you. Do you have any skeletons I need to know about? Game changers that would make me think you're another scumbag who's not what he appears to be?"

This was not the conversation for a drunk man teetering on the edge of an impossible love with a woman he could only hurt—or she hurt him.

"That works both ways, doesn't it?" he said, deflecting. "I don't know many of your secrets. Tell me one then. Get it off your chest, my child." he intoned gravely, "and I will decide your penance." That was the kind of thing she'd understand.

She bit her lip and took a breath. "My father was a senator from New York State."

"That's ten Hail Marys for a start." It got a smile out of her. "Tell me about him."

"He was an interesting man: a wealthy, liberal Catholic of all things fighting for a Great Society like Johnson. I just never saw enough of him. Always in Washington."

"Sounds OK to me. If you were a Republican, I'd be long gone."

Her smile was only temporary. "He was the incumbent running for the Senate when …" She paused to gather herself with a deep breath. "He was a shoo-in for re-election, comfortably ahead of Jeb Hamlish. That sanctimonious Jewish bastard brought up my father being a divorced Catholic to piss off the conservative Christians."

"Did it work?"

"Not enough. So he played the big religious race card to corner the Jewish vote—*zap!*—Dad had married a Jewess but brought his kid up Catholic and it still didn't work. He was damn lucky my father died," she said and dabbed her eyes with the back of her hands.

"Your mother's Jewish? And you were brought up Catholic?"

"Uh-huh. My mother was OK with it. She had problems with her own family." She stuck out her chin. "And I'm very proud of my Jewish roots."

"So you should be. The definition of survivors."

"You're not put off by that?"

"What? Being half Jewish blood? I love blintzes and you might get me some good deals."

She sniffed a laugh. "You *are* a *total* bastard."

He laughed too. "Now you know me far too well."

She stood up and helped him wobble to his feet. Something that had niggled away in his memory floated to the surface. "You mentioned David Hamlish before. Any relation to—?"

"Jeb's son."

"Whose father's running for president?"

"After my father died, he won the Senate seat and immediately put his money to work on running for president. Won—or should I say *bought*—the nomination and is leading in the polls. No grass grows under that bastard's ambitious feet."

"Why do Cruella and Hamlish dislike each other so much?"

"He dumped her at the altar." Charlie saw his expression. "She was quite something when she was a young woman."

God, she had to be. Or Jeb had a white stick.

"Talk about a family war breaking out between the Hamlishes and the Jacobs. The *dreck* hit the fan for years."

"How was it resolved?"

"The Hamlishes did some very favorable deals with the Jacobs and it was smoothed over."

"Smoothed over with Auntie?" Dan bet she'd never forgiven a kid who'd stolen her lunch in first grade.

"She doesn't talk about it." Charlie's voice became wistful. "David and I have started talking again and are sort of friendly. Forgiveness is next to Godliness I reckon. Hate doesn't do anyone any good, does it?"

Dan thought about his hate for Nadia that had taken years to be replaced by understanding. She was right. It had done him more harm than good. Hadn't he told her to let it go?

Charlie rested her head on his shoulder. "David's always asking after me and checking on me when he comes to visit Auntie. Every year he sends a birthday present. I did like the Corvette last year. Sweet of him really."

Dan puffed his cheeks and blew out slowly. A Corvette? "Is it guilt or love?" he asked, thinking it could be a happy ending if David Hamlish really did care for her and had just been a scared kid.

"Guilt!" She laughed bitterly. "He disappeared faster than his Lamborghini when I told him I was pregnant."

* * *

"We heard about Nadia," Gilly told Dan in the hotel's lobby where they'd found him swaying on his way out. "It'll be all right." She patted Dan's hand like his old school matron after scraping his knee in the yard.

Karen took a different approach: "Stop right there, you drunk bastard!" she ordered, angrily grabbing him by the arm only to sniff as she gave him a big hug. "You had us so worried. Don't do ever do that again," she admonished, eyes glistening under the bright lobby lights.

"This could get ... rough," he told her. It already was.

"Do you know how rough I can get?" Karen hissed, apparently willing to move up a weight class to take on Kanta. "Fuck Nadia and Lurch, you're not leaving!"

"I'm ... just going to the movies. Want to come?"

"The movies? What's on?"

"Who cares? We won't understand it anyway."

"Good point," agreed Karen and took his arm firmly in hers. "We'll all come to keep an eye on you."

* * *

How Jaipur had such a fabulous cinema as the flashy, white and green Raj Mandir was beyond Dan. It immodestly advertised itself as the "Show Place of the Nation" and invited him to "Experience the Excellence" but it could be right and he was ready if it was. Judging by the poster outside the cinema, a hunky man and voluptuous woman were going to be battling some kind of big monkey god but Dan's expectation was they'd only dance and sing with not even a kiss in the next ninety-five minutes of Bollywood.

Entering the warm kitchen of a cavernous foyer was entering a fabulous food hall where families loaded up on hot snacks and cold drinks for the show. No crappy popcorn with fake butter here. He recognized his appointment getting food and a drink at a counter. They climbed a type of wide staircase only found in royal palaces and sat in the front row of the sweeping crescent of a balcony. The aromas of spicy and fried foods drifted up from the plush lobby. He'd missed dinner and something non-liquid would go down well.

"I'm just going to get some food," Dan told Karen as he stumbled by her and stood on Bill's foot. "I'll bring you a samosa."

"You're on. Don't forget the chutney."

"Do they have any pizza?" asked Bill gruffly.

Dan laughed. Did they serve shit topping?

* * *

Elegantly dressed in a shiny sandy-gray suit and a cream, silk tie with a Windsor knot and a matching clip, Kapoor sat in the darkest corner of the balcony as far from everyone else as he could.

He'd texted Dewan the previous night: Evidence accumulating on Robert Stewart as the Harbor Murderer. There hadn't been a reply.

He sipped some cold Pepsi through a straw and munched on samosas. They helped with another hangover. Dan stumbled up the aisle stairs in the semi-dark and dumped himself into the plush seat next to him. "Hello, Dipak."

"Lovely to see you again," said Kapoor. He sniffed the air. "You're bloody *tallii*," he told him amiably.

"If that means drunk, you're right," Dan said with an angled grin. He sucked on the half bottle of whiskey he pulled out of his jacket pocket then held it out. "Like some?

"Why not?" Kapoor put down the Pepsi and swigged what he recognized as Royal Stag, a decent Indian blend. "Have some food." Dan took up his offer of a hot samosa. "What has happened to start you drinking?" Kapoor asked.

"Nadia, my nemesis, has shown with a giant of a woman to put a damper on my fun," explained Dan. He bit into a samosa packed with potato and chutney. "Mmm. This is good."

"And you tried to drown her out?"

Dan swallowed the food and took another drink from his bottle. "And still trying."

Kapoor took a drink too. "A giant woman?" he asked, wiping his lips.

"Someone named Kanta Suran."

"The famous Kanta Suran," interjected Kapoor.

"You know her?"

Kapoor pursed his lips thoughtfully. "Perhaps I should have said *infamous*. Besides skirting the edge of the law with her hedge fund and banking interests and various business ventures of dubious merit, she's India's most high-profile lesbian."

Dan stopped drinking. "She's a lesbian?"

"Very much so and very vocal about it. Any homos who put themselves out there and take the flak from the religious cranks who are blind to Hindu deities having always been interpreted as having variations in sexuality have a lot of balls. For a woman in India, far more than that. I admire her bravery. But then I would, wouldn't I?"

The green and white lights dimmed their glow and the movie started.

Kapoor continued: "However, I don't admire her business ethics—or lack thereof. I've investigated the disappearances or murders of rival businessmen but nothing has ever been proven against her." He shrugged. "With her wealth, she can buy whatever justice she wants."

"So she's the usual Mumbai financier?"

Kapoor smiled knowingly. "Very much so and very rich too. Strange to see her on a modestly priced trip like this one."

It didn't take long for the hunky man in a muscle shirt and tight white jeans to strut into the movie. He reminded Kapoor of George Michael—and Dan who was *jhakaas!* Perfect! The woman began to dance, throwing her veils around. He lost interest. "Anything about Mis'r Malik?" he asked.

"I can't be sure but there may be something going on between him and the Stewarts. There's something about the way they slip away together from the group to talk until someone gets close. Maybe Bob's working with Loki after all."

"Mis'r Malik doesn't seem angry that Mis'r Stewart foiled the kidnapping?"

"Far from it. They still chat together quite amiably."

"Now that is interesting." He started on another samosa. "Did you see a Doctor Pathan in Jaipur?"

"I saw him up at the Mehrangarh fortress."

"He was with whom?"

"Loki told me he was a guest of Missus Jacobs."

"Did you talk to him?"

"No. I didn't see him talk to anyone except Missus Jacobs."

Kapoor pursed his lips. "Mmm. Do you know why he was there?"

"Perhaps Missus Jacobs wasn't feeling well."

"He was a psychiatrist."

"Perhaps she needed treatment." Kapoor chuckled. Dan leaned closer. "Seriously though, he was there to find Charlie having a manic episode in public and have her hospitalized at his clinic."

"Did he?"

Dan smiled smugly and waved the bottle. "Not when I'm around."

"Miss O'Neill is *that* special?"

"Just think of me as her doctor, Dipak. I don't want her brains blown out with ECT if I can help it."

"A setup by her aunt to eliminate Miss O'Neill? Why?"

"That I don't know but I'll find out."

"Why here in India and not back in the States? Surely she could have done anything she could do her back there."

"Good question. I think she couldn't get away with it back there. Too much scrutiny from those who have an interest in Charlie."

"Such as whoever sent the Koepkes then the Drurys to protect her?" Kapoor was momentarily distracted by the buff man who had lost his shirt. For no apparent reason, he began to sing and dance with the woman. Typical mindless Bollywood. "Yesterday, Pathan was found at the fort by a security guard," he continued. "He'd fallen a hundred feet off a wall into a secluded ditch. Fatal, of course."

"No CCTV?"

"Not working." He exhaled noisily. "Typical India. It's a pity this is not New York."

Dan chuckled. "In New York, they would have been stolen, Dipak."

Kapoor smiled. He did that a lot around Dan and he loved it. "So who would want to kill Pathan to prevent this happening, *Dan?*" Kapoor asked, leaning into Dan, glowering like a pulp-novel heavy.

Dan gaped at him. "You don't—"

Kapoor laughed out loud, the whiskey getting to him. A barrage of *shhs* rose into their corner of the balcony. "Besides you, of course. I can only think of two people."

Dan's face fell. "Mark and Gilly?"

"They must have protected Miss O'Neill by eliminating Pathan. It's murder, Dan. I can't ignore it."

Dan drank heavily from the bottle and passed it back to Kapoor. He'd seen Mark and Gilly searching frantically for Charlie at the fort. Mark and Gilly were murderers? His heart sank. Kapoor passed the bottle back and Dan took another swig.

"Whose presidential campaign did Bob work for?" Dan asked to change the subject.

"A Senator Jeb Hamlish."

Kapoor's detective senses noticed Dan's telling pause and eye flicker. "How's he doing?"

"Odds on the next president apparently."

"Bob should have stuck with him. He could have been running his Security Service."

"Perhaps he should have." Dan knows this man, thought Kapoor. Next President of the United States? I'll have to find out more about him.

Dan placed a plastic bag containing orange, gray and white pills in his hand. "Is it possible for your CSI models to identify these? Shira Jacobs is being treated with them and I'd like to know what they are."

Kapoor fingered the bag. "Without asking her mother."

Dan nodded. Kapoor pocketed the bag before straightening his jacket and tie. "This film is for idiots. I'd love to take you for a drink," he said.

"I have to get back to the group," Dan said with regret. "They're expecting some food before the movie ends. Next time. OK?"

Kapoor had a final swig of whiskey and swallowed his disappointment.

* * *

The hotel didn't have a pool but out the back it did have a treed garden, sporting a gazebo and dried lawn bordered with dense shrubs with aromas of lilacs and hollyhocks. Dan wasn't there. Charlie checked her watch for about the tenth time. Her heart sank. Half an hour late already. She thought she'd played him along very well: non-threatening, not probing the reasons for his reticence and not overly affectionate, but she'd set out her stall to tempt him. Had she misread him? Had he been too drunk to remember? Had he deliberately forgotten in order to keep his distance? Could he have changed his mind and run off again?

She climbed the steps, biting her lips anxiously and entered the dark of the gazebo, a boxy wooden structure with a pointed pagoda-like roof, its latticed walls covered with spreading ivy. The beers she'd drunk hadn't settled her nerves. She swallowed more from her bottle and held back a painful urge to cry. She was shocked by how she'd fallen in love with Dan: it had gone far beyond such an unexpected, wonderful friendship into a physical yearning for him. She'd had no interest in sex since she'd returned from Las Vegas with the act depleted of any meaning beyond punishing herself and chasing love into blind alleys. The emerging interest in making love with Dan stirred an excitement in her she thought had maybe gone forever.

When they'd been dropped off back at the hotel, Dan had been called to a telephone at the front desk before telling her he'd have to go.

"Back of the hotel at eleven?" Charlie had asked.

He'd said nothing and it had set her nerves jangling. Her mind whirred a Pandora's Box of worries. Had ignoring her until Kathmandu already started? Had she annoyed him in some way? Too needy? Needy women frightened many men off faster than a case of the clap. Why had she blurted she was going to marry him? How she loved him?

She'd been like this all day: an emotional car wreck at the thought Dan had deserted her. Gone just like her mother and father and left her with her aunt and Shira. She'd taken taxis and tuk-tuks all over the city, to the bus station and out to the airport to find him. It had been searching for a needle in a haystack but it had kept her busy doing something, anything. She hadn't stopped to eat or drink and she felt drained but still not hungry. Only finding Dan outside the hotel had prevented her running off to get lost in India and damn the consequences.

Footsteps. Her heart jumped. A dark figure waving a glowing cigarette stumbled out of the shadows. *Dan!* She controlled her urge to leap down the steps to jump into his arms. Instead, she approached him slowly and raised her face for a kiss. He swayed before her, not taking up the offer, and threw away his cigarette. There was something different and it wasn't he was even more plastered. He could hardly stand.

"Only a cigarette … and … a drink, Charlie," he mumbled. "No … fuck … buddies."

"Let's sit down before you fall down," she told him and guided him up the steps into the dark of the gazebo. She didn't feel much better herself. On her empty stomach, the beer had gone straight to her head. They slumped together on a weathered rattan couch, its old legs creaking ominously as it bent to one side under their weight.

She put an arm around him and rested her head on his shoulder. She'd told him [Da]vid Hamlish had got her pregnant when she was only fifteen. Was that it? She'd [con]fessed what a drugged-up slut she'd been. Had he been thinking about that? Men [ca]n say it doesn't matter if their women were promiscuous but it does in spades. Had [she] come off as too much of a whore?

"Try one of these," he slurred, fumbling a hand-rolled, brown cigarette out of a blue [and] white, plastic pack.

"S'what … lower classes smoke. And the rich … when no one's looking." He lit it with a match for her at the third attempt. "Keep puffing on it. S'made of loose … leaves."

She sucked and burned her lungs down to her diaphragm, coughing on its hot, harsh smoke. She wasn't much of a smoker and these were like smoking rolled-up newspaper. "It's awful." She wagged her burned tongue.

He sucked hard on his beedie. "Shit, isn't it?" He threw it away. Its pinpoint red glow faded in the grass.

Charlie giggled when she threw hers. She found her pack of Marlboros, put one between his lips and lit both their cigarettes. Contemplatively, they both blew layers of clouds around them for a while, letting the warm air drift the smoke away but her anxiety still hung over her like a burgeoning black cloud.

"Have a drink." Dan struggled to extricate a half bottle of whiskey from his jacket pocket. He fumbled the cap off and held it out to her.

Charlie grabbed it like it was a wedding ring Dan was offering and took a deep swallow. Dan took another pull himself. Charlie felt the biting booze making a beeline for her already cloudy brain. A wave of relaxation rippled through her. She took another drink as much as the first time. It was even better. She closed her eyes and began to float.

Dan stood up shakily to step unsteadily to a post to hold him up. He watched the lights of a small plane rising into the night sky from the airport. She stood up too quickly and staggered into him, sliding her arm around his waist. She followed his gaze. How great it would be to fly away and start a new life. Was that what he was thinking? Was she on the plane?

The extra booze calmed her fears so much it loosened the bolts on the door to her secrets. She wanted to tell Dan everything—well, almost everything—and unload her heart into his. She'd been a lot worse than a slut.

"I've been up and down and up again ever since my parents died and I've been living with Auntie and Shira," she told him to break the heavy silence. "I don't know what's going on with me."

"You've been under ... a lot of emotional stress," he said. "Losing parents, especially when you're young ... is traumatic. Losing a baby when you're only fifteen is..." He shook his head. "I know you've been very brave and fighting it. You've had a tough time."

She nodded, tears welling. This was the understanding man she loved. But she still held back from telling him everything.

"No one's ... immune," he continued. "Emotions are ... most powerful force on the planet. They aren't easily controlled. Believe me ... I know."

She sensed him becoming more emotional so she pressed more into him. "I don't want to go back with Auntie," she told him with a deliberate catch in her voice. "I want to stay here with you."

"Don't ... don't go there, Charlie. Isn't she your guardian? She can do what she wants with you."

Charlie released him, her voice thick with anger. "She's my guardian until I'm twenty-one!" She stamped her shoes loudly. "Controls all my finances, my whole life. She chains me in the tower trying to *cure* me!"

Dan jerked to attention. "She's trying to cure you?"

"Shrinks." She moved into the light and stuck a finger in her mouth in a pretend gag.

"Drugs?"

Charlie blasted a flare into the night sky. "She's tried to force them on me!"

"She says ... you won't take your lithium. Is that wise? It'll—"

"I won't take it!" Charlie stumbled back and forth in the small space, an annoyed rat caught in Cruella's maze. "My hair fell out, my hands trembled. I peed all the time. I got spots like a teenager. It was awful. And it made me feel stupid!"

Dan pulled her to a halt. "These tranquilizers I'm giving you won't stop the manic depression. They're a Band-Aid, that's all. Remember the relaxation I taught you?"

"It does help."

But she liked the whiskey better. She took the bottle from Dan and swallowed more to loosen any remaining tension. She shocked herself with the highly erotic thought of being on her back on the lawn with Dan thrusting, thrusting, surged unexpectedly through her loins like a wildfire. It felt so natural after her years of disinterest in sex, hating the thought of it. After Dan finished off the bottle, she stepped into him. Should she? Her foot came off what little brake remained on her inhibitions and pressed hard on her libido. She held his eyes and gently took his bandaged hands and placed them on her breasts.

Dan blinked, mouth opening, tensing but not pulling away. She carefully moved his hands until he took over massaging her. The caress of his fingers and the scuff of the rough bandages across her breasts and nipples had her gasping, wet and enjoying what was meant to be enjoyed.

"This is ... more than friends," he rasped, hot breath on her cheeks.

"There ... are ... benefits," she said between pants, reaching up to kiss him on the lips.

She held his hips and pressed into him. What was wrong down there? She'd never felt any excitement below his belt but any lingering wisp of anxiety about his being gay was blown away by the thrill of him giving into her as his kiss deepened and his fingers tweaked her tingling nipples harder. Oh to be on her back on the lawn with her legs clamped around him, But all in good time, she thought. She'd told him she had patience. He wasn't getting away no matter what he thought.

* * *

A cloud of guilt descended on Dan after Charlie had giggled and sashayed away. Tired and drunk, he'd been seduced by a woman he wanted but couldn't have. Everything he'd suppressed for years was bubbling after Charlie had bulldozed through his weakened defenses. He was angry with himself for how far he'd let her capture his emotions. He stood against the post, smoking another cigarette to deaden his growing hangover.

"You bastard!" Cap askew, fists clenched, Duncan ran up the stairs at him, spitting mad. "How many women do you need to fuck, you ... you ... fucking adulterer!"

Adulterer?

Duncan sneered, wild-eyed. "Mom's so right about you ... you bastard!"

Ah. Adulterer. Biblical momspeak. Get out the stones.

"Oh fuck! What do you want?" Dan snapped. "Why aren't you face down in Shira's tits?" he growled, out of patience and energy to deal with Duncan any longer.

Duncan shoved his face at Dan. "I watched you groping Charlie!"

"What are you now? A fucking pervert?"

"Fucking the Kiwi. Then Shira? Now Charlie. Do you want to fuck that up everything in my life? You're pathetic! I hate you!"

Dan grabbed hold of Duncan with his both hands and shook him like an old teddy bear. "You listen to me! I've had enough of being a punch bag for you and your fucking mother!"

Duncan's eyes bulged with fear as Dan raged, smacking their foreheads together.

"You've every right to be angry but not with me! Your mother fucked it up! It cost you and Kathleen. You, in particular! I held that marriage together as long as I could for your sake. Your sake, you hear me? Not mine! How could I leave you with your idiot mother? You've never heard me say this but she became a vicious, vengeful, paranoid bitch! She's a fucking psycho I never wanted to see again! And here she fucking well is!"

Duncan shook himself loose, eyes blazing, shocked by Dan's tsunami of anger. "Mom told me all about you being a drug addict and fucking other women," he retorted, waving a fist. "She wasn't good enough for you?"

"Total paranoid bullshit! You prefer a crazy Bible thumper who fucks other women?"

"What?" Duncan dropped his fist as though it didn't belong to him.

Dan barreled on with the floodgates wide open. "I wasn't perfect but never, ever say I abandoned you! My father did that and I would never do it to you! I know what it feels like. It feels like shit!" Dan pushed Duncan away down the stairs but he came back at him like a rabid dog.

"You beat her up! I should beat the shit out of you!" He clenched a fist again.

Dan grabbed him by his t-shirt. "Punch me and I'll knock your fucking head off!" He shook him so hard his cap flew off. "I punched her when I lost control! I got to regret that, didn't I?"

"Why did you do that?" Duncan spat back.

Dan, angry enough, frustrated enough and drunk enough, yelled at him, "*Because you're not my fucking son!*"

* * *

Karen and Dan lay on the twin beds stuffed into the small room, with a picture of Mahatma Gandhi hanging lopsided from a nail, two standard lamps with dried-out, yellowed and holed plastic shades stuck in baby elephants' feet and no air conditioner. They'd have gladly traded the wrinkled feet for an air-conditioner any day. Karen left him alone to pop pills, drink several cans of lager, sip whiskey, smoke cigarettes and generally wipe himself out. He lay back blowing smoke at the cracked ceiling that swam across his vision.

What had he done? Charlie. Oh Jesus, what had he done? But the thrill of her deep kiss and twirling her nipples in his fingers remained—and the guilt. He drank more beer. Guilt? His angry explosion at Duncan reverberated over his concerns about Charlie. That had ended any hope of reconciliation with him. Nadia wasn't going to have to put in any effort at all. Dan had done it for her. He drank even more beer.

Dan felt no shock about Nadia and Kanta—and it wasn't the booze. She'd returned to the free love of her upbringing and in Nadia's mind it was not just for heterosexuals. As long as she was happy, he didn't give damn. He just wished she were far away with her new love, munching canapés and drinking champagne on a motor yacht in Mumbai harbor.

Karen came over and sat down next to him on the bed. "How are your hands?" she asked lifting one.

"Great. I can't feel them."

Karen carefully unwrapped the bandages on both his hands and gently moved his bruised knuckles. "You'll live to fight another day, Clark Kent," she concluded.

"Thanks, Lois." He wiggled his fingers. "But fighting's off my agenda."

"Sure it is. Until Charlie gets into trouble again," she said wryly. "Now, would you like me to tell you a bedtime story to cheer you up, sweetie?" she asked.

"Not really."

She ignored him. "I was sent to prison for killing my husband."

Dan rolled his head at her. "Should I sleep with one eye open?"

"I'd suggest both, mate."

"They didn't hang you?"

"Whacker. Larry was a real pain at times but I loved the mullet. We had some good times."

Dan slid one of her loose sleeves up an arm and ran a finger over her old scar tissue hidden in the tattoos. "Anything to do with this?"

"Very observant." She pulled the sleeve back down. "Larry and I dealt drugs. We thought we were too smart to get hooked on our own product."

"How long in prison?"

"Seven years. I was put in Max Security so early on I had to learn to take care of myself. I bulked up and word got around I was a mean bitch with a shiv after I'd had a few scraps." She pulled down the neck of her loose nightshirt to show an impressive deltoid shoulder muscle. "See this?" A crudely etched dagger with "BiChis" below it had been poked in smudged, black ink into her skin.

"Jailhouse tattoo?"

"The dyke gang spelled it that way. Thought it was cute. Bloody illiterates. But they kept me alive—in return for a few favors," she added pointedly.

"The research?"

"Write what you know." She drained her can and opened another. "There was plenty of dope available in prison but I cleaned myself up. Nine years now and damn proud of it."

"I was five years clean of booze and proud of it too until this morning." Bleary-eyed, he waved his bottle at her and gave her a sloppy grin. "And now I'm pissed again. Five years down the drain and proud of it! Cheers!" he said, mocking himself. He drained the bottle and studied the empty. "It's like I've never been away. Pass me another, will you?"

Karen fumbled a can open for him and took a drink herself. "What do you think of Nadia's friend?"

Dan twirled his cigarette in his fingers for a moment then shrugged. "I dunno. Jockey?"

"And I'm a ballet dancer. I think she's a used lemon. Seen a lot of them." She raised an eyebrow. "Both of them in fact. The big one's a real bull dyke. Your Nadia looks like she's the wife." She held his half-closed eyes. "She's become a lesbian?"

"She was a sexual chameleon when I married her and it was part of her erotic charisma for a young kid," he said as he slumped against Karen. She put her big arm around him and held him up. "Doukhobors accept everyone as equal children of God so it's no surprise to find her with a woman now." He shrugged. "We were good together for a long time once she'd broken away from the community and her family in particular. Two growing kids and the usual trappings of the upper middle class: houses, cars, private schools and expensive holidays. We had ups and downs like all marriages but something happened in her mid-thirties when she became paranoid and suspicious of everything I did. She was convinced I was cheating on her and plotting to take her children away. She became dissatisfied with the materialistic life she'd wanted through marrying me and slowly regressed to her religious childhood. She wanted to take the kids back to the Doukhobor community to restart her life and, of course, I wouldn't let her." His chin sank onto his chest. Talking about Nadia had sucked the last remaining energy out of him. He took a big gulp of his beer as though it might replenish it.

She hugged him closer and held one of his hands in hers as though she could transfer some of her strength. "So all hell broke out?"

"How many marriages end, unfortunately. Violently when passions are unleashed." He had a sudden thought. "I don't believe you killed your husband. I don't see it in you."

"Thanks for saying that, sweetie. I didn't but the cops took the opportunity to kill two birds with one murder. All circumstantial bullshit but I was sent to prison anyway. He was mutilated. Shot in the back of the head. Dumped in the harbor."

"Auckland harbor?"

"Fremantle."

Letting that sink in for a moment, he drew on his cigarette and exhaled a curl of smoke at the faded yellow ceiling. He thanked his high-school geography teacher for those maps of Australia he'd filled in with stripes and solid colorings for the states and geographical sites and the names of the major cities.

"Is that why you're planning to kill Bob Stewart with an overdose of heroin?"

March 31st

THEY LEFT JAIPUR early before the heat gathered and headed along the flat road to the red-stone palaces at Fatehpur Sikri, the city Akbar the Great had built as a capital for his Moghul Empire and then abandoned when the place had run out of water after only a few years. Akbar hadn't been a great plumber.

Charlie smiled at him like she'd just had a proposal for a wedding with flowers and hash in Kathmandu as she climbed into the bus. When she sauntered down the aisle, her long body in a loose, cream blouse and white Bermuda shorts, with a mass of red hair and a beautiful face only slightly bruised, no longer swollen, he wondered how long could he resist a powerful and dangerous physical yearning to make love to her. He told himself yet again he shouldn't be there and should have left the tour after the thug's attack in Jodhpur. Out of sight, out of mind should have been his mantra. He was now enjoying Charlie too much as they got to know more about each other. She made him mad enough to fall in love again. Mad enough to risk his life for her. Duncan reached out to grab her arm and pull her down next to him. He gave Dan the kind of sly look that set off fights between Italian families. Charlie glanced and shrugged at Dan as she sat down with him.

Nadia and Kanta ensconced themselves with Loki at the front of the bus. Dan ignored any attempt from Nadia to make eye contact. Almost twenty years had been enough of that. He avoided Bill too as Karen rested contentedly under his arm again.

For far too long, Charlie sat deep in conversation with a stone-faced Duncan, her face gradually darkening as she flashed Dan occasional hard glances. Duncan was telling tales and he guessed what they were. After the high of last night, he could see the low on the way. He drank from his water bottle and savored a mouthful of Royal Stag to help dampen a pounding hangover.

The minibus hauled to a stop among other cars and tourist buses randomly parked in a gravel area in front of a flat-roofed, green-painted, wooden ticket office for Akbar's palaces. After the cool of the minibus, they stepped into dry air that hit them with a burning disregard for Caucasian skins. Dan's straw hat continued its slow browning desiccation on the top of his sweating scalp. He squinted through his sunglasses as Charlie startled Karen, Gilly and Mark by pushing them to one side in a rush toward him. She squared up to him, hands on hips, face on fire.

"My God! You went to prison for four years for beating up your wife and putting her in hospital for months? You didn't think that was worth telling me?"

Her verbal assault rocked him. It was Nadia all over again. The kitchen scene haunted him. He was drunk again. Fighting over how to deal with another eruption in Duncan's teenage rebellion. Dan had chased him around the house and threatened to kick him out if he talked to him like that again. Nadia wanted to smother him with unconditional love.

"Get out of this fucking house!" Nadia screamed. A cup crashed against the wall near his head.

"Leave the kids with a bitch like you?" Dan shouted back and threw his glass of vodka at her. It missed and smashed the window.

He glanced sharply at a smirking Duncan. Bloody karma. He lowered his voice and spoke to Charlie as evenly as possible: "Listen, it was—"

Nadia threw a bread knife at him across the kitchen and it luckily hit him handle first. "Why should you care, you bastard?" Nadia spat at him. "Duncan's not yours anyway!"

"Did you, damn it?" Charlie demanded. "*Jesus.* I don't know you after all. You were struck off the medical list too? You're not a doctor!"

"Not mine?" It staggered him. His anger boiled over at Nadia's vicious laugh.

"You want to hear my side?"

Charlie wasn't listening. "How could you tell Duncan he wasn't your son? Do you know how much that hurt him?"

"Sucker!" screamed Nadia and threw a dinner plate.

Charlie came at him again. "What else have you lied about?"

He leaned into Charlie so only she could hear him. "I'm a liar?" he hissed. "Tell Duncan about the teacher you screwed and killed if you want."

Her face collapsed in shock, as pale as though she'd slashed a wrist.

Nadia reached for a cast-iron frying pan. He leaped at her before she had a chance to brain him and hit her with an uppercut that lifted her off her feet and threw her back against the edge of the kitchen counter. She thumped onto the tiled floor like a shapeless sack of spuds and didn't move. Blood trickled out an ear.

"You bastard! You're a lying scumbag like all the rest!" Charlie slapped him, sending his sunglasses flying.

* * *

Inside the grounds, Dan let it all out: he spat blood at Charlie and Duncan—and at himself for his spiteful riposte that had crushed Charlie. He angrily rubbed his face, now stinging again after her slap on the same cheek struck by Duncan and Nadia. Despite the dry air searing his throat, he lit a cigarette and tried to burn off his frustration by striding around the perimeter of the football field-sized courtyard and its low red-stone buildings. He sweated in rivers under his straw fedora, his shirt sticking to him as he roasted in the blazing sunshine. He spotted the pink and white blob of Cruella under a parasol dawdling with Nadia and Kanta. Charlie, Duncan and a few others of the group stood nearby, waiting for Loki to produce their guide. Shira fanned herself as she tottered on her stilettos. He drained the Royal Stag in one big glug. *Fuck it all!* He headed straight toward Shira with only one thing on his mind.

A one-legged guide in aviator sunglasses and on two crutches tapped up to them. Dressed in a flowing white robe with a hood covering a thin frame, he gave an introductory chat in fairly understandable Hinglish in the slow monotone of one he'd given a thousand or more times. There had been nothing new to tell visitors since 1573 anyway. Dan didn't listen to a word. He just had eyes for Shira, red-faced, her blouse glued to her in dark patches. He stayed close to her as they strolled through Akbar's red-stone palaces and around shallow, warm pools of greenish water reflecting the brilliant sunshine. The guide pointed out various features of the low-level palaces and living quarters for servants as the group wandered back and forth across the stone-paved courtyard in and out of the buildings. When they ended up in Akbar's bedroom, an enormous slab suitable for a dozen occupants raised high on stone pillars into the air above a cooling pool, Shira eyed him as she drifted to the rear of the group.

"Mother's told me to stay away from you," she told him, chewing on her favorite thumb.

"I don't think that's a good idea. I've got to like you."

"Goody! I knew you'd be my friend."

"What do you think of this place? Romantic, isn't it?" he said guiding the conversation. "The emperor had three queens. Must have got laid a lot, don't you think?"

She giggled. "Why three?"

"Each a different religion. It kept it cool with the locals. Each queen had her own palace," he explained. "That one," he said, pointing to a flat-roofed, dark-brown, stone building the size of a tennis court, "is the biggest and it went to the Hindu queen, even though Akbar was Muslim. The smallest one was for the Christian queen from Portuguese Goa." Dan pointed to the small palace with the peaked roof that resembled a church of only a few rooms. "Let's have a look inside."

Dan took Shira's hand and led her into what must have been the chapel. The room still had a large crucifix on a wall and a stone altar that resembled a large fridge on its side. Ancient dust motes floated in the hot, dead air. A shaft of intensely bright light streamed in the only window opening high above them onto the altar.

She giggled again as he held her waist and helped her up onto the thick altar slab. "What did you bring me in here for?" she asked, fingers in her mouth.

He held her broad hips, sliding between her knees. "A bit of romance?"

"Mother says we're not to do that anymore. But since you're my friend, it'll be OK."

"I won't tell her if you don't."

"Oh goody!" She put her arms around his neck, squirming on the slab. Shira giggled as he tore at the buttons on her blouse to reveal the overloaded red lace bra. "Do you like them?"

"You better believe it." He ripped up the bra and her breasts tumbled out like monster eggs from a golden goose. My God! He cupped them in his sweaty palms, in awe of pink areolas the size of small fried eggs before sucking ravenously on the swelling nipples as Shira squirmed and gasped at his ferocity. Plunging his face deep into a cleavage moist with American Beauty roses, he licked every inch of skin of its salty perspiration as he swam in the heat of her magnificent, fake breasts. His pulse thudded. His head pounded.

Have you learned nothing? Do you need such an empty craving? You're abusing her and hurting yourself.

He jerked his hot face from her cleavage's womb-like embrace.

"What's wrong?" she asked, confused gold-brown eyes meeting his and he bizarrely noted she wore contacts.

What was he doing? She was such damaged goods, an abused child who didn't know who the hell she was. She was mentally ill and on medication and here he was groping her, exploiting her, for a few minutes of ephemeral lust.

"Let's have sex instead!" Shira exclaimed, squirming her skirt to her waist and sliding a red thong down her thighs. He caught sight of a strip of black pubic hair.

He grabbed her wrists. "Don't!" he snapped.

"I'll hold my breath until you do!" Shira crossed her arms under her breasts, took a deep breath and puffed out her pink cheeks.

He shook her hard by the shoulders until she blew out and gasped. "Don't do that!" he scolded. "Stop acting like a child!"

"Oh!" Shira covered her face with her hands, shoulders bobbing in great heaves as she wailed, "You ... don't ... like me!"

It made him feel sicker. He pulled her bra down and covered her breasts with a blouse that needed a couple of new buttons. She needed a lot of help and he wanted to help her get better. It was what he did—or was meant to do.

Her wet face looked yearningly into his. "You ... don't ... want me! No ... one ... does!" she cried, shuddering with sobs. Her face collapsed into her hands. Tears flowed in streams down her pink cheeks. "Aren't ... you ... my ... friend?" She fell hard into him when he reached for her shuddering shoulders.

His throat froze at the human wreckage before him. His own anger rose as he held her shoulders wracked with sobs. Her mother was an evil monster to have created such a tortured soul—a psyche without its own identity, a psyche trying to live in two worlds.

"Nothing could be further from the truth," he told her softly. "You're a lovely woman," he told her with a kiss on her forehead in a kind of personal baptism. "Never let anyone tell you otherwise. If you ever need someone to talk to, for any reason, I'm here to help you. I want to be your real friend."

"Men ... haven't been nice to me," Shira sniffed. She raised her wet face into his. "But I like you. You're nice. You do care about me, don't you?" She kissed him lightly on the cheek.

"For as long as you need me," he said stroking her hair. "C'mon, let's get you dressed." Thong up and skirt down, he removed her thumb out of her mouth. "Don't do that. No thumbsucking around me. You can be the real Shira for me. You don't have to be a child." She blinked at him. "I won't treat you like your mother. Would you like that?" She nodded slowly, lips tight together. "And for Duncan? He's your friend too, isn't he?"

She smiled angelically. "He is."

"Does he treat you like a child?"

She shook her head.

"Good." He held her close again. "Duncan and I will never harm you like other men," he vowed. "Everything's going to be fine. We will take care of you. I know it's hard after all you've been through but will you trust us?"

Her return smile said "yes" and he saw the contacts were brown with gold flecks. Black pubic hair? Her red hair was naturally dark at the roots too. He checked the label on her bra: Howard Hughes was in New Delhi not New York and working for Adorable Me Lingerie. Shira had bought the red underwear to copy Charlie. He looked at the beautiful face resting on his shoulder. It was the best face money could buy—Charlie's but to perfection. Add a show-stopping pair of fake breasts and she was a sexual bombshell. A creation of Cruella's laboratory, there was nothing real physically or mentally about Shira.

Agra

The group arrived at its brown-brick Indian hotel near downtown Agra about nine. The narrow, three-story building with small wrought-iron balconies stood tilting toward Delhi near a market bustling with buyers and sellers and the spicy smells of roadside food stalls that made their stomachs gurgle. A crowded dip in the hotel pool barely bigger than a large hot tub after the long day on the road was a blessing. Simply too tired to challenge Agra looking for decent places to eat, they cooled off in virtual silence, drinking in the lukewarm water. Bill couldn't resist pawing Karen occasionally and leering when he caught Dan's eye.

Dan was delighted when he shouted: "Some bastard stole my camera!" and threw his bath towel in the air. "It was right here! I left it on the lounger under the towel!"

Karen looked around. "Not here. Perhaps someone will find it and hand it in."

"It was never lost!" Bill fumed. He stomped around the pool lifting towels and searching under loungers and chairs. No luck. It was a sour Bill who finally dried off and joined the rest of the group for the cold buffet Loki had persuaded the hotel to set up that late at night. It spoiled Bill's evening. He ate quickly before storming off in search of his camera, leaving Karen behind with Dan. Dan thought it wasn't that spoiled.

* * *

Dan slammed the grill closed and rode the rattling elevator to the third floor. He paused for a full minute of slow breathing to reign in his anger over what Cruella was doing to Shira before turning the door handle slowly and quietly. Across the bedroom, outside an open sliding glass door and a closed screen, Cruella sat on her balcony having a drink, an open bottle of Jack Daniels on the low plastic table by her side. Next to the bottle, Shira's doll lay crumpled like a knocked-out boxer.

"How are you this evening, Elaine?" he asked, snapping the screen open.

He was going to screw this bitch over big time. Charlie was gone again. It was final. It relieved him of any decision-making about her. She was just too damn complicated—falling in love with her was the last thing he or she needed. Now, he had nothing—and no one—to lose. Some good was going to come out of this.

Cruella's puffy, half-closed eyes regarded him with distaste. "Come in, loser, why don't you? Wanna celebrate my victory?"

The bottle was half full and her glass half empty. It was a good time to talk to a psychopath—she might have a drunk human trying to get out if he irritated her enough. He leaned on the stone parapet, looking out over the lights of the city. Behind him, he heard the bottle glugging into her glass. He lit an Indian cigarette, turned and blew a gray cloud of harsh smoke at her.

"Oh please, smoke if you want," she harrumphed, waving her hand at the smoke.

"Last bastion of the witless?"

She snorted and more than sipped. Dan watched most of her whiskey disappear—he could get lucky here.

"What do you want?" she asked displaying the boredom of the *noblesse* that would *oblige* if it felt in the mood.

"I want to make a better deal about leaving Charlie alone in exchange for Shira and the cash."

She blew out fiercely. "Funny man. Charlie hates you. Shove off." She dismissed him with a wave of her glass. "Want me to call hotel security?"

"Go right ahead. Want to take the risk I can't get her back?"

She emptied the rest of her glass into her maw and eyed him afresh as she leaned back to bend the plastic chair out of shape. He picked up the bottle from the table and drank from it.

He smacked his lips. "Mmm. It tastes even better than I remembered." It actually did. Bourbon had been in his top five.

"Why don't you have a drink?" she asked sarcastically.

"Thanks."

"Would you mind using a glass?"

He drank from the bottle again and topped up her glass. He'd re-run his confrontation with Charlie at the Akbar's palaces and been struck by one thing: Duncan had told her about his being struck off for drugs and assaulting his mother, telling him he wasn't his son but not that he and Nadia had divorced. Hadn't he shouted "adulterer" like he'd leaped out of the pages of the Bible? Nadia was in denial and Duncan never talked to Kathleen. He didn't know or he'd have thrown Charlie that choice piece of meat to chew on. He had to act before the window of opportunity closed. It quickly crossed his mind how Duncan must think he was screwing around with all these women while he was still married to his mother. No wonder he was pissed off and thought him such a bastard.

"I've got news for you: I'm not married," he said with his best patronizing smile.

"Yes, you—" She stopped abruptly, her rheumy eyes freezing. "But Nadia—"

Dan copied her dismissive hand wave. "We divorced years ago but she can't deal with it. She still sees us married in the eyes of her God. Nadia's nuts. Haven't you realized that? And I thought you were smart." Dan stayed resting against the rail blowing smoke. "Perhaps I'll ask Charlie to marry me right now. Or at least run off with her to the wilds of Kashmir and you could do zip about it."

"Bob and Rani would. You wouldn't get far," she said coolly.

"You're going to rely on them after what I did to Bob in Udaipur?"

Cruella took her time sipping from her glass. He could see the options running through her cold mind. "So what's your price?" she eventually asked.

"Two hundred thousand. You can afford it. It's probably in your purse."

"True but I could have you neutralized."

"Haven't we been there? You're far too smart for that with your Empire State Building IQ, aren't you? And too risky now Detective-Superintendent Kapoor is snooping around? Plus, I'm hard to get rid of." He changed direction abruptly. "Has Shira missed her medication today?"

"No, she—" Her heavy-lidded eyes batted.

Dan smiled at her while her cogs whirred again.

"Ah, my bathroom."

She was swift even when pissed. "How long have you been doping Shira? Tell me about all those bottles of pills."

"She's always been an anxious child," she explained. "I pop her a few pills now and then. They keep her calm."

My God, pop her a few pills? Dan stayed calm. "She needs the right treatment."

She suppressed a yawn. "And what treatment would that be?"

"The one for Dissociative Identity Disorder."

"Speak English."

"If you were a real doctor you'd know, wouldn't you? Multiple Personalities."

She wrinkled her nose like she'd smelled something disgusting. "I don't think so. There's only one useless Shira."

"Is that what Jewish history taught you? You have no idea what's wrong with her." He stabbed a finger at her. "You're giving her Xanax? See that on late night TV with the juicers? She needs the right drugs and a lifetime of psychotherapy after what you've done to her. You've now got two daughters. One's lapdog Shira and the other hates you."

Cruella sneered, breathing slowly in loud rasps. "What have you been smoking?"

Dan lit another Gold Flake and leaned over the parapet, looking down two stories to the pool on the left of the hotel's barb-wired wall, cars and the milling crowd in the busy street to the right. With the help of her stick, Cruella creaked herself up out of the chair with a lot of effort and unsteadily leaned on the parapet next to him, a glass in hand. On the sidewalk below, two men had a huge pile of chapattis and naans they were selling to passersby for their evening meals. He knew she wouldn't survive the fall. Neither would the guys selling the chapattis.

He turned to her. "You haven't seen her other personality, have you?"

She shrugged carelessly. "You have a twofer then, don't you?"

Her callous indifference to Shira really got to Dan. He grabbed her arm and shook it. "She's your daughter for God's sake. How can you treat her like this?" The glass slipped from her fingers and seconds later it smashed into pieces on the flagstones far below. Angry voices shouted up at them. Bourbon and chapattis were not a pairing apparently.

She twisted her ugly smile. "Take it easy. You should take a pill. You're losing it."

Dan pulled back from the parapet and thoughts of throwing her over it. He'd run out of levers. He knew appealing to her good side was like climbing Mount Everest wearing Speedos and flipflops but he gave it a go. "You need to save her not destroy her. There's a young woman in there who needs help."

A lead veil descended in her bloodshot eyes but a smile flitted on her pursing lips. "My, my, you're really sweet on Shira," she purred.

"She needs taking care of," Dan insisted. "But you punished her again, didn't you?"

Cruella snapped the doll off the table and threw it over the balcony rail. A few seconds later, it landed with a *plop* in the pool. "Stupid little cow," she muttered. "She gets easily stressed out. I need to see her." The words cascaded like coins from a chiming and flashing video slot machine. He was heading for the jackpot as long as the wheels remained spinning. She sat down again and poured herself another glass of whiskey.

What would harpoon her bloated ego? Dan poured scorn on her. "Isn't Shira meant to be *you* with a super brain molded for success?" he snarled stabbing a finger into her shoulder. Her mean mouth whitened across her teeth. He'd pressed on a very sensitive nerve. He pressed again. "Shira's always been your lab rat, hasn't she? But she turned out useless except for marrying alter kockers to make lots of bucks?"

"And hasn't she done well? Those boobs were the icing on the cake. Did you notice them?"

"She's become a great meal ticket for you."

"And it's going to get much better." She tried an enigmatic smile that slid down her chin.

"Better?" asked Dan, hoping her mental safe stayed open for an audit.

"Stay tuned," she bragged. "Much, much better."

He sharpened the barb and shoved it home. "You're *useless* and you *failed!*" He kept pulling the lever. "She turned out *stupid!* A hundred stories short of your Empire State Building IQ! The heir to the throne's a dope? As dumb as a bag of potting soil!"

Cruella's nostrils flared. "She's not stupid! And you'll find out how smart we are when she—!" She slammed her mouth shut.

"Becomes what? First female president? Don't make me laugh!" he mocked.

Come on! Flashing lights! Ringing bells. Hit the jackpot! But Cruella rapidly cooled as she collected herself. She went as silent as a plant and stared at him impassively again.

"Shira needs taking care of with the right drugs until we get to Kathmandu," he told her. "She's close to cracking up. Don't you care?"

"You want to take care of your girlfriend? How sweet. Do it."

She held her head up with a hand, her elbow on the table. A fog rolled in to cloud her eyes. He'd lost her. He took out his wallet, tore off a check and nudged her. "My bank account. Two hundred thousand tomorrow."

Her heavy lids fluttered open and toasted him by wobbling the almost empty bottle into the air. "Don't ... cross me," she warned.

Dan prised the bottle from her fingers and drank the last dregs.

* * *

Dan drank alone in the shallow end of the light-dappled pool after Karen had finished a beer and a cooling swim and gone off to bed with Bill. He gazed up at a clear, black sky with its twinkling carpet of stars, feeling dry, scented air drifting in from Central Asia, and thought there were worse things than relaxing in warm water, smoking a tangy cigarette and drinking a cold beer. He just wanted to get to Kathmandu and then on to Namche to get the trip over with. Money from Cruella would be a bonus he could put to good use but it would make no difference. He was a lusting fool for getting involved with

Shira and a love fool with Charlie. But now that he had, he'd help them as best he could while he could.

A figure moved unsteadily out of the glare of the hotel lights and stopped above him at the side of the pool. Shira stumbled as she pulled her t-shirt over her head and removed her pants. Naked, she slid into the water beside him like a silver seal. When she swayed drunkenly into him, he smelled vodka and beer—and trouble. Dan tensed and considered leaving the pool quickly might be a good idea but instead he stiffened his resolve and took a deep breath.

"Is that you, Carla?" he asked quietly, sliding an arm around her waist to hold her up. Close up she looked beyond awful—a face painted by Munch when he wasn't feeling very well. He felt no lust, just empathy for a mind in turmoil.

She wrested the bottle out of his hand and chugged it. "That bitch Elaine saw you together at the palaces and punished her!" Fierce eyes burned into his. The hairs on the nape of his neck paid attention.

"She took her doll away?"

"Forever! We've been together all our lives! Fucking cunt!"

"Shira tells you all her secrets, doesn't she?"

"She talks to me every night." She tapped her bottle on his chest. "Drink with me," she ordered.

Dan thought he'd better. He unscrewed another and took a big pull.

Her bleary eyes narrowed at him. "Why didn't you fuck her at the palace? She wanted you to."

"I had a headache."

Carla laughed harshly. "Congratulations! You're the first man to turn down fucking Shira," she told him, with a sharp edge that could cut his throat. "They've treated her like a fucking pin cushion and thrown her away."

"Isn't that Elaine's fault?"

"I'll kill that bitch one day for what she's done to Shira." She glowered into the rippling water.

Carla's aura of violence had him ready to defend himself. She was Shira's dark side, the anger and frustration she wasn't allowed to express and had forced underground where it had grown and grown to its current critical mass. She was nitroglycerin on a top shelf and it only took a simple shake for her to blow up. The priest and a lover had discovered that.

"You killed a man to protect Shira, didn't you?" he asked quietly. He knew Shira would have thrown her toys at him.

"He was a brute who deserved it," she mumbled. "The perverted bastard! What he wanted to do to Shira! The next one better watch out." She raised her dull eyes to Dan. "So be careful with her," she warned and drank more beer before she rambled on. "No man has ever cared for her but her father. And he wasn't around enough. There's only been that bitch of a mother. And that duplicitous teacher."

"The one Charlie killed in the motel?"

"Charlie?" Her eyes popped as she laughed. "Shira had been competing with Charlie as usual. I'd fucked the teacher for her—he seemed a good guy and really wanted her—but she was distraught when Charlie ran off with him. Shira and Elaine tracked them to a motel in Vegas. I got my revenge for what he'd done to her. Her mother covered it all up claiming the teacher had abducted Charlie and she'd killed him with his own gun in self-defense. She got off. No trouble."

"Charlie took the rap?"

"Even though I shot her when she tried to protect him and got in the way."

Charlie's spleen. "That was you? Not an attempt on her father's life?"

"You believed that crap?" She chortled and took another slug of beer. "After killing another man, even the scumbag lawyers would have had trouble keeping Shira out of prison or the loony bin for sure. Charlie couldn't let that happen to her no matter how much she hated her. So she said she'd killed the teacher with his own gun trying to escape and bingo Shira was available for her mother to find another rich guy. She doesn't remember a thing, of course."

"I'm sure Elaine has done a lot. Right?" he asked.

Carla snorted loudly. "For one, she killed Charlie's mother and father."

Dan's heart suffered a misstep. "In the car accident?"

"Accident? Ha!" She drained her bottle. "Got 'nother?"

Dan quickly provided another Kingfisher. Talking to alter egos required a strong stomach and a stronger backbone. He reached back into the dark and pulled out a soggy doll from where he'd slid it. "Elaine threw her in the pool. I gave her CPR and voilà!"

Carla's harsh face melted into a tearful smile. She dropped the bottle in the pool and grabbed the teddy with both hands. "Shira will be so happy!" She laughed wearily, crushing the teddy to her chest. Her narrowed eyes studied Dan. "You're different. You haven't taken advantage of Shira. She likes you and I like you too. I'm glad I haven't had to shoot you for abusing her."

"That goes for both of us." Dan liked her less murderous mood.

"I've ... seen a lot, believe me." She slipped an arm around his waist and sagged into him. "I can trust you, can't I?"

"Yes. I want to help Shira get better." He handed her another bottle to keep her well lubricated.

"Want to know how I saw Charlie's ... mother and father die?" she asked.

"You were there?"

"In the car ... with Shira and her mother. They ... drove the other car off the road. She was told never to tell anyone about the ... accident. Ever. Or she'd go straight to hell and her mother would send her there."

Dan felt shocked into sobriety. "Elaine was driving?"

Carla breathed deeply several times. Dan crossed his fingers. *Don't pass out!* Dan chucked her under the chin and she wobbled eyes at him. "Who was driving?" he repeated.

"Bob."

Dan's mind whirled. His stomach twisted with shock and excitement. Bob Stewart had murdered Charlie's parents? He'd been working for Cruella as well as Hamlish? What had she to gain from her ex's death? Had Hamlish made an agreement with her to kill off Charlie's dad and share the benefits of him winning the Senate race—and going on to the presidency?

Carla's bleary eyes blazed. "Why don't we get ... the bitch together?"

April 1st

"YOU MUST NOT be of missing this incredible most amazing event!" Loki had exclaimed, wanting them on the bus at five in the morning to get out to the Taj Mahal for the sunrise spectacle.

The only good thing about this was it was dark at five so it didn't matter Dan's eyeballs weren't working. He couldn't face breakfast. The thought of more fried eggs had his stomach playing the concertina so he took a slug of whiskey and ignited a Classic, drawing the smoke in deeply until he felt better. Cigarettes always helped his headaches. Lung cancer or headaches. He chose the pain relief and liked blowing smoke rings and fiddling with the things in his agitated hands. He had no worries about cancer. Cigarettes were his worry beads.

Arriving shortly after dawn before the bulk of the tourists, the immaculate Taj Mahal rose before them, glittering pink and white, changing its colors in the dawn sunlight as the sun rose and brightened above the tall trees. The reflecting pools beyond the green lawns and rows of flowerbeds that stretched ahead invited them to wear out their cameras. Loki climbed onto a marble bench and waved an arm toward the glittering mausoleum.

"Ladies and gentlemen," they chorused before he had a chance to speak and broke up laughing.

Loki laughed too. "Well, there it is. Twenty years to build. It was Shah Jahan's celebration of his dead wife."

Dan thought he knew how the shah might have felt.

"Is the Taj better than the Jain temple at Ranakpur?" asked Loki.

There was a mumble of "yes's" and "no's." Dan liked Ranakpur better: the Taj was clinically beautiful while the Jain temple was exuberant.

"Did you know a black mahal was to have been built across the river for the Shah himself?" Loki asked.

Dan did. The piggy bank was empty and one of his sons having checked where his inheritance was going gave dad the push. Sons. Dan saw Duncan leave Shira with Charlie by a pool and walk off with his camera toward the arch of the massive entranceway of the red sandstone mosque to the west of the Taj. He didn't look happy, walking head down, kicking at leaves and scuffing the gravel. Dan wanted to rush over and hug him but held back. He had avoided Duncan all morning, feeling awful about what he'd blurted out and how hurtful he had been. There was nothing like alcohol for unlocking demons from the dungeons of his anger. Hadn't it happened with Nadia? It was an opportunity to bite the bullet and apologize to a kid he loved and would never know it unless he told him. It shouldn't matter if he wasn't his biological child. He bit the bullet and zigzagged toward Duncan around the lawns and pools and newly arriving cohorts of camera-clicking tourists.

"Duncan," Dan called in a friendly voice deliberately tinged with remorse.

Duncan looked up sharply, his face hardening as he approached. He flinched as Dan tried to put his arm around his shoulders.

"I'm so sorry," Dan said. "I was angry and—"

Duncan moved quickly. His punch to the side of Dan's face wasn't particularly hard but it caught him unawares. The next thing Dan knew, he was falling backward. *Thud.* The back of his head hit the stone flagstones.

Duncan bent over him and Dan saw several twisted faces and heard a garbled "Now you know how Mom felt! Leave me alone!"

Dan lay there on the cool floor. He'd deserved it. Perversely, he felt better—except for the sore cheek and stunned sensation—blinking up at the waving, red-brick ceiling as it began to fuse into a single image. Punched by Duncan. It was a son-like-father moment he'd never imagined possible. But hadn't he threatened to punch Duncan when he'd been out of control? Dan heard a voice: Karen loomed over him.

"Dan, Dan! What happened?"

She kneeled down and gently lifted his head. Blood on her fingers. He groaned like a KO'd boxer as she sat him up. "Did you faint again?"

Karen had given him an out. "Uh-huh," he mumbled rubbing the back of his head and his face.

She held him around the shoulders. ""What's wrong with you, sweetie?"

He was in no mood for mothering. "I'm a fuck up."

"That goes without saying. But what's medically wrong with you?"

"I told you. African parasite."

"Oh, that African parasite?" she asked with heavy skepticism. "You mean the HIV, don't you? Isn't that what the AZT in your med kit's for?"

Dan flashed his annoyance. "Who said you could do that?"

"Fair's fair. Who looked through my luggage?"

Dan grunted.

"Like some heroin for your pain?" she asked sweetly.

Dan gave her a sour look.

"I'd like to know about the AZT since I have your blood on me. Am I going to get AIDS?" Karen asked with exaggerated patience.

* * *

Karen soaked her hankie in the cool but dubiously greenish water of a reflecting pool and gently pressed it on the back of his head then on his cheek.

"There, that's better." Karen dabbed his face dry. "You'll have a bit of a shiner."

"And I won't be able to get my hat on." Dan didn't feel sick so that was a good sign. No concussion from playing dice with his brain—yet. He washed down a few pills to dull the headache and the stinging cheekbone.

"Gonna share?" asked Karen. She took a swig from his water bottle. "Scotch? Getting pissed at the Taj Mahal is on your bucket list?"

"It is now."

"I'll get pissed anywhere." She took another swallow.

He held the cool hankie on his cheek as he looked around somewhere that had been on his bucket list since he could read. The Taj Mahal. One of the true Wonders of the World. The stuff he'd thought about ever since he could read his grandparents' encyclopedias. He'd missed the Library of Alexandria by two thousand years but he wasn't going to miss this one, concussed or not.

Watching the colors of the Taj Mahal's marble dome, the four corner towers reaching for the sky and the high walls change from shades of pink to white as the sun rose was a dream come true. Walking inside the extravagant memorial to a man's wife, the exterior decorations of calligraphy and painted geometric forms and the interior lapidary of precious and semi-precious stones added that extra bit of romance to fabulous architecture. The great moment was dulled by his self-loathing, the aches from his various injuries and the fact that if he did have a concussion he wouldn't remember he'd been there. And he was a little drunk.

Without Karen to support him, he'd never have made it inside and outside the mahal. They squeezed through the crowds and she sat him down at the edge of a reflecting pool to finish the Scotch. She lit a cigarette for him. Dan had been counting cigarettes but now he couldn't remember.

"Surprised to see me?" rasped a familiar voice.

Dan looked up slowly as he angrily rubbed the lump on the back of his head. A prune head on a coat stand covered with an ill-fitting khaki trouser suit added to his annoyance.

"Thought I'd make it a family affair." Nadia sniffed the air. "Are you drunk again?"

"Why not? You're ugly again," he retorted ungraciously before he caught himself.

"Asshole." Nadia looked at Karen like she'd spotted a pile of cow dung. "What's *this*?"

Karen tensed by his side. Dan spoke deliberately, slowly. "Karen … this is Nadia."

Karen's stare at Nadia grabbed her by the throat. "Is this the bitch who won't leave you alone?"

"And never will!" barked Nadia.

"Gotta real fruit loop here," mocked Karen exchanging eye rolls with Dan. "Aren't you going to introduce your husband?" she asked, nodding toward the tower of muscle in a hideous purple Adidas tracksuit on the other side of the pool.

"Husband?"

"Where'd you meet the big fellah? Lurch?"

Nadia's wrinkled forehead became an angry sheet of corrugated iron. "Don't call her that! Her name is Kanta and God joined us together at the ashram!"

"Sure it wasn't the zoo?"

Dan's spontaneous laugh triggered even greater fury in Nadia. "Fatty doesn't look your type," she sneered, eyeing Karen up and down with distaste.

Karen got to her feet as ominously as Godzilla rising from the deep. "Why don't you beat it, Skeletor?" she growled.

Nadia took a step back toward the pool thinking better of taking on Karen and laughed at Dan. "I enjoyed Duncan punching you. Now you know how I felt, you shit."

Karen looked sharply at Dan. "Duncan punched you?"

"You told him you weren't his father?" Nadia hissed with glee. "That really ticked him off. Pity it's not true! But it got you to punch me, didn't it? I didn't expect to be almost killed but it got you locked up and I got the kids!"

Karen gasped. "You set him up?"

Nadia's evil chortle penetrated Dan to his rebuilt core, a life based on trying to achieve the tenets of Buddhism. He'd been duped: robbed of his kids and four years of his life. Thrust into a world of violent criminals and almost killed. Murdered someone and was now on the run. There weren't many bigger tests. He refused to let her laud it over him.

Dan stood up, keeping his hands down by his sides. "It's OK, I forgive you," he said channeling Gandhi, Buddha, Jesus and anyone who might help him avoid strangling her.

"What? She's a fucking monster!" raged Karen.

"Forgive me?" Nadia cackled. "You sad bastard!"

"Your Jesus wouldn't think so." That shut her ugly mouth for a moment. "Why did you join this trip?" he asked evenly. "Just to be insanely vindictive?"

"I'm not insane, you bastard!" Nadia slapped him on the face where Duncan had punched him.

Despite the pills and Scotch, it hurt like hell but he tried not to show it. "Careful," he warned, holding his stinging face. "You could go to prison for that."

"Wimp!" She raised her hand again at Dan.

Karen exploded forward and thrust two Popeye arms into Nadia's puny chest. Nadia left her feet, arms flailing, as she tumbled backward over the low wall onto the mirror-surfaced pool. *Splat!* Her pancake landing abruptly silenced the tourist hubbub, setting cameras clicking and security guards running. Across the rippling pool, Kanta gaped at Dan and Karen and the spluttering Nadia. When she saw Karen was fired up to put her in the pool too Kanta threw a long leg into the water and decided saving Nadia was a better move.

Karen's turn to laugh. Dan really liked his violent, non-Buddhist friend. He joined in as Kanta jerked Nadia to her feet, her wet clothes clinging to her scarecrow frame.

"I have the last laugh, you bastard," she shouted gleefully. "It's Kathleen who's not yours! I screwed you over from the beginning!"

* * *

Kapoor smoothed his hand back over his well-oiled hair, nervously fingering his straw hat as he paced in the shade of the crowded trunks and spaghetti network of surface roots of a sprawling mass of banyans. He adjusted the jacket of his cream, raw silk suit. It was of impeccable cut with a pale blue handkerchief folded neatly in its breast pocket. It fitted his slim frame like a male model in GQ. He wanted to look good for Dan but it had been a poor choice when sweat began to trickle down his back. His shirt and trousers were sticking to him like flypaper. Reluctantly, he took off his beautiful jacket and slung it over his shoulder to cool off.

In the fields around the banyans, horses galloped on the great expanses that the Victorian British had left as a legacy of their rule. Teams of men in white ignored the burning sunshine while playing cricket. It was sweltering hot and vendors selling anything cold from their carts and covered stalls were making a killing. The park was packed with families relaxing on the dry, brown grass in any shade they could find, playing children's games and enjoying assorted foods on their array of blankets.

Dan approached Kapoor along the path. A bruised cheekbone? He ran out of the shade to meet him. "What happened?"

"Duncan hit me."

Kapoor didn't ask why. Dan would tell him if he wanted. Families. "I think a dysfunctional family is any family with more than one person in it," he said quoting someone he couldn't recall.

Dan laughed and winced simultaneously. He touched the injury. "I deserved it." He rubbed his bottle of cold water across his forehead and gently over his cheek. "Good to see you too, Dipak. Let's get out of the sun."

"Let's go this way," said Kapoor, feeling the spark of his arm as he guided him toward the lake.

"So this is what's left of the gardens?"

The rusting, iron-framed greenhouse the size of two tennis courts and several times the height of an elephant was missing panes of glass and hadn't been repaired. Orchids of many colors pressed their tiny faces against the glass. Vine-like philodendrons trapped inside were making a break through openings while curious strands of ivy wondered what was inside. Palms had burst their tattered fronds through the netting of the aviary, the birds long gone. It was a botanical and zoological wasteland.

"Not enough money for upkeep?" Dan asked.

"The British liked to build such things. We Indians wonder why they bothered when India is a wonderland itself."

They walked along the gravel path by the ice cream and water sellers toward the lake and the pavilions along its shore.

"I have something about Major and Missus Drury's company that may be of interest to you," Kapoor told him. "He's employed by the Indo-American Financial Group, where his wife happens to have a position too."

"And is owned by Jeb Hamlish."

Kapoor stopped abruptly. "How did you know?"

"I'm a genius detective?" Dan caught Kapoor's droll headshake. "OK, maybe not. Hamlish is a senator. The US Senate is in Washington. Ergo, it was Hamlish who sent the Drurys to protect the Americans.

"OK. But why would Hamlish want his own bodyguards on the trip without Missus Jacobs knowing?"

"He mustn't trust her. Charlie said they dislike each other."

"Or perhaps he doesn't trust Bob Stewart. He had employed him, hadn't he?"

Kapoor remembered something about the Stewarts he wanted to mention to Dan. Since he'd dug up so much information in such a short space of time, Hosseini had now ruined his chances of ever leaving the Maharashtra police force. "What was the date of the accident that killed Miss O'Neill's parents?" he asked.

Dan thought for a moment. "I'm not sure. About Christmas two years ago."

"The Stewarts moved to Mumbai just after that. And they had plenty of cash to start up their business."

Dan rubbed his cheek, managing a small, smug smile. "No accident. Bob Stewart was driving Missus Jacobs in her car when he drove Charlie's parents off the road."

"How do you know that?" Kapoor asked incredulously.

"You wouldn't believe it if I told you."

"But you have evidence that would stand up in court?"

"Not a chance."

Kapoor shook his head despairingly. "Perhaps you won't make a detective after all."

Kapoor let Dan's news simmer for a few minutes while they strolled on toward decrepit brick pavilions with holes in their tiled roofs. The murky lake with its muddy banks hadn't been cleaned since Independence. A battered red cricket ball bounced their way pursued by a panting, gangly teenager in whites. When Dan lobbed the ball to him, he turned immediately and threw it about thirty yards straight to the wicketkeeper who smashed the wicket to pieces with a mighty "Howzat!" The umpire waved a finger at the despondent batsman stretched out on the grass.

"Great throw," shouted Dan.

The teenager turned and grinned a set of piano keys. "Thank you, sah!" then ran off to his game.

"Great game," Dan said.

"Apparently," said Kapoor. "What if Hamlish and Missus Jacobs colluded in murdering her ex and his rival?"

"Hamlish gets a shot at the White House while she gets revenge on her former husband and obvious political benefits? They may dislike each other but ambition makes strange bedfellows, does it not?"

"Stewart followed their orders and then did a bunk with a big wad of cash from them to set himself up out here. But if that's the case, why are the Stewarts still alive? Hamlish and Missus Jacobs are taking a big risk having him around."

"Mutually assured destruction?" suggested Dan. "They both could take the other down? Bob's a sharp character. He'll have insurance stashed away—"

Kapoor stopped again and held Dan's arm. "I think we should take a deep breath and think about what we are getting ourselves into. Hamlish is probably the future President of the United States and we're suggesting he ordered the murders of a political opponent and his wife."

"It's even worse than sending photos of his genitals to an underage girl," quipped Dan.

"Be serious, Dan," Kapoor said sternly, looking at him until Dan's crinkled eyes met his icy ones and cooled. "This is a Rubicon moment. We back off or we cross over into extremely dangerous territory. If Hamlish gets wind of our investigation we're as dead as the senator and his wife. Want to carry on?"

Dan's eyes reflected his. "We have no choice."

"Let's carry on then. You'd make a real policeman."

And a wonderful lover, thought Kapoor. What they could talk about as they relaxed, smoked, drank and made love. What a life they could have if ... He could never leave Nasma and his children and Dan would never come to Mumbai. Basking in the warmth of Dan's sunshine, he could see heavy black clouds gathering. If it was to be, so be it. Enjoy what they had while he could. It was a gift from Lord Ganesha to be treasured. Kapoor felt a surge of sweat that was due to more than the heat.

They entered a pavilion that was in danger of collapsing on them. A stone bench lined the space that smelled of urine. The usual colorful graffiti daubed the walls. The Hindi would be lost on Dan but the drawings needed no explanation. Kapoor lit a cigarette to mask the stench. Dan joined him.

"So what now with Bob Stewart?" asked Dan, wandering around the empty space with one hand in a pocket and the other waving his cigarette.

"The evidence is building but we must be patient. We watch and wait. We'll get that *haramzada!*" Dan smiled broadly at him, a cat that had got the cream. "And what's amusing?"

"Someone might beat us to him."

"What do you mean?"

"Karen's husband was murdered."

"I know. She went to prison."

"He was mutilated and tortured."

"Not uncommon."

"Fingers and toes removed. Cigarette burns."

Kapoor blinked.

"Dumped in a harbor."

Kapoor's eyes widened. "Please tell me Mumbai."

"Freemantle."

He frowned. "Where's that?"

"It's a port in Australia."

"Keep going."

"The port of Perth. Our Bob's home base."

"By all the gods!" exclaimed Kapoor, eyes dancing with excitement. "Any direct link to Stewart?"

"Karen has evidence of his involvement. He was her husband's drug supplier. Hubby distributed in Freemantle around the docks. He kept recordings of their meetings and taped phone calls for insurance. Never got to use it. He sampled his own product and ended up a junkie himself. Bob didn't like that. She only found the evidence when she'd got out of prison and went through their stuff that had been warehoused."

"Why didn't she take it to the police?"

"Afraid it wasn't conclusive and he'd get off and come after her." He paused. "She has her own justice in mind."

"My God. She's on the trip to kill him?"

"I can get her to hold off if we can nail the bastard before—" Dan abruptly paused.

Kapoor looked at him expectantly. "What is it?"

"I've remembered something that escaped me at the time. I heard an attacker shout something at Bob before he started shooting. *Haramda* then *desrodi* or something like them. Was it what you just called Bob? *Haramzada*? What does it mean?"

Kapoor frowned. "*Haramzada* means bastard. *Desrodi*?" He mulled it over, muttering to himself. "Yes! *Deshdrohi!* Pity you didn't mention that before. He was shouting *traitor!*"

Dan held Kapoor's shoulders and shook him with delight. "He'd double-crossed them! The kidnapping was going to fail so he silenced them. It was the bodyguard in the sidestreet with a gun!"

Kapoor rubbed his hands together. "Now, we're really getting somewhere. Hamlish was right not to trust them. It's why he sent the Koepkes then the Drurys."

"I'll bet he attempts to kidnap Charlie before Kathmandu. She's worth a lot of money to crooks like the Stewarts."

"Oh, I think the Stewarts are greedy enough. It's a once in a lifetime opportunity for them to hit the jackpot. Next time, we'll get him for attempted kidnapping even if we can't get him for any of the other murders." Kapoor's excitement of the chase bubbled in his light brown eyes. "And I've got some very good news too. Vijay Gill won't be bothering you again. He was shot dead with all his family inside a Vancouver restaurant by a rival gang."

"Shot dead? The whole lot?"

Kapoor got ready for his reaction. "Six months ago. Someone else has been trying to kill you."

"Six months ago?" Dan grasped his head in his hands. "Six months!" he repeated. "So … so … who the hell wants me dead?" He paced the pavilion, kicking dirt and dried leaves like a caged tiger looking for someone to bite. "What am I missing?"

* * *

Kapoor texted Dewan: Robert Stewart now strongly linked to the Harbor Murders and the murder of three men in the attempted kidnapping of a rich American in Pushkar. Expect him to try second kidnapping.

He left out the two murders in New York and Stewart's involvement with Jacobs and Hamlish.

Shortly after Dewan replied: Keep me informed.

A few minutes after that Hara: Good going, boss.

* * *

"Dad!" A young woman with long dark brown hair bounded across the lobby and grabbed onto Dan.

"Kathleen!" Dan hugged her so hard she couldn't breathe. He held her away from him and smiled admiringly. "What are you doing here?"

"Our bus broke down so we got delayed. I don't have long."

"How's Safeer doing? Tired out?"

"Ha! These old guys!" She paused with a grin.

He winced. Safeer was a year older than him. She eyed his cheek with concern.

"What happened to your face?"

He touched the puffy flesh and laughed it off. "Next time, I'll open the door before I go through it." He moved on quickly. "Anyway, enjoying your trip as much as I am mine?"

"It's great. Just wait until you see Varanasi. That place is absolutely amazing."

"Can't wait."

"Any interesting women on your trip?" she asked with a smile.

She has no idea!

"Not happening. Remember where I'm going?" He'd told her about Nagarkot but she didn't know the full reason.

"You don't want to go out with a big bang?" she punned badly.

He laughed. "OK, I confess. There's a Kiwi lady I'm sleeping with. We share a room and have casual, meaningless sex to pass the time."

Kathleen chuckled. "Don't get her pregnant!"

"No worries there. She's seventy-two but spritely between the sheets."

Kathleen snorted. "Oh, that was bad! Are you really having a good time? You look tired."

"Yeah, it's all good." Mentioning attempts on his life seemed too much of a downer. Saving two women from death would be shameless bragging. "Love the temples in particular. Fabulous architecture. They make a good curry and a great cup of tea here too."

She laughed. "It must be the English immigrants. How's it going with Duncan?"

"Badly. We had a big blowup and ... I don't think he'll ever come around to understanding my side. The list of things to say to him gets longer and longer. I can't say them properly."

"You're overthinking, Dad. Just tell him you love him and he means the world to you. Worked with me after we had one hell of a time, didn't it?"

"He's a guy. Girls are different."

"Really? Who told me it's all about being kind to one another?"

"Sounds like something brilliant Buddha and I would say."

"Maybe I can see him before I go. Do you know where he is?"

"Probably with your mother."

Her face fell. "What? She's here in Agra?"

"Here in this hotel."

"Oh, God. How did she ... Duncan must have a big mouth."

"Unless it was you."

"Funny, Dad," she said without laughing. "What's she here for?"

"Keep Duncan unhappy with me?"

"Jesus, what a bitch!" She glanced at her watch. "I'll check at the desk and see if I can find Duncan." She kissed his good cheek. "Love you, Dad. I'll come visit you in Nagarkot."

"Do that, honey. Love you."

He hugged and kissed her as if it might be the last time.

* * *

Dan found Shira in the hotel restaurant, eating banana and mango pieces out of a fruit plate, sitting next to a white floppy hat above her mother. He was struck by how she was actually eating and how she was dressed: conservatively, a buttoned-up loose, cream blouse and comfortable matching slacks that didn't emphasize her curves. Her makeup was spare, a slight amount of blush she didn't need and a pale pink lipstick instead of her usual red slash. Her hair was tied back with a red ribbon into a ponytail. Dan ordered two cups of coffee with hot milk on the side, added a big spoon of sugar to each and smoked a cigarette waiting his chance. When Shira got up to go to the restroom, he slurped the last of the coffee, stubbed out the Classic and intercepted her coming back.

"How are you today?" he asked, feeling no resistance when he took her by the hand.

"I feel good … different," she said in a strong voice. No finger sucking. Her eyes had a morning sparkle. No drugs.

He led her into the shade of the hotel portico out of the morning sunshine. He took her sunglasses out of the bag dangling over her shoulder and fitted them over her squinting eyes. He noticed her doll's glass eyes peeking at him out of the bag.

She caught his gaze. "I thought I'd lost her forever. But this morning there she was. I must have been dreaming."

"You've been sharing your feelings with her?"

"She wants me to stop being so childish and jealous of Charlie. Grow up. Just like you said."

"I'm glad you got her back to share your thoughts."

She kissed him on the cheek then rubbed off the pink smudge with her fingers. "I'm glad we're friends. Carla told me I should trust you and Duncan."

"Carla's a smart teddy." He held her arm. "I'm sorry for what happened at the palaces. I was … " He hesitated under her gaze. "It was wrong of me."

She flickered a small smile. "Don't be sorry, Dan. I liked it as much as you did. Carla told me you didn't take advantage of me when I … " She blushed.

Dan was staggered by the change in her. But he knew it would be episodic: one moment a simpering child and another an assertive adult. More a child than an adult in the beginning but the open road stretched ahead for her with a long, long way to go. "I was sorely tempted," he told her. "It's not every time I visit Indian palaces I get that offer."

"That makes me know I can trust you to help me."

Dan basked in that while they walked along the road toward the bustling city center. The Irrefutable Institute of Computers beckoned them to enter its decrepit facility for an exciting career in outsourced programming but instead they decided to have a cup of tea outside the Zorba the Buddha Veg-Restouran, a crowded one-room facility open to the street with a slowly rotating ceiling fan and a slowly rotating waiter. The all-male customers cast furtive glances at them and made asides as they took in Shira. She was as close as this place would ever get to ever having Miss World stop by for a cup of chai.

They sat on a low wooden bench at a table where they could watch the cooks inside throw oil and vegetables into steel cauldrons and churn the sizzling contents with big wooden spoons. The aroma was delicious. Dan dropped a spoonful of a brownish sugar into the strong coffee then drank from a china cup in a big, mismatched saucer. Shira sipped her tea, smiling at him.

"Charlie told me you're flying to Varanasi from here," he said.

Shira's smile disappeared. Her voice weakened. "Mother's chartered a plane. We'll—"

Dan stopped her abruptly. "Oh, screw that. Come with us. The train will be a minor nightmare but what the hell? Take photos of the bloody mice and roaches! Down at the home, surrounded by those old Jews in Florida, you'll be able to tell them about the Agra-Varanasi overnight express! Beat Disneyworld any day."

Shira played with the handle of her cup, staring into it. "But Mother will be—"

"Duncan really wants you to come with us," he said casually, pouring some hot water into his coffee to weaken it. "He told me he's really fond of you."

Her eyes lifted quickly. "Really? He did?"

"He talks about you a lot. And it's all good." He laughed to keep the mood light. "The old bull has a young rival."

"I like him too." She smiled, lowering her eyes again with a captivating blush that made him so glad he was helping her find herself.

"But your mother expects you to be spending a lot of time with me, doesn't she? Not with him."

Her blushed deepened as her voice slipped back into a child's. "Mother told me ... what she wants me to do."

He reached out to pat her hand for reassurance. "Not going to happen. I know what's been going on. I know what your mother was making you do with the alter kockers." Shira looked anywhere but at him. "And she wanted to keep me away from Charlie—she was using you as bait."

"I'm sorry," she said in a whisper. "But I *have* got to like you a lot. Can you believe that?"

"And I like you too. She'll expect reports on your ... progress, won't she?" She nodded, biting her bottom lip as her cheeks burned. "Tell her anything you want to keep her happy." He held both her hands tightly. "Anything," he repeated. "OK? Tell her the sex is world class if you want. Hell, I won't mind. I don't want you stressing yourself out and making yourself sick."

"Sick?"

"Those blackouts? It's the stress of doing things you don't want to do. It's your mind protecting itself. Stop the stress and you'll stop those episodes. Let's be pretend lovers," he suggested.

She licked her lips nervously, her cheeks cooling. "OK."

"That way you won't get pregnant either."

Her frown relaxed and she forced a faint smile.

"Duncan's a secret between us, too. Live a little. Have fun with him. He's a great guy. Be the woman you want to be. Do what Carla would do."

Was he throwing Duncan into the lion's den with someone with two personalities? Don't like one? Try the other? But how would Duncan react to being warned off Shira just as they were beginning to get along better? Not well at all. Duncan was going to have to work out his own life and walk that tightrope on his own. Dan would stand by with a net. He recalled his time with Nadia's mental instability. In the Bible, Daniel had got out of the lions' den without being mauled to death but having God on his side had been useful. Dan saw a determined expression cross her tearful face.

She squeezed his hands back and said in a firm, low voice: "Do what my Carla would do. OK."

"I want you to take these," he told her. "One a day, every morning and never miss one."

She looked at the tube of pills in his palm. "What are they?"

"They're to help with your little episodes. It'll stop the blackouts." Maybe. He shook one into her palm. An antipsychotic. "It's important for me to take care of you and get you through this," he told her. "Trust me, it's curable." Maybe. She nodded.

The clinic closed. He slid the tube into Shira's purse and gave her the most sincere expression in his arsenal. "And nothing from your mother. You're going to be fine."

She swallowed the pill with some tepid tea. "Will it make me feel weird?"

He winked. "Weirder." Within a week, she might be much better but Dan worried what might happen in the meantime, especially if she continued drinking heavily. An angry Carla could reappear at moments of emotional stress. Add booze and all hell could break loose.

"Have some fun with Duncan," he repeated, "even if you're going to get married to another alter kocker when you get back to the US."

Shira's jaw dropped and her hand went to cover it but diverted itself to rub her chin and cheek. Boy, had he hit the right spot. Marriage it was.

"Are you?" he asked.

"Another alter kocker?"

"Is he rich?"

"Um … very rich."

"What if you refused to marry him?"

She swallowed hard, Cruella's's invisible grip still firmly around her throat. "I can't do that."

"Why not talk to Carla about it?"

She nodded. "OK."

"Dan! Shira!" Karen's husky voice rose above the general hubbub.

On the other side of the road, Karen elbowed people aside, pushing through the bustling throng to wave at him. He waved back. Charlie's straw hat floated high above the crowd nearby. Kanta towered even higher, farther up the road where she was watching a snake charmer who had no trouble clearing a space for his wobbling cobras. Mark and Gilly weren't too far away from Charlie, bargaining at a stall. Mark was in top form, scowling and waving his stick to swat away a one-legged beggar with a pet black and white monkey on his shoulder doing an imitation of Long John Silver.

"My father would have loved visiting a place like this. He was so into Eastern religions and cultures," Dan told Shira, just making it up as he went to direct the conversation going toward her dead parents. "Died far too young of a stroke. How about yours?"

She looked down and took a deep breath, exhaling slowly. "He died in a car accident."

Another one? "I'm sorry. What happened?"

"He collided with another car and he went off the road and …" Her voice trembled to a halt.

"How old was he?"

"Fifty."

"That's far too young. How awful for your mother."

She shrugged. "It didn't bother her. They'd been divorced for twenty years. They'd got along OK together which was good for me."

"How about you?"

"I miss him. He was very kind to me although I didn't see him very often. Mother wouldn't let me." She sighed. "But it hurt Charlie a lot more."

"Charlie? A favorite uncle?"

"Uncle?" She blinked surprise. "You don't know, do you? Charlie and I had the same father. He died in the car crash with her mother."

Dan was struck dumb. Two tall, beautiful women. Same father. Half-sisters. Cruella's dead ex-husband and former political rival to Jeb Hamlish. Murdered by Bob Stewart working for Cruella and Hamlish?

Tires screeched. A scream.

Dan jerked out of his daze to look across the street. People were running to a tuk-tuk and someone lying on the ground in the road beside it. It was Karen.

"Come on!" He grabbed Shira's hand and moved quickly, pushing through the gathering crowd. Dan grabbed anyone between him and Karen and threw them aside. Over Karen's sprawling body face down on the road, Mark and Gilly yelled Hindi at the milling crowd that probably would have made Gandhi blush.

Karen's forehead dribbled blood from a deep cut down her cheek onto her neck staining her white blouse. She was moaning, holding her right knee where her pants were ripped. The tuk-tuk driver and bystanders shoved and yammered like mad at one another.

The Sikh driver frantically babbled something Dan couldn't understand. He was beating his chest and his head alternately to save others from doing it for him. His eyes bulged with fear at the press of finger pointing, angry men around him. Dan had seen a taxi driver beaten senseless by a crowd in Kolkata and his vehicle wrecked when a boy walked into the traffic stupidly without looking and was KO'd. Indians were fond of instant justice for traffic accidents, personally delivered at the scene of the crime.

Karen was conscious and breathing OK. Her eyes were fine but wide as they looked up at Dan in shock. There didn't appear to be any neck or back injury.

Her arms and legs were in working order. Shira dropped to her knees and cradled Karen's head in her hands.

"Good job, Shira," Dan told her. She snatched a nervous smile at him.

"It's OK, Karen," he told her. "We'll get you to a hospital."

He took off his shirt and ripped off a sleeve for Shira to tie around Karen's head. Gilly wrapped the rest of his shirt tightly around the bloody gash on her exposed knee.

Dan jumped up. "Let's get her out of here. Mark!"

"Get back, you buggers!" Mark shouted alternating English and Hindi curses in his powerful foghorn baritone, waving his stick in great swooshes through the air.

The baying crowd used to ignoring excuses from drivers, reckless or not, was having none of this driver's. They wanted to lynch him by his turban to the nearest lamp post. A couple of youngsters rocked his tuk-tuk trying to turn it over. A piece of the roof was torn off and went flying over the heads in the crowd to great whoops of delight.

"Not my fault!" the driver screamed. "Save me, sah! Save me!" he yelped as men began to beat on him in anger. His turban disassembled like a roll of toilet paper. His head would be next.

"Back off, you bastards!" growled Mark, whacking a couple of troublemakers with his stick as an example to the others. They backed off sharpish from the old whirling white dervish. Gilly yelled in Hindi and thumped people with her swinging handbag.

The driver and Dan bundled Karen in the tuk-tuk trying not to do her any more damage than necessary. They roared off leaving the fevered crowd to seek another accident for entertainment.

* * *

Dan needed Mark and Bill's help to carry a dopey Karen out of the hospital into a taxi and back to their hotel room. She'd had her forehead bandaged, her knee stitched and strapped, and been shot full of painkillers and anti-inflammatories. Gilly and Shira washed and redressed her before tucking her into bed for a good rest until they had to leave for the train station in a couple of hours. The drugs had her so drowsy she had no trouble getting back to sleep instantly. Dan went out of his way to compliment Shira for her assistance and gave her a big hug and a kiss. Taking their cue so did Mark and Gilly as though she was the new Florence Nightingale. In his own gruff way, Bill gave her a hug and a "Thanks, kid. You done good." Shira's smile just managed to get out of the door.

After they'd all left, Dan took a few pills and lay on his bed to get some rest he desperately needed. He felt as much a wreck as Karen after his lack of sleep, drunkenness, hangovers and the physical assaults on his head but on the bright side, his cheek was bruised but no longer stung and its swelling had receded, his stomach felt less tender and his knuckles were working. The pills taking effect, he drifted off, his pains fading and his muscle relaxing. Kathleen, the shiny apple of his eye, floated into his dreamy mind. Nadia was trying to hurt him about Kathleen not being his child? Maybe she believed it herself but she was wasting her malice. At birth, Kathleen's blood group hadn't ruled him out as her father. He'd checked out her physical characteristics with his med school genetics a long time ago and known back then she *probably* was his biological daughter. It hadn't mattered to Dan since he'd fallen in love with his child. Duncan on the other hand ... A knock at the door.

"Who is it?" mumbled Dan.

"It's Duncan." He didn't sound angry.

"Come in." A groggy Dan sat up, yawning as he looked up at Duncan who didn't look angry either. "What's up?" he asked.

Duncan walked around the room touching things thoughtfully without looking at Dan. He looked like he needed to get something off his chest. It had to be about Nadia.

"Want a drink?" Dan asked to relax him.

"Sure."

Dan poured whiskeys for them and lit a mandatory cigarette for himself.

"How's the coffee business working out back home? The usual grind?" Dan asked to start the conversation.

Duncan sighed, still looking away. "I've heard 'em all." He drank half the glass in one go.

"I have more. Seriously, making a living?"

Duncan turned to Dan. "It's going well. Selling coffee to a few cafés. Working on my roast consistency. The café section is working well. Pays the rent," he said in staccato bursts. He stayed on his feet, his eyes wandering around the room again, not settling on anything.

"I have a name for a Jamaican coffee," offered Dan. "How about Roastafarian?"

Duncan cracked a weak smile. "I like it. You should register it."

"You can have it for free."

Duncan looked at Karen's comatose form. "Is she OK?"

"Dead to the world."

"I'll apologize to her."

"That's good of you. She's a very nice woman."

Dan let some time go by before he asked, "Have you talked to your mother much?" to open up a can of worms that had been sealed for far too long and let the truth fall where it may.

Duncan sat down on a chair, finished his whiskey, swallowed a knot and took a big breath. "I've changed my mind about her." He gave Dan a look of regret. "Kathleen talked to me … about … you and Mom … and us. Having you together again has been … strange. Especially since you don't talk to one another. We've never talked about what happened."

"It's not something men do easily, is it?"

"Kathleen told me a lot I never knew or thought about. You and Mom are divorced, for instance."

"Sort of. We never actually married legally. We had a Doukhobor marriage where God spoke through her people. She refuses to accept I could walk away from it."

Duncan looked aghast. "You mean Kathleen and I are bastards?"

"Only technically."

"Fuck."

"Want another drink?"

"Yes." Duncan rubbed his head in confusion. The glass emptied quicker than the first. "Kathleen said you didn't screw around and cause the breakup. Mom had told me that to make me hate you. When I saw you with Karen that first time, I thought you were still married and you were cheating on her with yet another woman. I'm so sorry about that."

"I recall the occasion very well." Dan smiled although it hurt. "Your mother *truly believes* I cheated on her. I didn't know what was wrong when she withdrew from me back then but I do now. You didn't notice a change in her at Kathleen's celebration in Kolkata?"

"Besides the haircut and looking like a scarecrow?" He rolled his eyes. "I dunno. She hung around with that big woman and didn't talk to me and Kathleen very much. When she did, she wanted to know if I'd talked to you. She wasn't interested in me."

"It's sad but she's mentally ill, Duncan."

"What's wrong with her?"

"She's developed paranoid schizophrenia."

Duncan's jaw slackened. "You mean ... split personality?"

"She's become delusional and hostile as well as suspicious of everyone around her."

"I'll have another drink," said Duncan. Dan poured him a suitably large amount.

They drank in silence for a while until Duncan turned his eyes up from his swirling whiskey. "Why did you beat her up so badly? *That* made me hate you the most." He watched intently for Dan's response.

"I'd been drinking too much but that wasn't it. I was already frustrated with your mother over how she'd withdrawn from me. I blew up when she told me you weren't my son."

Duncan's eyes lit up. "*She* said that? I thought you were just trying to piss me off."

"It hurt me more than you can imagine. All my frustration over how she'd changed and destroyed our family boiled over and I lashed out. She hit her head, fractured her skull and almost died. I was terribly wrong and I was punished, wasn't I?"

"She goaded you into attacking her? Why'd she do that?"

"I wouldn't let her return to her Doukhobor family with you and Kathleen. She could go but not you two. She had to get me out of the way. She got hurt far more than she intended but it certainly worked."

Duncan snorted. "Well, that didn't happen, did it? Kathleen took off and I lasted a month with them before busting out to join the merchant marine. Anything to get away from that bunch!"

Dan shook his muscular shoulder. How he'd changed from the snarly teenager he'd have given away to slave traders. The captains and crews of merchant ships weren't noted for mollycoddling spotty kids with chips on their shoulders. Except for the army, he couldn't have imagined a better pool of sharks to throw him into. "I can see it made a man of you, Duncan. I like who you've become. And how you've learned to box."

Duncan twitched a regretful smile before pain crept into his face. "Is Mom now a lesbian? There's only so much I can take of this crazy family."

Dan shrugged, keeping his voice level to play it down. "She may be bisexual. After all, you came from her," he said to lighten the mood. Duncan's distress stayed in his face. "But what does it matter if she is? She just loves another person who happens to be a woman."

It took a minute of heavy silence for Duncan to work the next question out of his tight throat. "She said you were an abusive alcoholic."

"Alcoholic, yes. Abusive? No. Did I ever harm you or Kathleen?"

Duncan shook his head. His eyes flicked over Dan's cheek and winced. "Does it hurt?"

"Only when I hear a good joke."

Duncan's rueful expression didn't crack. "I'm so sorry I did that. I've never hit anyone. I was—" Out of the blue, Duncan held his face in his hands and began sobbing.

Dan's own tears suddenly welling, he shuffled next to him, putting an arm around his shoulders. "It's OK. I understand how angry you must have been."

"I'm ... sorry too ... for making you look so bad to Charlie," he blubbed. "I ... exaggerated everything to make you into ... a monster. I hope I've made up for it. I've told her everything Kathleen told me."

"How is Charlie?" Dan asked to move away from the family trauma but he did wonder how she was,

Duncan wiped the back of a hand over his cheeks. "She's never been interested in me. And I've never been that interested in her. I was just angry with you and wanted to piss you off. All she wanted to talk about was you."

"How do you get along with Shira? She seems to like being with you."

Duncan sniffed and brightened. "She's turned out to be great. At first, I thought she wasn't quite all there but there's an extrovert side to her I'm getting to like. We've found plenty of things to talk about," he said wryly, "that don't include you."

It crossed Dan's mind it might be a good time to tell him to stay the hell out of the way of the Brit boys. Immediately be a concerned parent who picks his friends and tells him what to do? Maybe not.

"I see you're getting along with Arfa and Dazza," he said carelessly.

Duncan frowned. "Yeah, I like them. We have fun."

Far too soon. It was risky but he shelved it until another time or Duncan realized the danger himself. He came at Duncan and the Brits from a different angle. He stood up and went across to the heavy chest of drawers. He lifted up one end and used his foot to slide out the Glock he'd lodged in the space underneath it. He handed it butt-first to a wide-eyed Duncan.

"In case things get tricky," he told him.

"Tricky?" Duncan didn't take his eyes off the gun.

"What if someone tries to harm Charlie again—or Shira?" He didn't mention Cruella's threat or how he should stay well clear of drug deals.

Duncan looked up sharply. "Shira too?"

"She's not bargain basement."

Duncan nodded, hefting the Glock from one hand to the other. "Isn't Bob Stewart their bodyguard?"

"He'll need all the help he can get. Ever used one?" Duncan shook his head. "It's double-action," Dan told him. "Just pull the trigger and it'll reload for the next shot. Stick it in the back of your belt and don't shoot yourself."

"OK." Duncan carefully slid it into the small of his back.

"And there's more." Dan stuffed a wad of bills in Duncan's hand. "Go have some fun with Shira." He threw on a light jacket. "Let's get Karen on that train."

Duncan stopped Dan in the doorway. "You are my dad, aren't you?"

"Of course I am." Dan hugged him for the first time in more than five years. "I love you, Duncan. You mean the world to me."

Duncan held him tightly. "I love you too, Dad."

Guys aren't really any different from girls, are they?

April 2nd

Varanasi: The City of Lights

NEXT MORNING, LOKI gave a spiel to a bleary-eyed bunch on the bus into the city from the train station. Most of them were dozing and not listening. He stood with his microphone swaying to and fro as the bus twisted and turned and honked and roared through the late morning traffic, the heat, the noise and the dust.

"Ladies and gentlemen!" He laughed as they joined in with him. "Varanasi is the oldest city in India and the holiest city for Hindus. We believe those who die in Varanasi and have their ashes scattered on the Ganges will have their souls immediately liberated from the cycles of birth, death and reincarnation and unite with the Supreme Brahman. They will not have to be reincarnated."

"Saves a few thousand years," whispered Mark.

"Paraphrasing that famous American, Mark Twain, Varanasi is twice as old as history, tradition and legend put together," continued Loki. "Bathing in the Ganges remits sins …"

"If you survive," mumbled Mark.

"So many people arrive here for the dying … and tomorrow we'll be going for a boat ride to see the ghats … You will be truly amazed at what goes on there."

Much trepidation had surrounded the overnight train from Agra to Varanasi: tales of mice and cockroach infestations and crowded sleeper compartments had reached their ears and so with stiff upper lips, sheet sleeping bags and rolled up newspapers they'd entered the station for the night train.

George Henry

In the big warehouse of the carriage, beds were stacked crosswise three at a time above one another and on one side there were two. There must have been thirty fold-down beds of potentially snoring people. It wasn't been the Hilton so Dan's pills put him and Karen to sleep right up until the train clanked and shuddered to a halt. Now that the journey was over, the group's consensus was they'd only travel overnight on an Indian train again when the Ganges froze over and that Cruella had made a good choice in flying.

Duncan had been on the bed across from Shira and he'd spent a lot of time gazing, talking and smiling—and she'd hung on his every word, giving him that special return look, the one Dan had seen in Charlie. Young love that knew no limits, when men and women went irrational. Dan recalled that rush when everything was possible with another person and nothing else mattered. He'd never seen Duncan so happy. His first big, all-consuming love, he assumed. The scarred cynic in him knew first loves rarely ended well and with Cruella, he knew it wasn't going to end well.

"What did you think of the sleeper?" Dan asked a smiley Shira as she sat next to an equally smiley Duncan.

"It was great just to be with you all," she said in a strong voice to his delight.

* * *

They'd had snacks for the train and cobbled together a breakfast amongst themselves, but after warm showers and changes of clothes, Dan helped Karen into the hotel's restaurant for an early lunch, something not wrapped in plastic, or soggy or a cookie or a piece of chapatti or a piece of chocolate. She'd refused to listen to his advice on having several days of mental rest for her mild concussion—"Stop clucking around me like a bloody mother hen!"—but seemed to be recovering well and was as feisty as ever. He still kept an eye open for any problems that might develop.

Karen harrumphed impatiently. "I've been thinking about my accident—I think I might have been pushed."

"Are you sure? There was quite a crowd around you."

"It felt like a deliberate shove in the back."

"I was across the street. Honest."

"Whacker. Be serious." Her narrowed eyes met his. "Could it have been that bastard Bob? I've seen him giving me the stink eye."

He hadn't seen Bob or Rani but they had to have been close by Charlie. "I didn't see him near you," Dan said. "That isn't Bob's style anyway. He'd simply kill you if he knew who you were."

She mumbled a vague agreement. "Who else could it be?"

"I've narrowed it down to everyone but Bill and me."

"Arsehole." Karen thoughtfully drank more coffee, sitting with her strapped leg resting on a chair. "Cruella hates my fucking guts. Maybe she got Bob or Rani to do it just to get back at me."

"I suppose it's possible. She's a vindictive bitch."

Dan cast his mind back to the time of the accident. Kanta had been up the street. No Nadia. Mark and Gilly at the stall. Charlie's straw hat had floated above the crowd. Was she that jealous of Karen? He threw the thought away. Karen had just got caught up in the mayhem of India and not suffered too much damage. It could have been a lot worse head injury.

As Dan finished off his coffee, Hemal, one of the keen hotel porters who'd carried their bags up to their room, appeared to hand him a sealed, brown envelope with no identifying information. The slim young man in his oversized white jacket and striped trousers grinned as he received his second tip from Dan within an hour.

* * *

Dan found Charlie wandering aimlessly in the shaded loggia lined with cushioned, wicker furniture and forested with potted plants. She saw his controlled anger as he walked rapidly toward her clutching a sheet of paper.

"I'm ... I'm deeply sorry," she blurted. "I said all those awful things to you. Duncan's told me he made it all sound much worse than—"

Dan cut her short. "You're sorry? I feel terrible for what I said. But that's not what I care about—it's you."

"Me?"

"I think you should sit down. Have a cigarette." He lit her one for her and one for himself. He pulled out the police department report from Kapoor and unfolded it. "Read this," he told her.

"What is it?"

"An analysis of the pills your aunt has been giving you."

He watched her face as her eyes moved over the report. She ran her fingers over her lips. Her jaw muscles tightened. White globes of angry eyes flashed at him.

"LSD? PCP? Ecstasy?"

"And I found barbiturates to whack you out."

"They ... *make you crazy!*"

"Just need tiny amounts to make you appear that way. I should have seen it in you."

She jumped to her feet, ready to throw Cruella off the balcony in her fury before he could. He grabbed onto a trembling arm and pulled her back into her seat.

"How could she do this to me? I just can't believe it! She's been poisoning me!"

"She drugged you in Mumbai and at Ranakpur. And when you had tea at the fort where she wanted to have her pet doctor certify you and get you locked up."

"*What?*"

Dan wondered if she could get whiter without actually fainting.

"She's not the sweet aunt who came around to give you candies and chuck you under the chin. She wants to control you to get what she wants."

"I ... I ... just can't believe all this. She can be a brute but ... but she's been there for me long before my parents died."

Psychopaths and elephants never forget who pissed them off, thought Dan.

"Keep on accepting the pills but never swallow them. Flush any of her health drinks. Don't let her know you're onto her or she'll change tactics. You must stay calm."

She beat her fists on the table, not staying calm. "How can I? After she's done this to me for what? Two years?"

"Listen!" Dan grabbed her wrists. "Repeat after me, 'I must stay calm and carry on so I can nail the bitch to the highest cross we can find'. I'm going to help you do it. Are you in? Can you do that?"

Her fists clenched as her angry eyes met his. "I'll try."

"No, say *you will*. *Try* is not good enough. Your life depends on it."

"I will."

"The big question is why would she want you declared nuts and shipped off to a funny farm? But look on the bright side."

"What fucking bright side?"
"You're not a crazy loon and you'll never go to a funny farm. I like that."
She raised those golden eyes. "Really?"
Jesus. That look again.

* * *

Dan's watch read 02.34 when Kapoor called the hotel and the night clerk called him. Agitated by a thousand random thoughts, he hadn't been able to sleep. Karen and Bill. Duncan and Shira. Charlie. Charlie. Charlie. Steve and Bill. The dumb Brits. He went down to the hotel's lobby where he exchanged nods with the night clerk and onto the hotel's entrance steps where he breathed in the fetid, damp night air laced with wood smoke drifting up from the cremations on the ghats only a mile away. It was as quiet as Agra would ever get which wasn't quiet. It was another Indian city that simply didn't have time to sleep. Money needed to be made and there were plenty of people to try to make it. An Ambassador taxi with one headlight in search of a fare stopped outside the hotel when its driver saw him on the steps. He leaned a leather sandal of a face out the window and called out to him.

"Hey, *beedu,* friend! Anywhere! Three hundred rupees, sah!"
"Kolkata?"
"*Ghanta!* As if! But get in! I give you a deal!"
"The Palms Club?"
The driver made a face of digust. "Not *that* anywhere."
"Two hundred," Dan offered, "or I'll walk."
He laughed derisively. "Four hundred or walk and get yourself mugged."

The Palms Club wasn't far enough for even a two hundred-rupee fare but far enough for four hundred rupees of safety. It was a Red Light District that gave Red Light Districts a bad name: it reeked of drugs, prostitution, perversions, simmering violence and lurking disease. Neglibly dressed black and brown hookers in huge stilettos or cheap thigh-high plastic boots smoked joints paraded their goods between the pale lights of lampposts as curb crawlers cruised by eyeing them for the best picks. Some of the women wobbled their tits or lifted their short skirts as free samples to the cars' open windows. Big men wearing cheap suits and pugilistic smirks stood close enough to the girls to indicate who were the ticket sellers for the entertainment rides. The taxi driver barely came to a stop below the Palm Club's neon sign that crackled most of its cursive white script between flashing red palm trees before leaving quickly in a cloud of oily blue fumes in case he caught a bullet or the clap.

Dan descended a short flight of steps to where an African whore old enough to be his mother and with the body of a collapsed house held herself up in a semi-stoned state in the doorway. She pointed to his cigarette and mimed a blow job in return. He declined the payment, put a cigarette between her scabbed lips and lit it for her. When he slipped her a hundred-rupee note, he watched smoke blast out of her nose.

Behind the bar, a morose man with microscopes for eyes kept his hands below the counter and his eyes on Dan as he descended into the spartan room that could hold no more than twenty at five separate round, copper-topped tables and on long bench seats. The yellow wall lights shimmered on low through the fug and miasma of stale alcohol in the half-basement. The unemptied ashtrays were cemeteries of piled butts and the wooden tables not cleared of bottles and glasses. No air-conditioning but a fan rotated scratchily near the barred window to exchange the ganja that was as thick as dahl soup for the damp night air full of the day's sweet decomposition that smelled like cabbage soup.

Dan bought two beers to keep the bartender happy although he doubted anything ever would in this place—the bar was filled with a clientele that was the scum of the night. A bleach blonde Indian hooker whose best days may have been with Mahatma Gandhi sat next to a sweating, fat man, one of her hands moving under the table while the other passed the time smoking a cigarette. Two men kissed and fondled one another in the darkest corner. A smirking dealer passed a small package to a young woman with unkempt hair and a face from her future. Three drunks were engaged in that garrulous non-sensical babble known the world over. The Untouchables were the only Indians who would touch this place.

"Good choice," said Dan sardonically, sliding Kapoor a beer. Dan thought he looked and smelled freshly showered in his spotless, beige suit and as fresh as a daisy while he felt as sweaty and tired as a tourist-riding elephant after a long day at the zoo. They shook hands.

"Sorry about this place. Just close," Kapoor said, patting the beaten cushion. "Please sit next to me."

Dan slid close to him on the shiny, black leather scarred by cigarette burns and repaired with duct tape. "To what do I owe the pleasure?" he asked.

"Pleasure's all mine. I thought you might like some of the information I'm getting about your group."

Dan smiled knowingly. "Is that what you're really here for, Dipak?" He lit himself a fresh cigarette and added to Kapoor's gathering layers of cloud.

"It might be useful in keeping you alive and that is important to me." Kapoor darkened in a blush. "There are some dangerous men on this trip of yours. I have received reports on Schoenhoff and Loskota I wish had come through days ago."

"The Americans? You suspect something?"

"Schoenhoff has visited India and Nepal regularly the last few years. No criminal record. Former US Air Force pilot. Has the usual load of medals Americans throw around like confetti," he added with disdain.

"Nothing about him working for a US drug agency?"

"Is that what he told you? But they don't advertise their agents, do they?"

"I saw him watching a drug deal in Udaipur and he saw me."

"Watching whom?"

"The two Brit boys."

"Stevenson and Penney? They're new to India. Some minor juvenile misdemeanors in the UK. They're buying drugs?"

"But I think they're working for someone with a brain."

"Ah. Are we getting to Mis'r Loskota?"

"He joined the trip after we'd started and spends a lot of time following the boys around."

"A businessman in the tourist trade. No criminal record. Used to be in the US Air Force too. Military police. Rose to a colonel then left to open his own travel agency. Lots of those medals too. Seems to be legitimate."

Dan thoughtfully deposited ash in the tray stolen from another bar. "Happily married, all that American little pink houses stuff?"

"Three kids. Why do you ask?"

"Just interested. Were they in the military at the same time?"

"Yes. In Afghanistan but at different locations three years ago. Shortly after that, both of them left the Air Force."

"And here they are together on a trip across India? Isn't that odd?"

"Let it go, Dan. Not your job and it's not mine. Those NCB bastards can deal with them. Drug lords are the most violent of criminals. Life means nothing to those depraved thugs. Let's focus on Mis'r Stewart."

Dan nodded. "OK. Good night, Dipak." He leaned over and kissed him on the cheek.

"Good night, Dan." Kapoor positively glowed and kissed him back.

* * *

Dan climbed quietly to the top of the stairs that led onto the back street. The flashing neon sign cast little red and white light to illuminate the darkness—it was the perfect place for another attempt on his life. He waited a few minutes for his eyes to adjust to the dark, listening for movements, before he poked his head out to check for potential trouble. Only a few of the worst looking hookers remained available for what had to be the most desperate johns: it was the perfect place for stumbling drunks surfacing from the club to be relieved of their possessions—or gays have the shit kicked out of them by insecure homophobes. A cat blinked glass-yellow eyes at him before returning to snaffling through a pile of garbage. To his right, a parked taxi flashed its lights at him and the driver shouted out the window but he ignored him and walked quickly toward the main road to his left and hailed a tuk-tuk to carry him back to the hotel. He got out and was paying the driver when Charlie dressed in a jacket and jeans, hair covered with the red hijab he'd bought her, ran out the hotel's entrance, in a hurry to get somewhere. He hid behind a life-sized baby elephant statue and waited for Rani or Bob or Mark or Gilly. No bodyguards. She'd escaped again.

Keeping up with the fast-striding Charlie in the dark streets wasn't easy even though in the occasional streetlight and illuminated shop entrance Charlie's red head stood out tall enough to moor a zeppelin. Dan stumbled along the uneven pavement, avoiding careening, honking tuk-tuks, truculent bulls and other animal friends, beggars and vendors. Charlie knew where she was going and wasn't hanging about. At the butcher's on the corner, easily identified by the skinned corpses hanging from hooks on one street and the bleating goats marked with a red splash on the other, she paused to take a couple of flash pictures before being scowled at and chased away by the men in the store. It gave Dan time to get closer to Charlie before she strode off again at a cracking pace leaving him rubber-legged in pursuit.

Keeping his head up to watch Charlie made him trip on a curb and sprawl into a dirt-filled gutter. Cow shit all over his knees and hands. Damn! He scrambled back to his feet. Charlie had disappeared. He ran a whole block into a poorer district and reached a small park trapped between decaying brick buildings: an arid triangle of dirt under an old, semi-leafless tree. Charlie's red beacon was not to be seen. Dan cursed, lit a cigarette and dropped onto a stone slab next to a yogurt seller with his bowl of the white liquid sitting on the ground, flies dancing in a conga line along the steel rim. What now?

Strung with a few bare light bulbs, the area was home to a group of beggars that eyed him suspiciously. Three men in white shirts and wrapped in white lungis to their ankles sat smoking on a skinny plank held up by wrought iron rust, the remains of a Victorian bench. Partially in shadow, a heavyset figure in a ball cap and a long coat leaned against the scarred tree trunk. Bill, looking to Dan's right. Dan checked that way: the stalls and small shops with their bustle of sellers and buyers and an open-air eating area poorly lit by oil lamps under a tattered canvas awning and a roof of pieces of corrugated iron held down by car tires. Behind an assortment of scattered tables, bearded men raced to throw rice and vegetables into fuming, blackened pans over charcoal fires then onto paper plates as though it was an Olympic event. Spiced oil drifted across the park from the pans and to remind Dan he hadn't eaten lately.

Dazza, Arfa and—*Christ Almighty!*—Duncan sat at the table farthest from the street, talking to a gray-bearded man wearing a red turban. Dan cursed himself for not warning off Duncan but that was in the rearview mirror. No point. Thank God, Charlie had stayed away. But where the hell had she been going? Dan assumed the boys weren't buying the turban as they handed over a briefcase. The Sikh took it, looked inside, nodded and handed them a hefty backpack.

The Sikh shook hands with the boys and left with two bodyguards falling in step as he crossed the triangle. When one of the men on the bench waited a minute before following them, Dan sensed trouble. Who were they? Cops? Another gang? It didn't matter. The shit was hitting the fan. He looked back at the boys dawdling inside with the heavy backpack. "Get out of there, you idiots!" he screamed silently. What were they—? *Oh, Jesus.* Charlie appeared from a door at the back of the restaurant. She must have been in whatever passed as a toilet. He knew she was a brave girl. The nightmare was worsening. Hadn't he given a gun to Duncan too? This could turn into the OK Corral.

As soon as Charlie and the boys left the restaurant, the two men in white on the bench got up with their hands out of sight. The hair on Dan's neck bristled. Without thinking, he ran across the road toward the men without any idea what he intended to do.

"Run for it!" he shouted waving his arms like a total idiot.

Charlie, Duncan and the Brits saw him and froze in shock, dropping the backpack. The men stopped abruptly and pulled out their guns. Gun shots echoed between the buildings. Dan dropped onto all fours. The men went down like ninepins. Behind them, Bill held a gun. He quickly ducked behind the tree. The shoppers ran for cover. The beggars scattered. Charlie and the boys stared dumbstruck at the sprawling men.

"Run! Run!" shouted Dan.

The kids bolted like scared rabbits toward the hotel. Dan stayed down on the street hoping he wasn't going to get run over as tuk-tuks headed every which way out of the triangle. A loud roar of a motor behind him. Dan looked to his right. A car swerved out of a backstreet and squealed to a halt beside the backpack. A dark figure jumped out to scoop it up. The engine roared again and rubber squealed as the car accelerated, headlights blazing toward Dan. He scrambled to his feet to avoid getting run over. The big driver wearing a black ski mask saw him, swerved and skidded to a stop on the wet stone.

"Get in!" shouted another man, flinging open a rear door.

Dan scrambled in and slammed the door behind him. The man's rifle rested on the ledge of a rolled-down window. He turned to Dan as he ripped the mask over his head.

"What the fuck are ya doin' here?" Steve demanded, breathing hard.

Dan gripped the door handle and side of his seat as the bull of a driver drove at speed but not too fast away from the shootings. Several cop cars with red, white and blue lights flashing and sirens blaring shot by in the other direction. The big driver slowed when he turned off the major highway into a leafy area with brighter streetlights where the streets got wider, houses bigger and farther apart. No traffic. In the rearview mirror, he sized up Dan with professionally paranoid black eyes.

"Charlie and Duncan were going to get caught or killed." Dan's voice shook along with the rest of him. "I had to do something."

"Lahk get yerself killed, ya crazy bastard?"

"Who were those guys who got shot?"

"Ah'm bettin' cops," Steve said, turning back to the rear window. "Knew a deal was goin' down. The Sikh's men must've shot 'em. Wouldn't do a deal like that without some protection around."

"It was Bill."

Steve twisted sharply toward Dan. "Loskota?"

"He shot the cops so the Brits could get away. He'll be pissed you got his dope."

"Fuck! Ah knew there was somethin' not kosher about that dude!"

Outside the hotel, Steve took his time lighting cigarettes for himself, the Bull and Dan before he spoke again in a cooler tone. "He can't have recognized me but he must have seen ya. He'll come after ya, man." He reached under his arm and handed Dan a gun butt first. "Kill him before he kills ya. Ah know ya can do it, don't ah?"

* * *

Dan sat on his bed pointing the Colt at the door. Had Bill recognized him? Would he come to kill him? Should he burst in on Bill and kill him first? Steve thought so. Karen would be in bed with Bill. What if she got killed in a shootout? He couldn't let that happen. Instead, he slid a chest of drawers against the door and waited for Bill's move. He smoked a cigarette and let the fuzzy fragments of the shootout return to the forefront of his thinking. He revisited the triangle. Charlie, Duncan and the Brits with the backpack. The two men standing and moving toward them. Gun shots. Bill with his gun. Steve picking up the backpack. Why hadn't Bill shot him? He'd just shot two cops to save the Brits and maybe half a million dollars' worth of opium so why let Steve escape with it? He replayed the shots and diving onto the road. Suddenly the fog of war cleared and there was a shocking clarity. He snatched up the gun and took ran down the stairs, across the atrium, and up the other side to bang on Bill's door.

Scuffling, cursing and groaning before Bill growled, "Who the hell is it?"

"Get Karen out of there. Steve knows you're a narc."

* * *

Crash! The noise of splintering wood. *Pop! Pop! Poppoppop!* Shots echoed.

Dan jerked awake where he sat lodged upright in the corner of his landing ready to defend himself. If Steve came for Bill he reckoned there was a good chance he'd be next on his list. It was light enough to see across the atrium. A black figure bounded down the wooden staircase and dashed out of sight. From the street, a car's engine roared and its tires screeched.

* * *

The Bull's glassy, black eyes stared at the ceiling. As lifeless as if a matador had just delivered the coup de grace with his sword into his heart instead of a .38 bullet. His chest still oozing a mass of red onto the carpet, he lay on his back ready to be hauled away by his ankles. The door he'd charged through hung at an angle on one hinge. First come, first served. Bill sat on the bed with his gun dangling from one hand, breathing rapidly as his adrenaline boiled.

Steve had come for Bill after waiting the night for Dan to do his dirty work. It had been a damn close-run thing. The cops had staggered backward, clutching at their chests and bellies—they hadn't been shot from behind. The shots had come from Dan's side of the street where Steve's car had come from. Steve and his rifle.

"Steve got away," Bill said redundantly.

Dan poured him a big shot of bourbon and drank from the bottle.

Karen appeared white-faced into the doorway. She saw the body and covered her mouth in horror. "Bill!" she wailed.

She stumbled into his arms. How Dan envied him. But not with Karen.

* * *

Dan avoided Bill but when he went into a hotel toilet of white-tiled walls and a long aluminum trough, Bill followed. The toilet smelled of that ubiquitous and nauseating mint and was empty. Dan went to the end of the trough, farthest from the door. Bill arrived at his side, deliberately bumping into him like a docking cruise ship. Dan elbowed back.

"That was quite some interruptus," Bill said over a background of hale stones showering metal.

Dan scowled at the knife that stuck home as intended—painfully. "Next time, I'll wait until morning if you like."

"By that time, Karen would have killed me," Bill said, twisting the knife.

"Why haven't you shoved off to hunt down Steve and the Brits?" Dan asked sourly. "Isn't that your job?"

"I have a few days to fill in until I get a lead on them. I'm guessing they've gone into hiding so I thought I'd hang around with Karen as long as possible to piss you off."

A brief moment of water gurgling and the toilet door banging open and closed with new customers.

"You saved our lives," Bill said with unexpected sincerity.

"I'm glad Karen's safe," Dan answered curtly but relented. He did have Bill to thank for even standing at the urinal. "I did owe you one, didn't I?"

Bill's harsh tone softened in response. "It cancels out telling me she was a lesbian too."

"I thought you were a baddy—as well as an asshole."

"Weren't you shtupping Karen?"

"Too old for me," said Dan.

"Jeez. She's a walking double bed! What's wrong with you?"

Dan went to a washbasin. Several more men came in. Bill started to wash his hands while Dan was drying off with a paper towel.

"Who do you work for?" Dan asked.

Bill eyed the other men. "Not here. Did Steve tell you how he cottoned on to me?"

"Not here either," said Dan. "Do you know how happy she is you're not dead?"

"I noticed all right." He grinned in a lewd way that irritated Dan.

"Are your wife and kids as happy about it?" Dan left Bill swearing at him.

* * *

The massive, gray Mahabodhi temple loomed ahead: ten stories, two hundred feet up to its peak, the monument to Siddhartha Gautama's first preaching spot under the Bodhi tree nearby. With a crowd of tourists and pilgrims clogging the path leading to its entrance, Dan helped Karen limp with the aid of her cane farther away to take photos of the illuminated temple towering into the evening sky before they tried to get inside.

Karen lit up a joint, inhaled deeply and offered it to him.

"No thanks. Not here."

Not anywhere. No more drugs, no matter how casual. No more drinking. No more cigarettes either. He felt exhilarated, filled with an overwhelming resolution to change by just being at the temple and the Bodhi tree, the epicenter of Buddhism. No wonder Christian zealots threw away their crutches and ran home from Lourdes. He didn't need a different reality. He just needed to live this one better.

"More for me," said Karen and burned the joint again. "Good for my knee, you know," she told him then giggled.

He turned at the sound of footsteps. Charlie. After the scare of the shootout in the triangle, he'd searched out Charlie and Duncan intent on running over them like a rampaging mother elephant annoyed with her misbehaving calves. He needn't have bothered— when he'd cornered them at breakfast they'd been scared so straight neither of them was eating. Chagrined, unable to hold his condemning eye, they'd professed ignorance of another drug deal and apologized profusely.

Duncan wore the face of a man who wanted off a stomach-churning roller coaster halfway through the ride when he took Dan aside and held out the Glock. "Would you like the gun back? I was so frightened, I forgot I even had it. I don't think I could have used it even if I had."

"Keep it. Charlie and Shira are still in danger, Duncan. Everyone's afraid of guns including me. They deserve a whole lot of respect," Dan instructed to alleviate his fear and give him the motive to shoot someone.

To show confidence in his son and motivate him more, he explained to Duncan's increasing amazement what was going on with Bob and the Harbor Murders and Bob and the attempted kidnapping of Charlie and his worries about Nadia's malevolence toward Karen, Charlie and Shira.

"I need you to help protect the women. I know you can you do that." Duncan nodded slowly as though being ordered to be part of a firing squad.

"Next time, get out the gun, load it and don't be afraid to use it. Believe me, Bob will kill you in a heartbeat if you get in his way."

"What about Mom?"

He let that one go.

"Can I walk around with you?" Charlie asked.

She'd dressed Indian style in a brown and gold-patterned sari that matched her eyes. God, she was so beautiful and had that look of youthful excitement again that made his heart tap out a little dance.

"Can she?" he asked Karen. "I think she's too good looking to be with us."

Karen studied her. "She does make me look like a wombat's arse."

Dan put his arm around Karen's broad shoulders. "Have I told you how much I like wombats?"

She smiled and slipped her arm around his waist. "Of course, sweetie."

Charlie eyed them quizzically. "Get a room, you guys."

"Already have." Karen elbowed Dan and laughed and laughed.

Charlie gave them a wide smile as she shook her head. "Are you two stoned?"

Dan looked at a grinning Karen. "She is."

"Did she say stoned?" Karen broke up again.

Karen held out the joint. "Want some?"

Charlie glanced at Dan. "You're not smoking?"

"Not here at the Bodhi tree. Definitely verboten."

She shrugged. "I'll skip it then."

Dan smiled at her for doing that. Her return smile reinforced what he already knew: he was in a doomed love. He'd wanted to kiss her under the cannon in Jaipur but more so when he'd begun to negotiate with himself, just like when he'd been an alcoholic. Just one drink and that would be all. He'd alternate days drinking. He'd only drink on weekends. Only vodka. Only when socializing. It had been endless and he'd always surrendered to the temptation. He'd kissed Charlie after resisting. And stroked her breasts. OK, so now that was it. Absolutely nothing more. Well, maybe her breasts he could do again gladly but nothing lower than that. Leave her in Kathmandu. Go to Nagarkot.

He linked his arm through Charlie's and helped Karen toward the big Bodhi tree, decorated with strings of lights, the center of the activities in the garden. Under the leafless tree, a descendant of the original, a full-size model of Buddha sitting under a canopy talking to his followers was displayed. Pilgrims and tourists milled around it quietly, respectfully, some shooting flash pictures.

"This is Buddha's famous Bodhi tree?" asked Charlie. "Where he gave his first sermons, right?"

Dan nodded. "Very good. Where he achieved enlightenment—*bodhi*."

"I'd like to know more about Buddhism."

"I can tell you some. I read a lot of books about it and other religions in prison. I had a bit of spare time between making number plates." He leaned toward Charlie. "How has our friend Shira been today?"

"Real quiet. But she's better."

"You're a sweetheart for helping her after everything that's happened between you two."

"I've started a few novenas for her, too."

"Can't help yourself, can you?"

"Just a few."

Inside the temple, the blue and greenish wall paintings depicted the events of the prince's life from birth to enlightenment to death. It was full of pilgrims sitting quietly on rows of wooden benches in front of a large golden statue of Buddha. Dan felt a bit boorish taking photos of the walls in the crowded temple but he had to have the memories recorded in a form he wouldn't forget. Having spent years in prison reading about Buddha's Bodhi tree, he was a Christian in Bethlehem—the tree where it all began more than two thousand five hundred years ago. He was in awe and couldn't stop smiling his happiness.

"I'll stay here," Karen told Dan with a wink. "My leg needs a rest. Have fun you two."

Dan looked around. No Rani, Bob, Gilly or Mark. He took Charlie's hand. "Let's go."

He pulled her through crowds of pilgrims and tourists until they ended up on the north side of the massive temple where pilgrims had lit candles in glass jars and foil cups to decorate the Buddha shrines. Dan took out his lighter and re-lit two of the candles.

"Two?" asked Charlie.

"Are there more than two of us?" he said letting his great mood get the better of him.

"Two's real good with me," she said. She reached up and kissed him on the cheek. "Did you ever imagine you'd be here?"

"I've imagined it for years. I never thought I'd get here so soon." He slowly turned around with his hands cupped behind his ears. "Do you hear those insects, the birds?"

Her mouth open, she turned and turned looking up at the sounds and sights of the waving branches and leaves, and the chattering of the evening animal life. "This is amazing," she said, "and I'm not stoned!"

"If you relax and use your senses, you don't have to be. It's there all the time."

The strings of lights sparkled from one tree to the rustling dry leaves of the next tree. The chatter of the pilgrims became a buzz of crickets as he watched them huddled around small fires of charcoal, some animated, others eyes closed, calmly soaking up the sacred air gusting around the illuminated branches of the Bodhi tree. The atmosphere was electric, the lights on the temple pulsed along with his heart as it pounded its slow *thud... thud... thud* in his ears.

Charlie twirled around as she stared up into the mass of overhanging branches before grabbing his hand and leading him through the crackling, dried leaves toward the Dhamek Stupa that loomed ahead of them. It was just like in the picture books he'd read again and again in his cell. It was one of his Wonders of the World. He stared up at the silhouette of the blunt tip rising a hundred feet in the air, a huge phallus probing the jet-black night sky. Charlie approached the stupa with her arms wide. She hugged the rail that protected the rough bricks of the base, spreading herself against it.

When he stood beside her, she twisted around to hug him. "I love you so much," she whispered.

Dan swam in her golden-brown eyes and pulled her even closer. "Let's enjoy each other just for now."

"Why *just for now?*"

"*Carpe diem*, Charlie." Dan looked away into the night sky. He'd sat in prison not thinking about the tomorrow that never came. Being happy in his cell with Paul was all that mattered. If only Paul could have been here with him too. "There is no other time," he said to Venus, the brightest planet in the sky, floating above Charlie's head. An electric charge flickered through him. Tall, a simple beauty, slender, long red hair and small breasts, she was Botticelli's goddess of love.

"What do you see?" Charlie asked.

"You riding a clam shell."

"Sure you're not stoned?"

Charlie led him through the clusters of trees, wandering aimlessly until she stopped against a trunk. He didn't resist when she pulled him into her and he didn't need her to place his hands on her breasts again.

"I wore your red bra. Would you like to take it off?" she whispered.

He answered with deep rasping of hot breath on her neck. She kissed and licked his ears as he unhooked her bra and stroked her bare breasts. He stayed in control—it was as far as he let himself go. No lust here at the Bodhi tree, only wanting to please her and enjoy her in a mutually loving coupling. She squirmed against him as they kissed and talked about all kinds of things that sprang unbidden into their minds for what might have been an hour. Or maybe it was ten minutes. It was a timeless time. Two infinitesimal specks of energy enjoying each other suspended in an infinite universe, the cosmos he didn't understand and where he just had to make the best of it because he would never understand it.

April 3rd

AT SEVEN IN the morning, Dan and the others stood on the warming ghats under two circular water towers, each painted with a thirty-foot-high image of Lord Shiva: one purple and one pink, both of them looking to the south across the Ganges that stretched far beyond the haze of the horizon.

They'd just finished their morning cruise on the river that had seen thousands of years of coming and goings starting another day with its ghats swarming with Indians praying, swimming, washing themselves and preparing their relatives for cremation before sending them on their way to nirvana on burning piles of sandalwood, if they could afford it. A tsunami of sensations greeted them: clashing cymbals, tinkling bells, people talking and shouting, water swishing, motorboats puttering and musical instruments twanging and blaring; vibrant reds, yellows and oranges of buildings, clothing and flowers; the smells of cooking food, unwashed people, burning wood and sewage. The sweet smell and smoke of the sandalwood fires drifted by as they waited to board the flat-bottomed wooden boats for their voyeuristic cruise up the Mother Ganges. Funeral cruising had never been on Dan's bucket list but they'd caught glimpses of the Hindu ceremonies without being intrusive.

"What a fantastic morning," Charlie said aloud. She lowered her voice. "It was amazing last night too."

"What happened?"

"Lots of good stuff." She stroked his bare arm to stimulate his memory.

"Pity I missed it."

"We'll have to do it again to remind you then."

She walked off toward the boat swinging her hips provocatively. She was far too happy. Dan already felt the rising guilt over what was to happen. He glanced at Bob and Rani. They both wore the bored expressions of tourists who had seen too much of India's underbelly. They didn't look like they gave a damn about Dan, the Ganges or Charlie.

He sidled over to Karen sitting on a stone step to rest her leg. "Your look could kill," he told her.

"Better than a needle in his arse, don't you think?"

"Can we keep it that way until Kathmandu? Let's get him locked up for trying to kidnap Charlie." Karen snorted her annoyance. "Any way he could remember you from Fremantle? A photo in the newspaper, on TV?"

She shrugged. "Nah. Changed my name. Grew out my hair and dyed it. I've put on a lot of weight since I was a scrawny doper too."

Dan decided not to ask how much. He stood up and helped her to her feet. "Let's get you back to the hotel for a rest or you won't make it to the festival tonight. Forget about what happened and don't stress yourself. It'll speed up your recovery."

"Thanks for your help, sweetie." She tugged his arm and smiled warmly. "If only I'd met you thirty years ago. What we could have been."

"Lucky you didn't. You'd have been a pedophile."

Her cane swished dangerously close.

* * *

Dan held Bill back at the entrance to the hotel as they assembled for a fun ride in bicycle rickshaws to the festival at the river. "Let's ride together, Bill." A sharp look from Bill but he didn't say no, nodding as though he had something on his mind too.

"I need to talk to Bill," Dan told Karen under his breath as he helped her hop with the use of a cane to a bicycle rickshaw and climb in with Charlie.

"Race you to the ghats!" shouted Dan to Charlie and the other rickshaws.

"You're on!" shouted back Mark and prodded his driver with his stick.

Dan's scrawny driver, who looked like he'd just finished a forty-day fast, cranked his sandals hard on his one-gear bike's pedals to get about four hundred pounds of passengers moving. And they were off, trailing the others down a brightly lit, wide road teeming with traffic and people under the darkening sky.

Bill twisted his face with distaste. "What do you want, *rube*?"

"Now that you're leaving, I want to wish you a nice life."

Bill snorted. "Thanks. Now, why don't you just take a hike?"

"Before I do, you might want something."

"Yeah?"

"Do you want your memory card back?"

Bill's eyebrows reached for the sky. "You're the bastard who stole my camera? OK, what do you want for it?"

"We'll get to that. Who do you work for?"

Bill took a card out of his wallet and handed it to Dan. It was for a travel company named Exclusive Executive Expeditions. "None of your business but use the telephone number if you need me to save your *sorry ass* again."

"What happened in Afghanistan with Steve?"

Bill whistled softly. "You're well informed. How is that?"

"I own an ouija board."

"Steve and I never met. I sent the military police to arrest him once we had the evidence he was dealing heroin and other drugs from Kabul using Air Force planes into the US. End of story."

"Not quite. Why are you personally on his ass right now?"

"He got off easy. Pissed me off after a year's solid work. He turned state's evidence against some brass up the food chain and got a simple hash bust and a dishonorable discharge instead of a life sentence. Sweet."

"Too sweet for you?"

"You bet. As soon as his name showed up on a suspect list I got myself assigned to nail him."

"Since the Indians were doing nothing?"

"My report will state it's been another successful collaborative mission with the NCB."

"I hear you're leaving. Off to catch your Moby Dick?"

"You heard right. I'll harpoon that son of a bitch. Bet on it."

"Karen worries you'll go down with the whale. Should she care?"

"What's it to you?" he growled testily.

"She's my friend I care about and the silly bitch is in love with you. Do you give a shit?"

"Mind your own fucking business, bud."

"Here's something which is my business. Duncan and Charlie have nothing to do with this racket. You know that?"

"Do I?"

"You'd better or kiss your photo evidence goodbye."

Bill shrugged. "You want me to forget about them? That's all?"

"Arfa and Dazza are stupid kids who have no idea of the danger of the shit they're pulling. Wanna forget about them?"

He shook his head. "They're idiots but no letting off," he said firmly.

"Can you wait until they get back to the UK or wherever? They'll die in prisons out here."

"I don't have your sympathy. Maybe the Brits can have them extradited but that's up to them."

Dan held out his hand. "OK. Deal on Duncan and Charlie?"

They shook hands and Dan handed him the card. "I deleted all the pictures of Charlie and Duncan in case you forget."

Bill grunted. "Where's the camera?"

Dan shrugged. "You just contributed to the US aid program." He'd given it to a young man he'd seen outside the hotel in Agra. The youngster had been taking photos of his girlfriend with a forty-year-old, thirty-five millimeter Minolta. A basic functional camera but a free Pentax digital with a zoom lens had made more than his day. Dan hoped he wasn't now shooting her nude and slamming the pics up on the Internet.

"I'm so glad," Bill said with heavy sarcasm.

"Why did you follow me in Mumbai?" Dan asked. "Because I shared a taxi with him?"

"Uh-huh. See how connected you guys were. And when you both ended up on the same trip across India? I don't believe much in coincidence so I had you checked out. Not pretty reading but I ruled you out being an accomplice."

"More of a murderer?"

"That's about it."

"Why not turn me in?"

"Suspected for a revenge killing of a drug lord?" He shook a thumb and index finger he'd made into a gun. "I give medals for that! Kill a few more for all I care!"

Bill was definitely a Judeo-Christian Texan. Praise the Lord and pass the ammunition. Dan thought of Bob. If he didn't deliver a deal by Kathmandu, it'd be a shootout.

"I owe you for that," Dan said to be amiable.

"You certainly do," Bill answered dryly. His expression soured. "In return, you can shut the fuck up about Karen," he suggested less amiably.

The rickshaw shuddered and creaked along the flat road, the skinny driver up off his seat pressing down for all his worth with chopstick legs, gasping, slowing down to a snail's pace.

"Stop here!" Dan shouted.

The driver's head, bathed with sweat, jerked back over his shoulder, eyes wide in alarm.

"Get in the back!" Dan ordered and leaped out of the rickshaw.

The confused stick of a man replaced him on the bench seat but began to grin a fine set of gums as Dan climbed up into the saddle. The hardest part was getting the bike moving but when he did there was no stopping him—almost literally since the brakes were nominal.

Pedestrians and other cycle rickshaw operators whooped it up as Dan barrelled along the street in true Indian style—totally reckless, bell ringing. Passing Karen's rickshaw was the first target. The looks on her and Charlie's faces were something else as he steamed by. But Dan began to feel dizzy as his heart pounded. He began to slow, gasping, knowing he'd done too much in his excitement.

"Hey, give me a try!" shouted Bill seeing Dan tire.

He took over just as the road began to dip toward the river enabling the rickshaw to quickly pick up speed. Bill was strong and within two hundred yards had caught and powered by Mark and Gilly's rickshaw and by Duncan and Shira's, receiving a barrage of friendly insults in response. After wild steering to avoid collisions and pedestrian deaths, Bill used the high curb several times to bump the shaking rickshaw to a shuddering halt in the turmoil of people and vehicles near the ghats.

Seconds later, a beaming Karen's rickshaw rattled and screeched to a halt next to them.

"You crazy whacker!" she shouted at Bill and limped over to give him a big hug and a kiss.

Bill's glance over her shoulder at Dan was the strained look of a man with a dilemma he hadn't expected. Bill might be a better man than Dan thought.

* * *

The jostling long, wooden boats and broad, flat ones, loaded with excited camera-equipped tourists, formed a massed flotilla in the slowly moving Ganges just off the ghat where the ceremony was going to be held. Several fires burned in high metal stands as the band of musicians tuned up and a troop of dancers practiced a few routines to loosen up. Behind them, rows of seats were filling up with spectators and overhead umbrellas of green, red and white lights floated in the humid, smoky air like kids' balloons escaping their owners.

Where was their boat? Loki had disappeared as soon as they'd arrived, motioning to stay put and he'd find one. A group of nicely dressed children about ten-years-old offered them small candles in paper flowers. Dan bought six and gave two to Duncan. He motioned toward Shira.

"Give her one. Make a wish," he whispered.

Duncan looked at him like he'd always wanted a son to look. Or perhaps it was the free candle.

Nadia and Kanta hovered like lepers on the fringe of the group. Nadia continued to glower at Dan at every opportunity. Her face must have been getting awfully tired. It certainly looked it. He gave her a big smile and got a snarling scowl in return. Kanta stared at Dan like a gargoyle waterspout.

"Here we go, ladies and gentlemen!" Loki emerged from the dark, standing in the prow of a long boat. A young boy wearing expensive Ray-Bans to dim his incredible night vision and holding a paddle sat at the helm of the boat as it glided gently against the ghat. Captain Cool didn't look old enough to float a boat in a bathtub.

"Be careful getting in!" shouted Loki. "And this is Mohammed." He pointed to the boy who grinned back a set of flashing white teeth.

Dan and Mark helped Gilly and Karen down the ladder into the boat. Bill followed with an increasingly brooding look. Dan's empathy went out to him—he was being torn to bits by his conflicting emotions—and Karen had noticed. Charlie squeezed in next to him before Mark and Gilly scrunched up opposite.

Karen lit up a joint and offered it to him. He shook his head. She offered it to Charlie too and met the same response. He smiled approvingly at Charlie and she gave him the kind of look that told him they were on the same wavelength as she laid her hand gently on his thigh.

He leaned close to Karen. "Bill's a good guy. He's just helped me get Duncan and Charlie out of that bad situation. You have my permission to wear out what's left of him."

"Thanks for sharing, sweetie. And I intend to," she said with a strained smile. She lowered her voice even more. "Bill doesn't look very happy with me smoking hash, does he?"

"I think it's more than that. He doesn't want to leave you. He's in love."

Maybe it had been the wrong thing to say. Her face almost crumpled but she sat up, threw away the joint and turned to surprise Bill with a long, tender kiss. When she leaned her head on his shoulder, his arm went around her and he rested his head on the top of hers.

An exploding moon of blindingly white light flashed on the rows of seated spectators and the performers grouped behind a long line of flickering candles edging the ghat. Tablas and other drums erupted, banging out their eastern rhythms. Cymbals clashed and bells clanged and a troop of orange and white uniformed male singers sang and clapped their hands. Women in glittering costumes spun and jumped, dazzling with their virtuosic dance skills.

Dan's retinas fizzed and his eardrums buzzed. Charlie turned to look at him with huge eyes and a big grin. *Wow!* she mouthed silently. He wasn't a fan of endless ragas but he kept his camera clicking and enjoyed the pyrotechnics of the noisy light show. He took out his lighter, lit his candle and placed it gently on the water to join the many others drifting along with them. He gave one to Charlie, lit it and watched hers float off after his.

"Make a wish," he told her.

She smiled. "I have. And you know what it is."

Her hand stroked his thigh and he let himself enjoy the moment as the flotilla of dancing candles flickered away into the dark. Magical.

As the boat drifted toward the dark downstream, they took turns standing up to take photos or some video of the wild events on the ghats, or the massed boats. During the turn back upriver toward the lights of the show, the narrow boat rocked as a few of them stood toward the bow for their shots. Dan stayed on his seat to take a sweeping video of the entire scene from the illuminated buildings high up overlooking the ghats across the dazzling ceremony area to—

A splash. A shriek. Still turning, the boat rocked madly as people stood up and sat down.

"*Shira's fallen in!*" screamed Charlie.

Swimming in an open sewer wasn't on Dan's bucket list but he dropped his camera, kicked off his sandals and dove into the black water in the general direction of where she would have gone. It was the kind of crazy reflex thing men do without thinking. The fear kicks in later—if they're still alive.

"Shira!" he repeatedly shouted, breast-stroking, keeping his mouth above the water as much as possible to avoid gargling the Ganges. The darkness was frightening as the river moved him silently deeper into the maw of pitch-black nothing. Splashing behind him. Bill and Mark.

"I'll go this way!" shouted Mark and disappeared toward the southern bank of the Ganges.

"I'll go over here!" Bill stroked powerfully toward the ghats.

Dan swam on, calling out to Shira about every ten seconds, but felt himself weakening as his temples pulsed. Water splashed nearby. It was Duncan with a face from a horror movie.

A barely audible voice spluttered, "Help ... Help!"

Dan spun around. An outline of a head bobbed like a seal only five yards in front of them. Duncan plowed the waters apart in his rush to grab Shira. Dan grabbed both of them.

* * *

A gaudy, red and white-striped ambulance flashed its blue lights, siren dying like a dead cat as it braked heavily at the hospital's Emergency entrance. A man with his shirt ripped was rolled out on a gurney, a paramedic pounding on the bloodied chest. Dan counted five bodies, some ominously still, in the last thirty minutes. One dangling a leg with an extra knee had been carried out of a taxi screaming blue murder. He'd once worked in Emergency and he'd been prepared for whatever came through the door: bullet wounds, heart attacks, drunks, OD's, knifings, psychotics. He'd learned fast to play God: prioritize—not everyone could be saved. He'd got injured cops to the head of the line. They deserved it. He thought of Kapoor. Where was he?

Back at the hotel to shower and change clothes, he'd swigged Cipro and almost scrubbed his skin down to the flesh. Together with all those shots from Africa, he should have a good chance of staying alive. Nausea still lingering from swallowing too much of the Mother Ganges, he lit a Gold Flake to help settle his stomach. He blew a plume of smoke into the warm evening air but felt a chill at what might have happened to Shira. White-faced, breathing erratically and vomiting with a racing, feeble pulse, she'd been in shock by the time their speeding taxi had disgorged them at the hospital's entrance. Bellowing he was a doctor and throwing out orders, Dan barreled through the Emergency entrance and got Shira immediate attention: fluids, dopamine, a good stomach pumping and plenty of shots. She was so lucky not to have drowned and he felt great at having helped save her. It could have been Charlie. The thought chilled him even more.

A taxi cruised to a halt in front of him. He opened the rear door and froze at the gun pointing at him.

"Surprised to see me?"

Fight or flight? Outside a hospital would be a good place to take a bullet or two but Steve wouldn't leave the surgeons anything to work on. Dan controlled his breathing, calling upon his reserves of meditative calm. "Why wouldn't I be?" he asked in a steady voice. "You should be in China."

Arfa appeared behind him. "Get in," he said gruffly and pushed him onto the rear seat.

Steve swiftly patted him down. "Drive," he ordered. Dazza drove.

"What's with the gun, buddy?" he asked Steve. It was going to take all his wits to mollify him.

"Ah'm gonna kill ya, man," Steve said tonelessly with a grim smile.

"Give me a fucking break. You played me like a fucking finger puppet while you were the baddy and fuck off without saying thanks for the help? Kill me for what?"

"Rattin' me out to Loskota."

"Don't be ridiculous. You know I thought he was the bad guy. Turns out he already knew who you were. Guess who had you busted in Afghanistan?"

Steve's eyes flashed his surprise. "It was him?"

"He was military police. He told me he'd had you arrested for smuggling heroin to the US, got too light a sentence for *ratting* on your bosses and he'd vowed to make you pay. It was personal. Nothing to do with me."

"Interestin' he would tell you all that, isn't it? What was it? Shared pillow talk while the two of you fucked fat Karen in a cozy threesome?"

Dan forced a laugh. "That's your fantasy, Steve. Why would I give a shit about a guy who stole Karen from me? I hate the bastard. Did we act like buddies?" He didn't wait for an answer. "Not fucking likely. We got into a fight over her and he punched my guts in. Wanna see the bruise?"

Steve's eyes flickered some thinking. There was a chance. Dan kept talking.

"I tell you Loskota killed those men at the drug deal then I rat you out to someone I'd like to see dead? Why the hell would I do that?"

Steve nodded thoughtfully. "Ya're right, man. Ah don't see why ya would do that."

"Well, thank God for that," said Dan with a sigh from his feet.

Without warning, Steve buried the barrel of his gun in Dan's stomach as far as his backbone to show how unhappy he was. Dan doubled over, pain searing through him, unable to breathe. Acid rose in his tightening throat. He caught his breath with a mighty whoop of air.

Steve shoved his face close to Dan's. "Ah don't know and ah don't care but the bottom line is no one else could have warned him but ya," he growled. "He was ready for us when we came for him."

Dan spat out some vomit. "Warned ... him? Bill ... must sleep with ... one eye on his ... fucking door." He paused to gather some breath. "Think ... he doesn't expect night visitors ... in his job?"

"The Bull crashed the door and Loskota was in the corner behind an upturned table. Ah doubt he normally sleeps that way. He was ready that night. The night ah dropped ya back at the hotel. The night ah knew he was a narc. Ya must have figured who'd done the shootin' at the dope deal. He'd been screwin' that big girl every night and suddenly she's not there and he's behind a table in the corner waiting for us? So cut the shit. Ya cost me at least a million and ya're goin' to pay for it."

Dan's head pounded, his mouth burned and his stomach was on fire. Was it better to die trying to escape or just wait to die without a chance? Dan glanced in the side mirror when some headlights flashed but they disappeared as soon as he saw them. He was alone and on done for unless...

"I ... saved your life!" He groaned, twisting to look directly into Steve's black eyes for a sign of humanity. There was none.

Steve laughed mockingly. "Ya used up ya life, man. Who d'ya think killed that robber in the alley?"

"*It was you?*" Dan glanced at the revolver in Steve's fist. A Magnum. Make-my-day Steve. How could he have missed that? "Why would ... Harry Callahan follow me?"

"Same taxi? Same trip? Hell of a coincidence, man. Ah had to see if you were the tourist you were supposed to be."

"I am ... just a fucking tourist ... for Chrissakes."

"Bad trip then. Think ya way out of this one and ah'll give ya a Twix." He roared at his own joke.

Dazza's eyes danced white in the rearview mirror. Arfa cast an anxious glance his way from the passenger seat. His mind raced with increasing desperation. Could Arfa and Dazza save him? "Is murder what you signed up for boys?" he rasped just before Steve thrust the gun into him again and he threw up again.

"D'you have to ... er ... do this?" asked Dazza.

"Yeah," said Arfa.

"Shut the fuck up or ya're next," barked Steve.

The car turned off the main highway and bounced down a rutted trail toward a broad moonlit reach of the Ganges. A pack of pi dogs watched with glassy-eyed indifference as the car passed then went back to chewing on something lying at the side of the packed dirt. There was no human to be seen, no one to hear a scream.

"Left here," ordered Steve.

Dazza turned and the car slid from side to side along a smaller wet dirt track that ended under a group of trees near the river. Arfa opened the rear door.

"Gerrout," said Steve with another jab of the barrel.

Arfa and Dazza gave Dan pitying looks then nervously glanced at each other. They grabbed him by his shirt collar and by the arms and shoved him toward the river. Trembling, up to his ankles in mud and gurgling water, Dan turned to look back at Steve. He was definitely going to die ahead of schedule. Arfa and Dazza stood beside Steve, two scared kids staring at an approaching nightmare they hadn't seen coming.

Steve waggled the gun. "Head, heart. How ya lahk it? Ah prefer the face. Ya'll be unrecognizable."

Dan wobbled, dizzy, sick. Charlie. She flashed across his mind. What might have been. Too late.

Bang!

A bullet zapped into the mud by his foot. He was too numb and barely flinched. A migraine was now so intense he couldn't feel his stomach pain. He wanted to throw up even more. His tremble had become an outright shake.

Steve laughed. "Fuck, ah missed." He raised his hand and aimed straight at Dan's forehead. "Ya should've stayed the fuck out the way, ya dope."

One last plea to Arfa and Dazza. "I didn't know you were killers!" Dan shouted as loud as he could. Bone-chilling fear rumbled his bowels and opened his bladder.

Jesus, the last thing I'll ever feel!

Steve chortled. "Look, he's pissing himself."

Bang!

"Fuck! Missed again."

Dan sank to his knees in the mud. His ears roared with white noise. His head throbbed out of control. He closed his eyes.

Bang! Bang! Bang!

His eyes jerked open.

"Fuck! Jesus!" Steve writhed on the ground holding his thigh.

"Don't shoot! Don't shoot!" screamed Dazza and Arfa waving their hands madly above their heads.

"Dad!" A white-faced Duncan rushed up to Dan just in time to see him vomit into the Mother River.

* * *

Duncan sat with his arm around a shaking Dan in the back seat as Arfa and Dazza drove them in silence back to their hotel. They were all numb. No normal brain prepared its owner for an event like that. A stone-faced Arfa guzzled a can of Coke and shared a joint with a gray-faced Dazza like they'd never have another one in their lifetime. Sitting in his fouled pants brought Dan a certain sense of humility.

Dan shook hands firmly with Arfa and Dazza when they got out of the car. "Go home, boys. Get pissed on Ibiza with your mates," he told them. "I'll make a deal for you with Bill."

Their car disappeared into the night. He had the feeling they'd take his advice.

"Where did you come from?" he asked Duncan outside his room.

"I was coming back to see Shira and getting out of my taxi when I saw you being forced into the car. I told my taxi to follow yours. Another minute and I'd have missed you. We got lucky."

If Duncan had been a minute later, he'd be dead. If he hadn't given Duncan the gun to protect Charlie and Shira, he'd be dead. If Bill hadn't stopped the priest in Mumbai. If Shira hadn't thrust herself at the priest in Jodhpur. If Bob had shot him in Pushkar. Yes, luck was with him. Would it run out? How many lives did he have?

Duncan handed Dan the Glock. He looked deadly serious when he said, "I don't want to shoot anyone ever again."

"You almost didn't."

"I just kept shooting until he went down."

"Third time lucky for me. You saved my life." Dan hugged Duncan.

Duncan still looked serious when he said, "Would you mind if I skipped your next bonding trip?"

* * *

The exhausted face in the bathroom mirror stared back at Dan and he hated it. He ripped off his filthy trousers and flung them out the bedroom window. If he hadn't sat on a chair in the shower he'd have keeled over. As the warm water flowed over him, he began shaking again as images of Steve, the riverbank, frightened Arfa bobbing his Adam's apple, Dazza's pale face and finally wetting himself flashed in the dull throb of his head. He wanted to dissolve and be flushed away down the pipe.

Dan dried off, dressed in some clean clothes and summoned up all the energy and pride he had left to make his way to Bill's hotel door. He gave it a good thump. The gasping and moaning inside stopped abruptly.

"Who the fuck is that?" Bill was not amused.

"It's Dan."

"Not again!"

"It's important." He heard Karen's muffled swearing.

The door jerked open a foot. Bill kept his lower half behind the door and looked not only highly annoyed but also highly sweaty. He rapped his fist on the doorframe. "This better be good," he growled before noticing Dan was as gray as a corpse at an autopsy. "You all right, man?"

"Arfa and Dazza have brought in Steve."

"What? He's here?"

"In the trunk of a car downstairs. He's injured but he'll be OK if he gets to a hospital. It's a trade. Let them go, Bill. Deal?" He reached out his hand.

Bill shook it. "OK. Deal." He glanced back into the room. "Give me five minutes."

"Twenty for fuck's sake!" shouted Karen.

April 4th

Barabar Caves

THE PARCHED COUNTRY southeast of Varanasi flattened out like a well-done chapatti as the bus motored along a blisteringly hot, dusty road bordered by palms and ditches too deep to contemplate driving into and surviving. The occasional truck hinted at forcing them into one as overburdened and under-driven they used either side of the road on a whim. White brick farmhouses and tall waving palms dotted endless fields of drying newly cut wheat and millet. The bus hit a good piece of road and moved faster through forested hills and fields of green crops. Ahead of them above the heat haze, filthy black thunderclouds were gathering against the mountains. A storm was on the way.

Karen had forgiven Dan's interruptus. Bill had flown out after delivering Steve into the Indian justice system.

And good luck there, Steve. You'll wish you'd shot yourself with your Magnum.

"Miss him?" Dan asked a sad Karen.

"Already."

"Are you going to see him again?"

She went quiet so he shut up.

A storm had already blown through Dan and reorganized his emotions. He thought he'd steeled himself for death and had accepted its inevitability but the reality had been shockingly humiliating. It couldn't be that way. Things were going to change. Starting with Charlie. She'd been his last thought. He could no longer deny he loved her or avoid acting on it. It had never been lust for her young body. He'd connected with her at a deep emotional level, one of really caring for her as a woman: intelligent and independent, strong yet vulnerable, worldly beyond her years. She *interested* him and he wanted to know her far more. They could discover each other. She wasn't another daughter like Kathleen. He'd do anything for Kathleen, including giving up his life so she could enjoy hers, but with Charlie it was different: he didn't need her to complete him—that was a romantic fool's mission—he wanted that shared kindness that blended souls and made them one: true love. But he wanted the pleasure of sex too as long as it didn't control him and he didn't misuse it. He wanted to make the right kind of physical love with Charlie.

Charlie caught his eye and she came over to join him. She wore an NYU crimson t-shirt with a pair of shorts. Cruella must have got a bulk deal on the shirts. Lovely tanned thighs crossed next to him. He stared at her lovely face as though he'd never seen her before.

"You OK?" she asked, catching his look. She rested her hand high on his thigh.

"Not here for Chrissakes," he hissed and removed her hand.

She followed his gaze. "Like my gorgeous legs?"

"Go away."

She ignored him. "Have you noticed Shira and Duncan are getting very friendly?"

"Good for them. I suggested they have fun until Kathmandu."

"She's in love." Her hand reached for his. "I know the signs of a woman. Don't you?"

"I'm a guy. Write it down."

She gave his hand a big squeeze. "I've never seen Shira enjoying being with a man so much. Pity no good can come of it."

Dan thought Duncan missing out on a dual personality woman who'd killed two men wasn't too much of a downside. "I know. Her mother's lined up another alter kocker."

Charlie laughed. "David Hamlish is no alter kocker."

Cruella's gloating "she's taken" resonated. David Hamlish, heir to a billionaire who's probably the next president? *Ka-ching!* Hats off to the psycho. The ambitious, evil collaborators had sealed their deal suitably—in blood.

Charlie leaned in closer. "They're getting married as soon we get back. What do you think of that?"

"She isn't pregnant is she?"

Charlie giggled. "You kidding? Her boobs would explode!"

The thought of how enormous they'd get made Dan chuckle. "How long have Shira and Hamlish been dating?"

"They haven't. Just came out of the blue before we left on this trip."

"Isn't David sweet on you not her?"

She frowned. "Sweet on me?"

"Birthday presents? The Corvette? Not exactly a box of candies. I know men's signs. Don't you?"

She shrugged. "Maybe there's something there."

Dan took the opportunity to ask something that had been concerning him. "Remember you told me about you and David Hamlish?" he asked gently.

"Uh-huh."

"How's your child doing? Must be about five now. Boy or—?"

"Auntie got me an abortion in Canada," she said in a rush.

Charlie the Catholic had an abortion? A mortal sin? That's what had turned her away from the Church?

"Auntie did?"

She fingered her necklace's gold cross. "I didn't want to go but Auntie said my parents, especially my devout father, would disown me. Especially having a Hamlish baby. A family they hated. I trusted her to take care of me. I now think I made the wrong choice but I was confused, afraid and so young." She glanced at him. "I'll never know, will I?" she said softly and went silent.

An impossible choice she'd had to make? Was that the attraction of *Sophie's Choice?* She identified with Sophie and the self-destructive guilt she'd carry with her forever? He reached over and held her hand against his thigh.

"Do you think they really would have disowned you? Parents often only appear harsh because they're worried as hell about their kids. I always was. Still am."

She shook her head. "My parents would have forgiven me. An abortion? Never in a million years."

Dan went quiet, thinking about Cruella, Charlie and her aborted baby. Charlie rested her head against his shoulder. His heart went out to her. An abortion for a young Catholic woman? Devastating. It was hard to believe Cruella had done it out of the generosity of her heart. She didn't have one.

"Are you over it?" he asked.

"I get through a lot of novenas."

"You didn't go to California, did you?"

"I'm sorry I lied to you. After the abortion ... I felt awful. I was terribly depressed and hid out in Montreal for that year. It wasn't an awful time."

"You suffered and you came through it. It made you a better person. I'm proud of you." He squeezed her hand reassuringly. "How did David Hamlish deal with it?"

"The abortion came as a great relief to him."

Dan bet Hamlish thought differently now. Birthday cards? Corvettes? Guilt or lingering love? But he worried about the effect on a young Catholic girl like Charlie. She must have thought she'd killed her child. Her guilt must be enormous.

A sudden thought about Cruella and Jeb flew around in Dan's head. Was that it?

* * *

Dan's head grazed the roof of the minibus when it bucked in a particularly bad section of the pot-holed road toward the Barabar Caves. They hung onto the seats as the minibus tried to break its suspension, bouncing and banging in washouts from the last heavy rains. The bus slowed to almost a stop as the driver carefully maneuvered around holes the size of refrigerators. Obstacles had developed in size and increased in number in direct proportion to our distance north from the Ganges. Dan calculated they'd disappear completely into the magma if they stayed on the road another hundred miles.

They rose into the barren foothills, the metalled road turning into a bumpy dirt track. On either side, boulders grew into the size of small houses, gathering into flocks of giant gray-brown sheep. Cliff faces disappeared as the piles of boulders rose ominously, threatening to roll down and crush them at the slightest provocation. The track climbed higher into mountains that looked like they hadn't had a drink since the caves had been chipped out in Emperor Ashoka's time, more than two hundred years before Jesus sucked his thumb.

The sun punished them on the flights of concrete stairs that led up to to a sweeping arch of pink-brown rock that contained the four caves and overlooked fifty shimmering miles over brown land to the green, fertile plain near the Ganges to the south. It was a pleasant surprise to find they were the remote caves' only visitors.

Dan caught up with Cruella, Nadia and Kanta taking photos on the edge of a cliff that fell way to nowhere, cut almost vertically from a sheet of gray rock. Cruella, sweating profusely under her parasol, puffed like a dog sticking its head out of a car window. Nadia had dressed her bones in a loose khaki safari outfit from King Solomon's Mines, only missing a pith helmet and a flywhisk. Kanta towered over both of them, her green headscarf and multicolored sparkling kaftan reminding Dan of a Christmas tree. They all grimaced when Dan approached.

Nadia smirked. "If it isn't the hero."

"Hello, Elaine. How are you today?" he asked cheerfully, ignoring Nadia.

Cruella eyed him impassively. "Nadia's been telling me what a violent man you are."

It struck Dan she might be more impressed than bothered. "I don't do that anymore. I just rescue your girls from kidnappings and drownings, don't I?" Cruella smiled thinly. "You know you've got nothing to worry about with me," he said pointedly. "It's someone in the group killing Shira and Charlie you should worry about."

Cruella impassivity cracked. "In the group?"

Dan turned to Nadia. "You almost killed Karen. You pushed her into the road, didn't you?"

Nadia twisted a smile.

Cruella blinked at Nadia. "You tried to kill Karen?"

"What for?" Dan asked. "She's not my lover. When are you going to get it through that thick head? We're divorced! I got rid of you, you insane bitch!" he goaded, shoving his face into hers, his turn to get a violent response.

A glowering Kanta stepped forward and her big hand shoved him back.

"Don't call me insane, you fucking bastard!" Nadia spat. "We'll never be divorced! I swore to God you were forever and I keep my promises to God!"

"She's a religious maniac," he told a wide-eyed Cruella. He jabbed a finger at Nadia, poking at a mad bear in a cage. "You won't kill yourself but will kill any woman who gets near me?"

"Any woman!" Nadia blurted before biting her tongue.

"Any woman. Hear that, Elaine?" He deliberately glanced at Cruella, whose head had been flipping from side to side like a tennis umpire as she followed the hostilities.

He turned back to Nadia. "Shira? Charlie?"

Nadia trembled, fists clenched, mouth clamped shut. Cruella shot Nadia a look that was only missing a black hood and a double-bladed ax.

"Killing women keeps your promises to God? Why don't you kill me and get it over with?"

"Killing you wouldn't be justice! I'll make you suffer first! Suffer! Like I do!" She flashed her scarred wrists at him. It was the first time he'd seen the dark pink scar tissue.

"You cut the wrong way," Dan said coldly.

Nadia exploded. "You did this to me!"

Cruella stepped forward and shoved the end of her stick into Nadia's puny chest. "Go anywhere near my girls and you're dead," she growled.

Nadia staggered back but Kanta grabbed the end of the stick. She waved it in the air for a moment then broke it across her thigh like it was a dry twig. She threw the pieces over her shoulder into the abyss and glowered at Cruella like a pitbull in need of a leg to chew on.

"Goodbye, ladies," said Dan and left under a torrent of Nadia's abuse. Mission accomplished.

* * *

Dan's head grazed the roof of the minibus when it bucked in a particularly bad section of the pot-holed road out of Gaya toward the Barabar Caves. They hung onto the seats as the minibus tried to break its suspension, bouncing and banging in washouts from the last heavy rains. The bus slowed to almost a stop as the driver carefully maneuvered around holes the size of refrigerators. Obstacles had developed in size and increased in number in direct proportion to our distance north from the Ganges. Dan calculated they'd disappear completely into the magma if they stayed on the road another hundred miles.

They rose into the barren foothills, the metalled road turning into a bumpy dirt track. On either side, boulders grew into the size of small houses, gathering into flocks of giant gray-brown sheep. Cliff faces disappeared as the piles of boulders rose ominously, threatening to roll down and crush them at the slightest provocation. The track climbed higher into mountains that looked like they hadn't had a drink since the caves had been chipped out in Emperor Ashoka's time, more than two hundred years before Jesus sucked his thumb.

The sun punished them on the flights of concrete stairs that led up to to a sweeping arch of pink-brown rock that contained the four caves and overlooked fifty shimmering miles over brown land to the green, fertile plain near the Ganges to the south. It was a pleasant surprise to find they were the remote caves' only visitors.

Dan caught up with Cruella, Nadia and Kanta taking photos on the edge of a cliff that fell way to nowhere, cut almost vertically from a sheet of gray rock. Cruella, sweating profusely under her parasol, puffed like a dog sticking its head out of a car window. Nadia had dressed her bones in a loose khaki safari outfit from King Solomon's Mines, only missing a pith helmet and a flywhisk. Kanta towered over both of them, her green headscarf and multi-colored sparkling kaftan reminding Dan of a Christmas tree. They all grimaced when Dan approached.

Nadia smirked. "If it isn't the hero."

"Hello, Elaine. How are you today?" he asked cheerfully, ignoring Nadia.

Cruella eyed him impassively. "Nadia's been telling me what a violent man you are."

It struck Dan she might be more impressed than bothered.

"I don't do that anymore. I just rescue your girls from kidnappings and drownings, don't I?" Cruella smiled thinly. "You know you've got nothing to worry about with me," he said pointedly. "It's someone in the group killing Shira and Charlie you should worry about."

Cruella impassivity cracked. "In the group?"

Dan turned to Nadia. "You almost killed Karen. You pushed her into the road, didn't you?"

Nadia twisted a smile.

Cruella blinked at Nadia. "You tried to kill Karen?"

"What for?" Dan asked. "She's not my lover. When are you going to get it through that thick head? We're divorced! I got rid of you, you insane bitch!" he goaded, shoving his face into hers, his turn to get a violent response.

A glowering Kanta stepped forward and her big hand shoved him back.

"Don't call me insane, you fucking bastard!" Nadia spat. "We'll never be divorced! I swore to God you were forever and I keep my promises to God!"

"She's a religious maniac," he told a wide-eyed Cruella. He jabbed a finger at Nadia, poking at a mad bear in a cage. "You won't kill yourself but will kill any woman who gets near me?"

"Any woman!" Nadia blurted before biting her tongue.

"Any woman. Hear that, Elaine?" He deliberately glanced at Cruella, whose head had been flipping from side to side like a tennis umpire as she followed the hostilities.

He turned back to Nadia. "Shira? Charlie?"

Nadia trembled, fists clenched, mouth clamped shut. Cruella shot Nadia a look that was only missing a black hood and a double-bladed ax.

"Killing women keeps your promises to God? Why don't you kill me and get it over with?"

"Killing you wouldn't be justice! I'll make you suffer first! Suffer! Like I do!" She flashed her scarred wrists at him. It was the first time he'd seen the dark pink scar tissue.

"You cut the wrong way," Dan said coldly.

Nadia exploded. "You did this to me!"

Cruella stepped forward and shoved the end of her stick into Nadia's puny chest. "Go anywhere near my girls and you're dead," she growled.

Nadia staggered back but Kanta grabbed the end of the stick. She waved it in the air for a moment then broke it across her thigh like it was a dry twig. She threw the pieces over her shoulder into the abyss and glowered at Cruella like a pitbull in need of a leg to chew on.

"Goodbye, ladies," said Dan and left under a torrent of Nadia's abuse. Mission accomplished.

* * *

Loki rolled the ten-foot-high, wrought-iron gate away from the cave entrance to the biggest cave, the Lomas Rishi, and Charlie closely followed Dan under the archway carved with latticework and lines of elephants paying homage to Buddhist stupas. Loki's flashlight led the group into two cool rectangular rooms, a smaller first and a larger second deeper into the rock with a cavity that disappeared above them. It was a godsend, chilly after the pounding heat outside. Charlie took advantage of the dark to slip her arm around Dan's waist. She trembled with warmth when he responded by slipping his arm around hers. She'd thought about Dan since she'd awoken in a sweat from an erotic dream in which they'd made love in total darkness, only able to feel one another's bodies. Had it been a premonition of what was to come? What she desired? The thought was driving her mad with anticipation.

"Ladies and Gentlemen, these are the caves that Mister Forster used in his very famous book, *A Passage to India*," Loki informed them with a sweep of his arm. "He called them the Marabar Caves. They are the most famous caves in the world," he added with typical Indian hyperbole.

"Are they in *The Guinness Book*?" asked Mark with no hint of mischief.

"Yes, sah, I think they must be."

When the group filed out behind Loki, Charlie held Dan back. Her arms went around his neck and pulled him into her. She kissed him for a long time, her excitement intensifying when his hands slid voluntarily under her t-shirt to set her nipples pulsing.

God, how she wanted him! She deliberately hadn't pleasured herself since she'd met Dan and the desperate need she felt in her loins had reached critical.

"I'm ... not wearing any ... underwear," she whispered and sucked in her belly as she slid his hand down the front of her shorts. Dan tensed, his breathing quickening. She tensed too. Would he pull away and ruin the moment? A hot glow suffused her pelvis when his fingers started working. She moaned so loudly, the returning echoes surprised and thrilled her even more. Echoes like Adela Quested had heard and triggered her delusion of being grabbed by Doctor Aziz.

I'm Adela Quested with Doctor Aziz! This time Miss Quested will make love! What could be a better fantasy?

"Wouldn't you ... like to be Doctor Aziz ... and make love to me ... here? " she panted. "I won't ... freak out ... like Miss Quested."

She moaned again as an exquisite wave set her legs trembling. *Come on, Dan, or I'll explode!* Unable to wait any longer, she slid her hand to his zipper.

* * *

Dan stayed in the dark of the cave until his breathing slowed and his pulse returned to normal. Charlie's fantasy of sex in the cave had been one hell of a shock. He'd never had a woman be that aggressive. My God, young women weren't what they used to be. Outside the cave in the heat and blazing sunshine, Charlie was nowhere to be seen. Karen, Shira and Duncan were sitting as close as possible to the cliff edge for views of the valley so he re-checked his zipper and went over to join them.

"How are you today, Aquagirl?" he asked Shira.

Big sunglasses looked up from under her big brimmed hat. "The antibiotics are upsetting my stomach a bit," she said in a strong voice Dan liked. She held her belly and grimaced. "I need to be close to a bathroom all the time—and I don't see one."

"There's a cave up there you can use."

She giggled and made a face. He liked that a lot. "It's great to see you looking so much better."

"Thanks to you."

"And Duncan," he added, looking at Duncan dozing. "Father and son. We're a team, aren't we?" He nudged Duncan's foot.

Duncan knuckled his eyes. "Yeah," he mumbled.

He can't be my son, thought Dan. He's an idiot around women. But then at twenty-one, he'd been a dolt around them too.

There was something that had surfaced after Nadia's rant—and it smelled as bad as a bloated corpse rising from the depths to spoil a pool party. He turned to Shira. "I didn't ask you how you managed to fall out of the boat."

"I feel such an idiot. Loki told us not too but a few of us were standing when that big Kanta stood and really rocked the boat. We bumped into one another and over I went."

"Do you think someone might have deliberately bumped you off the boat?"

"Bumped me?"

Duncan woke up. "Bumped her?"

Karen flashed him a look. "Like me?"

"Like you," said Dan. "Who was standing with you, Shira?"

"Bob and … um … Nadia."

Karen gasped. "Oh, fuck!"

"Yes, fuck. Same as you. Who hates any woman who gets near me?"

Duncan jumped to his feet. "Mom? Surely not."

"She said she'd kill any woman who got close to your father," said Karen.

"Where's that twat?" Karen growled, striding ahead of Dan across the stone shelf.

Dan caught up with her and held her arm. "Take it easy Karen."

She tried to shake him off but he held on. "She's a bloody monster!"

Flashes of lightning forks crackled in the darkening sky. Thunder rolled like a heavy wet blanket across the mountains. A sniff of pungent nitrogen oxides. Loki called to get them on the bus because he could see the rainstorm coming.

Mark and Gilly waved to him as they headed back early to the bus. Cruella followed muttering to Bob and Rani and jabbing her finger at Nadia and Kanta ahead of them.

Nadia better watch out, thought Dan smugly now that she had been placed in Bob's gunsight. Dan didn't want him to kill her but he knew Bob had no such scruples, especially if he wanted to protect his own investment in Charlie. If she were collateral damage, so be it.

Where was Charlie? He wasn't looking forward to seeing her again. He'd jumped like a startled cat when she'd boldly unzipped him. He cursed himself for losing control and letting her lead him on too far. "Not here for God's sake!" and swatting away her hand had not gone down well.

"Jesus Christ! You must be fucking gay!" she'd seethed.

Humiliated and angry, she'd scampered out of the cave leaving him feeling far less of a man. If only she knew how he'd wanted to make love too. *What a disaster. Where the hell did "fucking gay" come from?*

Flash! Bang!

The roar of pounding rain rocked Dan before it hit him. Funneled and amplified against the cliff face, it was ball bearings cascading onto a silver tea tray. He hung onto Karen as they moved quickly in the rain that threatened to dimple their heads into the surfaces of golf balls. Rivers of it formed beneath their feet making the smooth rock into an ice rink.

Dan heard a shriek and spun around. It was Charlie, all arms and legs running toward them from a cave entrance. She was naked below the waist.

"He tried to rape me!" she screamed.

Gaya

The minibus rushed a chalk-faced Charlie along the road back to Gaya. Karen fulminated in gruesome detail what she'd like to do to the rapist's anatomy while she and Gilly, gritting her teeth with more British reserve but no less malevolent, dried her off and wrapped her in any spare clothing and towels to keep her warm. Loki looked as pale as Charlie. This must have been the group from hell. He looked grimly at the drenched Bob and Rani who'd rushed off with Dan and Mark into the pounding thunderstorm to scour the area for her attacker only to return empty-handed. They wore the humiliated expressions of bodyguards looking at the dead body of someone they were meant to protect, if just for themselves. Cruella had initially boiled with anger and excoriated Bob and Rani for their incompetence but Dan was chilled by how she'd cooled and become ominously smug—Jabba the Hutt drooling over her delicious frog appetizer. What was her cold-blooded mind up to?

Dan held one of Charlie's cold, trembling hands while a rock-faced Karen gripped the other one. Charlie's disturbed state of mind when she'd fled his rejection was still fresh in his mind when he said quietly, "Keep your eyes closed. Tell me what happened. Slowly. Take your time. Visualize it. Just talk to me." God, he sounded like a cheap CD advertised on late-night TV.

She squinched her eyes and tightened her grip on his hand. "I... was in the dark," she mumbled tremulously. "A... a man came at me from behind... held a knife across my throat." She caught her breath. "He was so big... he threw me to the ground like I was a doll and held the knife against my throat... I was so scared I just froze... I pleaded with him not to hurt me." She momentarily choked and sipped blindly on a shaking bottle of water.

"You're safe now," Dan said. He slipped a reassuring his arm around her shoulders.

"I let him do what he wanted... like we're told. He pulled off my shorts... I couldn't stop crying. I wanted him to do it and get it over with... I just didn't want to die. That's when I felt the knife slide under my arm."

"You had a knife?" gasped Karen, her voice rising sharply in expectation.

"More a toy." Dan held up a gap between a thumb and forefinger to show the size of the knife Charlie had bought at Ranakpur.

Charlie shuddered a deep breath. "When he looked down to pull down his pants... to get out his..." She shivered violently as though a blast of Arctic air had rushed into the bus. " It was so big... I got the knife ready. I... I was so afraid and shaking I almost didn't do it."

"You stabbed him?" growled Karen, her hand thrusting an invisible knife into the air.

Charlie's eyes flashed open, her lips tight over her teeth. "I slashed at his dick as hard as I could!"

"Oh! Bloody ripper!" chortled Karen.

Charlie hit a hand on her chest, swallowing hard. "Blood squirted... he screamed like hell and ran."

"She might have cut the bastard's dick off!" Karen shouted gleefully to the others.

It was met with a growl of approval from Mark, his livid face matching his mood. Nadia and Kanta exchanged sneers of indifference that roiled Dan's stomach and made him want to wipe their sour expressions off their faces—as did a glowering Duncan, who was only held back by Shira's restraining hand.

"Jesus, you're a brave girl!" exclaimed a sniffling Karen before she hugged the life out of Charlie. "Taking on a rapist with a toy? Bloody great!"

But foolhardy, thought Dan. He shook his head at Charlie's remarkable bravery under terrifying circumstances but women who fight their rapists often end up dead. She was a lucky one and wherever the luck had come from to her to buy the kirpan for protection from" rapists and dangerous fruit" a trip to a Sikh temple to say a short thank you wouldn't go amiss. He'd join her.

The pills he'd given Charlie earlier began to relax her and she stopped shuddering. When she slumped, burying her face in his shoulder to doze against him, he gave up his place to Gilly to professionally mother Charlie the rest of the way to the hospital. Karen allowed a tearful Shira to give her a break too. Dan gave Shira an appreciative smile. She was trying.

Cruella stopped tapping her way up the aisle to sigh her bulk onto the seat next to Dan while he was trying to dry himself off more with a damp towel.

"Still think she doesn't need ECT, *doctor*?" she asked snidely.

"Why would I?"

She blew out between her thick reptilian lips. "No one's seen this man but Charlene?" She flapped a hand. "He doesn't exist."

"Why wouldn't he?"

She twisted a cruel smile. Any moment she'd offer him a shiny, red, poisoned apple. "Because she's just like Miss Quested. One of the more pathetic products of Western civilization," she said, quoting Fielding in *A Passage to India*. "It's a hysterical fantasy of a self-absorbed girl. She needs treatment and she's going to get it." She chortled her way back to her seat.

So that was it: Jabba's main course was Charlie. Straight to Jodhpur drugged and in a straitjacket if necessary. Thanks for the gloating heads-up, thought Dan. She wasn't going to Jodhpur even if she'd claimed to have been raped by all 360 members of the Mormon Tabernacle Choir but Cruella left him with disturbing thoughts about Charlie. Her description of what had happened in the cave was plausible: the rapist and his knife, and how she'd cut him with her own knife to make him flee but she'd read Forster's book earlier in the trip. She and Dan had talked about it. "I won't freak out like Miss Quested," she'd panted as he'd stroked her passion before she'd fled from the cave in humiliated frustration. Had she been disturbed enough to hallucinate almost getting raped? *Jesus.* Was it his fault?

* * *

With the dark clouds lumbering away to the north, crackling and banging toward Nepal, the rain had stopped and heavy, humid air smothered the valley bottom by the time the minibus pulled up sharply, skidding in the wet gravel at the entrance to the white-walled and gray-tiled Railway Hospital in Gaya. Loki had phoned ahead to the police and the hospital as soon as they'd got within cell phone range of Gaya so a nurse and two burly attendants with a gurney were waiting for Charlie. Inside the hospital's sweltering receiving area, sweating patients and family members lounging on rows of wooden benches flashed their annoyance at her, Cruella and Shira being rushed by them.

An intimidatingly tall policeman stepped out of his blue and white cruiser, fitted his red-banded cap onto his large head and his black stick under his arm, and listened to the diminutive Loki's story with a thundercloud growing in his face. After punctuating a furious barrage at Loki with jabs of his stick to release his anger, he marched off into the hospital with Loki in his wake. Half an hour later, he sauntered out looking a much happier man, shook hands with Loki and departed. Dan guessed what had happened. The jaded cops had no interest in driving hours to the caves to search for evidence. Been there, done it, waste of our time for neurotic women. Case closed: there'd been no rape attempt and Charlie was another crazy from the Excited States who should be locked up. Dan wondered how much Cruella had donated to the police to grease the slipway to launch Charlie on her way to Jodhpur. Even if she had been raped, thought Dan, what would she have mattered to the cops anyway? One hundred rapes of women were reported every day in India although it was likely 1000 a day weren't. Rape was almost as popular as cricket.

Standing in the aisle at the front of the bus, a smiling Loki glanced at Bob and Rani who still looked like they were attending a funeral—their own. "Good news! Captain Shukla is not going to press charges!" he called out joyously.

"Well done, Loki," muttered Bob with a deep sigh.

The relief on his and Rani's faces was palpable much to Dan's expectation. They had no part in the rape attempt but it disturbed him that it was so damn convenient for Cruella. Could she have set it up on her own because she didn't trust them any longer? The only alternatives were the highly unlikely chance of it having been a random rape attempt or, far more likely, Charlie had been delusional.

"Not pressing charges?" Duncan frowned his confusion. "On the rapist?"

"No, no. On Miss O'Neill."

"*What?*" Duncan leaped to his feet so close to Loki he made him step back.

A startled Loki held his open palms toward Duncan. "Sorry, sah, but this kind of thing has happened so many times before," he explained in a placatory tone. "The captain is tired of hysterical … ladies … coming to the caves due to that damnable film and living out their … fantasy."

"*Fantasy?* Why the hell think that?" Duncan barked like a salivating Doberman eyeing an intruder's throat.

Loki gulped like a goldfish. "There's no evidence, sah, that anything happened except Miss O'Neill's statement. No witnesses. No one at the caves but—"

"Weren't her shorts ripped off?" growled Duncan.

"Yes but …" Loki shrugged his resignation. "The doctor hasn't been able to confirm any … um … there had been … er …"

"Penetration and semen?" Dan suggested, the doctor in the room who could use words like that and not be an offensive pervert.

Loki winced.

"She said he'd *tried* to rape her," Dan continued in a measured tone. "She never said he *had*."

"Quite so," said Mark firmly. "I'm with Charlie on this. We all should be."

Gilly jutted her chin by his side. "Hear, hear!"

Nadia croaked from a back seat: "She's just lying to get attention. They should lock her up."

"What's up with you?" Duncan yelled at her. "Why do you have it in for Charlie? You badmouth her and Shira whenever I talk to you!"

Nadia ignored him. "She cut this man, didn't she say that? Was there blood on her?"

"None … I'm afraid," replied Loki warily.

"How's that possible when a man's between your legs?" scoffed Nadia.

"*Jesus!*" Duncan despairingly threw his hands in the air. "Did you notice the fucking rain? She was soaked!" He viciously jabbed a finger at her. "And how would a lesbian like you know about men between your legs anyway?"

There was a collective gasp from the group. Christ, thought Dan. Duncan's suppressed anger at his mother was exploding. He'd never seen Duncan so mad at anything—except him. Son like the father.

Nadia jumped to her feet. "You ungrateful little shit!"

"Ungrateful for what? Lying to me about my father? You're the one I should hate!"

Nadia snarled at Loki: "Does she have a psychiatric history?"

Dan laughed. "You mean like yours?"

"Fuck you!" she yelped. Kanta stood up and hit her head on the bus's roof. The two them looked ready to tear Dan apart.

Duncan balled his fist. "You're the one who's nuts, *mother!*"

Too much like his father. When Dan shot to his feet to intervene, Duncan pushed Loki out of the way and stormed off the bus. Dan followed quickly to keep a fatherly eye on him. Also, he wasn't going to leave Charlie with her aunt no matter how nuts she might be. She wasn't going to Jodhpur. The Glock might come in handy.

* * *

Orange and white streetlights flickered on above Dan's head as darkness descended quickly. Far from the sky-blanketing pollution of Varanasi, constellations regained their luster in the pitch-black sky. The buzz and hum of racing tuk-tuks and cars gradually faded to be replaced by the clicking of insects. Dan batted away a squadron of mosquitoes that defied his smoke screen as he walked the hospital's grounds keeping his eye on the building's entrance.

Dan came across Duncan still cursing, kicking at the dry, brown ground between spiky succulents and tough-as-shit thorn trees. He put his arm around Duncan and together they walked without saying anything, each of them lost in their own tumbling thoughts. They sat on a plank of splintered wood resembling a bench under the shade of a dead tree rustling its dried-out branches. Dan smoked a Classic and gave one to a passing beggar with no muscle and a death rattle cough who should have been dead already. Wouldn't do him any harm. He inhaled and smoke never came out as he shuffled away.

"Is she crazy?" asked Duncan, glumly resting his chin in his hands, elbows on his knees.

Dan shrugged and avoided answering. "Hysterical like Judy Davis trembling with repressed passion in the dark womb-like cave with the Indian doctor entering her tunnel?" The possibility he'd triggered her to have a breakdown by his failure to satisfy her sexually haunted him.

"Um ... something like that." Duncan studied Dan for a moment before he asked, "You're in love with her, aren't you?"

"Like you are with Shira?"

"Isn't that deflection?"

Dan pensively blew a smoke ring that did nothing to sort out his Rubik's Cube of thoughts about Charlie. "It's complicated," he admitted with a rueful smile.

"So it's like me and Shira."

"Yeah, they're both handfuls."

Duncan grinned. "You mean Shira is."

Dan laughed awkwardly to lighten the mood further. "Sorry about that. Little happened between us."

"No worries. Charlie and I didn't get up to much either."

"So we're quits?" Dan held out his hand. Duncan shook it. "Have you told Shira you love her?" Duncan's grin said it all.

"And she loves me. Isn't that great?"

Dan slapped Duncan on the back and laughed: "You bet it is!"

Duncan looked so happy. Dan didn't have the heart to mention Shira was engaged to marry the son of an extremely rich man and was getting married in a few weeks. He'd let it ride and hope for the best. Love conquers all was a stretch but who knew what might happen?

"Tell me more about what happened with Mom," said Duncan.

He did. It was one of the best conversations of his life. They shared memories, some that they'd personally forgotten. Good times, bad times. It was a time for confession. Why he'd married Nadia in the first place. Their relatively happy marriage until Nadia had told him God wanted her to start a new life. How he'd carried on the family tradition of becoming a doctor and an alcoholic. How bad prison was for a man who'd assaulted a woman. Why he'd turned to Buddhism. Duncan told him about everything in his life for the first time and it brought Dan to tears. How Duncan had been hurt by his crazy parents.

"So life with a woman can be hard?" Duncan asked.

"Even when they're sane. Shira's going to take a lot of work from both of you."

"Why is that?"

Dan got through another cigarette by the time he'd covered the ground on Shira's personality disorder and what he was doing about it. Duncan sat listening carefully to every word. Maybe it would dissuade him and let him down gently.

"Are you ready to handle all that?" Dan asked.

"I don't know."

"I gambled on my future with your mother. I was in lust and too young to understand the consequences of getting it wrong."

Duncan nodded slowly. "And you did, didn't you?"

"In the end, I got it wrong but two good things came out of it: you and Kathleen. Without my bad choice, you wouldn't exist."

"There is that," said Duncan thoughtfully. "Now, what about Charlie? Is she worth the risk?"

* * *

A glass door swung open in the brightly lit hospital entrance. Cruella emerged with a bounce in her heavy step, followed by a downcast Shira. For a malevolent sociopath, Cruella looked far too happy. She shoved Shira into the back of the waiting taxi that roared away as soon as she got in herself.

"Work to do. See you later, Dad," said Duncan quickly and waved down another taxi.

Dan stubbed out his cigarette and re-entered the hospital where he was directed to a Doctor Gupta. At the end of a long corridor that smelled of a mixture of a pine forest and a laundry, he entered a staff room with assorted sofas, chairs, tables and kitchen appliances. A young woman with short black hair wearing a white coat lay with an arm folded over her eyes on one of the sofas. Dan recognized the exhaustion.

"Sorry to interrupt, Doctor Gupta," he said and meant it. "I'm Doctor Palmer."

She removed her arm and blinked tired eyes in dark sockets. He walked across the room to stand over her.

"How's the battle going?" he asked in his most charming doctor-to-doctor mode.

"I ... can't tell smallpox from dirty socks," she replied with great effort. She yawned as she sat up and reached for a cup of steaming tea from a side table.

"I'm Miss O'Neill's personal physician."

Doctor Gupta raised her eyebrows.

"She's rich," he explained.

"Lucky you. Please sit." She patted the sagging sofa before rubbing her eyes.

He sank into a sofa that had supported many a doctor's sleepover. "How is she?"

"Hysterical, uncooperative, won't take her pills."

"Miss O'Neill's just a spoiled, rich girl trying to get over an unconsummated love affair. She's still a virgin and desperate to lose it."

"And she read that book in preparation for this trip to the caves?"

He nodded. "You guessed it."

Doctor Gupta sipped more tea before tiredly shaking her head. "Another girl who identifies with that repressed Miss Quested. If I had a thousand rupees for—" She stopped herself.

"How about I get her off your hands?"

She studied him over a sip of her tea. "Her aunt offered me money to diagnose her as essentially a hysterical incompetent and release her into her custody. She assured me her niece will get first-class care at the psychiatric clinic in Jodhpur."

"And you accepted?"

She nodded. "A whole year's salary."

He knew she was thinking if he knew how much doctors earned in India. He did. It was why Indian GP's he'd known had moved to Canada to earn twenty to thirty times the amount. Cruella wasn't getting generous in her old age. She still wanted a good deal.

"She's paid you?"

"Tomorrow morning. A check when she collects her niece."

"A check that could bounce higher than Everest? You'd be taking a risk."

Doctor Gupta's eyes wandered as she thought that over.

"How would you like it in cash?" he suggested, pausing as he reached into his jacket pocket. "Right now?"

She continued to sip her tea but her heavy mascara cracked as Dan peeled off ten five-hundred-dollar bills. She didn't reach for them. He added another two and said, "She escaped, didn't she?"

She scooped up the bills before Dan changed his mind. "Please take her away, Doctor Palmer. I'll be glad to get another of these Barabar women off my hands. I'll leave a release form for you at the nurses' station." Her pager beeped. "The Black Plague has broken out on the second floor," she said wearily. "Drop by if you'd like to help before you go."

* * *

Charlie sat up, rigid against a pillow on the bed. "They don't believe me! Auntie's taking me to a clinic tomorrow!" She banged the bed with her fists. "They think I'm crazy! They think I just made it all up!"

Dan sat on the bed, unclenched one of her fists and held it between both of his. "First of all, let me get something off my chest. I'm sorry about what happened in the cave. I just wasn't prepared for you."

"So you should be!" she retorted, cheeks reddening. "I was so embarrassed!"

"I got that," he said with deliberate harshness. "I just didn't want you on a stone floor in a cold cave no matter how romantic it might seem," he lied. "Do you know how much I wanted to make love to you—proper love—in a big, comfortable bed? Not just a role-playing fantasy in a cave?" It was the best excuse that came to mind.

Charlie blinked, speechless, the wind taken out of her sails.

"And by the way, I don't know what men you normally lust after but I'm not *fucking gay*," he snapped, not holding back on his annoyance.

She paled under his glare. "I ... I'm ... so—"

"Listen! You have no idea how much I enjoyed what we did in the cave. We'll make love soon in Kathmandu. I promise. And it will be more special than you can imagine."

She pulled him to her and began to cry. "Oh, Jesus. How do you do this to me?"

He held her tightly and ran his fingers through her hair. He was back where he wanted to be.

She sniffed. "You believe me, don't you?"

No blood on her. No penetration. No semen. No one else at the caves. No knife marks on her throat either. It was an easy call.

"You bet I do, Miss Quested," he deadpanned.

"Oh, you ass!" Charlie held his face in both her hands to kiss him. "Thank you for believing me. Another reason to love you." She coyly fluttered her eyelashes like exotic black butterflies and ran her finger over his lips. "One day you'll say you love me," she said with a fierce determination.

"You think?"

"I know."

"Well, today's the day," he said nonchalantly.

"Oh!" Her hands covered her mouth below her wide eyes.

"I love you, Charlene O'Neill." It felt great to say the most dangerous three words on the planet and he hoped he didn't regret them. She threw her arms around his neck and held him tightly, her shoulders wracked with heavy sobs. He held her at arm's length. "Damn, I thought that would make you happy."

"Of course, it does!" She wiped her fingers on her cheeks. "Why are men so stupid?"

"It's hereditary." He passed her a tissue from a box on her nightstand.

She wiped her face dry and dabbed her eyes before throwing the covers off the bed to reveal long legs that briefly attracted Dan's eyes. "Now, how do I get out of here and get those bastards? I'm not going to any fucking clinic! I'm OK. I really am!"

"You *are* out of here. I've just arranged it."

"Fantastic!" She launched herself out of bed in her white gown. "Throw my bag of clothes over here, please!"

Dan passed her the bag and reached for the door to leave.

"Before you go," called Charlie.

He turned to find she'd lifted the gown to reveal where her red and green serpent ended in a dark red, bushy tail. "Look at what you'll get in Kathmandu," Charlie said throatily, her cheeks hot enough to barbecue steaks.

Jesus. Catholic girls.

* * *

Dan approached the nurse tapping on a computer keyboard at her station. She looked up at him expectantly. He checked her nametag.

"Good evening, Nurse Allad, I'm Doctor Palmer. I'm here to sign out Miss O'Neill."

The pristinely uniformed young nurse in a long white robe, wearing a light blue hijab over her long black hair, searched her desktop then slid a form with two carbon copies onto the counter for him to sign.

He slowly paced the hallway for a few minutes impatient to get outside and light up. Where the hell was Charlie? Women! After scanning a noticeboard and not needing a second-hand bicycle or play in the interdepartmental cricket game, Dan turned to the nurse to pass the time.

"When I was in Emergency we had some of the strangest cases," he said. "Ever had someone drill holes in his head to let the demons out and angels in?" He decided not to reminisce about those who'd *accidentally* sat on light bulbs or the man who'd hilariously sucked his cock into a vacuum cleaner.

"Oh, we get all kinds of cases." She slipped him a bigger smile. "We had a good one today." She looked away then back at him. "A poor man had his ..." Her eyes showed a lot of white. "It was almost cut off by his wife!"

Dan stopped mid-breath. The nearest hospital to the caves? "How is he?"

"He's been stitched up and is in one piece, I believe."

"Where might I find him?"

She waved her hand to a corridor to the right. "Room ten, doctor."

"Thank you, nurse. Please tell Miss O'Neill to wait for me here when she's got dressed. I'll be back in a minute."

Dan walked around the corner and gently pushed the door open to Room ten. A large man with a boxer's face lay on his back with a bed sheet draped on a frame over his groin area. An IV drip fed blood into a hairy forearm. He went for shock tactics: he ripped off the bed sheet and the frame and had the man's bandaged cock in his hand before he had time to jerk his eyes open. He had the pinpoint pupils of a sedated man but eyes the size of tennis balls as he gasped.

"You tried to rape that woman at the caves, didn't you?" Dan growled close to his face.

The man's mouth opened wide as he squealed in pain. His hands flayed the air. Dan gripped harder.

"Yes, yes!" He writhed in agony. Dan felt his pain but gave him more.

"Get your jollies from raping women do you?"

The man squealed louder. He had a very limited vocabulary until Dan eased off. "I ... paid ... so much! So much! I couldn't—"

"What?" Subconsciously, Dan must have tightened his grip. The man writhed and screamed. "Who paid you or I'll rip it off and flush it!" Dan squeezed even harder. If the man's eyes had not been wired into his head, they would have bounced out. He hit his head back on the pillow again and again.

"No name! Woman! No name!"

"Describe her!" Dan demanded with a vicious twist.

The metal bed-frame creaked as the man's hands tried to bend it into a pretzel. He shrieked a staccato babble amidst streams of snot pouring out of his nostrils.

My God! Her? Dan let go and the man curled up the bed, whimpering as he grasped himself.

Footsteps clicked rapidly on the corridor tiles. The door banged open. Nurse Allad's wide eyes darted from Dan to the patient and back to him again.

Dan brushed past her. "I told him it was too early for a wank."

At the nursing station, Dan phoned Captain Shukla.

Rapist. Room ten. Career cut short. Retired. Arrest the bastard.

April 5th

Lumbini

FOR THE FIRST time, Bob sat next to Cruella on the bus. With a face of dried cement, he fidgeted uncomfortably like a badly behaved schoolboy as Cruella the headmistress leaned on him and poked a talon into his chest. As low as her voice was, the sharpness to her muttering was obvious to everyone and Bob knew it. But Dan knew Bob deserved an Oscar: why be unhappy when Charlie hadn't been whisked away and she was still in play for a megabuck ransom?

Cruella shot a withering glance at Dan. Someone had got a morning surprise that was knitting next to Gilly. Within thirty minutes, Charlie's clacking needles had churned out a blue and white shawl a foot square. Impressive. Rich, owned a Corvette, knew some literature, interested in history and religion, loved old movies, politically involved, knew geography outside of New York State, good looking, sense of humor, not a murderer, bipolar or delusionally hysterical, and in love with him. He hadn't forgotten the thrill of her in the gazebo, at the Mahabodhi temple and on the edge of consummation in the cave either. He wondered how well she cooked.

To stay on the right side of his deal with Cruella, Dan moved over to sit down next to Shira when Duncan left for a visit with Mark.

"Mother's so angry about Charlie," she said keeping her voice down. There was glee in a strong voice.

"Why's that?"

"She had a flight arranged to fly Charlie to that clinic in Jodhpur. She almost had a stroke when she found she'd escaped Bob and Rani. Too bad, huh?"

"A terrible shame—she didn't have a stroke." Shira giggled. "I'm glad you and Charlie are getting along so well together. Sisters should be that way."

"I like it too."

"Has Elaine been asking about your sex life?"

Shira choked and bit a finger to stop laughing out loud as her cheeks burned. "You'd be surprised at what we get up to."

He squeezed her hand. "I can only imagine what you made up." He kissed her cheek trying not to imagine it.

* * *

Leaving India along the crowded road, they drove into a shambolic circus, the entertainment being the swarm of people walking with luggage, riding bicycles piled high with sacks and bags or in overburdened vehicles played out to a cacophony of car and truck horns thrown in for good measure. The old cars creaked and rattled, full of families and food supplies, with TVs, computers and assorted boxes piled on the top; massively overloaded yellow, orange and green trucks tilted over on their bald tires with their unbalanced cargoes. The line-up stretched for a mile along the road to the border crossing gates.

Dan sat on the edge of his seat chewing a nail as the big ENTERING NEPAL sign on the border arch got closer. Still no Kapoor. No cops approached them as they got out of the minibus and walked the last few hundred yards to have passports checked and visas issued. Dan would normally have smiled smugly having pre-paid for a visa as the others lined up and were overcharged four dollars each by sweating officials surrounded by piles of paperwork, stuffed into a cash cow of a small, wooden building. But he began to worry not about himself getting to safety in a few yards but about Kapoor. Something had to have happened to him because his disappearance made no sense at all. He looked back as he entered Nepal through an open gate and felt an odd pang of regret that he'd never see Dipak Kapoor again: the witty homo had grown on him. He'd have to take care of Bob himself. For Dipak, if no one else.

A half-hour stop at their hotel to unpack and have a quick wash or shower and they were off again, driving another half hour along another narrow, bumpy road to the World Heritage Site that housed Lumbini Gardens, the sacred birthplace of Prince Siddhartha Gautama, the Buddha. A wave of relaxation enveloped Dan—he'd been looking forward to this special moment for four years.

At the entrance to the Lumbini Gardens, a faded brown sign proclaimed the five precepts of Buddhism:

I observe, refraining from killing all living beings
I observe, refraining from taking what does the owner not give
I observe, refraining from committing sexual misconduct
I observe, refraining from telling lies
I observe, refraining from taking any intoxicant or drug

"Two out of five isn't bad, is it?" quipped Duncan.

"That many?" Dan replied.

Two security guards in t-shirts and camouflage pants with Uzi submachine guns and hands of playing cards got up from their plastic chairs and came aboard to check them out. If guards had examined their luggage, they'd have found Dan's Glock in his bag at the back of the bus; it would have been sacrilege to take it with him to visit Buddha's birthplace. The site hadn't had any trouble since 550 BCE so the odds were pretty good he wouldn't get into any. The guards waved them through and went back to their card game and listening to the sound of a cricket match on the portable TV with a long antenna they'd set up in the shade outside their hut.

Multi-colored prayer flags flapped on a spider's web of sagging wires, stretching from leafy branch to leafy branch of the old trees that shaded parts of the expansive, green lawns from the golden rays of the fading blood-orange sun. Dan had decided he was nothing. What did he matter in a universe bigger than he could ever understand, one with billions of suns setting in it just like this one? He mattered not and nor did anyone else. It was a place to sit and hear and see nothing—and think nothing.

He obliged, letting his simmering anger at Cruella and her minions continue to subside as he walked as far as he could across the swath of close-cut lawn and lay down near the thick roots of one of those heavily leafed trees. He rested his head back into his hands. The air smelled of freshly cut grass. Closing his eyes, he relaxed and ran through his meditation routine he hadn't used for a few days. He thought of the Buddha statue in his pocket to give him a focus. With the light breeze rustling the tree branches and fluttering the strings of flags, his heart rate slowed, his breathing became shallow. He melted into nature.

Someone approached, their feet crunching on the dry leaves. The person sat down by his side and leaned close. He kept his eyes closed and smelled the sweet rose scent drifting his way. Charlie or Shira? He had to be careful or he might end up in the pool where Buddha's mother, the Maya Devi, went for a swim before the prince was born. A hand stroked his cheek. No rings—Charlie.

He didn't open his eyes. "Feeling good?" he asked.

She whispered in the way mothers use on their babies. "Very good. Because I'm with you, someone who loves me."

A pair of lips barely touched his. He opened his eyes to hers. Magic. He quickly looked around for voyeurs.

"It's OK," she said. "No one's around to bother us here." Her lips touched his again and dwelled longer. The tip of her tongue danced the salsa across them. He did the rumba on hers.

She rested back on her elbows and sighed as she looked at the spread of the peaceful gardens. "This is a special place for you, isn't it?"

Dan rolled over onto his stomach. He tore a few blades of grass and smelled their freshness, thoughtfully playing with them as he considered how Buddha had changed his life and brought him to this spot with Charlie. He glanced at her. "Absolutely special."

She rolled closer to put an arm around his shoulders. "I'm so glad we're here together to enjoy it," she said softly and kissed him on the cheek.

"I have something important to tell you," he said.

"You really, really, really love me?"

"You know I do."

"I do but I need to hear it frequently." She peppered his face with kisses before he managed to speak again.

"But," he said.

She stiffened, steeling herself for disappointment. "But?"

"But ... it's complicated. I'm complicated. You're very complicated."

"Ah."

"I arranged to become a monk at Nagarkot monastery after this trip is over."

She drew back. "A monk?"

"I had thoughts of spending some time trying to be a better person. Maybe come back to do better too."

She narrowed hopeful eyes. "*Had* thoughts? You're not going to do that now?"

"No." He tightened his hold on her. "You've made me want to enjoy my life as long as I can. Do good things here and now. Not lock myself away from everyone and everything."

"So what are you going to do?"

"I'm not going to Nagarkot. I'm going to be a doctor in a Sherpa village called Namche Bazar." He shrugged. "When I die, getting myself chopped up and flown away in bits by eagles and kites sounds good to me. I've written it in my will."

"Where's Namche ... whatever?"

"It's on the trek up to Everest Base Camp. A few hundred houses. Maybe a thousand people at most. Delivering babies, curing coughs and wheezes, fixing trekkers' twisted knees and dealing with their heart attacks. I'll feel really useful."

She chewed her lips and took a breath. Her arm tightened over his shoulder. "Am I in it?"

It took all his resolve not to say *yes* immediately.

"Let me stay with you." Her eyes pleaded with him. "I could be ... ," her voice leaped, " ... your nurse! How about that? We could—"

"And what do you know about nursing?"

"I could learn, couldn't I? You could teach me."

"I don't think Namche has cable or malls."

Charlie hit him on the shoulder with a closed fist. "I don't need those things! I need a man like you!" She tried to smile but failed. Her eyes bubbled. "I love you more than I can tell you and you're going to send me away!"

"Isn't that what we agreed a long time ago?"

"That was before we fell in love."

Dan kissed her again and tasted the salty tears at the corners of her mouth. "You're young, Charlie. Don't waste your life on me without thinking long and hard about it. Couldn't this just be a vacation romance?"

"Oh, it's far more than that." She ran her fingers over his lips, an intimate gesture that had him wobbling. "I don't want to go back home. I hate it. How can I go back to live with a woman who's trying to drive me nuts!"

Dan had thought about this. "You'll be safe from your aunt in the States."

"How?"

"I know a way." He had no idea how. He had a few days to work on it. "And when you're twenty-one, you can come back and live with me if you're still interested."

Her eyes expanded to match the gathering O of her mouth. "I *am* in it!" The peace of the gardens was broken for a few seconds as she yelled to the trees that rustled back their happiness for her. Dan knew a lot could happen in the next year but he'd made her very happy right now.

She eventually sat up, the beaming mouse that had got a moon of cheese. "And only two days till we make love in Kathmandu too?" She chuckled. "You'll need an ambulance after I've had my way with you!"

Dan hadn't forgotten his promise. He'd got carried away and it worried the hell out of him.

One last long kiss before she stood over him. "I told Auntie I'd meet her at the temple in a few minutes. I'll see you back on the bus!" Charlie skipped off across the lawn like a spring lamb. She turned beneath one of the low-hanging boughs of a huge tree wrapped in strings of fluttering prayer flags and saw he was watching her. "Namche! *Whoo-hoo!*" she called, waved, blew him a kiss and disappeared. It hit him. A crushing pain in his stomach. One day soon, he might never see her again.

* * *

Shira looped her arm through Dan's as they strolled along a gravel path toward the white house where Buddha had been born and the sacred pool where his mother had bathed beforehand. Shira had appeared from nowhere as he'd wandered head down among the trees letting Lumbini ease his anxiety over Charlie. No dark circles under her eyes. Mouth slack, almost smiling. No pinched eyebrows. She kicked at the gravel along the path like a kid enjoying life. He stopped walking and held her still.

"What?" she asked.

He admired her clear eyes through the pair of fashionably hip rectangular glasses she'd perched on her narrow nose. "You've changed so much," he said. "You have beautiful eyes without those brown contacts. And regular black-haired beauties are just fine with me too."

She smiled from her pink lips to her steel-gray eyes. "Thanks. I feel so much better." She primped her glossy, newly dyed hair, shoving long strands behind her ears. Dan sniffed her cheek. Not Charlie's roses but violets. It triggered thoughts of a small blue-glass bottle on his mother's dressing table.

"Is that Evening in Paris?" he asked.

"You know it?"

"My mother bathed in it. It smells great on you."

"Thank you. Time I found my own perfume, isn't it?" She tightened her arm on his. "I'm changing everything I can to what I want. I've been meditating and letting my anger go," she said. "It's been destroying my life."

"It's a long process," Dan advised gently. "Just take the drug and avoid stress." He held her in front of him and held her eyes in his. "What's going on in your head cannot be made better by simply thinking it will. It's not a rational thing. Eating properly and stopping drinking won't solve your problems. It's the other way around. Become you and you'll be better. Love yourself first. Help others. It'll be years, maybe decades but you'll get there."

"Stop thinking and live, you once told me."

"No need to compete with Charlie any longer."

"I've always been envious of her: so tall, stunning red hair, so beautiful. Boys were all over her like bees buzzing around a honeypot."

"You decided on a bit of surgery?"

"I was desperate. Always the ugly sister. Mother told me I'd never get a man if I looked like a hook-nosed, flat-chested wonder."

"Nice," Dan said sardonically. "But *she* did. Nose and all."

"She got pregnant with me. Deliberately I'm sure. Trapped her rich man. Poor Dad." A little girl crept into her voice: "I'll have another rich man soon."

He led her to a nearby bench seat and brushed off a few dead leaves. She rested against him. "How do you feel about Duncan?" he asked. Her face sagged. She bit on a red nail.

He gently took her hand away from her tight lips. "Why not run away with Duncan?"

Her shoulders drooped. "No one runs away from my mother. She controls all my money and would hunt us down. Do you know how much harm she could do to Duncan?" The tears began to flow. "I couldn't do that to him."

Dan gave her a reassuring hug while thinking he couldn't let her and Duncan be robbed of a chance at happiness together. There had to be a way beyond suggesting matricide but it escaped him just like how to protect Charlie back in the US. He was running out of time.

"My father ran away from her and look what happened to him," Shira said.

That caught him by surprise. Her memories—or Carla's—were returning. A good thing—if she could handle them.

She sniffed. "Mother never forgot what he'd done."

"Left her with you?"

"For her younger sister of all people. How she hated them. She waited almost twenty years to get her revenge, didn't she? And now she's after Charlie."

"*After* Charlie?" he asked.

"Charlie's going to be very rich soon. When she's twenty-one, she'll inherit a trust worth millions."

"How many millions?"

"About three hundred."

Dan's brain hit the pause button.

The crunch of feet on the gravel path. Two dark figures approached them: one thin and the other taller and wider. Double trouble, thought Dan, and they stood up quickly. Maybe leaving the gun behind had been too respectful. Shira gripped his arm tightly.

"If it isn't dickless," Nadia rasped, stepping into the light of the lamp high on the pole. "And who's this? Ah! You've moved on to the one with bigger tits." Shira stiffened. "Not to mention a bigger ass," she scoffed.

Dan heard a purring growl that bristled his neck hair. He shot Shira a sharp look. Breathing heavily with her fists clenched, Carla flashed her eyes back into his.

Nadia stepped closer. "He's my husband, you whore!"

"Pity she didn't drown in the Ganges when you pushed her in," Dan said, forcing his arms between Carla and Nadia. Kanta edged closer, eyes moving back and forth between Carla and him. Kanta who had hired the rapist. He tensed, ready to defend himself and she was the one to take out first.

Nadia laughed. "If only the bitch had drowned like she was meant to!"

Carla's sudden punch to Nadia's mouth sent her staggering backward. Kanta swung a pig's knuckle fist that missed a dodging Carla just as Dan released like a coiled spring. He caught her chin with the heel of his left palm, almost snapping her huge head off her thick neck—and fired a knife up his forearm. Kanta spun and bellyflopped onto the mirror surface of the pool with a splash that echoed like a gunshot off the building. A dazed Nadia sank to her knees, holding her face, blood flowing through her fingers. She spat out a tooth.

"Dan?" Shira said in her little voice.

He turned to find Shira wobbling, blinking rapidly. "Let's get you back to the bus," he said helping her stumble away from the pool. He glanced back at Kanta and Nadia. A dazed Kanta stumbled to her feet but fell back on her ass in the shallow water. Nadia still spat blood. They'd live. Shira had no idea what she'd just done. Dan knew he'd remember it fondly as long as he lived.

* * *

Having given Shira a sleeping pill so she could rest back on the bus and swallowed enough pills to treat the fierce pain in his wrist, Dan strode back to see Buddha's birthplace. He had twenty minutes to make a pilgrimage of sorts to the white building housing the site before the bus left. Seen a thousand times in books and videos, it couldn't be missed.

The wooden walkway that led through the white, stone building protected the foundations of a rectangular house. It worked its way in straight sections around three of the walls to an exit back to the gardens. Dan leaned on the rail, holding his throbbing wrist as he looked down at a shallow depression in the rock and thought how this extraordinary, compassionate and peaceful man had changed billions of lives for the better over the millennia—including his own. He dreaded to think where he'd be now if Paul hadn't schooled him in the simple tenets of Buddhism that required no god but the adoption of a personal code of practice to correct inequality and injustice in the world and lead to happiness. He breathed in another special moment that ranked alongside being at the Bodhi tree and it filled him with an even greater resolution to help others. Shuffling feet and a stick tapping behind him interrupted his reverie.

Cruella sighed, a bemused smile flickering. "You don't believe that's actually Buddha's birthplace, do you?"

"Probably not. More likely Santa's." He glanced at her. "Or King David's."

Cruella shrugged. "Doesn't matter anyway, does it?"

"Not a bit. It's the philosophy that matters." He took a few photos of what looked like a footprint and waited for what Cruella was after.

"You think you got the better of me, don't you?" she asked in a tone he didn't like to hear in a psychopath. "You haven't kept your part of the bargain. I should get my money back."

"Yes, I have. Shira's happy, why aren't you?"

"You haven't stayed away from Charlene."

"I didn't agree to have her shipped to a loony bin to have her brains blown out."

"How did you get her out of that hospital?"

"I bribed the doctor with your money. I like the irony, don't you?"

Cruella made a rude noise. She rested herself against the wooden rail that creaked its complaint. "Why do you bother when we'll be gone in a few days and you can get on with your godless existence? Charlie will be under my control and I can do whatever I want with her."

"So why are you in such a hurry to lock her up before you get back to the States?"

Dan knew he'd hit home when Cruella's mouth clamped shut and her face slid into an expressionless wall. She waved a hand dismissively to change the subject. "So, are you really one of these weird Buddhists?"

"You mean the one billion, weird, pacifist Buddhists. You're lucky."

"Why am I lucky?"

"It's why I haven't killed you."

"Funny man," she said without laughing. "Still not too late for me to change my mind and have Bob bury you here in the park."

"Still playing that old tune?"

He walked farther along the walkway around the foundations, pausing occasionally to take photos of the cleaned stonework. He noticed the CCTV cameras keeping an eye on them from each corner of the building. He canceled his idea of running off with Buddha's birth rock. There were probably a thousand a day being made in China anyway.

She lumbered behind him tapping her backup stick. "I underestimated you. I thought you were another *shlemiel* who'd disappear as soon as he was threatened or paid off." She tapped his shoulder with her stick. A small smile flitted across her mean mouth like a scorpion.

"I've wondered if you'd get a bit physical but you seem to be smart. Not just one of those weak Buddhists."

"You think they can't fight back when needed? They don't murder people but they can defend themselves against people like you. Some God-fearer, you are. You'll go straight to hell for what you are."

"And what am I?"

"A text-book psychopath. We're all just stupid, aren't we? Not fit to share the same planet with a genius like you?"

"I said you were smart."

"You had Charlie's parents killed by Bob in a car accident, didn't you?"

She blinked slowly at him.

"Your ex was rich and had screwed you over long ago. You hated your sister because she'd taken him from you. You waited almost twenty years to get your revenge."

Her face became even more impassive.

"The money would have gone to his wife but whaddayaknow she's dead too. What luck! Money will go to ... Guess who? Charlie when she's twenty-one. Unless she's dead or declared incompetent, of course. So where would the money go then?"

"His loving daughter Shira?"

"Not if Charlie'd had her baby. You manipulated her away to have an abortion in Montreal. A mortal sin. You disgust me."

She waved his disgust away with her hand. "Mortal sin? What garbage. Give me some credit for not simply killing Charlene. She's my niece, my Jewish blood but she couldn't have a child who would have been in line to inherit. It had to go."

She made the child an annoying puppy she'd kicked to the curb. Dan restrained an urge to beat her senseless with her own stick. "You used Shira to keep away men who showed any interest in Charlie. *Jesus.* She killed two of them!"

She smirked. "You're lucky you weren't the third, weren't you? Now take that two hundred thousand and I'll forget about you."

"I want half."

"Half of what?"

"Half of three hundred million." A glint in her eyes as a megamillion-watt light bulb clicked on but she barely blinked.

"You think I'd give you one hundred and fifty million dollars to keep quiet? Now, you're the crazy one," she said in the tone of a gravedigger sharpening a shovel.

"I'd hate you to miss out on the billions from David Hamlish. The pot of gold at the end of the blackmail rainbow? I don't think you want me to screw up that, do you?"

Dan thought her face stayed impressively blank as she blinked slowly. The control psychopaths exert over what emotions they have is remarkable.

"I could have you killed ten thousand times over for that money," she finally said.

"It wouldn't take that many tries." Dan brushed her off. "But I thought you were smarter than that. All the information I have on you, Bob and Hamlish will be delivered to the police and media if anything happens to me or my son. Want to be in the *Washington Post* first then prison later? Or do they still have the chair in New York State?"

"You've been reading too many detective stories. You're bluffing."

"Call me if you want." Dan stared back at her, equally impassive.

"Five."

"Twenty."

"Eleven."

"Agreed." He didn't offer his hand.

She wobbled the chins under her twisted lips. "You're just a piece of *drek* like the other gold diggers."

"A smart piece of *drek*, please." His turn to rub it in. "Get over it. I've outsmarted you. Just take your millions and run along, you evil hag," he added with supreme condescension. "Bank account tomorrow," he ordered.

"This isn't over," Cruella said as cold as a sheet on a corpse in a mortuary.

Crash! The door swung open wildly and banged against the stone wall. A security guard waving a big stick braced himself in the doorway.

* * *

The gray, concrete-block police station with its shiny metal roof had small, barred windows that only skinny criminals could escape through. At least they let in a light night breeze to cool the heat within it. The cells were above the usual Indian standard with a metal toilet without a seat a welcome replacement for the usual bucket. Stripped of all his clothes and provided only an itchy blanket, Dan sat on the metal bench that doubled as a bed suspended on chains from the wall, shivering despite the mugginess of the evening.

Through the opened viewing slot in the cell door, the immaculately dressed guard with glistening hair coaxed smoke from a long cigarette while munching on a late supper of chapattis and stir-fried vegetables. The tape player on his desk oozed the piano of Barry Manilow. At any other time, having missed dinner, the spicy aroma of the hot food would have been as much torture as the music. This time, Dan's stomach and intestines had ceased practicing knot tying but he felt sick right down to his bare feet on the dirty floor tiles. Being back in a cell did that to him.

"I demand a lawyer," he told the guard.

"The captain will be here after he's finished his dinner," the guard replied riffling through the wad of cash he'd found in Dan's cargo pants. "The boss will be most interested in this," he said, no doubt thinking of his cut.

"I have more of that if you like."

"Really? The captain will be glad to know that."

"I have the right to a lawyer," Dan insisted. He knew he could kiss the money goodbye but it wasn't what worried him. With Shira nowhere to be seen, Nadia must have reported only him for attacking them. His swollen wrist throbbed with pain again to remind him there was no denying he'd hit someone. His word against Nadia's as to who'd started it? Was there any CCTV? The camera on the light post by the pool! It would show what happened! He'd be OK once they checked that. But what if they held him long enough to find out who he was? He needed to get out pronto.

"You haven't been arrested." The guard smiled smugly. "You've been detained as a suspect."

"How long can I be detained?"

"At least twenty-four hours. But up to six months if we feel like it."

Dan hit his head on the door. "Six months?"

The guard laughed a high-pitched, effeminate whinny. "You can have a lawyer when you're questioned," he volunteered with a sly smile.

"When will that be?"

"When the captain has finished his dinner!" The guard applauded himself by slapping his hand several times on his desktop. Dan had a feeling he'd had that conversation many times with head-banging detainees.

He decided not to bang his tin cup on the bars to annoy the guard and instead slowed his breathing and tried to lower his pulse rate to zero. Let his anxieties float away like a child's helium balloon up the valleys toward the mountain tops. Unshaven, his leather face lined with the furrows of an irritated man, half a beedie hanging beneath a shaggy tarbrush mustache on a scarred top lip, the police captain lumbered into the cell as subtly as Huns entering a convent. With a revolver stuck in a holster under his sizeable paunch, he was a heavy Raymond Chandler would have written into a bar fight. The guard leaped to his feet and saluted crisply.

"Found this in his pocket, sah." The guard handed him the wad of cash. The captain grunted, peeled off a good chunk of bills for the guard, and stuffed the rest in his trouser pocket.

"And he tried to bribe me," whined Desai sycophantically.

"The bastard did, did he?" Khan wiped some sauce off his chin and greeted Dan with a belch of beer breath. "Stand up!" he ordered Dan and swatted him across the head onto the floor as soon as he did. "I'm Captain Khan and I eat shits like you for dinner!" he said, spitting liberally into Dan's face.

Dan assumed Khan was the bad cop.

"Get up, you bastard!" Khan jabbed Dan with the sharp toe of his shoe.

Dan stood up, wrapping the blanket around him and keeping an eye on Khan's hands: big with the enlarged knuckles of a bruiser. "What am I supposed to have done, Captain?" he said with forced politeness considering his ear was ringing for the butler. He kept a hand over his groin.

"Done?" He was promptly whacked on the same side of the head before he could get an arm up and knocked down again. "What's wrong with you? Can't stay on your feet?" The captain's mocking laugh wobbled his big belly. "Confess and I won't beat the living shit out of you. Didn't I tell you to get up?"

Dan warily rose to his feet, rubbing at the pain in his face. "Confess ... to what?"

Khan shoved his face into Dan's. "You murdered a woman at the sacred Maya Devi pool!"

Dan gaped at him. "What?"

"You punched her into the sacred pool! She drowned!" Khan seethed showering him in spittle. He grabbed Dan's swollen wrist and twisted it enough for Dan to yelp in agony. "Look at this! What kind of fucking arsehole, are you?"

He answered his own question by pinning Dan against the wall with one thick arm up his throat and punched him in the stomach. A firestorm of pain reached every part of Dan's body before Khan dropped him onto the floor. Dan choked, mouth filled with bitter acid, *murdered* splashing across his mind's front page.

"One of the women identified you as their attacker so you're fucking toast, *gandu*. Admit you murdered her, you piece of shit, and I'll go and have another beer and you can take less of a beating. I'm only getting started. What's it to be?"

Dan decided to stay down. It was where he always ended up. "I ... didn't murder ... anyone. It was ... an accident. They—"

"*Accident?*" Khan roared and swatted him across the head again.

"They attacked ... me! Check ... the camera at the pool ... for God's sake!"

"Hear that, Desai?" Khan laughed derisively. "Check the camera? Never thought of that!" Desai whinnied. "None of those fucking cameras work." Dan's writhing stomach burned more at the news. Khan grabbed his hair and pulled him to his feet again.

"I ... have more ... money," Dan stuttered between retches.

Khan let go of his hair. "Where? Maybe I should look for it up your lily-white *gandu!* Fucking white men. You *goras* still think you own the fucking place, don't you? Buy anything you want. Buggered us for centuries and you can't stop, can you? Now, it's our turn." He pulled his revolver out of his belt and waved its stubby barrel at him. "Desai? Bend him over!"

"Bastards!" Dan got in a few kicks but his blanket was ripped off as the two men overwhelmed him. He screamed, writhing, but couldn't stop them from folding him over with his face pressed into the tiles. Desai had him down by the neck while Khan had his legs under the full weight of his knees.

He bucked and squirmed for all his worth. "*Chodnas!* Fuckers!" Dan yelled. "*Betichods!* Daughter fuckers!"

"Hey, the pussy *gora* knows a few words of Hindi!"

"Stop that right now!" A commanding voice thundered in the small space.

Dan looked up through a haze of angry tears at the cell's doorway—a battered face peered down at him. The man boiled in anger, a Browning shaking in one hand and a camera clicking in the other. He'd been through a meat grinder: a stitched right eyebrow over two black eyes, a swollen nose wearing a broad plaster. His lips were split and stitched. Dressed in a beige raw silk jacket over an open-necked white shirt and impeccably creased trousers from a night out at the Tropicana, Kapoor hadn't let the beating alter his sense of sartorial splendor.

"Who the fuck are you, semi-dick?" growled Khan, turning to point his gun toward Kapoor.

"Drop that before I drop you!" Kapoor barked with a waggle of his own gun.

"You won't shoot me. Just a bit of fun with the *gora*."

Kapoor lowered the gun's aim. "Willing to risk your cock?"

Khan didn't have to think twice about that. His gun clinked onto the floor. He heaved himself to his feet.

"I'm Detective-Superintendent Kapoor from Mumbai. This is my case. I'm taking over."

"Mumbai cop?" Khan spat at Kapoor's feet. "Like fuck you are! It's my—"

"That's right! Like fuck I am!" Kapoor waved his camera. "Unless you want the police commissioner to see a photo of you raping a Canadian doctor and spend the rest of your life as a cop getting buggered in prison with broom handles."

Khan's surly face quickly lost all its arrogance.

"You!" Kapoor snapped at Desai. "Get him dressed. Now!"

The skinny officer moved quickly to help Dan get into his shirt and cargo pants. Dan staggered, holding his belly, the agony in his guts almost unbearable, his head aching, a wrist throbbing painfully and his pride on fire. He launched his barefoot up between Khan's legs from behind. Dan couldn't kick him as hard as he wanted but he got in a satisfying squishing hit. Khan went down headfirst, his bulk hitting the tiles with a sickening thud. He writhed, groaning in pain as he retched.

Kapoor frowned. "Tsk, tsk. I didn't see anything. Did you officer?"

Desai shook his head, his Adam's apple bobbing.

"Get my money," ordered Dan holding out a hand out to Desai, "or do you want the same?"

Desai scrambled to remove the wad from Khan's pocket and quickly added his own.

"Let's get out of here, Dan," said Kapoor. "You look like you need a shower and a real drink."

* * *

Kapoor's king-size bed with its duvet and plumped pillows as colorful as those in a Turkish harem filled a third of the room. The air-conditioning hummed a quiet cool. Five-star hotels are like that. Kapoor didn't slum it. Maybe he was on expenses but Dan had a feeling Kapoor would pay the extra to stay in a room like this.

"I hit Kanta Suran, Dipak," said Dan, wincing at the pain in his belly as he slumped onto a sofa. "She fell in the pool and must have been too disoriented to get out. She drowned. I'm in big trouble."

Kapoor patted his sagging shoulder. "Let's have a drink first. We can clean up and talk about it later."

"Just a cold juice for me. I've stopped drinking. I was beginning to like it far too much—again."

"Really?" Kapoor sighed as he eyed the mostly empty bottle of Scotch on the dresser. "You're not the only one." He took two small bottles of fruit juice from the fridge and handed an opened one to Dan. "You're a bad influence, damn it!" he said with a chuckle.

"Great to see you," said Dan, raising his bottle in his working right hand. He washed down a few painkillers to dull the pain in his swollen left wrist and where Khan's fist had twisted his intestines already crushed by Bill's blow into a throbbing pretzel.

"Wonderful to see you again!" said Kapoor, smiling semi-toothlessly as he clinked bottles.

"What happened to you?" Dan asked. "Fell off a bar stool?"

"Have a shower first then I'll tell you. You'll feel much better." He went over to the closet and returned with a gaudy red-and-green Indian robe. "You can wear this until I find you some clean clothes." He looked Dan up and down with admiring eyes. "I'd love to see you in a nice silk shirt of mine and one of my best suits."

"It's a deal, Dipak. Well be the Beige Brothers, right?"

"What a lovely thought!"

A slow grin formed on Dan's lips. "Will you help me off with my shirt?" he asked.

Kapoor laughed semi-toothlessly. "I thought you'd never ask!" He unbuttoned Dan's dirty shirt and blinked his shock at the massive red-brown-purple bruise spreading across Dan's abdomen. "That bastard Khan did this?"

"I feel like I've been stood on by an elephant."

Without asking, Kapoor undid Dan's trousers. Dan stepped out of them and stood in only his shorts. "Who's a naughty boy?" he asked wryly.

"Who me?" Kapoor grinned sheepishly.

After a hot shower to wash away the grime of the cell, Dan emerged from the bathroom relaxed and beginning to float pain-free. Kapoor grinned at him even more than when he'd unzipped Dan's trousers.

"What is it?" asked Dan.

"Now, I need you to get *my* trousers off," Kapoor told him. "Not like my shameless come-on at the Turkish baths, of course. I haven't been able to shower for several days. I'm beginning to smell like the Ganges. Will you wash my back again?" he asked with too much of a grin.

Dan barked a laugh as he put his right arm around Kapoor's shoulders and helped him limp into the bathroom. "No problem. I'll wash your back again, you rascal!"

Kapoor's face darkened in a blush. "Not my finest moment!"

When Kapoor was stripped of his clothes and standing in the shower, Dan shook his head with disgust how badly beaten Kapoor had been. His bruises dappled his body in various shades of brown, blue and yellow from head to toe.

"I see part of you still works," Dan commented as he ran some body wash over the damage.

"And thank Ganesha for that!" Kapoor exclaimed turning more toward Dan. "See how much I like you?"

"And this isn't another come-on?" Dan grabbed his hips to turn him away and slapped his thigh. "Now, tell me what happened."

Kapoor giggled. "Only if you do that again."

Dan sighed. "Get on with it, Dipak!"

"When I left that club in Varanasi, I was lured by a group of homophobes into a car. They took me to an out of the way place, stripped me, abused me and beat the hell out of me. I'm lucky they let me live."

"Bastards!" Dan roiled with anger.

"Three cracked ribs. Severe stomach and groin bruising, as you can see. I lost three teeth. And they humiliated me with a bottle." He flinched when Dan sponged his buttocks that were more black and blue than the rest of him. "Careful."

"Sorry."

"It was a big bottle."

Dan laughed. "You silly bastard! How can you maintain such a sense of humor?"

"It's fate. Life goes on. I'm not dead, am I? Bruises and bones will heal. I'll get my teeth replaced. My soul is not damaged, that part of me that is part of Brahman. The homophobes will return as garbage and suffer while I'll continue to do all the good I can to gain nirvana," he said in a determined voice that radiated through Dan and made him feel so much for the man who was Dipak Kapoor.

When they both stood outside the bathroom in their robes, Dan said, "You were extremely angry in that cell."

Fury returned to Kapoor's face. "What they were doing to you? Those bastards cops give all of us a bad name. Their corruption burns me to the core. No wonder the people distrust us so much. Now, let me put some ice on that wrist."

Kapoor filled a plastic bag with ice chips from the fridge and used a bandage to wrap it around Dan's left wrist. "There, that's better. Now, please help me to the bed."

Dan held Kapoor's arm to hop him on his good leg across the room and lie him down on the bed. He climbed on next to Kapoor and rested his sore wrist and its ice pack over the dull pain in his abdomen. He hoped Khan's balls felt a lot worse.

"So what the hell are you doing here?" asked Dan. "If you hadn't shown up, that bastard would have buggered me silly with that gun until I'd confessed to murder."

Kapoor smiled. "For you. What else?"

"Besides wonderful me? Bob Stewart?"

"Secondary," he acknowledged. "I have unfinished business with Mis'r Stewart too. Now, if you've relaxed a little, shall we discuss how you killed someone tonight? Nadia Gorkoff's memory is fragmentary but she told the police you attacked them. You punched Miss Suran into the pool. The next thing she knew she was looking at the guards giving CPR to Miss Suran, sadly to no avail."

Dan hung his head and turned the misted bottle in his fingers. "Believe me it was an accident but I should have stayed and ..." He shook his head. "There's no damn CCTV at the pool to show they attacked us first. Just like in bloody Jodhpur, another bloody camera wasn't working.

"I want you to watch this," Kapoor said, fingering the VCR remote. "I think it will put you in a better mood."

"Movie time? It's not gay porn, is it?"

Kapoor laughed.

The VCR clicked below a flat-screen TV. A tape whirred. A night scene in a park. Maybe it *was* gay porn. The tape had a fuzzy line along the bottom and the pictures must have been shot in a light snowfall. A dimly lit path snaked through trees toward a far-off whitish building. Dan shot Kapoor a glance to find him smiling smugly. The Maya Devi pool could be seen if you looked hard enough. It was video from another CCTV camera in the park about one hundred yards away from Buddha's birthplace.

"Khan hasn't seen this, has he?" asked Dan getting down from the bed to get a close view of the TV screen.

"No. He's a lousy cop."

The camera took a frame every few seconds so there was a Charlie Chaplin flickering quality to the video. Kapoor gave the tape a little fast forward until two blurred figures appeared strolling arm-in-arm along the path toward the pool.

"That's Shira and me," Dan told him.

"I guessed as much."

The figures sat down on a bench. Two others appeared beyond them.

"Nadia and Kanta," Dan muttered.

They approached the seated figures that stood to meet them. Then one of the new figures fell backward as a scuffle broke out. Then the other one went into the pool. Kapoor stopped the tape, backed up and freeze-framed through the action.

"What happened?" asked Kapoor.

"I hit Nadia after she'd thrown a punch at Shira and then Kanta after she'd swung at me. She went into the pool."

"I've seen Miss Jacobs' swollen hand."

"She tripped and fell on the way back to the bus."

Kapoor let the tape run.

After Shira and Dan left, Nadia managed to get onto her knees, holding her mouth, swaying like a boxer wondering what the count was. Kanta sat holding her face in the water. Barely a minute went by before a black figure appeared from the trees. It wasted no time in quickly approaching the two women. Nadia had just struggled to her feet when the figure launched her into the pool. The figure jumped in after her. Kanta was first to get held under the water, barely struggling in her dazed state. As soon as Kanta went limp, the figure moved to the floundering Nadia who'd made her way to the side of the pool. The figure caught her and held her under for only a few seconds before it let Nadia go, scrambled out of the pool and disappeared into the bushes. Two other figures appeared.

"Security guards," said Kapoor.

One guard jumped in and dragged Nadia out onto the grass. He went back in to help the other guard pull out Kanta. One guard stayed to pound on Kanta's chest while the other ran off out of the screen.

Kapoor stopped the VCR. "Who's the last figure?" he asked.

Dan felt a surge of regret—Kanta had lost her life and he was to blame, even if indirectly. He couldn't believe Cruella had ordered Bob Stewart to eliminate Kanta and Nadia. It wasn't her style—bribing and threatening were. "My money's on Bob Stewart protecting his investment in kidnapping Charlie."

"I better get surveillance on the Stewarts from the Nepalese police. We're getting to crunch time in Kathmandu."

Dan noticed a framed photo of a pair of young men in police uniforms stood by the alarm clock. One had to be Kapoor. The other was Dan looking in the mirror.

"Monty?" he asked, indicating the frame.

Kapoor nodded. "Monty and I in the Fourth Form. We were inseparable." His voice hardened. "He became a policeman in Mumbai like I did until he was murdered by a gang boss."

"Did you get him?"

"I got him all right."

Dan raised his bottle. "To Monty."

"Monty," Kapoor replied.

They finished their juices in silence. Kapoor studied Dan. "Have you got to like me?"

"I can't lie to you," Dan told him sadly, took a deep breath then grinned. "Yes, you old bugger. I missed you the last few days believe it or not."

Kapoor laughed. "You worried?"

"Yes, I worried."

"That's so sweet!" He kissed Dan on the cheek.

"Now tell me about Monty," Dan said, sliding closer to Kapoor.

Kapoor rolled toward him. "And you can tell me about Paul."

April 6th

Kathmandu

KANTA'S DEATH CAST a pall over the group. Her body was to be autopsied then flown back to Mumbai. Nadia was in the hospital with a concussion. Dan's nightmare of Nadia's vindictiveness was over but Charlie wasn't out of danger from Bob—and he still had to find a way for Charlie to go home safely out of the clutches of Cruella.

No one wanted to stay in Lumbini any longer than beyond the almost silent breakfast. Sighs of relief and some applause greeted news of the police chief allowing them leave to Lumbini on the bus as scheduled. Dan knew Kapoor was to thank for that. He'd have shown the chief the tape and given them all he had on Bob, Rani and Loki. The trip ended the day after tomorrow and if Bob still planned to kidnap Charlie he'd better get a move on. With the cops following his every move, Bob's days were numbered. Hopefully fewer than two since Dan hadn't forgotten Bob had promised to kill him too.

Initially scenically impressive as the unairconditioned, public bus climbed the mountain pass and descended through the terraced foothills into the fertile valley, the long eight-hour ride became mentally and physically draining when it extended into thirteen. A diversion to Pokhara farther north caused by Maoists blocking the direct road from Lumbini to Kathmandu forced their bus far out of its way. It was a group of hungry, bedraggled tourists who glimpsed the lights of Kathmandu in the valley ahead—and they could smell it too: smoke and exhaust fumes after the pristine winds in the mountains.

A salivating pack of hungry wolves awaited them: locals with offers of a bed for the night and taxi drivers pushing and scrambling for the best position at the side of the road. It was close to eleven at night, five hours late when the bus eventually entered a maze of dark back streets and came into their sight. As soon as the bus stopped, the wolves blocked the doors and clambered onto the roof, throwing down bags and cases before looking for their owners.

Everyone relied on Loki to sort it out: the exhausted group couldn't wait to get to bed. Charlie stayed with Shira and Duncan while Dan jumped into a taxi with Mark and Gilly. A young man revved the motor to the red line while his friend in sunglasses for the bright moonlight rode shotgun. The smoke in the car smelled familiar. The driver took off, swerving and accelerating quickly as he raced another taxi along the dark, narrow road deeper into the city. Mark and Dan made faces at each other as they braced themselves.

Shotgun twisted around to look back at them crowded in the rear seat. "Where you from?" he asked.

"Canada," said Dan.

"Oh, Canada! Canada! My life here is shit! Please, adopt me. Take me to Canada with you. Please!"

He was as stoned as a gravel driveway. And so was the driver: the barely controlled, four-wheel drift around a sharp turn confirmed it. He had his window down yelling at another taxi as it roared by then slowed down to run alongside. Dan glanced across at its open windows and dark interior. A figure moved. A gun poked out the window.

"Get down!" he shouted and ducked, pulling Gilly down with him.

Bang!

The bullet shattered their window into fragments. The driver screamed as he swerved and skidded the car into a tight corner.

Bang!

The driver's stoned friend stuck his head out the window, waved his fist and yelled Nepalese obscenities.

Bang!

Shotgun's head flew back from the window. The driver screamed again.

Mark kept down while he fired his pistol through the shattered window.

Bang!

Mark's gun flew out of his hand. "Fuck!" he shouted at his bloodied fingers.

Dan cursed himself for having left his Glock in his bag. All he could do was cover Gilly as best he could and keep his head down.

Bang! Another single shot from the other car.

Gilly yelped.

They lurched from side to side as their still screaming driver swerved wildly along the road. Headlights flashed in their interior as another car raced up behind them. A machine-gun burst. None of the shots turned Dan's taxi into a pepper pot. Tires squealed. Engines roared. The driver slammed on his brakes and did a ninety-degree slide into the dirt at the side of the road throwing a cloud of dust swirling into the air. The car teetered on two wheels on the verge of flipping onto its roof. Mark fell onto Gilly crushing Dan beneath them. It crashed back to earth with a metallic thud and vibrated on its suspension. Two cars careened off down the road, guns firing at each other, swerving their red taillights into the night. Dan shoulder charged the jammed door open and fell out onto the stony ground. He got to his feet and helped Gilly and a shaky Mark climb out after him out.

The driver was wailing in the front seat, beating his head and hands on the steering wheel. Dan patted him on the shoulder through the open window. "Good man," he said before he saw his friend slumped face up on his bloodied lap. He was still wearing his sunglasses but a bullet had passed through one of the lenses.

Gilly knelt beside Mark, her wrist dripping blood. A dark streak across Mark's shirt showed where a bullet had given his chest a close shave. She pressed hard on a rapidly spreading stain on his thigh.

"Y'all reet, lad?" Gilly asked Dan. Definitely Yorkshire, he thought.

"Me?" He still shook with shock. "How are you?"

"Ah'm fine. Did ya get those fookin' bastards?" she asked Mark.

* * *

On a side street made out of crushed bricks and pieces of broken concrete, they piled gratefully out of the police car and fled with their bags through an open wrought-iron gateway into a five-story hotel of gray concrete. Dan pushed open the room door to find Karen in her big t-shirt, smoking a cigarette and holding a bottle of beer, sitting with her strapped knee up on a double bed with a pronounced valley in its thin mattress. The carpeted floor looked more inviting. Her rosy cheeks and four empty bottles of beer by the bed indicated she hadn't waited for him.

"What kept you?" she asked thickly.

"Car trouble. Started the party without me?

"After that ride from hell?" She nodded at the three full bottles left on the table. "You'd better get one before I finish them off."

"I'm still on the wagon so they're all yours." He sat down on the bed next to her. The bed springs creaked ominously.

Her cigarette smoke hit his nostrils like it had descended from Mount Olympus but he resisted the urge to light up—no booze or ciggies for four days: his epiphany at the Bodhi tree at the Mahabodhi temple Lumbini hadn't worn off. He was determined it never would.

She patted the mattress and smiled sloppily. "Pity it's only got one bed, sweetie."

He stamped his foot with a loud thump on the thin carpet. "I'll see the manager immediately. This is an outrage!"

She giggled. "If you want your arm broken, you mullet!"

"Whatever, dear."

"Good answer, dearest."

She ruffled his hair and limped to the bathroom. Dan cracked open an orange pop and kicked off his shoes, suddenly dog-tired. The bottle shook in his hand as he drank deeply from it. It had been more of a ride from hell than Karen yet knew. He lay back on the lumpy pillow with his eyes closed and listened to the sound of Karen brushing her teeth. His neck muscles slackened as he relaxed. Karen's flush of the toilet's cistern sounded like the death throes of the Titanic. She returned swinging a small bag of white powder in her fingers.

"Want a nightcap?" she asked sitting down on the bed and swinging her leg back on it.

He shook his head. She dipped her finger into the bag and withdrew a small dusting of the powder. She sniffed it up a nostril before licking her finger clean. "Mmm. Sweet," she said and looked at him again. "Sure?"

"It's organic sugar."

"Uh-huh." She tilted her head at him, waiting.

"What if there'd been a random search at the border? You'd have been in big trouble with heroin. Jail sentence for sure."

"So you were worried about me?"

"Yes."

"Anything else?"

"I don't want you to murder Bob. Revenge won't bring back your husband. I know about murder, don't I?" Her expression remained blank. "It'll destroy your karma like it did mine."

"Lucky I don't believe in karma then, isn't it? I want revenge."

He held her hand. "You could get caught and imprisoned for a long, long time. And I don't want that to happen. And neither would Bill."

"Bill?" She lost control of her face. "He's gone."

"No, he isn't."

Her eyes locked anxiously on his. "What's that mean?"

"He told me he's coming back for you when he's cleared up the drug business with Steve and the Brits."

A hand went to her chest, catching her breath. "He did?"

"You have a lot to live for," he said slipping his arm around her shoulders. "Don't throw it away on a piece of shit like Bob Stewart. He'll try again and we'll be ready for him," he said as confidently as a life insurance salesman smiling in her doorway.

She rolled away to her side of the bed. Dan turned the light out and maintained a safe distance from Karen. During the night, he felt her shuffle her butt into him and pull one of his arms over her. He'd lied about Bill but he felt no remorse. It had been for a higher purpose: Karen wouldn't kill Bob—but she might kill him instead.

April 7th

NEXT MORNING DAWNED as hot as the over-hard fried eggs with burned white toast on Dan's breakfast plate and unexpectedly blindingly sunny. For a brief time, a breeze from the north had cleaned the smog out of the valley and the surrounding snow-capped mountains had shown themselves. Dan squeezed himself through a human zoo of international tourists of all shapes, sizes, colors and accents milling in the lobby, cameras at the ready. They were packed into the city to witness the Kumari festival due to take place in Durbar Square that afternoon and the group wasn't going to miss the spectacle either. It was a major event Dan was looking forward to. It wasn't every day he'd see a living goddess.

Dan made another call to his bank. Another eleven million had been officially deposited. Cruella hadn't tried to have him killed last night. Pay him off then kill him didn't make sense and Cruella wasn't one to waste her money. Who had shot at their taxi? It certainly wasn't the late Bohan Gill reaching out from the grave. Or Steve. Had another hitman been hired to kill him? And Mark and Gilly just happened to be with him? Had someone tried to kill Mark and Gilly and he would have been collateral damage? God, who else might want him dead? For the first time, Nadia crossed his mind. Would she hold him responsible for Kanta's death? But his thoughts gravitated to the single gunshots, no wasted effort—Bob's trademark. He must have drooled when they'd piled into one taxi. Three birds in a bush. *Bang! Bang! Bang!*

Every table in the hotel's restaurant was taken. Cruella sat having breakfast in deep conversation at a table with the Marlboro Man, two-hundred-plus pounds of tanning bed, aftershave and razor commercials, square jaw and broad shoulders neatly packaged in a pec-hugging gray, light woolen suit and bluish silk tie. He'd look great on Mount Rushmore. If you can tell a man by his shoes, this man owned a factory in Rome where sculptors produced one pair a day and had them polished by Sophia Loren. Two other men, each over six feet tall with short hair, earpieces, close shaves, each wider than a regular doorway, stood close by in Armani suits designed to cover up a gun under an armpit, with their hands crossed at their crotches. One hovered by the doorway while the other watched the room like a slowly scanning radar dish.

Cruella caught Dan's eye and twisted her pumped lips. At least that had cost her eleven million. She leaned forward, said something to Mister Hunk and nodded her head in Dan's direction. Marlboro Man put down his coffee cup and penetrated Dan's soul with blue eyes that matched his tie. Dan was a person of interest. He held Dan's eyes waiting for him to look away first. Dan refused to. When Marlboro Man was forced to blink first, his face hardened as quickly as Portland cement.

* * *

Dan followed a limping Mark down the crowded streets from the hotel by the Nadiapurna temple, where a fish was supposed to have landed and left its impression in the stone slabs, and past a towering Buddhist stupa, its multi-layered spire raising its Buddha eye to the heavens. Small shops, some the size of a phone booth, sold everything from scarlet bindis to stick on Hindu foreheads to posters of Western rock stars next to those of the various depictions of Shiva. Street vendors hustled their Nepalese flags and every possible size of wooden and metal statues of Buddha, Shiva and Parvati. The narrow street opened out onto the wooden house that had given its name to the city. Inside its dark brown timbers, flashy tourists in an assortment of colorful shirts and shorts swirled with the better-dressed locals. Women decorated the rail surrounding the house with garlands of bright saffron-orange marigolds, the symbol of both success and surrender to the divine.

A tall man with a straw fedora, beautifully dressed in a light tan suit, white shirt and cream tie fell in step with Dan as he followed Mark toward the city's center, Durbar Square.

"Well, Dan. What a to-do, last night," Kapoor said crisply. He was in a very good mood.

"We're lucky we're not dead."

Kapoor's voice cooled. "That boy isn't and I don't like that."

Dan stopped and looked down at Kapoor. "That was you in that other car last night, wasn't it? You saved our bacon."

"What an interesting expression. I'll have to remember it. Not that we have much bacon in India, of course." He rubbed his chin. "That surveillance almost worked but the Stewarts got away."

"Have I been used as unpaid bait to see what everyone has been up to?"

"Not exactly bait. I don't use loved ones like that," he said warmly. "An insider and not unpaid."

"OK. You kept me alive and out of jail."

"Priceless, don't you think?"

"Where are Bob and Rani now? Tibet?"

"That boy was murdered. We'll find them wherever they are. It is their fate."

"What about Loki?"

"We're watching him but we have no evidence to arrest him."

Dan breathed a very deep sigh of relief. Bob was gone and Charlie was safe. Only Cruella was left to worry about.

* * *

Durbar Square hummed with the buzz of excited spectators and the vibrant drums and sitars of Nepalese music played over a PA system. People arrived early to get the best seats for the Kumari ceremony, an event held only every six years or so, a god-girl's menses permitting. Shiny, black limousines delivered their contents into the Devi Palace at the south end of Dubar Square and to the old Royal Palace on the east side where a covered grandstand had been erected to provide shade and the best views for the royal family and government officials.

Mark paused to take photos of the twelve-foot-high, gray stone statue of a kneeling, winged Vishna on its red-brick plinth and a colorfully robed and face-painted *sadhu* holy man before crossing the crowded square to stand under a side temple's elaborately carved wooden eaves. After five minutes, Dan guessed he was waiting for someone. To get a better view, he climbed the steps of a stone pyramid, passing parents spoiling their excited children with clouds of cotton candy to sit in the shade of the triple roof of a small pagoda temple.

A well-polished, gray limousine with black windows and an American diplomatic plate cruised slowly toward the square in a narrow side street. It edged its flashy hood ornament into the sunlight then stopped. The motor idled, no doubt keeping its occupants cool with the air-conditioner. No one got out. An SUV also with black windows parked close behind. Mark, all ruddy face and upright military gait, stepped from the shade. Scattering pigeons into a mass flight and dodging the sacred cows, he approached the Lincoln and got in.

Something metallic pressed into Dan's head behind his right ear. A hand lifted his loose shirt and pulled his gun out of the back of his belt. After the car shootout, he didn't leave home without it.

"Nosey bugger, aren't thee?" A female voice. Definitely Yorkshire.

"OK. Kill me and get it over with Gilly," Dan said, faking boredom.

She patted him on the shoulder and sat down next to him. "Good morning, love. Lovely day for a new Kumari? Watching Mark take care of business?"

"You're not going to shoot me."

"You're right." She handed the gun back.

"How many British accents can you and Mark do?"

"Hundreds. Don't get me started. Mark's better. We were in amateur theater and Christmas pantos. You should have seen my Desdemona. Have you liked his Field Marshall Montgomery?"

"A bit over the top but highly commendable.

"Good. I'll let him know."

"Who's in the car?" he asked.

"Hillary and Bill."

"How long have you been working for Hamlish?"

"Who? Marvin Hamlish? The songwriter?"

"Jeb Hamlish."

"Never heard of him."

"The one who pays you to keep an eye on Shira, Charlie and Cruella? The one in the car over there."

The rear door of the Lincoln opened and Mark got out. He put on his sunglasses and shaded his eyes, looking around the square.

Gilly stood up and waved to him. "*Yoo hoo!*" she called until she got his attention. "Somebody wants to see you," she said.

"I'm happy here."

"Want me to shoot you?"

"Whatever you do, don't let Missus Jacobs take Charlie back to the US."

"Relax, Dan. *That's* not going to happen."

* * *

After frisking Dan and relieving him of his gun, a bodyguard opened the limo's rear door. Dan sank into the plush backseat of the cool car, breathing in pine, cigar and rum vapors. Up close, Jeb Hamlish was more rugged than ever. The lines across his cheeks and jaw and around his blue eyes were in just the right places to indicate power and experience. His gray hair was the right shade of gray. His tan the right shade, too. His eyebrows were trimmed to avoid too much of an intellectual look. He was lean, a daily jogger Dan guessed, indicating a healthy body but not the self-indulgence of a well-honed muscle man. His suit fitted his broad shoulders perfectly. A small, gold US flag decorated its lapel. This man was a patriot who could afford the lifestyle of the rich but didn't overdo it. An American success but not too far removed from the middle-class voters.

"I've heard about you, Senator," Dan told him.

"And I you." He gently shook Dan's bandaged right hand with Superbowl ring-encrusted fingers. Several of them looked like they'd been broken more than once. "And I like what I've heard." His voice was Tony Bennett's without the melody.

Beyond Jeb Hamlish was Son of Marlboro Man, similarly dressed. The same chiseled Hollywood features on a square-jawed head and the younger body morphology of a more athletic All-American powerhouse. All he needed was a Coke and a burger.

"Hello David," Dan said.

"You know me?"

"Saw you on a Wheaties box."

David actually smiled as he held out a hand big enough to encircle the pigskin and hurl it sixty yards for the Hail Mary winner.

"Pleased to meet you, sir," he said.

Damn, Dan wanted to hate him and here he was thinking he might actually like him.

Hamlish Senior slid the dividing window closed to give them privacy from his guards. He was straight down to business. "What's going on with you and Shira?"

"Didn't Missus Jacobs tell you?"

"That vicious, old cow?" Dan warmed to him instantly. "Let's not waste time, Dan." His first name and he wasn't even a voter. "Tell me."

"Nothing's going on."

"Have you fucked her?"

Dan shot a glance at Junior. He seemed calm enough.

"No. Felt her tits though. In mitigation, at the time I didn't know she was engaged to your son here." Dan turned to David. "Sorry about that."

David shrugged.

Jeb smiled. "You'll get a pass on that then. What about your son? Is he banging her?"

"Duncan?" Dan shrugged. Maybe he had. He looked again at David, the person most likely to hurt him. "Friendly but no more than that." David waggled his head, still looking indifferent. Dan moved the conversation away from that. "I've got some bad news for you though. She's got a personality disorder. How many daughters-in-law would you like?"

"What?" said David.

"Seven Faces of Eve?" asked Jeb. "She's not only stupid?"

"Only two. She's really fucked up—and stupid."

"And you know because you're a psychiatrist, right?"

"I'm a doctor. Seen similar cases. I know about fucked up."

"How fucked up is Charlene?" asked Jeb. Dan felt himself out on a pond in late spring wondering how thick the ice was. "She's been having these"—Jeb tapped a finger at his bronzed, botoxed forehead—"whacko moments back in the US. I've been keeping a close eye on her."

"She's had them again a few times." Dan knew Mark and Gilly would have fed him all the news on that. "Pretty fucked up too. That whole family's a fucking mess. Charlie and Shira need a lot of therapy and Missus Jacobs needs shooting."

Jeb nodded gravely. "Tell me about it."

David interjected. His voice had dropped and he was staring at Dan for a reaction. "Did you fuck Charlie?"

So he didn't care if Shira had been gang-banged by the Red Army. It was all about Charlie. "David, you know she's bipolar," said Dan in a confiding tone. "A beautiful one with a great body. No tits, good for a bit of action but fuck-ups like her are not my thing."

"Bullshit," he snapped, leaning closer. "Charlie's really into you."

"I admit touching her up a bit but no fucking ever. Plug my dick into that cigarette lighter and I won't say anything different. I'm not getting on that train."

David's eyes narrowed. "You like fucking the Kiwi more? What's her name?"

"Karen." Dan smiled lasciviously. "Now there's a real woman. Great piece of ass."

Jeb took over. "And you've been fucking her since Mumbai." He was telling not asking.

Dan kept smiling broadly. "You're right. No time for anyone else. She's exhausting."

"If you like them butch and chubby ... You were struck off the medical registry, weren't you?"

"Yes."

"You did hard time for assaulting your wife."

"Yes."

"Why should I believe a criminal like you?"

"And you swim in the Washington swamp?"

Jeb smacked his knee as he laughed. "Good point!"

"What have I got to gain?" Dan continued. "I've been treating both of them with drugs as well as I can but they both need lifetimes of medical interventions and psychotherapy."

"So my son would be the crazy one if he married Shira?"

Dan looked at David, who'd calmed down. "Or Charlie. My medical opinion? You'd be out of your fucking mind." Jeb nodded. "You have the marriage with Shira arranged for when she gets back," Dan asked.

Jeb sighed his resignation. "That's the deal."

Dan glanced at David who gave a resigned nod.

"You have no choice, do you?" stated Dan.

Jeb raised his eyebrows. "Because?"

"You're being blackmailed by Lucrezia Borgia." Jeb Hamlish's face slackened into someone much older. Even Marlboro Man had his limits. He needed a cigarette. "David got Charlie pregnant five years ago when she was a minor." David seemed to shrink in his suit. "And she had an abortion. Unless Shira marries David, Elaine will go public and there goes your chance of the presidency."

Jeb's face formed a dark cloud. "And David's future chance at it."

David turned his stone face to the window.

"We can deny it," Jeb said without conviction.

"Good luck with that. Thought of paying off the clinic? Lose the records? Burn the building down?"

Jeb smiled wryly. "Their computer records have been hacked as it happens."

"But Lucrezia still breathes."

"If only she'd take money instead. I've offered her plenty but she wants the name and a lot more."

"She has high ambitions for Shira. President's daughter-in-law? Maybe future First Lady? Looks good on the dinner invitation. She has good leverage. Looks like you're screwed."

"That woman is the bane of my existence," he mumbled to no one.

He'd been cornered, outwitted by a psychopath and the promiscuity of his son. Dan didn't envy him. Being a billionaire's not all gravy.

"The irony of this is David's in love with Charlie, not Shira," said Jeb. Dan sat up. "He's never got over her or the abortion and what that meant to my wife and me." He shook his head looking at David. "What it did to Charlie and my stupid son." He talked about David as though his stupid son wasn't in the car. David returned dead eyes.

"You *love* Charlie?" Dan asked David. "Or is it just guilt? She was only fifteen when you gave her a Stingray special. Isn't that statutory rape? Not too late for jail time on that I assume."

David closed his eyes and ran his hand across his forehead. It was old news. Marlboro Man paled beneath his healthy tan. The wrinkles were now more of an old cowboy's at the end of a long cattle drive. And the Indians were running off with his stock.

"If only I could get rid of Shira and Elaine, he'd marry Charlie if she'd have him." Jeb glanced at Dan sounding like Henry the Second talking about that irritating priest, Thomas à Becket. Dan knew how it had worked then. Was Jeb now looking at him?

"And her three hundred million would come in handy?" Dan asked.

"Very nice," admitted Jeb. "But chunk change in my world."

"Missus Jacobs doesn't think so."

"She's a greedy bitch." He spat it out like he'd bitten into a chili pepper by mistake.

"And she's trying to put Charlie away as insane to get it."

"Well, she is, isn't she? Didn't she go nuts in those caves?"

Dan nodded several times for emphasis. "Yeah, she's crazy all right." He turned to a deflated David. "You'd be wise to stay away from her. Not an asset on your Dad's campaign trail to have your wife jump off the Empire State Building and bite a seagull's head off on the way down. Lose the bird vote."

Jeb snapped out of his doldrums and laughed. "That's a good point but don't knock insanity. It's not Thomas Eagleton anymore."

Dan recalled George McGovern's first running mate in 1972 getting exposed in the press as having had electroconvulsive shock treatments and suffered bouts of depression. Apparently, a lying thug of a veep like Spiro Agnew had been a better fit with the lying, paranoid Tricky Dicky in the White House.

Hamlish continued with a shrug, "Now, there's the sympathy vote. Rehab. Heroic comeback. Mental health advocate. Yadda yadda, yadda." He went silent, tapping his rings on his knee.

Dan focused on David, the All-American hunk sadly slumping his broad back into the leather seat. "Charlie told me she'll hate you until the day she dies and hopes you rot in hell for what you put her through."

Jeb thought about that for a moment while David turned as gray as his father's hair. "I'd like you to do something for me to make up for your more than fondling my future daughter-in-law's boobs," Jeb finally said. He took a few photos out of his inside jacket pocket and slipped them one at a time into Dan's hand. "Nice camera work?" he asked. "I particularly like this one. Mark or Gilly got the lighting just right."

The photo was of Shira holding a man's head deep in her bare breasts. Yes, Dan thought, that movement in the doorway. He'd had other things to think about. Jeb chuckled as he passed a few more. The one of Dan's startled full face emerging from Shira's cleavage was priceless. It was like he'd discovered the Holy Grail.

"Would you believe photoshopped?" Dan asked without conviction.

"Sure. And she made you do it."

"You got that right." Dan handed the photos back. "It really wasn't as bad as it looks."

Jeb guffawed. "Ha! Or as good, buddy!"

Dan glanced at David but he was looking away again. He just didn't care what had happened to Shira. He was probably thinking about how long he'd have to hate being with her.

Jeb flicked through them again before putting them back in his pocket. "I can only say I'm envious. I'd almost give up the presidency to go diving like that."

"No photos of me fucking Shira," Dan pointed out.

"But your son is." Jeb held out a few photos. "Shira *and* Charlie? You're quite a duo, aren't you?"

Dan winced, holding up his palm at the photos. "Believe me, neither of us have fucked Charlie. Duncan had a couple of dates with her but nothing happened. He's genuinely fond of Shira."

"That's very good to hear." More photos appeared from a different pocket. "I do believe you as a matter of fact."

Dan wondered if he had white doves and bouquets of flowers in other pockets waiting to impress him. One showed Charlie and Duncan doing nothing more than kissing goodnight. The other showed Charlie straddling Dan on the lawn at Lumbini.

"Is that the best you've got?" Dan asked.

"How about this one?"

It was a night shot of Dan giving Charlie a tutorial on garden design against a tree trunk at Lumbini. "I still haven't seen any fucking."

"You must have fantastic self-control then. Or your dick doesn't work." Jeb turned more toward him. "However, to business. If I were an Italian father, I'd have your nuts in a jar on my desk by now but I'm a Jew. Let's do some business."

"Do I have a choice?"

"Sure you do. Should we go into the options? Want me to become an Italian Jew?" Dan winced. "Don't worry, I don't kill people. Not good on the resume for the White House. But," he took his time grinding out the words, "I can make life difficult for people—and their sons—who get in my way."

Jeb and Cruella were definitely cut from the same sociopathic cloth. Doesn't kill people? He'd wait until he had his feet up in the Oval Office before he got into that.

"How would you like to be well rewarded? Enough for the rest of your life on a tropical island you actually own?" Jeb asked.

Dan's ears perked up. "Drinks with umbrellas?"

"Ha! Big drinks with big umbrellas, buddy." He gripped Dan's arm with strong fingers. "It's third and inches. I need that final push for the TD." Jeb didn't need speechwriters.

"You want someone to be less of a problem?"

"No, no. Nothing like that, of course. Although if someone we both know happened to fall over a cliff?" He shrugged carelessly. Jeb was definitely presidential material. Plausible deniability was in the air.

Jeb withdrew an envelope from his inside breast pocket, unfolded a single sheet and showed it to Dan. It was an official certificate typed in Nepalese and English.

"Well?" Jeb reached into the walnut humidor recessed in the front console next to the TV. Dan didn't know Cohibas came in that jumbo size.

"Shira might need a lot of persuasion," Dan said, watching Jeb roll the cigar in his fingers by his ear. "To be kept in the manner she has become accustomed?"

"OK. Ten million will cover it."

"My expenses?"

"Take a ten percent cut."

"It'll be tight but I'll manage," Dan deadpanned, mentally ordering a seventy-piece marching band and a squadron of buxom cheerleaders. Jeb probably had the money in his pocket next to his favorite chunk of the Hope diamond.

Jeb threw his mane back as he laughed, flashing his set of ultra-white teeth. He smacked Dan on the shoulder. "Excellent!" He lit the cigar with the electric lighter and blew a cloud of blue smoke at Dan. He waved the smoldering cigar. "Like one?"

Dan thought he would since he was already inhaling Jeb's. "Only if it's not Cuban. Hate to break the embargo on those Commies."

Jeb laughed even more. "Have one, you cheeky bastard!"

Dan took one and Jeb cut and lit it for him. It was like smoking a broom handle. He puffed the most expensive cigar he might ever see never mind smoke.

Jeb leaned back enjoying the cigar and blew an enviable smoke ring that floated toward the divider until he poked it with a gnarled index finger. "You know, I'll throw in a bonus, kid. Like me, you're worried about Charlie and what her mother might do to her. Right?"

"That's why you sent Mark and Gilly along."

"Exactly. Keep her alive for David here"—Dan glanced at an attentive David—"and away from that asshole Bob Stewart. I'll hide her out at a guarded compound I have in Florida. No one will know where she is. She can get the very best treatment. When she's twenty-one, she can do what she wants. Whaddayathink? You can convince her?"

"I'll convince her," Dan told him. Safe from Cruella? She was going. David's amorous intentions he would have to get over. Charlie came first. He thought if David Hamlish smiled any bigger, he'd start humping his leg.

"You're on," Jeb said, extending his hand again. "After this, you'd better run for the hills or the Jacobs bitch will string you up by your nuts."

Dan knew that would be the least she would do to him and Duncan. And he knew the hills to run to. He was going there anyway. They shook. Jeb looked very pleased. So did Dan.

Jeb beamed as he blew a volcano's plume of smoke. "Pull that off, my man, and I'll throw in another mill!"

Two marching bands, a division of cheerleaders with never-ending, high-kicking legs and perhaps Beyoncé's ass! Dan put the cigar back between his lips to avoid smiling far too much.

David crushed Dan's hand, his expression the relief of a man sitting strapped in an electric chair hearing there was a call for him from Governor Billy Bob.

"I'll have a cigar too, Dad," he told his father. Dan flinched: the bastard was figuring out how to get in Charlie's panties already. Easy, of course, since she didn't wear any.

"One last thing, Senator," Dan said, turning back as he stepped out of the door. "You didn't know Missus Jacobs had Bob Stewart murder her ex and her sister, did you?"

Jeb's crashing face and dropped Cohiba told him what he needed to know.

* * *

Karen grabbed Dan's arm. "The Kumari's only a kid!" she cried. "How old is she?"

The huge, three-tiered, wooden chariot, decorated with garlands of marigolds and gold paint, and glittering statues of the Ganesha and Bhairab gods, swayed as it rolled and creaked its enormous solid wooden wheels. It wobbled through the dark brown, elaborately carved doors of the Kumari Ghar, the living goddess's home, into the bright sunlight. The crowd buzz grew as the Kumari's tiny face, her forehead painted red and yellow with a central ruby, her eyes heavily brushed with mascara, came into sight. The young girl swayed on her high throne as the chariot pulled by about a hundred men with ropes rolled into the swirling mass of people gathered on the Durbar Square expanse. The vibrant gold, red and brown flags, banners and ribbons dazzled.

"Ten. They consider her perfect," he told Karen.

"And she's a goddess?"

"Until she menstruates."

Karen's reddened eyes gave Dan a look right out of the Feminist Handbook Weapons section. "*Chroist.* What then?"

"I dunno. Legal secretary, social worker, pole dancer. Who knows?"

Poor kid, he thought. Even before her first period, a minor cut releasing blood could cause her to be dumped out of the palace and replaced pronto.

Karen pushed on ahead while Dan paused to take more photos of the chariot as it ground its way noisily by the old Royal Palace, its white-painted edifice decked to its Greek Classical roof with a mass of red and white ribbons and streamers.

A hand touched his arm—Shira, shaking, crying.

"What's wrong?" he asked.

She pulled him through a partially open, wooden door into a room so dark, he couldn't see a thing but he heard her sniffling.

"Something happened with Duncan?" he asked, gripping her trembling shoulders. His eyes adjusted enough to see her collapsed face staring at him, her breath coming in rasping sobs. Her hands began beating her head.

Dan grabbed her wrists. "What's the hell is going on?"

"Mother ... she ... she," Shira stuttered in her child's voice. Tears poured down her cheeks. "I'm real, real sorry!"

"About what? Look, I've got something to talk—"

With a sudden burst of movement, she tore open her blouse and ripped at her wrap-around skirt. No underwear. She ran to the doorway.

"Rape! He raped me!" she shouted above the roar of the crowd.

* * *

Dan assumed rapists didn't receive the red-carpet treatment when surly guards stripped him, clumsily cavity-searched him and threw him Nepalese-size pajama pants and a top to wear that left his arms and feet sticking out like a scarecrow. After the arresting cop had used his long stick to beat him like an old carpet, the guards kicked him into the worst cell they had. Yet another cell? He should begin to rate them on TripAdvisor. He'd give it half a star: a single, rock-filled mattress of dubious hygiene on a metal frame and a bucket in the corner for his sanitation needs. Inedible slop congealed on a metal plate with a cup of water for company appeared through a slot. He ignored them. The single fluorescent light flickered occasionally, providing a modicum of light for flies to eat his food by. It wasn't a Kodak moment. He eased himself down into the cleanest corner to rub his new wounds and think.

He felt no anger toward Shira—Cruella must have asserted control over her fragile psyche again. An apologetic Shira had been distraught at what she'd been made to do. Was it outwitting Cruella and taking her for more millions of dollars had burned a hole in her narcissistic brain and she had to teach him a lesson? Was it a taste of what might happen if he thought he could cause her any future problems? He instantly worried about what she might think of doing to Duncan—which was, of course, part of her intention. Had she called his bluff over his revealing what he knew about the deaths of her ex and her sister? She could have had him killed but this was much better—she was controlling him and there were side benefits: would Charlie believe he'd raped Shira? He trusted Charlie would see through that. But with him out of the way, Cruella could spirit Charlie back to the US without his interference. Here he was impotent in a cell while he worried Mark and Gilly wouldn't be able to prevent that from happening.

He wondered what he would do if he were in Jeb Hamlish's expensive shoes. What was in Charlie's head about her abortion and David Hamlish was political dynamite but Hamlish knew she was sane and would roll with the wishes of the potentially most powerful man in the world. On the other hand, kidnapping Charlie himself might be a good idea. Was that his intention in giving her sanctuary back in the States? It was Cruella with her psychotic delusions of blackmailing him for her own aggrandizement who was the ticking bomb after Dan had told him about the murders of Charlie's parents. Eliminating Cruella would solve a lot of problems for Jeb.

His dark thoughts were interrupted by the view-slot in the metal door sliding open. A pair of eyes stared at him briefly before the door bolt clanked back. An ascetic man with an immediate bureaucratic air due to his smart attaché case and charcoal business suit carefully entered his highly polished black leather shoes into the cell. He momentarily held a white handkerchief over his pinched face. Urine wasn't everyone's favorite scent.

"I'm Mister Ponjijee. I'll be representing you, sir, when your trial comes due in about six months," he informed Dan, his voice sharp and efficient.

"You're being funny, aren't you?" Dan replied sourly from his corner office.

"Not a bit, sah. Could be longer. The law here grinds ever so slowly ... depending on circumstances."

"Please have a seat," Dan told him, indicating the floor.

"I think I'll stand if you don't mind."

Dan stood up, wiped his right hand on his pants and extended it. Mister Ponjijee's soft, office hand barely touched it. "Thank you for coming."

Ponjijee immediately wiped his hand with the handkerchief. Dan couldn't blame him—he knew where his hand had been.

"I'm glad to be your representative, Doctor Palmer. I'll do all I can to get you out as soon as possible."

"I appreciate that. How about today?"

Ponjijee chortled politely.

"You've seen the evidence?" Dan asked.

Ponjijee opened his attaché case and took out a brown folder. He didn't put the case on the ground. He flipped some typewritten pages. "Yes, in her statement she says you forced yourself on her and raped her."

"She's been checked over by a doctor?"

Yessir. No semen anywhere on her."

"Or penetration?"

"Nossah."

"So, no semen and no evidence of forced entry? Have the police checked the CCTV in the square?" He crossed his fingers it was working.

Ponjijee made a face of profound regret. "It's such a pity there isn't any, sah."

Dan groaned. "I was set up, Mister Ponjijee." He sighed as he spread both his hands wide in an act of openness. "Nothing happened. Doesn't she have to prove I raped her?"

"Yes, but—"

Dan groaned. "Here it comes. But what?"

"Her mother says you've been harassing her for the last two weeks."

"Bullshit! How about my witnesses that I wasn't harassing her?"

"And who would they be?"

"Everyone else, damn it. Go talk to them!"

Ponjijee nodded gravely. "I'll get onto that but I can assure you, sir, the more evidence and witnesses and the more complicated the case the longer it will take to come to trial and the longer and more expensive the trial."

"Isn't Nepal somewhere that rape cases like this are most likely thrown out and never come to trial?"

Ponjijee nodded. "However, there have been some high profile rapes lately and the authorities are getting a little twitchy about it." He paused. "But it has been known," he conceded.

"Ah, so the wheels of justice may be lubricated?"

Ponjijee frowned professionally. "I'm not sure what you mean."

"How much of an apology to Nepal is required to make up for the shame I have brought the nation?"

"Hypothetically, in this type of case, let's say one hundred and twenty thousand dollars. Give or take."

"That's quite a take." One-twenty thou? Relief flowed through Dan but he kept his face grim. Ponjijee and his legal cronies probably thought he might be one of those rich Western doctors making oodles of cash from breast enlargements, nose jobs and facelifts. They were wrong—he was richer except for those reconstructing aging movie stars in Beverly Hills. He'd give all eleven million to get out of the prison if needed but he wasn't going to give these corrupt bastards any more than he had to.

"If you're found guilty, sir, you could get ten years. And the accommodation can get a jolly sight worse, Doctor Palmer," said Ponjijee encouraging his decision-making.

Dan rubbed his chin thoughtfully. "I can probably get some scumbag to handle it for say sixty thousand."

"There are some who might accept one hundred and ten."

"Any ambulance chaser could get me out for eighty, I'm sure."

"For one hundred? Definitely, some dirtbag will do the job, sah. And a damn fine one too. Probably."

"Probably?"

Ponjijee waved an open palm that was used to collecting money. "As you can imagine, negotiations are always tricky on a serious matter like rape. It might cost a little more," he continued. "Do I have your permission to go a little higher if required?"

"How high?"

"Say, another twenty thousand?"

"Ha!" Dan laughed and hit his head against the wall just for fun. "Make it so, Mister Ponjijee. Make it so."

"Are you able to borrow the money, sir? Have it sent from America?"

"Canada."

"Oh, American dollars are best, of course." Ponjijee put away the file and closed his case. "I'll be back tomorrow and see what we can arrange to expedite the payment and start negotiations."

"I have to sit in this hole?"

"I'll have you moved."

"How much will that be?"

"I'll add it to the bill." He left.

Dan was back in a cell. His heart sank. It would take more than paperbacks about Buddha telling him how to be cool and antidepressants to get him through this if it all went bad. But within twenty minutes, his smiling jailer moved Dan to a clean cell with a washbasin and running water, a comfortable bed and a working toilet. A plate of much better food arrived too: rice, chapattis and a curried vegetable. The jailer must have been doing well out of the deal with Ponjijee since he gave Dan a pack of Gold Flake and a box of matches. But the claustrophobia of the cell brought out old anxieties and he didn't sleep well. He awoke to scratch at an occasional flea bite and played football with a centipede the size of a lobster before he found Buddha—no future, no past, just now—and floated away like a balloon. Time is a human construct so he constructed his own.

April 8th

THE DOOR OPENED and Mister Ponjijee appeared again. He looked down at Dan who was hurting his knees in his attempted Lotus position on the hard mattress and broke into a big smile.

"You're free, Doctor Palmer!" he exclaimed. "The police have dropped the charges. Come, sah, let's get you dressed and out of here."

Dan de-lotused faster than Buddha ever had and got quickly to his feet. "What a surprise," he said with barely concealed sarcasm but was relieved nothing had gone wrong and he wouldn't be spending another night in the cell. "Well done, Mister Ponjijee." Not surprisingly, his attempt to hug Ponjijee to his odorous body was rebuffed.

"Thank you," said the little man taking a quick step backward to safety, "but one hundred and thirty thousand will do nicely, sah."

"Credit card?"

Ponjijee laughed for the first time.

* * *

Dan stood in the lukewarm shower for a long time, washing the prison dirt off his irritated skin and any bugs out of his hair. He came out of the bathroom naked with the towel over his shoulder to find Karen sitting on the bed, bagged with teary eyes. She looked up at him without getting excited.

"Relax, my raping career is over," he quipped wrapping the towel around his waist.

Using her cane, she rose as quickly as she could to hug him. "Oh, Dan. That … that was terrible! I was so worried!"

"It's OK, it's OK," he repeated, patting her on the back gently.

Her eyes ran over the dark welts on his arms and legs. "Look what they did to you!"

His arrest in the building at the square had been less than civil as a mob of men had detained him with rough vigilante justice before the policeman had saved him from them and beat him with his stick instead.

"I'm OK. Just a misunderstanding," he joked darkly.

"They wouldn't let us see you, the buggers! Mark went ballistic at them! I thought they were going to jail him too!"

Dan thought of an enraged Mark pounding his walking stick, red-faced and imperious, berating the poor cops who got in his way.

"What did that bitch do this for?" Karen seethed. "If I could get my hands on her!" She beat at an invisible Shira with her waving cane.

"You don't know? She got me out."

Karen abruptly stopped beating Shira to death. "She did?"

"Ponjijee told me she'd withdrawn the accusation this morning. Go figure." He didn't mention the big bribe Ponjijee had used to move the justice system into top gear. Shira had turned on her mother. Or Carla had.

"Jesus Christ! The bitch is as insane as her bloody mother!"

"Where is Cruella?"

"Flew out this morning. She's lucky she did or I'd beat the shit out of her."

Dan's face must have tightened as much as his stomach. Karen grinned at him.

"It's OK. Charlie's been with me, Mark and Gilly ever since this shit hit the fan. Never out of our sight. Charlie refused to go with her aunt back to the US."

Cruella flew out without the golden goose? That didn't sound like the psycho Dan knew.

"And fuck me, you should have seen Charlie go at Cruella and Shira last night. She wanted to kill the pair of them she was so mad at what had happened to you. She and Shira had a screaming, hair pulling catfight you wouldn't believe. It was fucking great!"

Way to go, Charlie! "Cruella left without Shira too?" He crossed his fingers.

"At breakfast, Cruella and Shira got into one hell of a fight themselves. I couldn't believe what Shira was like. She completely flipped out. She came close to punching out her mother she was so bloody angry. When Cruella buggered off, Shira refused to go with her."

Carla strikes back, thought Dan. "Where's Shira now?"

"She left in an airport taxi about an hour ago."
"How's Duncan dealing with this?"
"How do you think?"
"Where is he?"

* * *

Duncan stared into his beer on a lounger, no smile within a hundred miles of his face. A dozen empty beer cups were scattered nearby. When he turned his miserable face at Dan, his red-rimmed eyes narrowed into angry slits.

"You ... bastard!" he shouted, staggering to his feet. "You raped Shira ... she's gone!"

Someone hadn't got the news bulletin, thought Dan. He looked pissed all right—and pissed drunk.

Duncan stumbled toward Dan, fists ready. "Fucker! Shithead!"

"He didn't rape her, you mullet!" shouted Karen. She glanced meaningfully at Dan as she waved her cane, stepping closer to Duncan. "Punch him and you'll have to punch me!"

Duncan turned sharply toward her. "Shut the fuck up!"

It was enough distraction for Dan to move quickly to push Duncan into the pool.

Duncan surfaced, spluttering. "You ... you ... fucking bastard! I'll ... kill you! I'll kill you!" he repeated between coughs, struggling toward the side of the pool.

Karen towered over him. "Shira got him thrown in prison. She framed him, you bloody dolt!"

Duncan held onto the pool's edge. "Why the fuck would she do that?"

"Her bloody mother," said Dan. "She wouldn't do it on her own, would she?"

Karen tapped him not so gently on the head with her cane. "Do you have any fucking brains in there? It's not that poor kid's fault! It's all her fucking mother's doing. To put your dad in jail. It's revenge. She's a nutter, you miserable little spawn shite!"

Duncan darted a wide-eyed glance at Dan. "Is that true?"

Dan nodded several times. "Shira's in love with you. What are you going to do about it? Get drunk and cry or go get your woman?"

* * *

A money-incentivized Nepalese taxi driver is even more insane than the rest. They gripped the shabby upholstery as their driver swerved and braked the old black and yellow Ambassador like an enraged wasp. A cardinal rule of Nepalese driving is not to hit anything and the cardinal rule of Nepalese pedestrians is to get out the way. No gap between cars and trucks was too narrow for their speeding Ambassador and the natural selection of pedestrians over the generations ensured no one was hit, although they all screamed out loud when one man almost lost his ass, tempting fate as he dawdled in their flight path. The driver laughed maniacally at that. He'd been a good choice to get them to the airport in negative time. Dan glanced at his watch. *Guinness Book* stuff.

The driver grinned as they piled out and Dan fed him a wad of rupees. "Thank you, sah! Thank you!" He pushed a card into Dan's hand. "If you need me again!"

What a joker, thought Dan.

As they hurried through the crowded main hallway, Dan glanced at Duncan. He'd sobered up a bit but still ran as though most of him was still back floundering in the pool. His face was a mix of flushed cheeks, wide eyes and a tense mouth and he was breathing rapidly. Duncan skidded to a halt and threw up in a potted palm on the concourse to the surprise of an older couple having their lunch on a nearby bench.

Dan left him behind and only broke his run to look up at "Departures" on the monitor. Damn! Her plane was boarding to Kolkata to catch her connection to the States. People and their suitcases scattered out of his way as he forced himself faster through them. In the distance, a mane of glossy raven hair stuck up like a homing beacon above the hubbub of the crowd. She was on the other side of a rail heading for "Passengers Only" having shown her passport and ticket. Dan's pulse thudded and warned him to slow down before he fell down. Duncan appeared from nowhere. He shot ahead of Dan whose cigarette and alcohol-training regimen began to fail him.

"Shira! Shira!" Duncan screamed. She didn't stop.

Duncan headed for the gate. Dan headed for the waist-high rail. The last time he'd tried the high jump at school, he'd broken his coccyx on landing. His pulse thudded a warning he'd better slow down but he went for it—legs turning to Jell-O he vaulted the rail. He landed on one unstable foot, crashed onto the tiles and slid into the back of Shira's legs. She flopped onto her ass beside him with a pneumatic *thump*. Only her clutch bag continued, skittering down the walkway toward New York. She flashed wide-eyes at Dan, her mouth falling open as if she'd seen an unwelcome ghost.

"You ... forgot ... Duncan!" he stuttered between deep gasps.

Shira's face crumpled into tears when a beaming, out-of-breath Duncan slid onto his knees and crushed her in his arms.

* * *

They enjoyed a much slower taxi ride back to Kathmandu. Duncan and Shira held each other, crying and kissing in the back, while a teary Karen held both of them in her big arms. Dan took a check out of his pocket and passed it to Shira.

"*Ten million?*" She gasped. Dan had gasped writing it. He'd waived his agent's fee.

"Root me dead!" said Karen.

"You don't need your mother's cash. Screw her."

"My God, Dad!" said Duncan. "If I'd known you were rich, I'd have sucked up to you years ago!"

Dan laughed along with everyone else. "I have something for you."

"OK. What's the catch?" asked Duncan.

Dan handed him Jeb's sheet of paper.

"Holy shit!"

"You can refuse it."

* * *

It was a great afternoon for Dan on the last day of the journey to Kathmandu and they'd made it without any harm coming to Charlie or Shira—or himself. Now that Cruella, Bob, Rani, Steve, Nadia, and Kanta had all gone, he felt a huge weight off his shoulders. It was a pity Karen couldn't be with him to celebrate but climbing around the temples would have been far too arduous for her on one leg. She'd stayed at the hotel, leaving only Charlie, Duncan, Shira, Gilly, Mark and himself to relax at the complex of Hindu and Buddhist temples near the eastern edge of Kathmandu's sprawl. Shira sidled up to him and linked her arm through his. No silly heels, lovely mane of black hair, dark glasses and an aroma of something tropical and delightful.

"What are they doing?" she asked.

Dan hated to see the poor Nepalese standing in the murky waters of the shallow stream that ran between the temples. "They're panning for gold teeth," he told her.

"You're kidding?"

"Nope. Any metal of value that's survived the burning of the bodies over there." Dan pointed to the ghats upstream where one ceremony was still underway, a small group of relatives gathered around a smoldering pile of wood. "Perhaps the occasional artificial hip," he joked darkly.

"Ugh." She pulled him away toward a wooden temple but stopped when she noticed the human couplings and red and blue-painted genitals on the erotic carvings on its eaves. She exchanged amused looks with Dan and changed direction toward the small stone bridge over the narrow stream.

Her grip his arm tightened, drawing him closer. He glanced at her and saw tears glistening. "I'm so sorry about what happened. My mother …" She bit her bottom lip hard.

Dan could feel her anguish and wanted to hug her and tell her he understood very well how painful breaking away from such a tyrant of a parent must be. But he let her talk it out. Let out the guilt. Remove the infection. It was only the beginning of a long recovery process. She was lucky to have Duncan to love her and help her through it. It wasn't going to be easy for either of them but if they came out of it together, the world was theirs. He was well aware that's what he'd thought about Nadia a long time ago.

She raised a desolate face to him. "She said she'd disown me and leave me penniless, a social pariah unless I did what she wanted. Who loved me the most? My mother who had done everything for me, or others who would dump me as soon as they had no use for me? It was what I was used to." She beat her clenched fists on her chest. "After I'd … I'd done it. I … I felt so … awful. I couldn't sleep. I cried and cried. And … then … it just came in a rush into my head, water breaking through a dam. It was … like being born again. I knew what I wanted." She glanced away at Duncan watching then as he idled on the bridge. "Or who."

"You're winning, Shira."

"Winning?"

"Your mother's lost control of you. You're becoming your own woman."

Thank you, Carla, wherever you are.

Her chin firmed below clear, gray eyes. "I am, aren't I?"

"You chose to save me from going to jail." Dan hugged her hard.

"Mother ... wanted me to have sex with you. That way ..."

Dan had to hand it to the psycho. Cruella had it all worked out. "I'd leave evidence and the cops would definitely nail me for rape?" he thought out loud.

Tears flowed again. "But something told me I couldn't do that to you."

Carla. "Never lose that teddy bear," he told her and held her shoulders. "Well, now you're my daughter-in-law and I couldn't be happier for you. You've come a long way, Shira. I'm proud of you. Now, how does it feel to be married to Duncan?"

"Is it really legal?"

"Absolutely."

The official Nepalese marriage certificate supplied by Jeb had sealed the deal, saving three weeks of sitting around in Kathmandu waiting for Canadian and US documents of marriage eligibility. Shira was married and off the market. What was Jeb going to do now with the massive liability of Cruella? She'd lost control of both Charlie and Shira. What was her next move?

"I hope we can be happy," Shira said.

"Duncan knows a lot but he'll need to know everything about you."

She nodded. "I know he'll understand. Like you do."

"I learned the hard way. Glad to help. You've been his wife for two hours. How does it feel?"

"Wonderful."

"Love's the best we've got. Nothing else matters. I never imagined I'd say this but I believe you'll be great for him."

She hugged him very hard. "Thank you. You've been so good to me."

"You need to work very hard to find yourself. You have someone who wants to stand by you. Now go and be with Duncan." She let him go. "One last thing," Dan told her. She looked at him quizzically. "Never call me Dad." She laughed, and kissed him on the cheek. Watching her re-unite with a beaming Duncan and walk arm-in-arm together gave him a feeling as great as he'd ever known.

Across the bridge, the ghats were layered one after the other up to a set of Shiva temples, the mandatory stone bulls sitting on their enormous balls at the base of the steps guarding their entrances. Troops of monkeys ran around trying to steal anything they could get their opposable thumbs on but pickings for them were slim today with only Loki's group ambling around this side of the complex. It was hot on the ghats and Dan took a swig from his water bottle.

Charlie took a few photos of the cheeky monkeys as they scampered among the tourists and around the small temples.

"So Auntie's gone home?" Dan asked. "Refueled the Bitchmobile and buggered off?"

Charlie lowered her camera, linked her arm in his. "Isn't that great! With a bit of luck, I'll never see her again."

"And you and Shira are coming on the trek to Namche? That's what's great."

"I don't think I'll go back quite yet. I want to see my future home."

"Ha! Don't count your chickens, missie. I might meet a nice Sherpa lady while you're growing up back in the States."

"And I might meet a young guy who isn't a drunken jailbird."

"OK. Come and check out our stone hut. See how you like it."

She plucked the bottle from his backpack and took a swig of water. "I intend to. It better have a good bed. You'll need something special to remember me by."

He slipped his arm around her waist as they turned toward the steep ghats. He was happier than he'd been in decades. Perhaps the happiest. Something inside him worried it wouldn't last but it was a fabulous setting to be happy. He'd accept the glass half full and consider how beautiful it was. Live for today. He stopped Charlie.

She squinted up at him. "What?"

"This is the best moment of my life."

Maybe too Hallmark but she clamped him in her arms. He tapped her on the nose before he kissed her again. "And before you go home, I'll make sure you have something to remember too."

She giggled. "Sure you're up to it, old man?"

He wasn't sure at all.

Across the stream, it wasn't a busy day for worshippers at the temple with its blue Shiva on the gate lintel, only a few families entering and leaving. Shira and Duncan appeared arm-in-arm at the gate and strolled down toward the small Buddhist temple.

"Shira's very happy today, isn't she?" Charlie asked. "Now that she's *married*. A marriage certificate? How did you pull that off?"

Dan didn't want to mention Jeb Hamlish. And he sensed where this might be headed. Charlie looked more than miffed.

"Superintendent Kapoor arranged it with the Nepalese as part of my compensation." It sounded weak but it was all he could think of on the spur of the moment.

"Mm. Really? Sweet deal for Shira. That's her third marriage and I've yet to have one."

Dan digressed quickly. "She's remorseful about everything. There's a lot to like about her, isn't there? Give her time with Duncan. She's a half-sister but a sister. She values you a lot. She needs understanding people around her after the hell of a life with her mother."

They sat down on a step and looked down fifty feet into the stream below that was clogged with items of clothing for some reason. Kids fished for anything usable.

"I'll help her." Charlie shielded her eyes from the sun, twisting toward him. "She's very much in love with Duncan. I'm happy for her."

"So am I."

"I missed a real wedding though." She paused and shot him a glance. "I like those things," she added pointedly. "I don't want to miss her honeymoon, do I? Might pick up some tips for my own wedding night, don't you think? Couldn't get another of those certificates, could you?"

"It was a rush job. Duncan's pregnant."

She laughed. "Even though there's a big age difference?"

"Good one."

She snuggled up to him. "I'm a girl, Dan. I've dreamed about my wedding day since I could play with dolls and have them walk down the aisle together. It's a special day for me. Think about it."

Dan detected female water torture beginning. His head was a stone that the gentle drops would gradually erode him into submission. She'd begin to ask him what flowers he'd like and would he really mind a church wedding. Perhaps a Catholic one? Can our children be Catholic? Please? It would mean so much. He felt a restlessness shudder through him as he hauled her to her feet to go back and join the rest. They climbed the ghats shooting off their cameras at the myriad of small temples above them.

He felt a strong tug on his backpack. "What do you want?" he asked. "The water again?"

Dan glanced over his shoulder. A big monkey bared its teeth six inches away. "Jesus!"

"Oh!" Charlie jumped in surprise.

He twisted around to shake it off but it quickly pulled a bag of potato chips from his backpack and leaped away. He laughed. "You little bastard!"

The monkey ran between the small temples with the chip bag and sat with one of his mates to tear it apart to get at the salt and vinegar chips. He was sure it was grinning at him. Charlie laughed so hard she almost choked. Maybe it was the right time to mention Jeb Hamlish's offer to protect Charlie from her mother.

"Remember at Lumbini when I said I'd make sure you were safe in the States?" he asked after she'd recovered her breath and they were climbing the stairs. "I've made sure you can hide away and you'll never have to see Bitch Auntie again."

"I won't? Great! How?"

"Jeb Hamlish is willing to protect you from her."

She stopped as abruptly as if she'd walked into a brick wall. "*What?* Jeb fucking Hamlish?" she snapped.

"He'll guard you until you're twenty-one," he explained quickly. "It's only—"

"You arranged all this without me knowing?" Anger reddened and set her jaw. "What am I? A piece of meat to be bartered around? Jeb Hamlish is the bastard who said all kinds of nasty, vicious things about my father and you made a *deal* with him?"

Dan held out open palms. "Charlie, that was politics. Politicians say all kinds of shit to get elected. Grow up, smell the coffee! Who else can protect you from Auntie?"

"Fuck the coffee and fuck Jeb Hamlish!" "Have you thought about how Hamlish would like to keep me under lock and key until the election is over? One word from me and he's toast!"

Had Jeb Hamlish played him for a sucker? Had he almost delivered Charlie into his arms to keep her quiet? And David Hamlish's arms too? It was definitely the wrong time to tell her he'd get a million if she went with Jeb.

"I've done the best I can for you," he said firmly. "Or do you prefer being locked up in a nuthouse by Auntie if you go back to the States on your own?"

"I'm not going back!" Charlie hit his arm and ran away up the steps toward the white, conical-domed Shiva temple at the exit to the main temple area. She ignored the pesky monkeys running around her and never looked back.

Dan sat with his head in his hands as husbands and wives, lovers and children, all in their colorful outfits, walked the ghats, entering and leaving the temples, some wading in the waters below the bridge. It was *National Geographic* stuff. What a scene to remember if he could forget the previous few minutes. How did the Shakespeare quote and popular fifties song go? "Love is a many-splendored thing"? He could think of a different adjective.

A grim Loki stood outside the Shiva temple at the top of the steep embankment. He'd said barely a word all day. Not even his customary "Ladies and Gentlemen!" Charlie the treasure ship had sailed and left him on the dock.

Dan had no sympathy for him. Too bad. He was a criminal, robbing tourists on his trips and Kapoor would eventually nail him. Loki called and waved everyone into the entrance to the Shiva temple.

Where was Charlie? Dan saw her disappearing into the temple's entrance followed by Shira, Duncan, Mark and Gilly. He stuffed his sunglasses into his shirt pocket and jogged up the ghat steps to join them. Inside the small temple, there was only light from the open door behind them. Charlie was taking a flash photo of a six-foot-high statue of a many-armed Shiva standing on one leg.

"Go away," she said harshly.

"Listen, Charlie—"

The heavy door slammed behind them with a clang of old wood and iron and plunged them into total darkness. A powerful flashlight blinded them.

"Stay right where y'are!" called Bob. "If anyone tries anythin', ya'll be deed."

"Oh my God!" Charlie clutched at Dan's arm.

Bob pointed his Walther at Mark and Gilly. "Throw your guns over here you two."

The guns clattered at his feet. Rani scowled alongside Bob's, happier now with her Nano in her hand. Loki smiled smugly on Bob's other side. Too soon, you idiot, thought Dan as he reached for the Glock in the back of his pants.

"Charlie?" Bob waved his flashlight at her. "Get over here!"

Charlie gasped. "Me? Oh, God!"

Bob aimed his gun straight at her. "Come on, luvvy," he coaxed with a jerk of the barrel.

Charlie glanced fearfully at Dan, hesitating, tightening her grip.

"Do as he says," he told her. "He's not going to hurt you. You're worth a mint."

"That's right, Danny boy. Do as I say and no one gits hurt."

Charlie shuffled slowly toward Bob. Rani grabbed her, swiftly tied her hands behind her back with a plastic strap and wrapped duct tape over her mouth.

"All of you!" Bob shouted. "Down on your knees! Hands behind your back! Rani's gonna come 'round and tie y'up. Don't resist. I repeat no one will git hurt. We only want Charlie."

Mark glanced at Dan meaningfully then shouted, "You won't get away with it, you bastard! I'll hunt you down, you gutless Ozzie! Good for only kidnapping girls?"

Bob laughed sourly, swinging his Walther and flashlight toward Mark.

Bob snarled, "You pommie arsehole, I think I'll—" He heard the click as Dan loaded the breech. He turned too late.

Bang! Dan's Glock boomed and thudded back into his hand. Bob spun violently sideways as though hit by a passing train and went down. His flashlight hit the ground and shattered, plunging them into darkness again.

"Bob!" Rani's tortured scream.

"Stay down!" Dan shouted and dove onto the stone floor.

Bang! Bang! Warning shots from Rani's Nano whined over their heads and ricocheted off the walls.

He kept his gun pointing toward the sound of feet shuffling toward the heavy door. It creaked open and Dan squinted into the brilliant rays to see Rani, Loki, Bob and Charlie staggering out into the blinding sunlight. He fumbled his sunglasses out of his pocket, got to his feet and rushed to the door. Loki held onto Bob as they staggered along behind Rani and Charlie between the small temples above the ghats. Rani twisted around and saw Dan. She raised her arm. He ducked behind a Shiva statue.

Bang!

A bullet pinged behind him. He ignored Loki helping Bob since they had no guns and used both hands to aim the Glock at Rani. With only two bullets left after Duncan had already fired three at Steve, he couldn't afford to waste any. No clear shot without a chance of hitting Charlie—not that it mattered since he was trembling so much the bullet could go anywhere. Too much adrenaline pumped through his arteries, his breathing and heart rate rocketing. He ignored the pain in his head as it strained its gaskets.

Whap Whap Whap pounded in his ears. He looked up. A black helicopter passed low overhead.

He ran, taking cover behind one small temple after another. Rani recovered her vision and ran better, shoving the gun into Charlie's head as she pushed her toward the small bridge at the bottom end of the ghats. She fired over the heads of a few gawking people near the bridge to clear the way. Screaming, they took off in a hurry.

Whap Whap Whap.

The helicopter made one hell of a racket as it spun around and landed in clouds of dust in the parking lot on the other side of the bridge. Rani jerked Charlie to a halt at the bridge and waited for Bob and Loki to catch up. She saw Dan. He dodged beside a statue of a Shiva bull as it guarded the entrance to its temple.

Bang!

Stone chips stung Dan's face. Rani's aim was getting too good. He rested his gun barrel on the bull's tail and aimed it at Rani but she was too close to Charlie—he couldn't fire. Hell, he'd never won a teddy bear with an air rifle at a town fair. At this range, he couldn't hit Kathmandu.

Bang! Rani again.

When Bob and Loki caught up with her, Rani smiled for the first time on the trip. They'd be off with Charlie in the whirlybird in a few minutes. They almost had Charlie and a fortune in the bag.

The bull monkey jumped off a temple roof onto Rani's backpack as she began to cross the bridge. Rani screamed and released her hold on Charlie. She twirled around trying to brush the big monkey off her backpack. She thumped at it with her gun over her shoulder.

It was now or never. "Get down, Charlie!' Dan screamed as loud as he could. She heard him and dropped to her knees.

Bang! Bang!

Dan unloaded the gun at Rani and the monkey as they wrestled on the bridge, hoping to hell he hit anything but Charlie. The monkey and Rani went down in a squirming pile. Dan dropped the empty gun. Bob collapsed. Loki took off toward the helicopter. Where'd Charlie gone? Oh God! What had he done? He scrambled down the steps but Duncan rushed headlong onto the bridge ahead of him and took one mighty swing at Rani who was waving her gun and clutching at her thigh, struggling to get to her feet, It put her down for good. He jumped off the bridge into the water and disappeared.

Whap Whap Whap Whap

The helicopter's rotor whirled faster and faster. Loki silently screamed as it rose above him. A screech of tires as a brown and green Hummer roared into the parking lot and skidded to a halt in the gravel. A SWAT team of armored cops spilled out. The helicopter pilot gunned his motor to make his escape, the blades spinning faster.

Whap Whap Whap Whap

The cops riddled the helicopter with bullets. Out of control and smoking, it spun around and around before tilting over and crashing, its shattered rotor zipping killer shards of metal in all directions. Loki disappeared in a blinding flash of detonating gas tanks.

"Where's Charlie?" Dan shouted, picking himself up from where the blast had felled him. He ran onto the bridge, just as a grinning Duncan hauled Charlie out of the shallow water below. Charlie's white face exploded with joyful relief. Dan jumped in the water and hugged them both. Dense black smoke with its stench of burning fuel drifted over from the blazing helicopter.

"You couldn't hit a barn door from inside the barn!" Mark laughed, nudging the dead monkey off the bridge into the stream. He knelt next to a motionless Bob and rolled him onto his side. "He'll live. Pity."

Gilly ran up, pink-blotched cheeks, and kicked Bob. "Bastard!"

Dan left Charlie with Duncan and climbed back up onto the bridge. Rani lay on her back at Mark's feet, nose and mouth bleeding, her leg a bloody mass. Dan ripped out his belt and used it as a tourniquet to halt the streaming blood.

She rolled her head, her eyes flickering. "Bob?" she said anxiously, reaching to touch his head.

"He'll live," he told her.

She sighed and drifted off.

Dan almost felt sorry for the murderous couple. Almost. She and Bob had assured futures: many years in slimming prisons.

"Well done, Dan!" called a familiar voice.

Dan turned to find Kapoor in his protective helmet and bulletproof jacket, grinning at him, slightly blurred. His head pounded like an old hand-cranked water pump whose warranty was up. He felt nauseous.

"We've caught the buggers!" Kapoor hugged him.

Dan gave him a tight hug in return. "How did you know it was going to happen here?"

"We kept an eye on Loki Malik. As soon as we got a sighting of Bob Stewart, we were on our way. I almost didn't make it!"

"It was Bob, Rani and the guide with the gun at the temples?"

Kapoor laughed and pulled Dan closer.

"You'll collect a big promotion and a few medals for this!"

"I'd prefer to kiss you," Kapoor whispered, apparently forgetting hugs didn't have to last forever and they were in public.

Dan kissed him on both cheeks. "How about that?"

Kapoor beamed up at the beneficent gods. It struck Dan how pleased he was to see Kapoor's happy face and how he wouldn't see it for much longer. His only male friend since Paul.

"Hey!" Someone grabbed Dan from behind. He twisted around into Charlie's arms. He looked into a pale face with the wide eyes of a terrified baby seal that had just dodged a club. "What … about … me?" Her lips smacked his, two magnets obeying their Natural Law, glomming their poles onto one another and never wanting to part.

"I … love you," she gasped, sagging against him.

"I love you too," he said quickly, the most important reflex a man has to learn.

Her face grew a determined look. "So screw Jeb Hamlish. Screw … the lot of them. If I hide out anywhere … it'll be Namche. With you, damn it!"

* * *

Back to the hotel after dropping by the Kathmandu Police Headquarters for a grilling by a sour detective professionally irritated by Kapoor's coup and Dan's request for Kapoor to be given a medal, a smiling Duncan and a blushing Shira went straight to their room. He didn't expect to see much of them for a while. It could have been the last time he saw Duncan. He could see the death certificate: smothered, his face a smiling rictus. Charlie kissed him for a long time and left to rest and clean up for the evening. They'd meet in the lobby at eight.

He showered and shaved, rested on the bed and let thoughts, the aroma and the touch of Charlie drift through the fertile fields of his mind. He was excited about the future instead of preparing to die. Living for today like he'd blabbed on about to everyone else was a damn good idea.

In the lobby, a young desk clerk with slicked-back, gelled hair and coal-black *surma* that enlarged his choirboy's eyes took a few moments and fifty rupees to remember Charlie. The "tall, red model" had been "most stunningly dressed." A gray limousine had picked the lady up and whisked her away to the Radisson. Jeb Hamlish.Why hadn't she phoned him? A tightness grew beneath his sternum.

"The lady checked out, sah," the clerk informed him. "Would your name be Doctor Palmer?"

Checked out? "Yes."

"The lady left this for you."

He took the cream envelope from the boy's well-manicured hand. It had the red and yellow hotel crest and name nicely embossed in the top left-hand corner. "Dan" was written in the neat, arty script of a female hand. Black ball-point ink. It was sealed, the flap not simply folded inside. Maybe only one sheet of paper. He imagined her tongue licking it. He knew he'd remember the envelope for the rest of my life.

He used a sharp letter opener from the clerk to slit the envelope open. He scanned the single sheet quickly through misting eyes. "You bastard!" Underlined too. "How could you? ... Auntie left me a letter ... eleven million! ... to fuck Shira ... abandon me in Kathmandu ... Jeb told me ... more money! ... David Hamlish can't be worse than a bastard like you ..." It went on.

His heart not only sank, it kept on going deeper and deeper until it was crushed in the depths of despair. No survivors. He didn't read any more. The tightness became a big fist gripping his stomach. Jeb hadn't suckered him. Charlie had fallen into his lap after she'd read Cruella's letter. No Hamlish scandal unless Cruella said something. Would she and blow her blackmail? Not a chance. She'd just squeeze Jeb for lots of money over the abortion—and she'd come after Dan and Charlie. She'd want more than this—she'd want them dead. If only he'd told Charlie everything. He thought of taking a taxi to see if Charlie would talk to him then changed his mind. Stalking wasn't on his bucket list. Charlie was better off without him even if it killed him inside. He hated being smart enough to see both sides of a situation. Being selfless sucked.

It was maybe for the best that Charlie was gone, he tried to convince himself. He wouldn't have to worry about how long he'd have with her should she have returned. But it was a painful best that filled his head with a terrible darkness he never thought he'd ever feel again. In the bad old days, he would have had a beer or ten, his default behavior when everything went to shit. He didn't.

* * *

"I missed all the fun!" Karen shouted from the bathroom over the hiss of the shower rattling the plastic curtain. "Ding dong the wicked bastard's off to prison! I'd have loved to have been there to see Bob get shot and cuffed."

"I wouldn't have minded missing it. I think I've used up all my lives," Dan replied tiredly.

He rested against the balcony rail and looked down onto a boy selling Chinese knock-off walking poles, socks and sunglasses, bootleg audiotapes and cheap trek maps of the Himalayas. The hard-working kid would be there as late as possible then back at dawn to help support his family. It could have been him, struggling to make a living in a poor Third World country like billions of others. Tomorrow he'd buy something he didn't need from him. Maybe the whole stall.

Karen poked her head out of the bathroom with a toothbrush wedged in her mouth. "That temple shootout must have been wild. Saved Charlie again? What's that twice?"

He waved his hand in the air. "Practice, practice, practice."

"You should star in your own video game. *Super Dan to the Rescue?*"

"More like *Dupe Dan and Win the Princess.*"

Karen in a garish purple and yellow silk robe limped out of the tiny bathroom. "Well done, Dan. We got Bob and I didn't have to kill him."

"Could you have?"

"I dunno. In my darkest moments, I'd have killed him twice. You were right. It's better this way. Do you mind if I drink?" she asked, with a wave of her bottle.

"Go right ahead."

She toasted him with her beer before easing herself onto a plastic chair. Dan joined her and they sat in silence for a while listening to the general hum of the traffic and people crowded below in the narrow street. He lit her a cigarette.

"Bill phoned you?" he asked. She grinned the width of the Kathmandu Valley. "Told you so."

"Yeah, off to see him in Goa tomorrow." She laughed beyond happy and it made him feel great.

He'd phoned and managed to get through to Bill—miraculously the number on the card hadn't been a phone booth in the Philippines—and told him what a great woman he was missing out on. Turned out, Bill had thought the same thing. Dan had been surprised when Bill had opened up about his marriage and

Dan had been able to share his own problems. Misery does love company and men will always tell other men of similar experiences to make them feel better.

"You haven't asked me why I'm not out celebrating with Charlie," he said.

"Instead of hanging around an old biddy like me?" She shuffled her chair closer. "I thought something must have happened."

"She's checked out of the bloody hotel and moved to the Radisson with Hamlish. She left this for me." Dan handed her the folded envelope from his shirt pocket."

She took it from his fingers. "What does it say?"

"*You bastard* and it's downhill from there."

She smiled thinly. "A not-so-love letter?"

"She's gone. I fucked it up." He worked hard to keep his eyes dry.

She placed the envelope on the patch over her stitched forehead. "Ah, yes. It says 'Fuck off, loser. Thanks for saving me from getting kidnapped twice. Thanks for keeping me out of the loony bin for the rest of my life and making me rich. Sorry I was such a prick teaser. Nice to have known you. Found a billionaire's son, sucker.' Am I right?"

"Close enough."

She placed the envelope on his forehead. "What else does it say, sweetie?"

He exhaled deeply. "Cruella paid me to play her along and dump her in Kathmandu."

"She did? Blimey, that would hurt."

"It gets worse. Auntie paid me to stay away from Charlie and … offered me Shira on a plate instead."

"Oh, God. Did you fuck Shira?"

"Not even close." Dan smiled sadly. The monastery was beginning to be a great vacation destination. Bring on the kites. Sharpen your beaks, my friends.

"So that's where the ten million came from?"

"Actually, no," Dan explained his blackmail of Cruella and the money from Hamlish and watched her eyes widen as the numbers rolled out and the total grew.

"Crikey. What are you going to do with it?"

"Shira and Duncan got the ten. The rest? Donate to the monastery and build a proper hospital in Namche Bazar. Lots of ways to help the Sherpas with the rest."

"Very laudable."

"And a million to you for putting up with me."

She waved a palm at him. "Hold it, whacker."

He held her hand. "You've become special for me," Dan said seriously. "Don't refuse. It's a wedding present for you and Bill. Do something good with it."

She kissed his cheek. "OK, OK! I don't need that much convincing! I guess I'll have to invite you to the bloody wedding now." She laughed and hopped off to the bathroom again. "I'll celebrate with some Spanish plonk! Can you get it for me, sweetie?"

He returned with the bottle of dubious Spanish rioja she'd hunted down at a local bar and a plastic cup. He opened it and poured some for her.

"Cheers, Dan. You're the best!" She drank and kissed him on the cheek. She rested a big arm around his sagging shoulders. "You're very much in love with Charlie, aren't you?"

He nodded his heavy head. "But it's all over now. *Kaput ... Wiedersehen ... Sayonara ... Addio*," he rambled.

Karen pulled him closer. "You know, if it hadn't been Bill, it might have been you. You're my kind of guy. Even if you do have AIDS."

Dan laughed. She knew the AZT had been a prophylactic to keep him HIV-free. Not fucking anyone in Africa had something to do with it too. "I'm going to miss you too," he told her.

Karen kissed him on the cheek, limped to her closet and picked out some clothing. "I remember I have something to do." She changed into an elaborately decorated Nepalese shirt and white jeans before pausing in the doorway with her cane. "Thank you again for getting the Stewarts," she said. "I owe you big time, sweetie."

* * *

Dan and Kapoor drank cold orange juices in a private booth in a hip bar near Durbar Square. The lights were low, the music soft and the air cool.

"I must go back to Mumbai tomorrow," Kapoor said quietly. "I'm going to miss you so much."

"I'll miss you too," Dan said. "You're a great guy—saved my life."

Kapoor forced a small smile, squeezing Dan's fingers. "Paul didn't have HIV, did he?" Dan held his eyes for a few seconds before he shook his head. "You never told me if you'd made love to him."

Dan took a deep breath. "The last night I spent in the cell with him."

"You're no homo. Why did you?"

Dan waved his head from side to side for a moment, gathering his thoughts. "To make him happy," he said. "We loved each other and it was what he wanted. Also, we knew it might be the last time we saw each other." His eyes glistened. "And it was."

Kapoor let a quiet moment pass before he said, "This is my last night in Kathmandu and I don't think we'll ever see each other again either."

Dan looked into Kapoor's coy smile and laughed. "You are a persistent fellow, Dipak."

Kapoor grinned. "That I am!"

April 9th

"HERE, PUT THIS on," Charlie told Dan.

Dan pulled a face as he looked inside the scuffed helmet the rental store had provided.

"It's sprayed with DDT. It's good." She lied but it was for a higher purpose. Didn't count. Didn't Thomas Aquinas say that?

Dan put on the helmet and fastened the chinstrap. "I didn't know you were a biker."

"There's a lot you don't know about me."

"Oh God. I'm not sure I want to know. You're exhausting." He kissed her again and she liked it again. She knew she'd made the right decision—he was The One.

"Where did you get this?" Dan looked at the shiny black and silver, old-style Royal Enfield motorbike that Charlie had idling by the side of the road in front of the hotel.

"Cheap rental. I've always wanted to ride one of these—India's the only place that still makes them."

He threw a leg over the rear seat. "Where are we going?"

"You'll be surprised." He certainly would be. "Worried about my riding?"

"I'm OK. I brought Buddha along for back up." He patted his pocket. He caught Charlie looking intently at him. "What's the matter?"

"I can't believe you're here."

"Well, I am, aren't I?"

"I'm the luckiest woman in the world." She beamed like a lighthouse that had found its ship and stopped circling. He was all she wanted. She didn't want to search elsewhere. "Do you know how much we have to thank Karen?"

Dan nodded. "I do. She's a wonderful person."

"If she hadn't come to the hotel and talked me through everything, I'd be in the US today. Maybe with David."

"And unhappy?"

"And *very* unhappy."

"Why don't you kiss me again?" he asked, feigning shyness. "It must have been five minutes since the last one."

She didn't need to be asked twice. Off they roared into the streets of Kathmandu where even motorbikes could be stuck going nowhere as people, cars, trucks, buses and animals competed for the smallest space. No sooner had they moved off than she felt Dan's hands slip under her jacket.

"You bastard!" she called over her shoulder.

"Gotta hold on somewhere!"

Charlie used either side of any street and the sidewalks to wiggle the bike between cars and onto a bigger artery road where a leaping lion painted on the rear of a huge TATA truck full of construction workers of the truck warned her not to get too close. Here the main obstacle was the heaps of dirt dumped in the middle of the roads to be used for filling any of the holes that emerged on a regular basis. She took the main road east then turned off north toward the temple pool at Budhanlikantha in the Himalayan foothills.

The town square bustled with hawkers flogging every household item you could think of from pots and pans to electric plugs to electric toasters and toilet seats. Farmers fought over prices for fresh produce from the fields they displayed on carts and on sheets laid down on the ancient cobbles that the Moguls had trotted their horses on several centuries previously. Nearby, the small temples, some smoking with ceremonial fires, surrounded the Vishnu pool.

Charlie put her arm around Dan to make sure he was still there as they watched women laying wreaths of marigolds at the feet of the god Lord Vishnu. Carved out of rock, the most powerful Hindu god slept comfortably on a bed of snakes in a recessed pool of water.

"Tell me about Vishnu," Charlie said.

"He's stoned."

Charlie kicked his ankle.

"He's a biggie with Brahma and Shiva. He's the preserver of the universe. That's hard to beat!"

"I want to offer him something," she said.

Charlie bought a garland of marigolds from a shriveled woman near the entrance gate and walked down the stairs to the god's feet. She waited her turn then knelt and looked up at Dan before praying for a few minutes.

Back at the bike, Charlie jumped on the back seat first. "Now, you bastard," she said with a broad grin as she flexed her fingers. "Get on!"

"If I must!" he said with the biggest of laughs. "Where are you taking me?"

The bike wound its way higher and higher through fields being plowed by water buffalo and tilled by families with hoes. Patches of corn and millet ran alongside the narrowing road. They passed through Nagarkot's small collection of houses, restaurants and guest houses before descending into a wet valley of forests of junipers and rhododendrons and tall, waving pines before climbing steeply to the temple perched on the rocky hillside above the trees. Lines of colored prayer flags hung from red-flowering rhododendron trees up toward the temple.

"The temple at Nagarkot!" Dan called out when they stopped at the temple's gate and parked the bike.

Charlie felt a surge of joy at Dan's excitement. "Did I do good?"

"You amaze me, Charlie!"

They left their helmets on the bike. The monks weren't going to steal them.

"This is where I want to be released," he told her.

"Released?"

"From this mortal coil. Buddhists here chop up a dead body and put it out for the birds to recycle you into the universe."

She winced. "Sounds a bit like a messy butcher's shop."

"Look up." He pointed to a pair of kites that had heard their conversation and were circling overhead on the updraft. "Think of it as taking your pop cans back."

She held back an urge to cry, holding his hand firmer than ever, looking up at the temple's dome and at a few monkeys that were playing just inside the wrought iron gate.

"Do we have to talk about this?" she asked.

"Everyone has to some time. You'd rather be buried in a box to rot or cremated into a vase of ashes and put on a shelf?" He began to sing: "Feed the birds, tuppence a bag, t—"

"Oh God." Charlie groaned and shoved him toward the gateway that looked like the kind at an entrance to a Chinatown in North America, a rectangular arch with a couple of lions to guard it. Walls with embedded prayer wheels stood to each side.

"Come on," Dan told Charlie. "Turn them clockwise and it's as good as a prayer!"

They spun them and giggled as they got as many going as possible. It was like being at the fair. Charlie felt herself becoming as excited as Dan. A real monastery! In Nepal too!

Beyond the gate, they approached a white stupa, flags suspended across the entrance yard and got more thoughtful, sobering up from their giddiness. They climbed two small flights of stairs to a three-story box of a temple, glass windows in dark brown frames, a tapestry suspended in its entrance from a brown and white-painted overhang, its walls painted in a dark pink.

Inside, there were no windows to allow daylight, just subdued lighting from several electric lights suspended from a twenty-foot-high ceiling. Their eyes adjusted and they began to appreciate the splendid work of the Nepalese monks, their bold greens, yellows and reds splashing oriental life into the murals of Buddha's life on the walls and the decorated wooden posts. Dominating the room was a massive, ceiling-high, golden Buddha, placed at a higher level at the end of the temple. The Tibetan influence was easy to spot: Buddha guarded by wild dogs that had morphed into ferocious, red and green dragons. The ceiling of the temple was decorated with circular symbolic patterns between the elaborately painted crossed members supporting the roof. This was no dull bunch of God-fearing Calvinists on a miserable Sunday in Switzerland. These monks enjoyed their paint pots and their Buddha.

The murmur of Buddhist prayers droned softly from a group of five monks with shaven heads and maroon and saffron robes who sat on a carpet to the side of the room. They eyed their visitors but ignored their presence. Charlie motioned to Dan and they quietly sat on a red and white-patterned carpet on dark brown wooden planks.

"Close your eyes and relax. Don't think of Jesus," he whispered.

Charlie elbowed him. Dan began to mumble something and she knew she had to join in for the full experience. What was Dan attracted to? No god? No one to say how bad or good you were? No confession of sin?

"*Om Mani Padme Hum*," she whispered to herself. The path to enlightenment. To the perfection of Buddha.

Her mind drifted. Dan had told her how many million times he'd repeated it to calm himself in his cell. She sneaked a peek at him: something good was happening to him as he repeated the mantra—his constant practice now enabled him to drain all the tension out of him. She closed her eyes again and she felt it too. She didn't know what it was but a peace rippled through her as she let go of her anxieties, her pessimistic thoughts. Was it the eternal now? *Post-orgasmic* is the only way she could think of to describe it—when the powerful emotions had been released and the mind was left devoid of the pressures of life. It began in her head and flowed to her toes. Tears almost overwhelmed her. She took a deep breath and held them back.

"What did you say?" Dan whispered.

"*Om Mani Padme Hum.*"

"I didn't know you knew that."

"Didn't I tell you there's a lot of things you don't know about me?"

They closed their eyes again, this time holding hands.

* * *

An elbow from Charlie. Dan opened his eyes to find one of the monks kneeling in front of them. He was the oldest, probably the boss, a beatific countenance, a dark red-brown skin.

"*Namaskar*," he whispered. "You are welcome in our temple."

Dan and Charlie moved to get up.

He held up a well-worn palm. "You can stay as long as you want. Relax in our temple. Please, be our guests," he said in an accent he must have learned from the BBC World Service.

"*Dhanyabad.*" Dan reached out and shook a strong hand, one calloused by working in the gardens he assumed. "*Mero naam* Dan *ho.*"

The monk's eyes moved to Charlie.

"*Mero naam* Charlie *ho*," she said, extending her hand too.

The monk shook her hand before patting his chest. "*Mero naam* Tshering *ho*. Have you eaten?

"Why don't we?" Charlie asked Dan.

Tshering guided them out of the temple entrance and across the stone-paved courtyard to one of the single-story stone buildings nearby. It was barely bigger than a couple of rooms but the delicious aroma floating out of its half-open door led them to a wooden table flanked by long benches. They weren't handed menus or a wine list so they went with the veggie stew and naan-like bread that was brought by a stooped, round-faced monk with Buddy Holly glasses. He could have been the Dalai Lama undercover. He smiled at their *dhanyabad*s and left without saying a word.

Dan played with his stew a moment while Tshering observed them. "I started studying Buddhism a few years ago," he told him.

"Ah."

"And I would like to be ... recycled ... in Nepal when I die."

Charlie tensed at his side.

Tshering nodded impassively.

"It's such a special place and to be returned to the universe here, close to Lumbini, would be beyond special."

"Indeed it would."

"Is it possible for me to do that here?" Dan glanced at Charlie. She'd stopped eating and stared into her bowl.

"Of course." Tshering studied him. "But you are still a young man."

"Planning ahead. You never know. One day at a time."

"We never do know." Tshering turned to Charlie, playing thoughtfully with her spoon. "Do you need a rest, young lady?"

Charlie forced a smile. "I am a bit tired."

"Why not relax here while I talk with Dan in our gardens?" He glanced back at Dan. "And then she'll be good for your ride back. To Kathmandu, I presume?"

Dan nodded. "OK, Charlie. I'll be back soon." He ran his fingers across her head.

Charlie half-smiled but even that was a big effort.

* * *

Charlie pensively regarded Dan when he returned with Tshering from the garden and disturbed her reverie. Her red eyes must have told him what she'd been thinking about. Outside the temple, Buddy Holly and two other monks followed discreetly behind them.

Back at the gate, Tshering held his palms together and dipped his head. "*Pheri bhetaunla.* I hope we meet again, my new friends. But not too soon, Dan"

They dipped their hands and heads to him.

Charlie bent down and kissed him on the cheek. "You've been real kind. *Dhanyabad* so much."

Sharp laughter barked from Buddy Holly. Too late, he covered his mouth and scurried off with the other giggling monks. Tshering's wide eyes showed his surprise at the kiss but he grinned. It's not every day a Buddhist monk is kissed by a red-haired Amazon. Dan could imagine the table chatter in the refectory that evening. The boss was in for a teasing. Tshering strolled with them the short distance to the motorbike.

"You never know, Tshering. Maybe next time around!" said Dan.

"*Pheri bhetaunla!*" shouted Charlie as they roared off on the Royal Enfield.

Dan looked back at Tshering waving the check for three million dollars. He looked rather pleased for a man who didn't value money.

* * *

On the drive back to Kathmandu, Dan's grip almost broke her ribs as Charlie guided the thrumming Royal Enfield around the tight downhill corners and between the ox carts and bicycles down through the red-flowered rhododendron forests into the tiny village of Nagarkot. It was after they passed through the village that Charlie flicked her eyes at the rear view mirrors to see what the screech of tires behind her was all about: a dark brown Range Rover was rapidly approaching. She pulled more to the side of the road to let the idiot by. Her heart jumped as it loomed in the mirrors, heading straight toward them. It had no intention of passing.

"*Hold on!*" she shouted, dropping a gear and twisting the throttle to max.

The engine roared and the rear wheel spun as she snaked across the road to narrowly avoid being shunted by the Range Rover's grill.

Holy Mother! Who the hell is it?

Into higher gears and she was away at over eighty within seconds, leaving a spray of dust and gravel. She hammered the bike toward a bend that made her gasp as she took in the huge fall off into a canyon to nowhere if she misjudged it. Dan's grip took on a python dimension as she carved a turn hoping like hell she didn't lose it on the rough blacktop and plunge into the abyss.

The Range Rover's tires squealed as it braked heavily to take the turn. Its engine screamed closer. Charlie was up a gear and revving hard, the next turn approaching rapidly only fifty meters ahead. She had time to judge it and scrubbed off some speed to carve the turn.

The SUV took the turn much easier. It must be in four-wheel drive. It gained rapidly on them out of the bend. Behind the Range Rover, she caught a glimpse of another car swerving down the road. *Two of them!*

She hit a gravel patch and swerved crazily, losing vital speed. "*Jeeesus!*" she screamed as she tried to regain control, wobbling toward the next hairpin. The roar of the Range Rover was so close—its grill filled the mirrors. She gritted her teeth expecting a crunch any second and to be vaulted into oblivion. She wrestled with the jerking handlebars, willing the bike on.

Metal crunched and tires screeched above the roar of the bike's motor. The Range Rover shot by and spun over the edge of the road and disappeared into the bottomless pit of rocks and stunted trees.

Charlie braked hard, wrestling with the vibrating handlebars as the next bend loomed, filling her nostrils with the burning smell of overheated brakes and hot oil. The bike went down on its side. She let go, grabbing back to hold onto Dan. The bike spun several times before it attempted to fly. She and Dan bounced together along the road until they lay bruised, cut and gasping with relief on the edge of the jump to nowhere. Charlie's whole forearm seared with the pain of smashing her elbow onto the road.

Charlie's immediate thought: the second car will run us over! She heard its tires screech as it thundered by spraying loose grit. Her right hip throbbed in agony. She tried to take off her helmet. She couldn't do it—her bleeding hands shook uncontrollably.

Dan flipped up her cracked visor. "Jesus ... where the fuck ... did you learn to ride like that?"

Charlie's gray face looked up at him. She broke down, her whole body trembling, tears gushing.

"It's OK," he gasped, patting her helmet and holding her as though she'd never ever be lost to him again.

A shadow fell over them.

Dan looked up. "Where's ... your white charger ... you lovely man?" he asked.

"I prefer a BMW these days, old boy."

Mark kneeled down and removed Charlie's helmet. "Wonderful riding, Charlie. You saved this bugger's life. You should be damn proud of her, Dan."

Charlie retched onto the gravel. Mark helped remove Dan's helmet. They checked out Charlie's bits before they lifted her onto her shaking knees. She couldn't stop shaking in Dan's arms. He didn't mind when she vomited on his shoulder.

"There there, dear," soothed a reedy voice. Gilly appeared to cradle Charlie and wipe her mouth with her hankie.

Mark put a powerful arm around Dan's shoulders as they stumbled over to the cliff side of the road. Far below, a cloud of black smoke rose out of the valley.

"Who ... was it?" Dan gasped between his own urges to puke.

"We kept track of Missus Jacobs after she checked out of the hotel. When she was picked up by a couple of thugs and didn't go to the airport, we knew Charlie and you were in danger." Mark smiled his satisfaction at the burning vehicle. "The psycho won't be found for years—if ever."

Dan stared at Cruella's funeral pyre. Killed in a road accident. Karma.

"I guess she couldn't find good help," Mark mused. "She must have gone over the edge."

Dan laughed at the dark pun. He reached out and shook Mark's hand. "Thanks, you saved our lives." Dan kissed him on the cheek and made him blush like the embarrassed good Brit he was. "So you were following her and we got lucky?"

"Lovely day for a drive, wasn't it?"

"Jeb Hamlish will be a happy man."

The revelation of Cruella killing Charlie's parents had hit Jeb like a megawatt advert blinking at midnight in Time Square. Dan hadn't missed the horror in his face—and the mix of fear and anger. The opportunity for Mark to shunt Cruella to her death had been serendipitous but the irony of Cruella being driven off the road to her death wasn't lost on Dan—and he was sure wouldn't be on Hamlish either. Cruella, the psychotic loose cannon, a danger to his political ambitions, was no more. If he had ordered the hit, it was the presidential right stuff even before he had his feet up in the Oval Office.

* * *

Kapoor texted Dewan: Robert Stewart arrested for the Harbor Murders, kidnapping attempts in Pushkar and Kathmandu, and for the murders of three men in Pushkar, one in Australia, two in the United States and the murder of Kanta Suran at Lumbini. Admitted to all of the murders on condition wife is prosecuted for only the Kathmandu kidnapping attempt by Nepalese. Acceptable?

Dewan: A mass murderer! *Jhakaas!* I'll get right on it. Come home, all is forgiven!

Hara: Way to go, boss!

* * *

Dan came out of the incident relatively unscathed if a sore knee and a reinjured wrist were ignored. He was far more concerned about Charlie. No broken bones but a severely bruised hip, a cracked elbow and damaged fingers on one hand added to the shock of the whole event had rendered Charlie exhausted physically and mentally. Dan undressed and slipped behind Charlie's long body under a single sheet. He slid a hand around her waist and pressed into her rose-scented warmth. He cuddled up to her and didn't need anything more.

April 10th

FROM FIVE THOUSAND feet above Kathmandu, the entire sweep of the sprawling city lay below in the dawn sunlight as the Yeti Airlines flight hummed its way east over the lower foothill ridges toward the towering mass of the Himalayan peaks. The chatter of the group rose into an excited buzz, a combination of excitement and fear as they prepared themselves for Lukla airport, a destination with a reputation of a theme park-rollercoaster landing. It made a change from the shocked silence when Nadia had suddenly appeared and boarded the plane last. An anxious murmur rippled through the passengers after she took her seat at the rear of the small two-engined plane and stared dead-eyed at them out of a stone face with bruised, stitched lips. Charlie audibly gasped and flashed her fear at Dan from across the aisle. It was a re-run of that hotel lobby in Jaipur—Nadia's malevolent glare wishing he were dead. Dan handled the shock as best he could: he ignored her looking by out of the window while a car crashed in his guts.

"My God! Check her for weapons!" said Mark, alarmed from the seat in front. "Can't our guide stop her from being on the trip? Call the cops?"

"What could we tell them? She's ugly?"

"She is, isn't she?" fumed Gilly. "Inside and out. We'll have to take care of her ourselves, won't we?"

"Pre-emptively?" asked Mark.

"Only if we have to," said Dan wishing Mark and Gilly had been able to carry their guns on board. He'd been out of bullets anyway—he'd left them with Rani, Bob and the monkey.

It wasn't long before the snow-capped Himalayas stretched across the horizon. The group's buzz got more excited as cameras clicked. Nadia was the only one who showed no emotion, a stone head suitable for Easter Island. Her hooded, dull eyes flicked from Dan to Shira to Charlie as though making a list and checking it twice. Dan didn't doubt she was back for revenge on Shira for the punch but more so on him for punching Kanta. No matter Bob had drowned her she'd blame him for putting her in the pool in the first place. How about harming Charlie? What better way to make him suffer?

Besides Santosh the guide, brave Duncan was the only one to have spoken to Nadia. Dan heard him share the news about his marriage to Shira, receive no response at all, and retreat grim-faced to hold Shira. Dan admired him for trying. The engine noise changed as the plane began to descend into a deep green valley, flying between steep slopes below the peaks.

"Here we go!" called Santosh, with a mischievous smile. "Cameras out!"

Dan looked down the aisle between the seats as the postage stamp-sized airstrip nestled between folds of vertical ridges made its daunting appearance. There was a collective anxious silence as the plane buffeted by the air currents waggled its way down, screeching its tires, landing with a thump on the airstrip that angled higher before it.

Santosh laughed at their discomfort. "Don't worry. If we overshoot, the mountains will stop us."

Relieved cheers from everyone when the plane braked quickly enough to prevent the flight turning into a mountaineering expedition. An hour's walk with their heavy backpacks along a slightly descending path brought them to the two-story, wood-framed inn at Phakding where they were going to spend the night before beginning the trek proper.

Nadia almost didn't make it. It was a nothing walk but she had to stop every ten minutes to recover her breath and gather her strength. Dan watched from one of the dining area's windows as she arrived last with Santosh helping with her pack. Maybe she wouldn't make it to Namche after all.

* * *

In the warm dining area of the inn that smelled of *moo moo* pork dumplings, spicy Sherpa soup, burning oil lamps, and stove smoke, Nadia's soup spoon trembled as she raised it slowly to her bruised lips as though the effort was too much. Dan sat down on a chair across the table from her and felt oddly empathic with a crazy woman who wanted him dead: the woman he'd spent half his life with, the mother of his children and someone who was now totally lost to all of them.

"Tough walk?" he asked. She didn't look up. "It'll get much harder tomorrow. Think you'll make it to Namche?"

"I'll make it," she rasped, her voice cracking like a much older woman.

Nadia was physically weak but he sensed the hate in her that would drive her on. Face to face with her, his anger over what she'd done rose in his throat like a bad street curry. He'd come to terms with malicious Nadia putting him in prison and costing him his medical career, and with her turning Duncan against him but the murderous Nadia who had pushed Karen into the road, tried to drown Shira and collaborated with Kanta to have Charlie raped at the caves was a new poison he couldn't swallow.

"Try anything tomorrow and I'll throw you off the mountain," he threatened, leaning into her for emphasis. He could take her outside for a walk right now and make sure she never came back but she wasn't Bholan Gill, she was the mother of Kathleen and Duncan. He couldn't bring himself to kill her unless it was absolutely necessary.

"You're still a violent man, aren't you?" she sneered revealing Carla's punch had left her with only fangs of teeth. She looked hideously evil.

"You sent the assassin to kill me," he told her. "There's no one left who'd like to see me dead but you." Nadia smiled crookedly into her soup. "Was it Kanta's idea or yours? Kanta from Mumbai. Kanta who rubbed out rivals. A Christian nutter who set me up with the Club, a Christian hitman? He failed so you joined the trip to do it yourself?"

Nadia gripped her spoon like a knife, chilling him with a venomous glare. "I loved Kanta and you killed her," she hissed, her voice as cold as the hate in her eyes.

"It was Bob. You know that."

"If you hadn't punched her, she'd still be alive."

"You're here to kill me, Shira and Charlie, aren't you?"

"I'm here for a breath of fresh air," she said with a thin smile on her swollen lips.

"It might be your last," he warned.

"And yours." She went back to spooning her soup.

One of us won't be sipping Sherpa soup tomorrow night, thought Dan.

* * *

Charlie shook with nervous excitement, the intense desire for Dan suffusing her entire body, as she primped herself in front of the full-length bathroom mirror. She held open the black silk, kimono-style robe she'd been saving for this moment. Her small breasts embarrassed her. Was she good enough? She smiled nervously, her cheeks as flushed as much as her chest and neck. She was ready for Dan but she bit a knuckle worrying if he would be ready for her. Was there anything wrong with him? Could he satisfy her? Would it just be a wham-bam-thankyou-ma'am? God, what if she couldn't satisfy him?

"You idiot!" she told herself. "Snap out of it. Go out there and give him your best!" One last look in the mirror and she took a deep breath.

She moved slowly into the dark room and a thrill vibrated down to her toes when she glimpsed Dan naked on the bed near the window. With the curtains wide open, he was propped up on a pillow looking out over the deep valley to the southwest watching the moon slowly rising. It was a beautifully clear, crisp night, stars blinking. The room was warm and a thin mist of moisture gathered on the cold glass. It was magical and tears of happiness bubbled down her cheeks as she moved quickly toward him. The silk kimono was long gone by the time she slipped onto the bed. He wrapped his arm around her and she felt in heaven.

"Remember it," Dan said huskily. "I will … as long as I live."

"I remember everything we've done together," she said, snuggling into his chest, "and I'll remember everything we're going to do." She caught his face in the moonlight: anxiety showed in his narrowed eyes and the tight set of his mouth. Was he as nervous as she was?

"Isn't this wonderful," he whispered as his fingers began to caress her.

Stars that had hidden from them all their lives twinkled at her from a pitch-black sky. The moon continued to arc higher and higher in the void, luminously white and as big as a dinner gong. She was in love with this man, more than she'd ever imagined possible, by a window on a moonlight night in the Himalayas. Not in the life brochure. Nirvana.

"Everything OK?" she breathed softly, stroking his rippled forehead. She loved it when his fingers played with her breasts.

"There's something I haven't told you. The medicine I take for the disease I caught in Africa, doesn't only keep the parasite down."

There was a moment's silence only interrupted by the mountain wind and her breathing. She mentally gasped: a disease! Temporary impotence!

"That's why you—" She stopped abruptly.

He laughed nervously. It wasn't the kind of thing men easily told anyone, especially their lover.

She pulled him closer. "When can you stop taking the pills?"

"I stopped yesterday."

Charlie swallowed her relief. *Thank God for that!*

"It might take me a while to rise to the occasion," he warned.

As long as he gets there! "We'll just have to take it slowly with our love-making, won't we?" she said, not expecting an answer.

Charlie touched, stroked and fondled him as though he were made of glass and could shatter at any moment. She wet his fingers and stroked them where she wanted. "We have all night, lover," she soothed. "Give a girl a chance to warm up too." It wasn't her she was worried about. She was on the edge of flying solo.

"I'm going to love our home in Namche," she whispered, squirming under his gliding fingers. "I can't wait until tomorrow to get there. What's it like?"

"Think stone hut," he mumbled with a nipple in his lips.

Charlie had read the guidebook on Namche. She knew what she was getting into. The village of stone houses with their blue, red and green metal roofs clung to the terraces on the steep hillside in a dish between snow-capped Himalayan peaks. Djopkis, the yak-cattle hybrids, loaded with sacks of goods staggered up the stone steps while small, muscular men with backs of steel and legs made from tree trunks climbed under the weight of full basket backpacks, plywood sheets and pieces of lumber that would have crippled lesser humans. There was a good job for a chiropractor at Namche. The stonewalled field below the center of the village would be full of workers mixing in the djopki and yak waste to enrich the soil for their vegetables. Namche was a happening place where the high-altitude yaks took over from the djopkis to carry loads even higher, another six thousand feet to Everest Base Camp, and where all the trekkers paused ascending and descending. It was the Paris of the trek. Charlie felt a surge of happiness—she couldn't wait to get there with Dan.

"Sounds cool," she said and was thrilled to feel him getting excited under her fingers.

"Especially ... in the ... winter."

"We'll just have to huddle together in our bed for warmth, won't we?"

His fingers found a place that took her breath away. All conversation stopped for several minutes as their rapid and deep breathing temporarily synced.

Dan told her softly, "Believe this. You're a beautiful, beautiful woman. You are Lhamu. You need not fear anything."

"Lhamu?" Charlie noticed him wincing in some kind of pain.

"A goddess."

She gulped. "I've always wanted to be someone's goddess"

"You certainly are mine," Dan said and Charlie was treated to the gamut of gasping, shuddering and moaning as he showed her he didn't need tantric training. She was floating in the clouds when he raised his bobbing head. "Are you … ready?" he asked, his face strained, his shoulders heaving with his effort.

Climbing to a Himalayan peak she'd never thought within reach, Charlie hummed and gulped and shuddered as she came in rising waves of pleasure as Dan's increasingly powerful thrusts shoved her back up the bed into the headboard. She sensed Dan's whole body stiffening, muscles taut as much as hers as another intense wave of ecstasy coursed through her abdomen taking no prisoners. She almost ripped his ears off when she threw her head back and growled like a feral cat in heat.

"Ooooh! … I'm melting!" she panted, dissolving from the waist down.

Dan rhythmically convulsed. "*Aaaaaaaaaah! Aaaaah!*" With a final agonizing groan, Dan rolled completely off the bed, thudding onto the floor.

"Dan!"

Muscles knotted in his neck as he knelt head down on the wood planks. She leaped after him and pulled him into her. His heart pounded on her chest. His erratic, labored breathing rasped in her ear.

"Oh my God!"

"I'm going … to … throw up," he groaned, between stomach heaves.

She helped him shuffle on all fours to the bathroom where he repeatedly retched into the toilet bowl.

"My … bag," he said, blindly reaching out a hand to the counter.

She snatched several bottles of pills out of the bag. "What are these?" she asked, dropping to her knees. Anger surged through Charlie. She'd been lied to. It wasn't some parasite! What wasn't he telling her?

"Just give them to me!" he snapped flexing his fingers impatiently.

"What are they? I'm frightened!"

"Got ... any water or ... should I drink from the bowl?"

She hurriedly opened a plastic bottle of water. He *swallowed* a couple of each type of pill.

Charlie read the labels. "Percodan? That's a powerful painkiller, isn't it? Metasomething? Nimowhatever? What are these?" She was overwhelmed by a sudden hysteria. "What's wrong with you? Are you going to die?"

"Not now!" Dan shouted. He held his head between his hands, rocking to and fro.

Charlie sat down beside him and tried not to cry as she held him under her arm. She began to pray to God to save Dan: *Don't let him die! Not now!*

It was ten minutes of sitting on the hard tiles running through her novenas over and over again before Charlie slowly eased him to the bed.

"We shouldn't have done that!" she blubbed in a voice laced with guilt at her selfishness. "Look what it did to you!" She covered him with the duvet and knelt by the bed with her hands clenched together as though she were before an altar.

Dan rolled his head toward her and said, "Are ... you ... kidding? Wouldn't have ... missed it." He lifted the duvet. "Get ... in." He folded her into his arms as she gripped him like an anchor in a storm. "Just let me ... lie still for a while."

Charlie trembled, repeating "sorry," sniffling against him as they lay sipping some water from time to time and tenderly stroking each other. When she felt his heartbeat slowing under her hand on his chest and his breathing becoming shallower, she kissed him all over his face. Relief flooded through her when the pain in his eyes receded in a warm wave of the narcotic.

Finally, Dan talked slowly through a fog. "You know I get headaches from time to time? They're a warning sign."

"About what? You've been drinking a lot?" she asked holding down her anxiety about what was wrong with him. He flickered a small smile.

"About my brain."

"You have one in there?" She stroked his forehead.

"Everyone's a comedian. About my blood pressure."

"Uh huh."

"If it's too high, I get severe headaches. So I take powerful antihypertensives."

"Uh huh."

"They stop me from getting my blood pressure up. If I stop taking them I could blow an aneurysm."

She looked into his warm eyes again, caressed his forehead and ran a finger down his nose to his lips. "Sounds painful."

"Do you know what one is?"

She shook her head.

"It's like blowing a tire inside your head except there's no spare."

She felt a chill. "A stroke?"

Dan nodded. "My father blew one and that was the end of him. I inherited it."

The seriousness of it began to dawn on her. How childish of her to think of only sex. "So it could be …?" She felt a dam about to break and wash away this special moment.

He breathed deeply several times as though preparing for a hundred-meter dash. "I'm a time bomb. I could disappear from your universe at any time," he said.

A surge of emotion flooded her eyes until she saw the tears pouring down his face. What the hell was *she* crying about? "You're afraid you'll die soon," she said, her voice breaking. "It's why you haven't wanted to get … intimate with me, isn't it?"

Dan nodded, wiping his face. "Couldn't resist you, could I? It's my decision. I want you no matter what. Get over it."

Her grip tightened if that were possible. "I love you," she told him firmly. "We'll make the best of it."

Charlie knew Dan was essentially a block of concrete. Drop him off a tall building and shatter him to bits and he'd tell you it didn't hurt but here he was breaking down in her arms. This was the man she wanted.

He rolled his head toward her. "This moment reminds me of one of Buddha's sayings," he whispered. "When you realize how perfect everything is, you will tilt your head back and laugh at the sky."

He looked up and laughed, hugging her as tightly as humanly possible without killing her.

April 11th

"MAOISTS BUILT THIS," said Santosh with a wry shake of his black mane. Forty-years-old, the short, muscular Sherpa with copper-brown skin and a mass of black hair exuded the calm disposition and beatific smiles of his people.

About twelve-feet high, bedecked in hammer and sickle flags, the rickety, wooden arch produced by clueless carpenters proclaimed "Welcome to New Nepal" on red cloth, long ago ripped by the constant winds. Charlie photographed the arch of hubris in the early morning before breakfast just as the first men were heading down to Lukla to pick up their massive loads for the day.

Santosh bravely leaned against the arch. It wobbled its discomfort. "It's a shabby reminder we may be stopped on the trails by the rebels and *requested* to contribute to their cause."

"And we do?" Mark asked.

"Of course." His smile broadened. "They have AK-47's and we have walking sticks."

Charlie glanced at a quiet Dan standing off to the side of the small group. At breakfast, he'd been subdued. No surprise there—she felt like she'd been used as a wishbone, a very happy one, and it had been a struggle to get out of bed for the early start. She warmed at the memory of a remarkable night and she wanted a lot more where that came from but only when Dan was well enough.

"Had to take more pills than usual," he'd told her languidly. "They make me slow and stupid."

"I haven't noticed a change," she'd replied with a grin.

He'd smiled and kissed her but he worried the hell out of her. Not knowing what was wrong with him was now a lot better than knowing about his condition.

Beyond him, Nadia stood alone, her daypack ready and walking stick in hand, watching them like a vulture waiting for road kill. Only one more day and that would be the end of her, thought Charlie. She and Dan resolved to stay close to one another and knock her off the mountain if she tried anything.

Mark turned to Charlie and whispered, "What did you do to our Dan? He didn't eat his breakfast. He may not make it to the top now."

Charlie smiled politely at Mark's humor and walked over to Dan to hold him around the waist. She forced a chuckle. "Did you know the whole building heard us?"

"Really?"

"You didn't see the leers at breakfast? Perhaps we broke some kind of altitude record."

"I did mine."

"Mine too!" She held him even tighter.

At that moment, Duncan and Shira wandered over hand in hand.

"Noisy newlyweds," said Duncan with a silly grin. "Don't you know how thin these plywood walls are? Jesus, how long did that go on for?"

"What's your secret," asked Shira. "For a moment, we thought you were going to kill the old guy!"

A blushing Charlie fanned her cheeks and glanced at Dan.

"We got to page forty of the *Kama Sutra*," he said and got a good laugh.

"Not so loud tonight, Dad. Shira needs a rest. She's getting on and—"

Shira gave him a sharp elbow but laughed as much as everyone else.

Dan pulled Duncan to one side. "Watch out for your mother today."

Duncan blinked away a wave of anxiety, nodded and moved away with Shira.

Dan turned back to Santosh who'd decided not to continue leaning on the rickety arch. "What's the trek like today?"

"Easy at the start but then we have a hard climb up lots of stairs to a high bridge before another long climb to Namche. There are a couple of tricky spots where the path is close to the cliffs but I haven't lost anyone yet." He laughed. "You'll sleep well tonight."

"Zoom! Zoom! Wankers!" Maya, Santosh's young assistant, called out from his position ahead of the group. They laughed as usual at Maya's misuse of English swear words and they were on their way. Maya was a constant source of amusement having an English lexicon compiled from the utterings of exhausted tourists wondering why they hadn't chosen a beach resort instead.

Charlie was glad Santosh was along to keep an eye on Nadia too. No one had a gun but they had Nadia well and truly outnumbered. They'd agreed to position themselves so that Nadia was always boxed in by Duncan, Dan and Mark, unless she was at the rear or highly unlikely at the front. If she wanted to harm Dan, Charlie or Shira, she was going to have a hard time doing it. Nadia remained at the rear of the group with Santosh taking up his position behind her. He briefly caught Charlie's eye and almost imperceptibly nodded.

* * *

After a morning's slow climb along uneven paths and up and down stone staircases, and an hour's stop at a tiny village to rest and eat a lunch of pork dumplings with a spicy *achar* chutney and tea, Maya called to them again and the group was off on the last part of the journey to Namche.

Only three hours to go, thought Charlie.

After more taxing stairs and a walk between rock faces covered with colorful Hindu paintings, Maya pointed up at a long, swinging cable bridge wreathed in fluttering prayer flags, several hundred feet above them in a tight gorge. Flights of almost vertical stone steps invited them to commit suicide climbing to it. Charlie looked at Dan and wondered if he'd make it.

"Rest your arses now, you brilliant wimps," Maya ordered, flashing his almost permanent grin.

They laughed and applauded while he smiled proudly at his use of English.

"Easy peasy," intoned Mark.

"Eessee peeseee?" Maya frowned.

"It means this trek will kill us," Gilly told him.

"Ah!" said Maya filing that one away.

"Why am I doing this?" asked an out-of-breath Shira.

"Ha!" Mark waved his walking stick at the bridge. "Because it's there," he exclaimed, channeling the great climber Mallory's comment on why he wanted to climb Everest. Charlie recalled Everest had killed him.

"Mother Mary. Why does it have to be there?" Charlie asked gazing up at the bridge.

"What are you a man or a mouse?" asked Mark.

"Is there a third choice?" asked Charlie. She cast a look at Dan who'd sat resting, not joining in any conversation. She put her arm around his shoulders. "Are you OK, old man?"

"Don't fuss," he said, irritated, but quickly flashed a small smile to compensate for his snappiness and squeezed her hand. "Sorry, you tired me out."

"It's my fault?" She chuckled. "Serves you right for being such a stud," she whispered in his ear. "That was the best ever. You'd better have more or I'll have to find a horny Sherpa."

Dan hugged her. "I've had better but you—"

She lightly smacked his face and laughed simultaneously. "But I'll let you rest in bed tonight," she told him, gently caressing his hair. "Think about that as we get closer to Namche. I am. You're a dream come true, my love."

He pulled her closer and stroked her cheeks as he kissed her gently. He smiled a lot more. "Well, I'd better get going, shouldn't I?"

Charlie helped him to his feet before glancing around for Nadia. She was surprised to find her moving to the front of the pack. The bitch wasn't as weak as she was making out, she thought. No matter, it would be easier to keep her in sight and stay between her and Dan.

* * *

Santosh appeared at Dan's elbow. "Feeling tired after last night's exertions?" he asked innocently but Dan could see a look of concern more than humor. "Charlie is a lovely woman inside and out. You are meant for one another and I can see you being together in many future lives. Her soul is happy like yours. I see how much she loves you." He put his arm around Dan's shoulders. "After what she told me, I searched Nadia's room and baggage. No weapons." Dan nodded. "There's no rush to Namche. Let's get there together and enjoy the journey. Does the destination really matter?"

"Zoom! Zoom!" Maya called. "Come on, you buggers! It's bloody there!"

Mark cracked up. "Yes, it's bloody there, you wankers!"

Gilly hit him with her stick.

"Only an hour to go," whispered Charlie with an encouraging rub of his shoulder, adding, "The bitch won't stop us now" before striding off ahead of him.

Dan took the steep, stone steps slowly, carefully avoiding a descending train of unloaded, snorting djopkis that could easily have nudged him into oblivion. His pulse and breathing remained under control but it alarmed him when he and Santosh broke away from the group. Losing sight of Charlie, he felt a surge of panic and forced himself on as fast as he could up steps as high as two feet. Where was Nadia?

He paused, pulse pounding, gasping the thin air on the deserted platform at the start of the swaying cable bridge, its strings of prayer flags snapping in the strong breeze. He sighed his relief: Charlie was OK, taking photos from the middle of the bridge. Beyond her, Mark stood between her and Duncan, Shira and Maya waiting at the end of the bridge. Off to Maya's side, Nadia watched them all, medusa-like and Gilly watched Nadia.

Charlie turned toward him, waving her walking stick. He read her lips: "Come on!"

Dan stumbled up to her, holding onto the wobbling rail that was shaking in the wind as much as he was. Two Charlies weaved before him briefly and then she was hugging him and brushing her lips on his ear as she hugged him.

"Don't kill yourself, you silly man! Not far to Namche!" Charlie panted. "We've almost made it! Our new home!"

Santosh put his hand on Dan's trembling shoulder. "Go as slow as you want, Dan. I'm behind you."

Dan took a deep breath to help clear his buzzing head. Namche. Because Charlie will be there. He'd plod on like Mallory.

Beyond the bridge, the trail wound around yet another Buddhist shrine—move to the left to go clockwise, the way the universe rotates—with its white-lettered inscriptions painted on the gray rocks. After that, a precarious route skirted a huge rocky outcrop that overlooked a deep gorge. With bells clanging, a long line of unloaded djopkis slowly lumbered its way down the narrow path toward them. Dan could smell them coming like a herd of wet rugs.

"Keep to the rock side everyone," shouted Maya, slapping the cliff face to get their attention.

Nadia stopped far enough behind Maya for the lumbering djopkis to separate them. Gilly stood not far behind her. Dan stayed as close as he could to Charlie but the monsters forced their hulks between them. Dan looked back. Mark, Duncan and Shira were close, followed by Santosh. The hairy beasts swayed by carefully placing their hooves on the uneven rocky trail barely six-feet wide.

Nadia suddenly grabbed Gilly and threw her off the path into the gorge. Dan stood paralyzed in shock as Gilly screamed before bouncing off an outcropping and sliding down a slope of scree. An anguished cry from Mark. Terrified cries from others. Maya leaped into action, shouting and frantically smacking at the djopkis but he couldn't get by them to get at Nadia, who beat a djopki with her walking stick, screaming at it until it panicked, pushing into the one ahead and starting a stampede. The frightened animal lunged to get by but slid over the edge, bellowing, crashing wildly through the boulders and thorny shrubs.

Charlie jumped out of the way of a wild-eyed djopki threatening to gore her but found herself on the wrong side of the beasts. Shrieking, she teetered on the edge of the precipice, her hands clawing frantically at a snorting djopki.

"Dan!" she yelled. "Dan!"

Trapped against the rock face by the jostling djopkis, Dan was helpless. Nadia rushed at Charlie, thrashing her on the head with her walking stick as Charlie screamed, clinging on to the djopki's mass of hair for all her worth.

Adrenaline pounded through Dan's arteries. A mighty kick with both his feet caught an unbalanced djopki and sent it, legs twirling, squealing madly, bouncing from rock shelf to rock shelf.

Thud thud thud.

The vision in Dan's right eye blurred rhythmically with his pounding heart.

"Die you bitch!" Nadia yelled, dropping her stick to tear at Charlie.

Dan launched himself at Nadia, grabbing her around the neck. With a mighty wrench made from desperation, he pulled her off Charlie.

THUD THUD THUD.

Nadia's screams in his ears, grasping at him, falling, falling, his head exploded noiselessly.

January 15th, 2017

Kathmandu, Nepal

THE BEDSHEET FLEW into the warm morning air. Charlie jumped off the lumpy mattress to stretch naked, gazing out at the shambles of the city awash in traffic noise, the bittersweet aroma of smoke and diesel fumes and the bright promise of a new day.

Good morning, Kathmandu! Today, Nagarkot! I'll be there in only a few hours!

Her skin tingled and she licked her dry lips anticipating what was to come. She couldn't believe how great she felt being so close to her goal—she was as excited as the first day she'd met Dan in Mumbai all those years ago. She'd made up her mind to escape a year ago back in Florida and here she was at last where David Hamlish and his numerous minions wouldn't be able to find her and return her to the family compound. It was an end to endlessly playing the dutiful Jewish wife with the frozen smile at brain-numbing social and religious events, raising funds for the senator's trough from the money-obsessed, culture-free, power elite to promote his political career. No more hiding her Buddhist leanings and an end to her loveless, childless marriage of convenience that had driven her into a Big Top of therapy and psychoactive drugs where she'd been the circus clown wiping the pie off her face.

Why had she suddenly decided to change her life? Was it the upcoming anniversary of the day she'd treasured in her own way for the last twenty years? A day when she went AWOL to be on her own to give herself time to think, to celebrate, to mourn, to love? What better place to treasure another special day?

At seven in the morning, acrid wood smoke drifted in her open window from house fires and street food vendors and she loved it. Gas fumes rose from the exhausts of the gridlock of cars and motorbikes. Men and women snorted and spat in the rubble-strewn backstreet three floors below her hotel room. A blanket of low, brick and wooden houses interspersed with elaborate Buddhist and Hindu temple spires and a forest of TV antennas stretched before her into the thickening haze. The valley gradually became opaque as the smoke mixed with the morning mist and fumes and faded out the sunlight. She'd been here two days and never seen a snowy mountaintop—except in postcards on the stands outside the shops. The memory of driving around the valley on a motorbike, her arms tightly around Dan, looking for a view of the Himalayas tickled her into a wistful smile that even the constant hawking in the street below couldn't wipe off her lips.

After a shower that almost flooded her room and throwing on a light cotton shirt without a bra—she still didn't need one—she pulled on a pair of big, comfortable panties—*How Dan would have laughed at them!*—and slid her long legs into loose cargo pants and her large feet into walking boots. A quick breakfast of coffee and a couple of fried eggs on toast set her up for entering the maelstrom of the city: streets choked with cars, minibusses, bicycles and motorbikes going nowhere, people going everywhere and lined with shops selling everything, legal and illegal. She ignored the clothing stores: although everything women wanted was available here for a fraction of the cost in the US, none of it fitted a woman six feet tall.

She narrowly avoided colliding with a much smaller woman and her head-born water jug outside the open doors of a motorbike rental shop. Above it, sexy Westernized women in tight tops and jeans advertised Nepali Idol—a glaring contrast to Nepali women in traditional yellow and maroon robes sold bright orange garlands of marigolds for offering at the many temples and altars big and small scattered throughout the area. One of several dusty black motorbikes parked in front of the shop caught her eye. Western music blared from an invisible radio inside where a young man with a head of tousled, black hair leaned on a counter reading a newspaper.

"*Namaste,*" she said quietly.

His head slowly rose to her then jerked up quickly, his eyes growing to the size of her morning's fried eggs in his round boyish face. She was used to it. Tall, white women with flowing, rust-red locks were in short supply in these parts. Two other men in oily coveralls tinkering with bike parts stopped what they were doing and stared, finding her far more interesting than greasy chains and sprockets. Even in her early forties, she could still draw a crowd, especially in a land of dwarves.

"*Na ... maste,*" stuttered the short brown man, looking up a foot at her chin.

"*Kasto cha?* How are you?" she asked.

The man's gapped teeth flashed. "*Thik cha.* I am fine. *Kasto cha?*"

"*Thik cha.* I'd like to rent the Royal Enfield, please."

"Nice bike you choose."

"I know it is."

She haggled over the price, paid cash and filled out some paperwork she assumed would never see the tax authorities.

"Do you need to see my American license?" she asked.

The man shook his head.

"Insurance?"

He smiled impishly.

Nepal hasn't changed in over twenty years. No one has insurance. The best policy is still "Don't hit anyone!"

"Be very careful on these roads," he warned. "People are crazy, madam." He pointed to a scratched, open-faced helmet on the shelf behind him. "I recommend one of these," he told her. "No charge for the lady."

It was her turn to shake her head. She'd brought her own protective jacket, leggings and gloves. In particular, she'd brought her expensive, newly painted helmet. Dan would have been delighted to see it sporting a big red maple leaf.

"You travel alone?" the little man asked, frowning. She nodded. "Nepal can be dangerous." He paused and smiled again. "Especially for a beautiful lady such as madam."

She felt herself blushing slightly at his compliment—she liked it. Compliments these days never went wrong. Only forty-eight hours away from her husband and she felt the crushing weight of her marriage lifting and the gloom she'd endured for far too long clearing in the warmth of Nepal and its charming people. She also felt the paring knife she kept at the ready in her pocket.

She returned the man's warm smile and said, "*Dhanyabad.* I'll be back shortly to pick up the bike. *Namaste.*"

She felt three pairs of eyes watching her butt leave the shop. She liked that too. She smiled to herself and gave it a little twerk as she walked back into the warm sunshine. If only she were twenty-one years younger!

* * *

On the city's bigger roads, the speeding cars dodged one another, motorbikes buzzed like bees, and wooden ox carts slowly rumbled as they had for centuries.

Mantra for the day: Don't hit anyone ... Don't hit anyone ...

The words of the young man in the motorbike rental shop echoed in her head as she slipped through the gears and gunned the motor on the more open highway farther from Kathmandu. She breathed in and out deeply letting Nepal work its magic and relax her. The oppressive heat of the day was over. She left the smoggy valley and with the evening drawing close, no longer had to put up with the dust thrown up by overburdened yellow, green, orange and red-painted trucks on the verge of collapse, vehicles of all kinds coming the wrong way and the omnipresent danger of people or animals wandering across the road. The late afternoon went by quickly as she sped along the narrowing road through scattered villages among the plowed fields and up into the mountain range toward Nagarkot. Only the occasional lumbering, creaking ox cart got in her way as the bike hummed along, climbing higher and higher.

The smells of wood smoke, cow shit, street food being grilled or simmering in pots, piles of fish glistening after a brief afternoon thunderstorm and occasionally the whiff of pungent human sewage from the rivers brought memories bubbling to the surface that had remained silent in her mental diary for decades. She whizzed by the enormous heaps of pancakes of dried cow shit, fires burning dried shit and houses built of dried shit. Swallowing hard, holding back tears.

She'd left it until late to leave Kathmandu but decided to stop at the stone buildings of Budhanlikantha that hadn't changed in probably ten centuries to revisit the shrine to Vishnu, where the god carved out of black stone lay covered in orange marigolds and rested on the coils of the cosmic serpent in the dark waters of his fenced pool. She purchased a small garland of marigolds from an old woman with the face of a walnut, a saffron robe and glistening, oiled hair crouched by the enclosing railing, giving her far more rupees than necessary. Dan would have approved. She took her turn in a short queue of devotees before laying her offering near the god's head with the many other fresh and fading flowers.

Her mind wandered happily through distant memories as the motorbike hummed through the cooling, farm-smelling air along what had become a thin strip of blacktop toward the hacksaw skyline of dark mountains. Heavy clouds reared ominously ahead of her. With darkness rapidly descending, the first rain droplets streaked her windshield. The motorbike's headlight beam swept back and forth across the potholed road curving ahead with a sheer rock face on the left and a thousand-foot drop down a treed slope to the right. With the black clouds lumbering closer, she twisted the throttle further. She tapped the rear brake lightly and leaned into the rapidly approaching tight corner.

An ox cart without a wheel collapsed in the middle of the road. The headlight beam flashed across a bunch of men gesticulating at one another. They scattered like bowling pins. She eased quickly on the rear brake. The bike slowed but its front wheel wobbled and skidded in the gravel. It went down on its side, crumpling the fairing. Her leg was trapped beneath it as she slid along. The engine roared. The smell of burning rubber filled the air. Gravel sprayed. The handlebars twisted violently. She gasped as her left wrist snapped. Her helmet hit the ground hard, ripping off her visor. The bike spun under the wooden cart. A snorting white ox. White and green flashing lights. No pain as her leg buckled. Darkness.

January 16th, 2017

CHARLIE SENSED HERSELF breathing and rising. Incense. A bell tinkled, went silent, then tinkled again. Warmth. Thick fur, soft beneath her fingers. The darkened room swam into focus as her eyes flickered open, squinting at the bright light. She looked up at a rough, wooden ceiling that disappeared into the dark far, far above her. Her eyes closed again as she let herself drift back deeper and deeper. Dan's rectangular face with its bent nose drifted across her mind between flashes of the ox cart and sliding on the motorbike. Something touched her hand.

"Hello," said a strong voice.

Her lips felt numb. Her heart pounded. "Dan?" She opened her eyes and looked into a smiling brown face with almost black irises. It wasn't Dan.

He tightened his hand on hers. "My name is Tshering."

"Tshering?" she repeated. It sounded familiar.

Charlie tried to move but the pain in her left arm and leg stopped her.

"You need to rest longer," he said.

His hand gently lifted her head and warm, deliciously scented liquid touched her lips. "Drink some. It will do you good."

She sipped the spicy soup and surprised herself by draining the bowl. With a cold cloth placed across her forehead, she slipped away again into the warmth.

March 17th, 2017

Two Months Later

THE GONG ANNOUNCED the monastery prayers at five in the afternoon. Five monks in their saffron and maroon robes sat on the patterned carpet in the smoky room and one began reciting to the others. Their shaved heads glistened, reflecting the light from the oil lamps suspended above them.

Charlie relaxed on a pillow on a divan at the side of the room, eyes closed, her breathing slowing with her pulse. She remembered every bit of the temple part of the monastery where she'd been with Dan so many years ago and fought back her tears.

It was the room she and Dan had watched monks at prayer. Its garishly painted high walls displayed Buddha's life from birth to death in shades of red, yellow and green. The enormous golden statue of Buddha reached twenty feet to the ceiling. She'd never forgotten the tiniest detail of it. In her mind's eye, it was the center of her universe and always would be.

After two months' recuperation from her accident, the details of the ceremony and muttered phrases of Nepalese had become second nature, something she'd never thought possible. She'd gone far beyond tourist *namaste* and *dhanyabad*. Tshering observed her from the group of monks. They nodded at one another. He always had a warm smile for her. And her for him.

What a star he's been to me. In the week after the accident, whenever I woke up he was there to feed me. Now, he visits me every day to check on how I'm doing. He must like me, or why would he come every day to bring food, drink tea and teach me Nepalese? I love everything about him: his calm personality, the way we easily talk together about so many worldly topics and there's his hard young body. She caught herself. *Christ, he's a monk and only about twenty. I'm old enough to be his mother!*

With the cast removed, her left leg felt weak as she stumbled back with the help of her cane along the rocky path to the small stone house with a wooden roof she'd occupied since the accident. Her left wrist occasionally throbbed but Tshering stopped by every day to have a cup of tea or some soup and massage her wrist, working on its flexibility. He brought her aspirin and some local medicines from the people of Nagarkot. The village had taken to her and various locals dropped by occasionally to drink her tea and to check on their tall, redheaded, alien American guest. Their generosity knew no limits. She realized more and more why Dan had loved the Sherpas.

Before prayers, she'd already done some of her work. Every morning, she helped feed the djopkis that were used for meat, leather, fur, milk and cheese, and their shit for fuel, building materials, fertilizer and God knows what else. A small solar panel propped up against a big pile of djopki patties by her door provided some electricity for a light bulb to supplement the oil lamps in the evening. She dried her clothes in the sun by laying them over the same pile. Her mother and father would have had conniptions if they'd seen how their expensively reared daughter now lived. In the evenings, Charlie was surprised she hadn't got bored but she practiced her yoga and Buddhist prayers, read what literature on the religion she could get delivered from the outside world and began to smile at everything and everyone around her. On a mainly vegetarian Sherpa diet, she delighted in losing the lifebelt that had grown around her waist the last five years. It was early to bed and very early to rise. The jaded, old bag in the mirror had gone—she was beginning to look like someone she liked. Being without her anti-anxiety and sleeping pills for weeks had left her more alive than she could remember. She didn't miss the vodka either. Her house became a place of tranquility where she spent a lot of time learning not to think. Not allowed to stay with the monks, of course, she spent most of her recovery time resting on a hard bed by a djopki patty fire in a metal stove.

The burning dung scented everything she cooked. And cook she did: momos, the steamed, meat-filled dumplings, with sesame sauces and hot tomato chutneys; potato curries; *shakpa*, the spicy vegetable stew; and noodles and vegetable soups, such as *thukpa*. She walked the trails and grew stronger and stronger and found herself smiling more and more. Being with Tshering, talking and learning from him, was her favorite activity. She knew she was falling in love with the boy. It embarrassed her.

April 1st, 2017

Two Weeks Later

OUT OF BREATH, some five hundred feet above the monastery, Charlie and Tshering stopped at a white prayer cairn of stones with its tattered and fading flags fluttering prayers up to the heavens. They sat cross-legged on the warm, flat stones in the morning sunshine after they'd trekked up the narrow diagonal path to the ridge. From its top, they looked down on the monastery with its stone walls and outhouses and the valley that rose higher to the north-east, houses scattered throughout fields providing grazing for the djopkis and for growing potatoes. Plastic hoses surfaced and looped from one home to another feeding water throughout the valley floor.

Charlie brought water, some fruit and vegetables and a few balls of dough she'd made from *tsampa*, a roasted flour. She unpacked it and shared her food with Tshering. Far below, wisps of gray smoke trickled from her chimney and the temple glowed in the intermittent shafts of bright sunlight. Kites soared in the rising warm air, gliding up the sides of the mountains toward their summits. Every day, Charlie had walked a little farther and farther up the path.

"Very good," Tshering told her between bites of his dough ball. "This is the highest you've climbed. You are getting so much stronger." He paused, considering her future. "Soon you will be able to go home."

"I'm in no hurry," she told him. "I like being here with you."

He smiled.

"You don't know I've been here before, do you?"

"You mean in a previous life?"

"No. Twenty years ago. I recall a monk named Tshering back then."

"Ah, yes. He died many years ago but his name lives on in me wherever his soul is now."

"Tshering sounds a nice name. What does it mean?"

"Good luck." He kept his gaze on her. "And I feel so lucky to have met you."

He feels the same way? "I'll miss you when I go."

"And I will miss you, Charlene," replied Tshering sadly, not looking at her. He stared across the valley at the high, snow-capped peaks that masked the even higher peaks of the Himalayas. "Do you know what nirvana is?" he asked.

"Yes. It's a state of perfect peace of mind, an enduring happiness."

Tshering nodded still looking away. "Meaning?"

"It's more than simply a peaceful mood free of anger, anxiety, sexual urges, things like that."

Sexual urges? How I love Tshering's boyish smile, beautiful eyes and firm body. I don't think I'm quite ready for giving up on that.

Tshering nodded seriously. "How is this achieved?"

"It requires a reordering of consciousness through meditation. And *carpe diem.*"

"What's that mean?"

"*Carpe diem* is Latin. *Seize the day.*" She swallowed an urge to cry that rushed out of nowhere. "A ... friend once told me that."

Tshering mulled the words for a moment. "That's a good start, grasshopper."

Charlie erupted in laughter. She coughed crumbs of bread over Tshering's robe, brushing off the mess she'd made.

Tshering grinned. "I saw re-runs of Kung Fu as a child. Loved it."

Charlie drank some water and patted her chest. "Oh, God. That was funny."

He grinned. "I'm so glad you're happy."

"You think so?"

"Of course you are. And I know you will be. The numbers have told me so."

"The numbers?"

Tshering shuffled closer. "Numbers are very important. Twelve months, twelve on a jury, twelve disciples for Jesus, a dozen loaves of bread, twelve signs of the zodiac, twelve days of Christmas. It goes on and on. Don't get me started."

"Mmm. I didn't think of that."

"I hope you don't mind but I looked up your numbers."

"What numbers are those?"

"Age, birth date, names. I found your driving license in your wallet."

"What did you find out? This is fun."

"It's not only fun. It's who you are."

"Tell grasshopper who she is, O Master?"

"You're nine, seven, five."

"Ha!" Charlie laughed. "Thank God for that. You had me worried. My parents knew me more as 911." She caught Tshering's quizzical look. "It a US thing. Never mind. Carry on."

"Nine is your destiny. In a nutshell, you are compassionate and generous. Romantic too."

"I like that number. Keep talking."

"Seven is your personality. You seek wisdom and religion."

"That's true. And the five?"

"You yearn for domesticity."

"Mmm. Not sure about that one. Hasn't shown up so far."

"And have magnetic charm."

"That's better."

"You believe in karma, don't you? We get recycled and return as something we deserve to be?"

"I'm working on that one. Do you think I'll be reborn too?"

"Yes. Whether you believe it or not."

"So I've already been reborn?"

He shrugged. "Maybe thousands of times and will be until you reach nirvana and you won't return."

"Maybe we'll meet in another life."

"I hope so. Maybe we've already met." Tshering studied her face closely and shrugged. "But I'd like to enjoy this life first."

"So would I." She touched his hand and he let it stay there.

He glanced at her shyly, letting her fingers run over his while they remained silent and watched the sun sink farther for a few minutes. He abruptly stood and brushed the grass and dust off his robe. After studying the robe for a few moments, he said, "Time to go" and walked off ahead of her back down the path.

On the way down the slope, it occurred to her what the total of her numbers was.

* * *

Recycled Love

At the end of prayers, Tshering walked slowly over to her house, thoughtfully kicking pebbles with his sandals, and sat cross-legged with her on the rough bed. His round face didn't have its usual beaming smile. At moments like this, she wanted to bundle him up in her arms and cuddle him forever. She made some Sherpa tea and they sipped the buttery, salted drink from small clay cups.

"You didn't tell me you're the one who fixed my broken leg and wrist."

Tshering nodded but frowned for the first time she'd known him.

"Where did you learn to do that?" she asked.

"I went to medical school for two years but dropped out and entered the monastery as a *samanara,* a novice." He took her wrist in his hands and began moving it gently. "You were lucky that the wrist was only dislocated. The ligaments and tendons were damaged and they'll take a while to heal but no broken bones. You'll recover much of its mobility if you do some exercises like this."

She tingled at the touch of his fingers flexing and extending her wrist. "Coming every day has helped a lot," she told him. Just being with him made it feel better.

He grinned back at her, beginning to look like the Tshering she was used to. "On my birthday, I may decide to become ordained as a *bikkhu.* Will you still be here?"

"When is that? We should have a celebration. I have a lot to thank you for." She wanted to kiss him.

"In just over a week."

"Of course. I wouldn't miss it."

"My parents didn't want me to become a monk. They were very disappointed I didn't become a doctor like them."

"Do you think you'll become ordained?"

"I'm not sure. There's such a lot of the world to see and experience. The good, the bad and the ugly."

"I could show you America. We certainly have that."

A new reality series: A Boy Monk in America. Tune in. Watch the disaster unfold as he gets trampled at the Blue Light Special.

He nodded. "America is rich in money, isn't it?"

"Very much so. In money, little else."

"Is it important for you to be rich? To have things?"

"It was. Not now. Not since I've been here with you."

He stopped rubbing her wrist and held her hand, staring at it. He smiled that beatific smile at her. She looked away feeling a little embarrassed especially when she realized how damp she was getting.

I wonder what he looks like out of that robe?

Tshering sipped his hot tea. "You like to attend all our prayers now."

"Yes, there's nothing on TV."

"There's nothing new in our prayers either."

"I noticed. All re-runs."

"Isn't it time you got back on the bike?"

Charlie laughed. "You think I'm nuts?"

"I know you're brave." His brown eyes fixed on her.

"No, I'm not." She looked away from those eyes.

"Think about where you are. Your journey here."

"The bike's a wreck."

"It's a pity."

April 10th, 2017

Nine Days Later

CHARLIE AND TSHERING bicycled and walked up and down the hills along the rough path through the blooming red flowers of the rhododendron forest and herds of djopkis into Nagarkot. They stopped at the café at the high end of the triangle where the three small roads to Nagarkot converged. They sat at a table in the warm sunshine and ordered fruit juices to help them cool off.

"You're a much fitter lady now. I can see that," remarked Tshering.

He's been watching my body? Well, why not? It's getting pretty good.

She flexed an elbow and pumped up her biceps. "What do you think of that?"

Goosebumps ran up her arm when he placed his hand on it and squeezed.

"Very nice," he told her with crinkling eyes.

"I think I've lost about fifteen pounds since the accident. I don't think I've ever been so healthy—if you don't count the wrist and leg."

"You look very good." He clenched his fists and bent his elbows to show his biceps too. "Strong lady. Not soft American now."

He was right: she felt muscle all over her. Two months ago that bike ride from the monastery would have killed her. She sneaked a look at him again while he sipped his juice. God, he made her feel so good: he was so energetic and happy all the time. And his teeth now looked good after she'd shown him how to clean them better. His hair was growing longer since he'd stopped shaving his head.

He got up and excused himself. She watched his hard, muscular body stride off down the square. It was a long time since she'd felt so aroused by a male presence—she liked it a lot. That bike seat hadn't helped as she'd followed behind the tight buttocks showing through his robe.

I really am a dirty old woman!

She'd started pleasuring herself after a ten-year break. *In a stone hut in Nepal? Write that in your* National Geographic. She smiled at her complete lack of guilt. Tonight she'd do it again. And think of Tshering.

Ten minutes later, wondering where he'd got to, the sound of a motorbike grabbed her attention from playing with her empty glass. Coming up the road, kangaroo hopping and wobbling from side to side, was Tshering on her Royal Enfield. He stalled it out halfway up the square and struggled to keep it up. Charlie leaped down the hill and helped him steady the bike.

"What the hell?" She laughed, half in amazement, half in excitement.

She stood it on its stand in the middle of the square as a noisy crowd gathered. The shattered fairing had been removed but the handlebars had been straightened and the lights and indicators were working. She hugged him for a bit longer than was really necessary and even kissed him on the cheek. He didn't push her away.

"This is so wonderful. Who fixed it?"

"We all did." He waved around him at the small crowd of smiling faces. "They did it for Lhamu."

"Lhamu?" she repeated. After all these years, the name had the impact of an asteroid landing in Nagarkot.

"They did it for the tall, redhead goddess. Lhamu. That's what you're known as around here."

Charlie ran her hand self-consciously through her hair. "Oh. Really?"

"They've come to love you, Lhamu. We all have."

Oh, those eyes and that smile.

Charlie squeezed his hand then let it go. "We need helmets."

They sat on her bike with the borrowed helmets strapped on. Charlie asked over her shoulder, "Are you sure you're ready for this?"

"As much as you are." She looked in her mirror. Tshering grinned back wearing an old, metal helmet that resembled a wok.

"Watch out for ox carts!" he yelled.

Charlie laughed when his arms wrapped around her waist.

April 11th, 2017

CHARLIE PREPARED HERSELF for the special day: to celebrate and to contemplate, to laugh a little and to cry a lot. Was it simply luck she was still in Nagarkot? Tshering meant "good luck" after all. Or had fate worked through her motorbike accident and brought her to this moment: the twenty-first anniversary of Dan's next life? First of all, she heated a bucket of water on the stove, then filled the one on top of the shower she'd built with Tshering in her backyard: just three posts holding up the bucket with a string to release the water through a hose into a watering-can nozzle she'd found in the village. She could stand there naked washing herself and, although she was in sight of the temple, she knew no one would watch her. She dried off with her rough towel and put on fresh clothes only slightly smelling of djopki and prepared her lunch for the walk up the mountain to the cairn.

* * *

She crossed her legs, held her fingers together in each hand and breathed slowly. All she wanted to think about was Dan: his face, hair, smile, laugh, the conversations, the lovemaking, how they'd met in that church and their first trip to Elephanta Island, how he'd taken care of her and protected her and how he'd saved her life. Tears welled as memories of smoking and drinking with Dan behind hotels and in gardens flooded her mind. His hands on her breasts. His kisses. The magical night in Phakding.

Footsteps.

She heard the noise on the bank below and Tshering's head rose above the rocks. He was wearing a white t-shirt and a pair of worn blue jeans with the usual sandals.

"I thought I'd find you here," he said.

"My favorite spot. Come join me. It's a special day." She wiped her cheeks with her fingers.

Tshering sat down next to her but said nothing, looking away from her toward the mountains tops. Charlie knew he wasn't one to ask many questions.

"It's special because a special friend of mine named Dan died twenty-one years ago today," she told him.

He nodded.

"He died saving my life. I loved him with all my heart and whatever soul I have."

Tshering looked at her with the eyes of someone much older.

"I'll never forget him." Charlie reached out and touched his arm. "Are you OK?"

He looked away again, drawing with a stick on the rocks as he spoke. "I entered the monastery because of a woman, my wife. Anza."

She took one of his hands in hers and didn't say anything.

"She ... had our baby and ... they both died in childbirth. It hurt me so much to lose her ... them. I needed to find ... to find ... some peace."

She put her arm around his shoulders and pulled him close. He rested his head on her shoulder as he sobbed softly. "And you found it."

"Yes." He turned his face up to her. "Until I met you."

Charlie's heart leaped into her mouth. She stopped herself from shouting how she felt to everyone as far as Nagarkot. In the gentlest way possible, she held his face in her hands and pressed her lips softly on his. He responded in kind, lips lingering lightly, enjoying the sudden intimacy. He held onto her and they lay back face-to-face on the thin layer of rough grass between the flat rocks.

"I ... watched you take a shower this morning." He blushed and couldn't hold her eye contact. "I'm sorry. I've watched you many times."

"Look at me," she told him. She looked into his wet eyes and ran her fingers over his lips. "I've been watching you too. Women do that, you know. Have a shower. I'll gladly watch." She caught her breath as she felt his hardness against her thigh.

She licked her dry lips. "I haven't ... in a long—"

"I haven't either."

She knew she'd have to take the lead. Loosening his jeans allowed her to gently touch him. She knew he would snap like a triggered mousetrap if she gave him too much cheese too quickly. She kissed his face and placed his hand on her breast. She shivered with delicious expectation. "Monks shouldn't do this, should they?" she asked as she tenderly stroked him.

"I've decided not to become a monk." He touched her lips, too. "When I saw you today, I knew then I wasn't ready to leave behind ... " He paused.

"Physical love?"

"More than that. I feel a spiritual love I never thought I'd know again with a woman. I love being with you. We don't even have to talk. Perhaps like with your Dan."

Charlie loosened her blouse and slipped out of the sari she'd wrapped around her waist. She exhaled deeply as she pressed his fingers rhythmically into her. Beginning to feel nervous after so long, she paused to look at him, wanting to relish what she knew might be a special moment of her life. It was beginning to overwhelm her emotional walls.

"I want you so much," she told him. "I want to stay here. I don't want to leave."

Tshering rolled onto her and she enjoyed feeling a man again. Charlie kept on using his hand on herself until she knew she was ready and Tshering could take no more of her.

"Now, Dan," she told him, pulling him into her and holding him between her thighs. She bucked hard against him, feeling herself melt from the waist down into a pool of delight. Tshering lasted far longer than she'd anticipated and she made the most of it, moving against him until she dissolved into him again.

They stripped naked and lay on their backs side by side as the warm sun moved over to its highest point. Tshering held her hand but neither of them spoke for at least an hour. Just being was what they were good at. Charlie really enjoyed that. She looked up at the swirling streams of cloud around the mountain tops, smelled the freshest air possible and listened to the light breeze kissing their bodies and carrying her thoughts to the heavens. Nothing else mattered but now.

Tshering eventually broke the silence. "You called me ... Dan."

Charlie frowned. "I did?"

"It's OK. I thought of my wife and child, too. People we've loved. They flood into our minds at times like that." He smiled at her. "Wonderful times like that."

Their love-making extended into the mid-afternoon until it was getting cooler and no matter how much body friction they'd created it was time to put on their clothes and get back down the mountain. With the anxiety gone, Tshering had made the subsequent couplings even better than the first. They'd talked about what their lives could now be together. She had money. They could do anything. Tshering told her his parents were happy he was going to leave the monastery. They had their lives before them.

"What a day. I'm leaving the temple and we have each other." Tshering kissed her again. "And something else."

She sat up, resting back on her elbows. "What's that?"

"It's my birthday. I'm twenty-one."

Charlie realized how perfect everything was, tilted her head back and laughed at the sky.

Acknowledgements

I wish to thank the following for their contributions in one way or another to the completion of *Recycled Love*:

Kathleen Martin
Diana Stevan
J.P. McLean
Dr. W.J. Loskota
Dr. Isabella Camilleri
Michael O'Neill
The late Joan Lane.
Mark Giglio

Also by George Henry

Trieste Series #1

Milo Marchetti, a club owner, smells a rat when an exotic woman asks him to arrange a murder with an offer he cannot refuse. He soon finds she's big trouble: the catalyst for confrontations with mobsters and religious zealots, and with police who brand him a serial killer. Drawn into a dangerous love affair and her criminal family, will Milo commit the murder for her? When shocking truths about the woman surface, he must choose: a deceitful lover and enormous power or a return to his previous life as a musician. Or is there another shock in store for Milo?

Blood Rain in Trieste's witty, morally pragmatic Milo Marchetti will appeal to fans of Philip Kerr's hard detective, Bernie Gunther, Robert Wilson's fixer, Bruce Medway, and Len Deighton's insubordinate Harry Palmer. If you want a furiously paced thriller with memorable characters, humor and uneasy love, this is it. Don't expect a pat ending.

Sequel due out in 2019

About the Author

George Henry was born in England. A graduate of Sheffield University, he has worked in scientific research and education in England, the United States of America, Canada, and Saint Lucia in the West Indies. He lives with his wife in British Columbia, Canada.

Connect with George Henry

Friend on Facebook: http://facebook.com/georgehenry47
Follow on Twitter: http://twitter.com/georgehenry47
Visit author website: https://www.amazon.com/-/e/B00GKCALR4

Made in the USA
San Bernardino, CA
10 January 2019